Meshka the Wise Woman

Volume I in the Seeder series

In a world of war and ethnic cleansings, it can seem almost impossible to find peace. And yet, somehow, step by step, one at a time, some people have worked their way through to a new life. Thus it was with Meshka.

Meshka
The Wise Woman

Volume I in the Seeder series

N*I*N Sharyn Bebeau

SPIRITBOOKS

Printed in the United States of America

SPIRITBOOKS
Is an imprint of Portal Center Press
Oregon, USA
www.portalcenterpress.com

ISBN: 978-1-936902-32-3

Other Books by the Author:
Soul Matrix
The Archetypes of Soul
How to be a Goddess in 28 Days
Looking Beneath Reality
The Book of Paradox
Haggadah

I dedicate this book to my mama
Liba Hanna (Love of Life) and
My father Shalom (Peace).

Table of Contents

The Old Meshka:
Meshka the *Kvetch*

In the little village where my mother was born, they tell the tale of Meshka. *Oy!* Poor Meshka, could that woman *kvetch*!

Meshka went to the baker. She bought a *challah* (bread) and a few *rugelach* (cookies). When the baker was counting out her change, he asked, "So Meshka how is it by you? How are you feeling?"

"Oy! You shouldn't ask. My feet are so swollen like ten pound melons. 'N my back, oy, my back! I feel like I'm carrying da wall of Jericho on my back." The baker smiled sadly, and walked away.

Later Meshka went to the dressmaker and the dressmaker asked, "So, Meshka, how are your children?"

"Oy, my children, vhat did I do da deserve such children? My Yonkela, he's soo lazy. All day long he lays around in da bed reading. He lays around like a pickle, like a bump on a ko-sher pickle.

"'N my daughter Rifka, she only comes to visit me once a month. Da rest of da time, she doesn't remember from who I am." The dressmaker smiled sadly, and walked away.

One summer day, Meshka was leaning out of the window. Along came the rabbi. "Good Mornin', Meshka," said the rabbi, "Vhat a sweet house you have."

"Sweet, shmeet," said Meshka, "How can you call dis liddle box a house? Why my late husband could not build me a bigger house, I vill never know."

The rabbi smiled sadly, and walked away. Always it was the same. To the rabbi, the baker, even the little dressmaker, always *kvetch, kvetch, kvetch.*

Meshka woke up one morning. She looked up at the sky and she said, "God, give me da strength to bear one more miserable day."

As soon as she said these words, she felt a strange little tickle on her tongue. She scratched it with her finger but there was nothing there, so she went to make breakfast.

When breakfast was ready, she called her son, "Yonkela, put down da books already. Come 'n eat."

"Oy, dat boy is soo lazy. He is like a bump on a kosher pickle!" she grumbled to herself.

Again she felt a strange little tickle on her tongue.

"Yonkle," she yelled. No answer, so she went to his room and opened the door. Oy vay!! There on the bed wasn't her son, but a huge kosher pickle -- with a bump on it!

"Oy! Oy! Vhere can my son be, in dis liddle box of a house?"

As soon as she said these words, the house began to moan and groan and shrink! Soon her head was sticking out of the doorway and her arms were poking out of the windows! She screamed and wiggled her way free.

"Oy! Oy! I must tell Rifka about all da terrible dings dat are happening to me today. Dat is if she even remembers from who I am."

Again she felt that strange little tickle on her tongue.

She ran to her daughter's house and knocked on the door. Rifka opened it and said, "Yes old woman, vhat do you vant?"

"Vhat is dis 'old woman' business? I am your mama!"

"I do not know from who you are. Go away old woman!" Her daughter turned her back and slammed the door!

Meshka was so shocked! She was reeling in the street.

She looked up at the sky and said, "God, it's not bad enough dat all these terrible dings are happening to me? But my poor feet are so swollen like ten pound melons 'n my back, oy my back, I feel like I am carrying da wall of Jericho on my back."

From her mouth to God's ear, suddenly her feet swelled up like melons and she toppled over from the weight. Out of a clear blue sky, came a big stone wall, and it landed (clunk!) right on her back! Meshka was sprawled out in the middle of the street. She laid there for a long time thinking about her *tzoris*, her troubles.

Along came the rabbi. He said, "So Meshka how is it by you?"

"Oy Rabbi, you wouldn't believe all da terrible dings dat happened to me today," and she told him her story.

He smiled sadly, rubbed his beard and looked like he knew something. "Tell me Meshka, vhen you woke up dis mornin', did you feel a strange liddle tickle on your tongue?"

"Yes Rabbi. Vhat vas it, a plague, a curse?"

The rabbi said, "Oy Meshka, I am afraid you have vhat is known as da kvetch's itch!"

"Da kvetch's itch! Vhat is dis kvetch's itch business?"

"Vell, it happens very rarely 'n den only to a *kvetch*. Meshka, have you been kvetchin' a lot lately?"

"Vhat is a lot? Maybe I kvetched a liddle."

The rabbi said, "Da kvetch's itch is very serious. Vhen you have it, everythin' you kvetch about comes true."

"Rabbi, you mean I made all dese terrible dings happen vid my voids?"

"I am afraid," said the rabbi "you vill have da kvetch's itch for da rest of your life to remind you dat once you va a kvetch. But if you learn to praise dings instead of complain about dem, at least all dese terrible dings vill never happen again."

"Praise?! Shmaize. Vhat do I know from praise?" she *kvetched*.

"Try, try Meshka."

"Alright. My son -- oy, he is soo lazy…"

"No, no! You must praise him," said the rabbi, shaking his head..

"My son lays around all day on da bed reading… but dat is because he is vise 'n vants more knowledge."

"Good" said the rabbi. "Come, say more."

"My daughter only visits me once a month, but dat is because da rest of da month, she is busy vid her own liddle ones."

"Very good," said the rabbi. "Say more."

"My house is snug 'n vell built 'n I am relatively vell for a woman of my years."

"Good," said the rabbi.

From her mouth to God's ears! As soon as she said these words, the melons disappeared and her feet became feet again. The wall vanished and she stood up. With her apron she wiped a little melon juice off her legs and a little dust off her shoulders.

"Rabbi, I must tell Rifka about all da amazing dings dat are happening to me today."

She ran to her daughter's house. Just as she got there, the door opened and Rifka walked out. "Hello Mama, I vas just comin' to visit you."

Meshka kissed her daughter and ran to her house. "I must tell Yonkle about all da amazing dings dat are happening to me."

When she reached her house, she found it just the way it was when her husband built it. She rushed to her son's room and there lying on the bed, was her son reading a book and smelling a bit like pickle juice.

And you know from that day on, if Meshka would even think of complaining, she would say, "Dings are vell 'n I am happy." And soon they were.

CRCRCR

Part 1

The Journey

Chapter 1

The Little Village

In the little Hungarian village where my mama was born, they tell the tale of Meshka. Meshka was a very wise woman for she had a good word to say about everything.

One day little Moishela, Meshka's grandson (such a little bundle of joy, all giggly and cute), he came running towards her squealing, "Grandma, Grandma, custard, custard."

He just tasted the sweet creamy stuff for the first time, and right away he wanted to share it with his Grandma. He was moving so fast on those plump little legs of his, that he tripped over a rock and went *plotz!* His little body came to a crashing halt -- b-u-t the custard kept on going! It flew straight into Meshka's startled face.

Dripping with sweetness, she licked some of it off and put on a weak little smile. With her big soft arms, she picked up the sad little boy and she cuddled him into her cushy breasts.

She didn't scold him. She didn't say, Oy vay, such a child, vild like a bear cub 'n clumsy like a duck. She did not moan and groan and say, Oy vay, my one good dress! Now it is a *shmata*, (a rag) good only for vashing vindows.

She may have thought these things, but the words never passed her lips. All she said was "Do not cry *Shainela* (my sweet one). Look you aimed vell. See how much you got near da mouth!"

Then there was the time, Meshka was walking through the market with Yonkle, her handsome young son. His arm was draped lovingly around her shoulder. When they passed by the butcher shop, a stall with all kinds of meats hanging from hooks, Meshka said quietly to Yonkle, "If your books make you as smart as Solomon, tell me, vhat I should do vid Isaac da butcher? His eyes are going bad 'n he does not see da scale. Last veek I asked him for a three-pound chicken 'n I came home vid a two-pound duck."

Meshka didn't say vhen dat pretty young Mrs. Cohen wiggles her big round *tush* (backside); he has eyes like a hawk, but da scales he doesn't see. Maybe the thought crossed her mind, but such words never passed her lips.

Yonkle replied, "Mamma, Isaac is as honest as his nose is long. Vhen he goes to weigh da bird say, 'Let me smell da chicken. If it is not a chicken say, 'Isaac you joker, always making tricks, dis is not a chicken. It is a duck,' 'n den you laugh.

"Before he weighs da bird say, 'Isaac, you have been a butcher for vhat, forty years maybe more? Let me see if you can guess da weight of dis chicken? Vhen he weighs it, he vill look at da scale 'n see if there is a mistake."

Meshka smiled and said, "Ahhh, my wise son da scholar." But when Yonkle broke his leg jumping off a rope into a rushing stream, Meshka asked him, "Did you ever swim in dis pool before?" He said, "No." She asked him, "Did you ever think to look first, to see vhere you would land?" Again he said, "No."

Meshka didn't say, for someone who sees into heaven, here on earth, sometimes you are blinder dan Isaac da butcher. She didn't say, For Solomon so wise, sometimes dis boy does not have enough *saykhel* (common sense) to crack an egg. She may have thought these things, but they never passed her lips. Instead, she shook her head and said, "You have a great sense of adventure. Such a free spirit! Someday, maybe you vill learn to look before you fly."

And then, of course, there was sweet Suryla, Meshka's granddaughter, a lovely little girl, only four years old, but wise beyond her years. She was standing by the road just staring off into a blank blue sky. Meshka's heart was *kvelling*[1] as she looked at her. *Kvelling* is when a mama's heart bubbles over with so much love.

She asked the child, "*Shainela*, (sweet one) vhat mischievous liddle thoughts are playing in your head?"

Suryla looked up at Meshka, her eyes glazed like she was waking from a dream. Suddenly with a pink puckered smile, she laughed like a pixie and said, "Grandmama, did you know love makes love?"

Meshka knelt down and looked into the mysterious wells of her grandchild's eyes. Suryla giggled. She threw her tiny little arms around Meshka's neck and nuzzled in. She loved the sweet smell and tender warmth of her grandma's neck. Lazily, she twirled one of Meshka's silver curls around her finger and bubbled, "Can you feel it? Dis warm fuzzy feeling? Whenever I hug someone, I get dis warm fuzzy feeling all over me."

Meshka didn't say, such a silly child, life is not so fuzzy. Some people vould rather hate you dan love you. Dey vould rather hit you vid a stick, dan eat a piece of your cake. Maybe these thoughts walked through her mind, but the words never passed her lips.

Instead, she looked into those sparkling little pixie eyes and said, "Suryla my sunshine, if only everyone could see da world through your eyes." Yes, Meshka always had a good word to say to everyone.

଼ଃ଼ଃ଼ଃ

---

[1] kvell – a welling up of joy as a mother's heart does over the sweetness of her children

Meshka was walking through the woods. Her short plump little body and big round breasts were bouncing up and down as she waddled along. The dappled light between the tall trees danced on her silver curls and kissed her sweetly dimpled cheeks.

Meshka felt free and alone. She lifted her chin defiantly and with eyes darting nervously around, she accidently let the shawl slip off her head. It was a rare treat to feel the cool breeze on her face. You know it was forbidden for a woman to romp about like a child uncovered, but the summer sun made her feel so young and she loved the warmth on her naked face.

Meshka was free and it was high summer, the best time for picking blueberries. She wandered through the forest she knew so well, for she had lived in this little village and picked blueberries around here, since she was a little girl carrying her mama's basket.

When Meshka reached the meadow with the crooked tree, her eyebrows shot up to the top of her head! Surprise, fear, and curiosity all raced across her face. There in front of her, was a strange caravan of gypsies! They were camped in the meadow where the best wild blueberries were growing! Meshka stood there like she was made of stone. One of the *goyim* (foreigners), a beautiful young maiden with flashing black eyes draped in exquisitely long silken lashes, strolled over to Meshka.

"Hello!" sang the Gypsy girl, her voice sweet and friendly. Meshka's eyes turned to look but the rest of her was frozen like a stone.

Meshka was blinded by the bright sunlight sparkling off the golden beads that playfully dangled along the edge of the maiden's scarf. And such a scarf! Such color! Brilliant red and yellow like fresh roses. She looked like a walking garden.

The young maiden glided gracefully towards her like a dancer on the ice. Her skirts swayed around her long shapely legs as she walked towards the old Jewish woman.

The Gypsy girl was wearing a bunch of skirts. They were every color in the rainbow, and such a *mishmash* of patterns! Meshka's eyes were used to dark somber tones; they could not even make sense of all these busy dizzy colors!

Meshka was still standing like a statue made of stone. She was so terrified!

"I am Joya," said the young maiden in a songlike voice. "Would you like me to tell you your fortune?"

She looked into Meshka's eyes and smiled. You could light up the world with such a smile. When the Gypsy girl reached for Meshka's hand, the poor woman did not even have mind enough to run away.

Meshka's mind was racing to make sense of this strange wild creature. Her accent was thick, a little hard to understand, but her tone was so warm, Meshka's heart softened.

Joya took Meshka's stony silence for consent and gazed into her palm. Suddenly the color drained from the young girl's face. She smiled weakly and said. "Good fortune, good fortune." Then she dropped Meshka's hand like it was a burning coal!

The spell was broken and Meshka scurried away. She never met a Gypsy before! Joya was the very first person, outside her village, who ever talked to her! Meshka ran home and bolted the door.

She promised herself she would never ever go near the meadow with the crooked tree, never ever again. B-u-t day after day, always she was thinking about the Gypsy girl! She could still feel the bolt of horror that flashed across those strange eyes! They must have seen something terrible in her hand! Meshka was haunted by the fear she saw in those eyes!

Everyday her mind argued with itself. Are you crazy or vhat!?! She screamed at herself, you! Old woman, you are going to talk to a stranger??? You dink you can just walk into a wild Gypsy caravan 'n talk to dat weird fortuneteller. Who ever heard of such a ding!?!"

But then her heart put in its two cents, saying, if vee can see da future, maybe dis time vee can soften da edges. Maybe vee can work together to prepare for da storm.

While Meshka's heart and mind were busy arguing back and forth, her legs courageously wound their way through the woods to the meadow with the crooked tree. On the way, scared old Meshka collected all her courage and found some she did not even know she had.

Meshka walked into the Gypsy encampment with leaden feet, each step was a struggle. She had to know the truth, but she was terrified of hearing a prophecy!

First she passed some children playing with a ball. They glanced at her and went back to their game. A group of men were arguing loudly, talking with their hands. They paid her no mind either. Old women can be invisible.

Then Meshka came to a young man with long curly black hair playing a violin. His spirited music danced through the air stirring a sweet place inside her. The handsome violinist smiled at the old woman and said, "Welcome."

Meshka let out her breath in a rush. Only then did she realize she was holding it. Her heart even started beating again! And oy was it beating fast!

With a burst of courage she croaked out the name, "Joya?"

The Gypsy man gave Meshka a warm friendly smile, shouted the maiden's name and went on playing the violin. His tune was so sweet, it kissed her soul.

From behind a nearby wagon the young maiden appeared, again dressed in a wild splash of shockingly bright colors! Meshka jumped back at the sight of her, but spoke before she lost the nerve.

"Hello Joya. Do you remember me? Before I vas a stone statue, now I can talk." Meshka took a deep long breath, breathing the courage up from her soul.

The maiden smiled, flashing white teeth and chimed, "How could I not remember you? You are the first Jewess I ever met! Oh what strange stories I have heard about your mysterious people and their great love affair with God."

Such words from such a young mouth! They took all the breath out of Meshka.

In silent panic, Meshka's mind begged her to run away, but the mouth opened and the words fell out, "Please tell me da part you did not vant to say da last time you looked at my fortune." The hand opened all by itself as she gave her palm to the Gypsy fortuneteller.

The smile of welcome melted off the young maiden's face replaced by honest fear. She gazed down at Meshka's fleshy callused palm hoping something new would appear, but the lines were just the same as she remembered.

Although Joya was a naturally honest person, she quickly looked for a lie to tell. But the sharp clarity in this sweet little old lady's steady gaze changed her mind. So she dared to speak the truth, "I see the mark of God written in your hand. God has touched your tongue. Be careful what you say. Your words have the power and the frailty of truth."

This made no sense. But it sounded important. Meshka quickly thrust a fresh baked loaf of her famous sweet challah bread into Joya's hands and squeaked, "May God bless you." The words spoke themselves and the old legs ran away as fast as they could carry her.

Meshka was right. At this moment, God *was* blessing Joya. The girl was intoxicated with the magic of being fourteen in high summer. She reveled in the joy of being young and free! Utterly free! She was traveling with her family from place to place discovering a wonderful world!

Everywhere they went she danced. People threw money and gifts at her feet. Everywhere she sang, people wept and applauded! She was a bright light among her tribe, a bright light on the verge of becoming an amazing woman. The blush of full life radiated from her soul. Yes, God blessed her.

CRCRCR

Meshka ran most of the way home. It was a long time before she could breathe again. Her heart was throbbing, her mind was racing, and her feet could not run fast enough.

Joya watched Meshka go. The girl smiled, amused to see the old woman's fleshly little body bouncing up and down, like a big squishy ball on little churning legs. Joya's smile faded, though, as she remembered the palm print engraved in her mind.

She ran over to Uncle Alberto, who was sitting by the fire with a beautiful blue quill in his hand. She ran up, looked at him with that cute troubled pout of hers.

He put aside his precious scroll and opened his arms. She crawled onto his lap and rested her head against his warm, sweet, musky robe.

It smelled of tobacco, sweet herbs, tangy wine and fresh ink all mingled with his powerful man smell. She burrowed in under his arm and felt warm and safe in the sheltering darkness.

He rocked her like a child. At thirteen, she was both child and woman; a little of each, and a lot of promise. He had rocked her like this since the day she was born. She was the shining star that brightened his life.

"What is troubling you my little peacock?" She heard him say. The words were muffled through the thick robe.

His wild musky smell lulled her into a feeling a safety, so she dared to tell him. "Uncle, I saw too much in a woman's hand! I wanted to lie, but I could not. She had the hand of a holy woman! But she looked like a little old hag. I saw something terrible! I gazed at the clashing lines in her hand and I saw a vision filled with fire and screaming!"

Uncle Alberto held her tightly to his heart. "I know my child, I know," he whispered and rocked her. "Enjoy each moment. Life is precious and fleeting." He had seen the visions too! That is why he led his little caravan down off the mountain to this quiet little green valley. The deer in the forest were plentiful and the fish in the stream jumped onto the hook. There were even fresh blueberries to sweeten their pies. Who could want for more? They came down the mountain and made their camp here to be safe. But even in this quiet sanctuary, terrible visions came upon him.

CR CR CR

Meshka reached her village and walked up the safe little road her feet had traveled all her life. It was a great relief, to be back in her own familiar world. She told herself she was safe, but she still wanted to crawl under her bed and hide like a little girl.

"God has touched your tongue!" The words rattled around again and again in Meshka's head.

There once was a time when Meshka looked at life through a dark veil. She saw the world always half-empty and that drained her. But one day, she felt touched by the hand of God and ever since then, she guarded her words with reverence and respect.

Meshka turned the fortuneteller's words over and around in her head for the next few days. While she was making breakfast for Yonkle, she had her eyes on the eggs but her mind was on the Gypsy girl until she smelled the eggs burning.

There was definitely something the girl was not saying. Meshka was sure of it. Then she got all aggravated with herself for running away so fast. She should have given the girl a chance to say more.

Later, Meshka figured this would be a good day to go hunting for mushrooms. The woods were carpeted with so many different kinds of delicious little treasures now that summer was coming to an end. Meshka padded along through the soft underbrush in the forest. In no time at all her basket was full. It was time to go back to the village, but her legs didn't go back, they went forward!

The loud crunching sound of the pine needles under her feet accused her of returning to the Gypsy camp. "No, no, no," she protested. But her legs defied her will, and disobeyed tradition. They carried her all the way back to the meadow with the crooked tree. She had to visit the forbidden fortune-teller, just one more time!

Meshka hardly saw where she was going -- her mind was making so much noise. Battered between hope and dread, she imagined the caravan had moved on and the fortuneteller would be gone. All this babbling, justifying, making excuses, it all kept her mind from paying attention to what the legs were doing.

Her heart skipped a beat when she reached the meadow with the crooked tree! The Gypsies were still there! Excited and nervous, she smiled at everybody she passed as she walked between the wagons looking for Joya.

Meshka was having a little trouble catching her breath, because her heart was beating so fast! She found Joya standing next to a wagon flirting with the handsome young man who played the violin. How could she miss her, dressed in brilliant beautiful colors, her head covered by a pretty magenta kerchief sparkling with golden beads. Such wild colors made Meshka's eyes swim. Whoever heard of a girl dressing like this!?!

Joya was laughing at something the young man said. She tossed her head back. Her velvet black hair cascaded from under the kerchief over her shoulders. Then she saw Meshka and her smile faded. Joya broke away from her handsome young man and glided over to the old Jewish woman.

"Hello, are you looking for me?" She sounded friendly, but she had a look of wary suspicion.

"Such a question! Who else? You dink I came all dis vay for my health!" Her words came out harsher than she meant to, so she smiled - sort of. Her lips gave a tight crooked twist, but it got the idea across. "Joya please, I know something big is coming. I can feel it." A chill ran up her spine at each word.

Joya led the old woman over to the crooked tree and they sat down. The curve of the trunk made a perfect bench for two people to sit side by side. Meshka knew this tree well. She used to come here after picking blueberries and share a picnic with the children. She would sit on the tree and knit sweaters, while little Rifkala and Yonkela played with the yarn at her feet. Usually such memories made her smile, but right now they just made her feel more scared.

Meshka sat down beside the young Gypsy fortuneteller and opened her palm. From the grimace on her face, you might think the girl was going to cut her hand off. Meshka's hands were always hot, but right now they were cold as ice.

Joya looked down into Meshka's big fleshy palm and trembled. She wanted to look away. She wanted to block out the vision that was standing clearly in her mind. Before she could compose her face and make up a lie, Meshka saw the horror flash across her eyes!

"Vhat!?!" The old woman croaked! "Vhat do you see!?!" she demanded. Fear was spreading through her body like a dark stain ruining a good dress.

Out of the strange Gypsy girl's mouth, came the most unbelievable words, "You are going leave your village and never return. No one will for a long, long time."

Meshka's eyes were bulging like they were trying to run away from the truth. The beautiful young Gypsy girl and the weathered old Jewish woman just sat there staring at each other like two stuffed birds on a branch. No one moved.

Dark angry clouds moved across the sky above them. The air felt still and heavy. Insects stopped buzzing and birds stopped singing. Within minutes the ugly clouds were dropping big fat raindrops on their heads! The two unlikely companions just sat there. They didn't notice. I don't think either one was breathing. Finally a loud crack of thunder broke the trance.

Meshka stood up and slowly walked away. Her eyes saw nothing. Somehow the legs found their way back to her village, but she did not remember walking through the woods. Safely back in her cozy little house, she realized that she left her basket of mushrooms back in the meadow. She began to cry because it was her favorite basket, but that was not really why she was crying. The big tears fell from her eyes, because the world was going to end!

Am I crazy or vhat? Why do I believe dis strange creature vid all those gaudy colors 'n her vild black hair!?! She scolded herself, but it did not make her feel better.

She turned the fortuneteller's words this way and that. In desperate panic, she grabbed for one meaning after another, but none rang as true as disaster.

രുരുരു

Within a month, the world turned upside down and nothing made sense anymore. A sickness came from the East carried by a weathered old bookseller. It rampaged through the Gentile village to the north. Many young children and old people died.

One Sunday morning in the aftermath, the priest of the village stood before his congregation cloaked in his usual long black robe. He cast a dark and brooding eye over his congregation. The deadly poison of hate filled his veins, exploding in a voice so harsh and loud, it could have come straight from God!

His face was screwed so tight, his brains didn't work. He was filled with wrath! This imposing figure slowly cast his dark gaze over the congregation. He looked each person in the eye. His terrible passion raked their souls, awakened their pain, and touched their suffering. He held their pain in the palm of his sacred hands and twisted it into hate. He betrayed God's holy trust.

The priest filled the people with his poison and told them the suffering of this terrible plague was a sign from God!

"God," he shouted from the pulpit, standing high above the simple farmers and their families. "God is punishing you for your wickedness!" His colorless eyes were cold as ice as he shook a long bony finger at the congregation. With the finger of God, he accused them, "You are being punished for letting infidels dwell on this land! God will not suffer them to live here in this pure place. They brought the sickness," which was a lie.

In his booming voice of doom, he read Judges and when he reached the part where it said, "And ye shall make no league with the inhabitants of this land; ye shall throw down their altars: but ye have not obeyed my voice," he hissed in a low deadly tone, "Why have you done this?"

He gave voice to a wrathful God! The congregation trembled. The sound of one whimpering child broke the absolute silence in the long tense moments that followed.

The priest read Judges 2:12 – 15 to let his people know what God expected of them: "Jehovah's anger blazed against Israel, so that he gave them into the hands of the pillagers, and they began to pillage them."

After that mass, the men abruptly left the church. They were of one mind and they knew what they must do. Burning with a mission they believed came straight from God, the angry roiling mob grabbed their tools and weapons. Burning with a fiery hunger for vengeance, they set out for the Jewish village!

On the way, they came upon the caravan of Gypsies camped in the meadow with the crooked tree. Some of the men with crazed eyes, carried burning torches. Soon all the Gypsy wagons were blazing! Screaming women and children were running in every direction trying to escape! The Gypsy men were fierce fighters, but there were too many angry villagers flaming with God's wrath! Loud shrieks and horrible groans tore the air in dying agony. The choking smoke of the fires offered a little cover but no one escaped!

In less than an hour, all the screaming stopped. The groans of agony stopped. All the dancing, singing Gypsies in the caravan were dead! By the end of that accursed day, most of the Jews were dead too.

Meshka survived. Maybe it was God who gave her the urge to go fishing in a pond deep in the woods, far from the village, and the meadow. Maybe her guardian angel was just doing her job. But that morning Meshka woke up with a strong desire for fresh fish sautéed with onions. So she went fishing on the last warm day of summer.

It was a beautiful day, but Meshka's skin was crawling. A strange terrible feeling made her uncomfortable. She prayed to the God of her foremothers, as her family had done for thousands of years. She begged the Holy One to give her a sign, to whisper on the wind, to do something to ease this terrible ache in her heart. But no sign came and no wind blew. God did not answer.

The terrible feeling got worse, so she headed home to cook the two plump shimmering fish she caught. She thought about how happy Yonkle was going to be. He loved fried fish with onions.

Every step felt exhausting, as though her legs were made of lead, as though they did not want to go home. If that was the sign she was waiting for, she could make no sense of it. Near to the village, she heard frightening screams. Her heart pounded like crazy. She ran in circles not knowing where to go.

Then she saw the big old hollow burned out tree. She used to hide in there when she was a little girl. No one ever thought to look for her in there. It had been her dreaming place. Trembling, she crawled in and waited forever and ever for the nightmare to end.

When the world was quiet for a long time, she crawled out of the tree and slowly walked in silent dread back to her sweet little village. She passed Leah, the lovely little dressmaker. She was lying sprawled out in front of her house. Someone had stabbed her several times in the heart with a pitchfork. They did the same thing to her three beautiful little children.

Meshka got very sick. Her stomach jumped out of her. This was the most horrible thing she had ever seen. But there was worse to come.

As she crossed the smoldering ashes of the market, she wondered why Isaac's little butcher shop was the only thing standing amongst the ashes. Then her eyes grew wide and her jaw dropped open! Isaac's body was hanging grotesquely from one of his own meat hooks. They hung him there next to all the other cuts of meat.

She could hardly walk, so blinded was she by bitter tears. Then she came to Eli, the sweet fat little baker. He was always so nice to her. He always asked about her health and gave her a few extra cookies whenever she stopped by, just so she should have a sweeter day. His bald head was broken and his blood was seeping out in little red rivulets flowing through the flour on the rolling board beneath his head. She wanted to erase these unbelievable things. She prayed that she was dreaming and these terrible things were not true. Not now and not ever.

She thought this was the most horrible thing that could ever happen, but the worse was still to come.

She found Rifka. Thank God, Rifka was alive! Her body was covered with blood and bruises, her face was all discolored, and her eyes were swollen shut, but she was alive!

She was babbling, screaming, screeching, and making no sense. How could Rifka tell her mama that sweet little Moishela and her pixie Suryla were locked up in the house by crazy people, who put a torch to it, and laughed at the children's screams? It was much too terrible to remember and she would never forget.

This sweet little village had thrived here for centuries and now it was only smoldering ashes. That evening was so cold, not just the night, but inside their souls. Ashes and agony, few people survived. Whoever was still alive gathered by a pile of rubble that only yesterday had been their beautiful *shul* (sacred temple). People held each other and wondered why they were still alive. Several women threw themselves on the ground and wailed pitifully. Meshka's daughter Rifka was one of them. They screamed, pulled out their hair in chunks and ripped at their clothes. Some people just sat in mute silence staring with frozen eyes.

Meshka looked from one familiar face to another. These were the wonderful people she had known all her life. Her heart broke in a million pieces. In the core of her soul was a huge gaping hole. She was falling and falling, trapped in a terrible nightmare. God had abandoned them! Her anguish was so vast; she just kept falling and falling. It was never going to stop. Never!

The broken bloodied Jews now faced the hideous task of burying their dead. All time had stopped! The day went on forever and ever as these good people buried so many sweet innocent victims of hate.

The rabbi was dead. Someone broke his head with a hammer and all his brilliant compassion and wisdom spilled onto the ground. Such a terrible waste!

A young scholar said the prayers over the dead. He stumbled on the words and choked on the tears running down his throat. Yonkle, with his beautiful deep voice, could have recited the prayers so much better, but he didn't, because he was dead.

Yesterday was just like any other day, not so different one from another. Today, nothing will ever be the same again! That night was so black, the world looked erased. Wounded, broken people huddled in groups and cried all through the night.

Morning begrudgingly dawned. The sun rose like a regular day, as though nothing had happened; but the world had ended. The Jews gathered what they could and began to leave. Some people had distant relatives elsewhere. Others just followed the road, assuming it would lead somewhere. They mourned their dead as they trudged down the road, each exiled into an unknown destiny.

Meshka and her daughter Rifka scavenged a few things they thought would be useful, a stew pot with a burning coal inside, a few cooking things, some blankets, some clothes, a rope, an ax, two candlesticks to light candles on the Shabbos (Sabbath), and as much food as they could carry. The two women packed all these things in long dark dresses and lifted the heavy weights, onto their backs. They pulled their drab shawls more tightly around their aching heads and quivering shoulders. Slowly they shuffled down the road.

"Mama, vhere vill vee go?" Rifka asked in a small voice, cracked and parched from too many tears.

"I do not know *Shainela*. (my sweet one) Everyone I ever knew, lived, married 'n died in our liddle village. I know from nowhere," and so they set out on a long journey to nowhere.

"Mama, how vill vee live?" Rifka asked softly looking up at her mama with little girl eyes.

"I don't know Shainela. Vee are in God's hands now."

A chill raked Rifka's back. It raised the short hairs and made her shiver.

ଔଔଔ

Chapter 2

The Journey Begins

The two Jewish women slowly shuffled down the road, bent under the heavy weight of their bundles. Around her neck Meshka wore a *mezuzah*, a tiny box with a written blessing inside it. For years, it hung by her front door to guard and protect her cozy little home. She kissed it every time she walked through the door. It was *supposed* to keep the house safe! It did not work! Now she had no home, no village, and no place to belong.

On Rifka's strong shoulders was a similar bundle of useful things wrapped in a long dress. She did not have a *mezuzah*. The one she had was lost in the fire when her life burned down. Tied securely around her thigh was a sharp knife and hidden in the folds of her dress was a pretty little doll.

Rifka was such a good mama; she was always making some little toy to delight the children. Just yesterday morning she finished the lovely doll with its delicately embroidered eyes and long braided locks of yarn. In the madness of biting flames, the pretty doll lay forgotten in the folds of her dress. Now her sweet little pixie was never going to cuddle the cushy little doll and giggle in delight.

The two women trudged down the road in silence. They had not gone far when they found Joya. The Gypsy girl lay twisted across the old crooked tree. She looked like a broken and discarded doll. Her body was a mass of black, blue, and purple bruises; her eyes stared blindly unseeing. What little was left of her pretty clothes were torn to shreds and covered with blood.

The poor girl was still alive, but she did not know from anything or anyone around her. She just lay there! She took refuge from the horror, by creeping into the darkness of her mind. Her eyes did not see and her ears did not hear. Too much sound! Too much pain! It pushed her into the darkness of her soul. If the breath did not breathe itself, she would be dead. She had no mind for nothing.

Meshka and Rifka were walking in a numbed trance when they came across her. At first, they thought she was dead, but then Rifka pointed out her chest was moving. Reluctantly, they walked through the meadow to the crooked tree. As children they both played on this tree, as young mothers they each brought their children here to play. On the way to the tree, they stepped around several pretty people laying on the ground in horrible broken pieces. Rifka began screaming madly when her foot slipped out from under her and she fell plop into a huge puddle of blood!

Meshka held her daughter and patted her like she was a little girl until she calmed down. They looked at all the burned wagons and gagged on the thick sweet smell of death. The meadow was littered with bloody bodies and massive clouds of ugly black flies.

Meshka's brain stretched very far to believe her eyes! It stretched even farther to accept that God could let such a thing happen? The Gypsies, like her own people, had done nothing bad. They celebrated life with their dances, songs, and magical powers.

Meshka stared at this abyss of wasted life! An agonizing wave of sickness came over her. She felt like she was drowning under crashing waves of death!

A strong wind blew, branches trembled, and several red maple leaves rained down around them. A magenta scarf fringed with tiny golden beads fluttered past Meshka taking flight. Seeing it took her back to a sunny day, not that long ago. While her eyes were on the scarf, and her mind was in the past, Meshka took a few steps forward. Suddenly a big black bird flew right up in her face in a wild panic of flapping wings. She startled him from his dinner. Meshka jumped back trembling. Her legs were wobbly and she almost tripped over a broken body. As she got her feet back under her, she looked down into the dead man's face. His mouth and eyes were frozen forever staring in horror. In the depths of his old eyes something reminded her of her pious papa's patient eyes.

Racked with terror and disgust, Rifka was pulling on Meshka's sleeve screaming, "Mama, vee must get away from here before da Gypsy ghosts tear our eyes out!"

Meshka stared at her in confusion. For a moment she did not understand the words. Then she gave a heavy sigh and said, "Vee must bury dem."

Rifka stared at her mama in horror. "No Mama. Vee must run!!!"

In a crusty tired voice, Meshka sighed again, "Shainela, these are not our people, but in death vhat does not it matter? Vee cannot in good conscience leave dem to rot 'n make more sickness."

"Mama, are you *meshugeneh* (crazy in the head) or vhat!?! Vee do not owe these people anythin'!" She shrieked.

"Dat is right, but vee are good people 'n vee must do vhat is right, or vee become like da dogs dat did dis." Meshka put down her bundles, stretched her back and went to look for a shovel.

She found one near a fire pit and another by a broken cart. The tools lying strewn about had a dark crust of blood on their blades. Heaven only knows what terrible stories the blood-stained shovels could tell.

Meshka handed one to Rifka. She was about to protest, but changed her mind and shrugged instead. The two women put their backs into the work. They were desperate to finish before nightfall. The idea of spending the night with the unburied dead was far too frightening to contemplate, so they just dug faster. By necessity they dug one really big grave.

With each shovelful of dirt that Rifka lifted, she grumbled. First she just muttered quietly to herself; but as the sweat poured down her body, the grumbling got louder. "God! Humph!" she muttered again and again.

As she lifted each load of dirt, her mind churned up one angry thought after another. "You know Mama, God makes war." The words tasted like bitter poison on her tongue. She turned her face away to hide her eyes.

Rifka was stuck in hell; condemned to endlessly dig ditches for innocent murdered people.

Rifka is right, thought Meshka. God makes war. In Bible stories someone is usually hurting someone else. Those tales are not good maps 'n vee keep passing dem down from one generation to da next. It is wrong!

Meshka put her slumped old shoulders to the task of digging. The dirt was heavy, but the loamy soil was loose and yielding. Shovel load after shovel load, her jawbone tightened until it ached. She felt heavy and tired down to her soul. In her mind was the nagging thought, if God's holy book vas filled vid stories of people helping each other to make everyone's lives better, it vould teach people to make a better world.

Muscles Meshka did not have, ached; but her anger fueled her old arms with the strength to keep digging.

"God should make life different. He should tell people how to live without hurting each other! He should give people a new book vid new maps," Meshka grumbled out loud.

Rifka was just as furious with God; but she could not yell at God, so she yelled at her mama, "Mama, are you *meshugeneh!?!* You dink God did dis! I do not believe in God anymore 'n anyway I am angry at him."

What could Meshka say? Nothing, so she bent her shoulder to the work. Hour after hour the two Jewish women stood side by side digging graves for the Gypsies. Their hands became blistered, the blisters broke open, and they ached all over, but still they kept on digging. Their exhausted arms and blistered hands went numb, but still they kept on digging. Too bad their hearts were not so numb; the grief was stifling.

Joya did not lift a finger to bury her people. She did not move an inch. She didn't even see what the two Jewish women were doing. She just sat on a log staring off at nothing, her mind was melted.

After several grueling hours, the big ditch was deep enough and long enough to put all the people in. Together, they lugged, dragged, and rolled each heavy body, bloated with maggots, into the ditch. As they moved each body, a cloud of flies rose up for a moment; then settled back to their morbid mission of devouring the dead. The two women wore kerchiefs over their faces, but they still struggled not to gag. The work was hard. Their arms stretched and stretched until they felt six feet long.

They reached for the old Gypsy man who looked like Meshka's papa, Rifka saw her grandpa in his eyes as well. It shocked her to remember! She shook her head to wipe away the wretched memory of the horrified look in her pious *zaideh's* (grandpa's) eyes when she buried him only the day before.

Rifka tried to recall the way her *zaideh's* eyes laughed when he used to tease her for being so serious, but the look of horror kept forcing its way back into her mind.

Zaideh vas always talkin' about God, she thought. He vas da one who taught me to have great reverence for da *Torah* (Bible) 'n to respect all its powerful words. He loved God 'n look vhat God did to him!

The anger kept her working long after all her strength was gone. It took forever and ever, but finally the last body was respectfully placed in the mass grave.

They carefully put one body next to the other, so the dead people would be comfortable in the forever. Then they shoveled even more, until the people were all covered with dirt. By this time, their arms were eight feet long and made out of something stretchy.

The women were exhausted, soaked with sweat, filthy, and miserably hungry. Rifka's back creaked when she tried to stand up. Meshka could hardly straighten up at all. She was afraid she was going to stay bent forever. It horrified her to picture herself walking around with her nose pointing to the ground. After several attempts, much to her great relief, *Baruch HaShem* (blessed be the name of the Lord) she straightened up. She was so grateful to be upright, she could have kissed God!

Rifka pressed her hands against her aching spine and leaned back as far as she could, grumbling, "I hope none of these ghosts come back to dank us." It was a lame joke, but Meshka answered her seriously.

"You are right. Vee have to put their souls to rest. Vee should say *Kaddish*." (da mourner's prayer)

Rifka stared at Meshka in horror and disbelief! "Vhat! *Oy Gevalt!* (Heaven Forbid!) Mama are you completely *fertummelt* (befuddled 'n confused)!?! You cannot recite Jewish prayers over dead *Goyim!*" (Non-Jews)

"Why? You know some Gypsy prayers?" Meshka chided. She flashed a twisted smile at Rifka that held no humor.

The air felt much lighter once the mound was firmly covered. They patted the last bit of dirt down the way you pat a baby's back when he goes to sleep.

CRCRCR

The day was gone and twilight was rapidly descending upon them. Meshka was too tired to take another step. She helped Joya lay down and curled up next to her. She drew her shawl tightly around the two of them and fell right off to sleep.

Rifka was hungry, but did not have the strength to do one more thing, so she curled up next to her mama and fell asleep in exhaustion.

Shrieks of terror and a fierce loud hissing startled them awake in the middle of the night! A snake and a cat were locked in a battle to the death. The cat's terrible screams tore through the night; followed by foreboding silence. The three women lying curled together were wide-eyed and two of them were trembling!

Though miserably exhausted, they were now wide awake, listening to the eerie whispering of the night and all the creepy little sounds. The night was quiet, except for the scampering of small feet. Everything was still until shadows scurried right by them. Leaves crackled in the wind and an assortment of living creatures made themselves heard, all around them in the dark.

Rifka was sure the scampering feet, the crackling sounds, and the scurrying shadows were all angry ghosts! She jumped up and urgently tried to convince Meshka to leave the caravan and camp in the forest.

Meshka gave her a weary look, shook her head, and mumbled, "I am sorry Shainela. I am too tired to be scared." She stayed right there, curled up where she dropped, and fell back to sleep. Rifka laid a blanket over her mama and Joya, and wandered off to sleep as far away as possible from the eerie haunted grave.

B-u-t she came right back. Being all alone in the dark forest was more frightening than these dead people rising in the night!

�

The next morning, the three women were still alive. Not one ghost even tried to eat their eyes out in the night, Rifka was afraid for nothing. After a few hours of sleeping like a rock, Rifka woke up famished.

She wandered around the caravan scrounging up whatever food she could find. Most of it was burned or trampled, but she found some fresh food: flour, onions, oil, salt, potatoes and even a few eggs. Perfect! She could make *latkas*....if she had a frying pan.

It did not take long to find the perfect stone. It was flat and only as thick as a mouse's belly, a perfect frying pan. She scrubbed it with sand and rinsed it in the creek.

Meshka was also awake. She wandered off at first light and returned with an armful of branches, also a pot of water to make tea. Now for the fire!

Meshka wanted to make the fire right on the dirt, but all the twigs everywhere made it dangerous. She shuddered at the thought of lifting more dirt, but felt she should dig a little pit. Once that was done, she lined up a few sticks side by side inside the pit. She put the living coal hidden in the pot on top of the sticks. One or two branches caught fire, but soon burned out. Meshka put a few more sticks neatly one next to the other and tried again. The branches kindled and caught flame but the wind blew it out.

Feeling inspired, she piled the branches together in a bunch so each one could share its warmth with the other, and tucked her precious coal in the center. Soon the flames were warm and blazing.

Meshka sat by her first fire and took pride in its warmth. At home, Meyer always lit the fires. It was a part of his charm, how he liked to take care of her. She liked him doing things for her and he enjoyed doing them so......she never learned.

The fire burned down to nice warm coals, the pot of water boiled, and the tea leaves were brewing by the time Rifka returned with the food she scavenged and her nice clean new stone frying pan.

Rifka set to work quickly, chopping three handfuls of potatoes and a nice big onion into very fine little pieces with her sharp knife. She added a handful of flour, an egg, a pinch of salt and mixed it all together with a short thick stick.

She moistened the stone with oil, and placed it firmly on the hot coals. When the oil on the rock was sizzling hot, Rifka made big flat patties and cooked the latkas on the stone until they were crispy, delicious, and done. With careful maneuvering and a big knife she found, she adeptly turned them over to crisp on the other side. The two hungry women gobbled the delicious latkas down in a gulp, drank their hot tea, and patiently fed Joya. Not a word was spoken.

The women were toasty warm sitting by the fire on this chilly morning. Meshka's tongue and her belly were *kvelling*. "Ah, *mekheye!*" (pleasurable)

She felt full. She was tickled that God gave them just the right ingredients to make such a feast.

Suddenly Rifka broke the silence, Meshka was roused from her thoughts by Rifka's voice.

"Shainela, vhat did you say?" Meshka asked.

A little irritated, Rifka repeated, "I said, '*Chaval!* (too bad) There are no apples. Latkas are perfect vid applesauce. Without apples, the latkes taste too greasy."

The early morning chill was burning off and the sun was now high enough to warm them. They faced their second day outside of time.

Another search around the caravan to see what survived turned up a few more treasures like a big brick of cheese and a hungry goat. The rascally little creature had run away, frightened by the chaos, and now returned to be milked and fed. Rifka relieved the goat of her burden.

In a gentle but firm voice, Meshka whispered in the Gypsy girl's ear, "Listen my dear, vee are going away now. You must take some dings." Joya did not blink an eye. She did not say a word. She just sat there staring at nothing.

All the wagons were burned. All the horses and mules were either dead or stolen. But over near the forest lying overturned in the shadows of a big elm tree, Rifka found a small push cart in good repair. This was a really exciting find! Gratefully they piled all their bundles in the little cart.

 Meshka and Rifka both wiggled their shoulder at the same time in the same way, both feeling the freedom and relief of putting down the burden of their weight.

 Meshka walked around the caravan gathering whatever interesting treasures survived the fire and the pillaging. Rifka collected a few practical things as well. They packed everything up and put it in the little cart. They also tied the goat onto the handle with a long strong rope.

 Meshka put her arms around Joya and lifted her to her feet. The girl stood there like a limp rag doll. Meshka took her hand and pulled her along. The girl slowly walked beside her. Thank goodness Meshka did not have to drag her. Once Joya was on her feet, she ambled on down the road beside them.

 Rifka put her shoulder against the cart and pushed it; then she pulled it. That worked better. The wheels turned and the cart rolled on down the road.

C3CRCR

The three tired, droopy women walked along hour after hour all day long, stopping at every stream and pond to drink or share a bit of pungent cheese. As they walked along, the women filled their pockets with almonds, chestnuts and mushrooms, little gifts from the land. Rifka found a wild bird's nest and borrowed an egg. When darkness threatened to descend upon them, they made camp in a thicket under countless unseen but threatening eyes. Meshka bundled the wood this time when she made the fire and was quickly rewarded with a roaring blaze.

 Maybe Rifka could make a different kind of *latka*. She crushed the nuts with a heavy round rock that fit nicely into her hand, diced the mushrooms, added a handful of flour, put in the egg, and added a pinch of salt. She mixed it all up with her now favorite stick, pulled her trusty frying stone out of the cart, and made a very decent dinner. She served it with fresh warm goat milk.

The night was chilly and the wind was whistling through the trees, but their blankets kept them warm. Close to the fire, Joya lay cuddled up next to Meshka. With the flames in front of her and Joya behind her, Meshka was warm enough. Rifka was wrapped in her own blanket beside them, but as the night grew colder, Rifka drew closer until she lay wrapped around Joya. The fire kept them warm, but no amount of heat could soothe the icy dreams pursuing them.

Screeching hoots from a barn owl shocked them awake in the middle of the night! He flew out of a nearby tree and then the night returned to quiet, but Meshka could not sleep. She felt cramped and her bladder ached, so she crawled out of her warm blanket into the cold and dark.

Once Meshka was finished with her business behind the bushes, the idea of returning to her cold blanket on the hard cold ground, lying squished between Joya and the last of the glowing embers, did not appeal to her; so she walked off to be alone.

She found a relatively comfortable spot on a pile of soft leaves under a big birch tree. Pulling her long homespun shawl tighter around her shivering shoulders, Meshka called out to heaven, "God!" She started coughing, choking, and tried again. "Holy God!" The intensity of the last few days was crushing her. She felt weary down to her soul.

Suddenly a tide of rage swelled up in her and she cried out, "Oy God, how could You do dis to all da good, religious people who obeyed Your commandments 'n honored You?"

There was no answer.

"God, I know you are not sleeping! You must do something!" Meshka desperately urged. "People are killing each other down here!"

The words popped into her head, "I have given you free will. Now we shall see what you do with it."

Her voice grew more intense as she cried out, "But Most Holy Von, You have given us a view of da world dat sees only good 'n evil, Jew 'n Gentile, us 'n dem. Vhen You chose Abel over Cain, vhen You set brother against brother because you favored one over da other, look at da terrible force You unleashed. Do something!"

She clearly heard God's reply; "I will not interfere with your free will. You must find your way to virtue by yourselves."

Meshka was furiously angry, but since it was not safe to be angry with God, she went off to gather wood for the fire.

She brought back an armload of branches and dropped them near the fire. She added a few of the thicker sticks to the smoldering embers and fanned them into flame, hoping it would last the rest of the night. Utterly weary, she crawled under the blanket just as the dark was fading into light.

That was when the birds woke up all excited. They made such a racket with all their chirping! Two very noisy squirrels chased each other up and down the trees, chattering the whole time; and Meshka had a headache. The day had not even started and she was already fed up with it!

Sitting by the morning fire warmed away the chill in their bones. Rifka made a nice hot pot of tea and warmed up some of her wonderful nut latkas.

The women gathered up all their things, piled them in the cart, and continued on their way to nowhere. They walked all day and only stopped for a brief midday meal of more nut *latkas*, pungent cheese and sweet goat milk.

The road got rougher and then disappeared altogether. They kept going and found themselves walking through a thick forest, stumbling over big roots and stubbing their toes on hidden rocks. Meshka was just glad it was daytime. When the sun began its slow descent, she was relieved to find a small clearing hidden among the thick trees. Meshka's legs felt like rubber and Rifka's legs felt like they were going to fall off! Meshka never complained and Rifka never stopped complaining. Joya, of course, said nothing.

The clearing was a gift from God. It was bordered with ber-ry bushes overhanging a small stream. Rifka and Meshka picked plump red ones, big juicy black ones, and luscious blue ones. They put them all in a bowl and added a little goat milk. Joya was very weak. It was hard to get her to swallow. Patiently Meshka fed her one berry at a time, to keep her from choking.

That night, the women made camp and had a fine fire go-ing before the dusk stole all the light away. The sun was swallowed up by the velvet darkness and the crickets began their endless clicking babble. Cuddled close to the flames, they stared up at a vast cold sky.

All the sinister stars were staring down at them. Invisible eyes watched them from behind every tree and boulder. The wind gave an eerie whistle and the trees shook angry arms at them. Rustling leaves laughed at them, mocking helpless wom-en cast adrift in a threatening world. The haunting silhouettes of silver trees waving in the dappled moonlight, made every shadow look dangerous.

Somewhere in the night, God decided to drop rain on them. They needed that like they needed holes in their heads. They jumped up and scrambled under a big tree. The embers sizzled as fat rain drops stole their warmth and cooled the coals.

Meshka slept restlessly. Her hip hurt from the cold hard ground and her neck was stiff. At first light, she got up and went off to gather wood in a wet forest. Only the branches un-der the thickest trees were still dry. It took longer than usual to find a big armful of usable wood.

While she was gathering sticks, she gathered her thoughts. Then she put her bundle of branches aside and sat down under a big ash tree. After a few deep breaths, she felt ready for her morning talk with God.

"Vell Most Holy Von, have You come up vid a new plan yet?" She chided.

The Good Lord was quick to answer, "Meshka, you are a troublesome woman. Haven't you learned? Women should be silent and respectful?"

That shut her mouth! But arguing with God was in her blood. It is what Jews have done since the beginning of time, so she answered Him, "Most Holy Von, vhat vill silence get me? You gave me a mind! Do You dink a woman's mind is just for memorizing recipes 'n repeating gossip? I may be an old woman, but my mind is sharp 'n clear."

She felt like a grandmother with a naughty little boy who needed a good straightening out. If she did not set God on the right path, who would? Her rabbi once said, "If not me, den who? If not now, den vhen?" The words came from the *Talmud*, a very sacred scroll. So with the *rabbi* and the *Talmud* behind her, Meshka scolded God!

"You dink I do not see vhat You are doing? First You turned brother against brother. Den You told men dat dey have a natural right to boss women around. You are a troublemaker! If my son, you know da one You killed, if he fought vid all da boys 'n bullied all da girls, I vould have taken a birch branch to his *tush!*" (buttocks)

Oops! Maybe she said too much!?! Meshka held her breath trembling. B-u-t when fire did not rain down from heaven, she figured God wasn't too upset with her little tirade.

ରେଉଇରେ

The world ended on Sunday. They buried the Jews on Monday and the Gypsies on Tuesday. Wednesday and Thursday were a blur, just one foot in front of another. They were not hot or cold. They were just days. The women walked from morning till night. They stopped only when they had to. They were wearing holes in their shoes and wearing down their feet. Meshka was sure she was now an inch shorter. Still they kept on going. What else could they do? They wanted to get far away from their memories, but the pictures in their minds chased them wherever they went.

Today was Friday and tonight the *Shabbos* (Sabbath) would begin. Rifka woke up early, just like she always did on Friday mornings. This was the day she always cleaned the house until it shone like a jewel. Then she would cook a delicious chicken soup with fluffy *matzoth balls* (dumplings), bake two huge golden *challahs* (braided bread) and prepare a special dinner for her family.

But today, when she opened her eyes and saw the rain falling all around the big oak tree, where she was laying curled up stiff and cold, she moaned and groaned and closed her eyes. There was no house to clean, no chicken for soup, and no children to cook for. The rest of the morning, she choked on her tears.

That night, a huge full moon lit up the sky and made the clearing where they were huddled together, almost as bright as day. Meshka begged Rifka to get up and at least, light the Shabbos candles. It was hard, but she roused herself.

Rifka and her mama drew their long shawls over their bowed heads, lit one Shabbos candle each with a precious live coal, drew the flaming light into their souls, covered their eyes with their hands and recited the prayers. As always, after the customary words, Meshka added a few of her own, "Please Holy Father, dis is a good time for a miracle. Shabbos is supposed to be a day of rest. Could you please give us some rest?"

A few minutes later a blustery wind blew the candles out. Rifka was going to relight them, but Meshka put out her hand to stop her and said, "Let it be Shainela. God blew dem out because He knows these candles have to last us a long time."

A light rain began to fall. Meshka tried to build a fire, but it was a challenge. The flames sputtered and went out several times. Each time Meshka put aside one precious coal and went searching for more dry wood. In the rain, even the dryer branches were hard to light. Meshka could not bear to face a wet, cold, fireless night, so she wandered off determined to find dry wood and kindling.

At first she thought she was imagining the smell of smoke, but she followed her nose and soon came to a small cabin and a well-built barn. Meshka was shivering terribly. Even when the moon was kind enough to light the way, the rustling trees dripped big splats of rain down on her. She was soaking wet.

Quietly, she tip-toed over to the cabin window and peeked in. Three strong young girls and a tired looking man sat around a table. She crept over to the barn and very slowly opened the door. Inside was warm, dry, and inviting. There was even a lit brazier burning in one of the stalls. She edged her way through the door and stood by the brazier warming her hands. It felt wonderful! It was hard to tear herself away from its warmth, but she had to share this good fortune with the others.

Meshka led the bone weary women, the cart and the goat out of the wet woods and into the warm dry barn. The two women changed into dry clothes and dressed Joya. Once everyone was in clean dry clothes Meshka took their blankets and made a nest in the hay near the brazier. Then they hung their wet things near the warm fire. Meshka crawled in and watched the steam rise from the drying clothes. She closed her eyes and in her heart she thanked God for this gracious gift.

In the stall beside them was a mama cow heavy with calf. She looked pretty ripe. The birth could come sometime soon. They hoped it would not be tonight. The hay was sweet and clean. Meshka lay down in the soft comfortable hay and *kvelled*, "Ah *mekhiyeh*." (very pleasurable)

They were just settling in for the night, when the door flew open! Meshka and Rifka instinctively dove into the hay to hide themselves, but Joya just sat where she was put and there wasn't time to grab her.

A young maiden with flaxen hair, maybe the same age as Joya, entered the barn. With long strides she walked over to the cow and was startled to see Joya sitting calmly beside her.

Joya was shivering despite the dry clothes; her long thick hair was still wet. The flaxen maiden relaxed, Joya was obviously no threat.

"You look hungry. I will bring you some food," the maiden said in a language they did not understand. She walked over to a dark corner in the barn, pulled down a heavy horse blanket hanging there, and wrapped it around Joya's shivering shoulders.

Seeing this act of kindness, the two Jewish women crawled out of their hiding places. With words and motions, the kind maiden asked them if they were hungry. They nodded. The maiden smiled and signaled for them to wait. She left, and returned in a few minutes with bowls of hot soup, warm bread, and three hunks of roasted chicken!

Rifka looked at all the delicious food. It smelled sooo good! Her mouth was watering. A thought dashed through her mind, "Is da food kosher?" but she was too hungry to catch it.

She devoured the food before she could convince herself not to eat it. The maiden left, but returned quickly with some dry blankets. Meshka thanked her again and again. They had no language between them, but they had no trouble understanding each other.

In the middle of the night, the cow began moaning. Sure enough the calf was coming. She was making a loud racket! The women were afraid the father was going to come, so they slid under the hay. This time they made sure Joya was well hidden. The door flung open. The women held their breath. Then let it out with a loud hiss when they saw, to their great relief, it was the kind maiden.

The cow was having trouble because the calf was not in a good position. If Rifka, the milkman's wife, knew anything, she knew cows. She pushed up her sleeves, grateful to be able to repay the maiden's kindness. Meshka and Joya went back to sleep lulled by the warmth and softness. Meshka was so bone weary, even the noisy birth did not keep her awake. As for Joya, who knows if she even heard anything?

A healthy calf was born, the cow was relieved, the young maiden was grateful to Rifka for her help, and everyone finally got some sleep. All in all, Meshka got her Shabbos miracle.

CRCRCR

Meshka, Rifka, Joya and the goat walked and walked and walked forever. Eventually the food they took from the caravan and the little bundle of goodies the flaxen maiden gave them when they left; were all gone. The women survived on goat milk and whatever berries, fruit, and nuts they found along the way. Their bellies often ached with emptiness.

The next Shabbos came and went without a redeeming miracle. Hunger rattled around in Rifka's belly and only her temper was fed.

They were making their way through an endless forest when a white bird flew right by Rifka with a juicy worm in its mouth. That was the last straw, she spat out the words, "Mama, look at dat bird! God gives food to a stupid bird, but for us He has nothin'!"

Meshka nodded, "Shainela, so now you vant to eat worms?" She stepped over a big fallen tree, with long spindly branches. Like clawing fingers, it grabbed at her skirt. Entangled, she turned this way and that, until she managed to free herself. She was grateful she did not tear the skirt.

"I am hungry enough to eat worms! I would eat grass like a cow, but I tried dat yesterday 'n it made my belly hurt. God is so unfair!" Meshka was hungry too. What could she say to comfort her daughter? "Shainela, God helps those who help themselves."

Annoyed with her mama's pat sayings, Rifka barked, "Oy Mama, if you have nothin' good to say, say nothin'!" and stomped off.

Rifka was tired of feeling helpless, so she went hunting. True, she never killed anything before, not even a chicken. She used to buy her chickens from Isaac the butcher. He not only made them dead, but he neatly burned off all the feathers too. She knew nothing from hunting, but she could learn.

Rifka marched off on a mission, Joya sat on a big rock where she was put; and Meshka rested on the ground with her big fat feet up in the air against a tree trunk.

Feeling like a great hunter, Rifka collected small rocks and dropped them into the folds of her dress. She aimed her rocks at trees, at pinecones, at plants. Anything and everything became a target. She missed most of the throws, but the rumbling in her belly sharpened her eye. Soon she was hitting things.

Then all of a sudden, her moment was at hand! She surprised a flock of ducks feasting on grubs in tall swampy grass beside a shallow little pond and they quickly took flight. Could she kill something? Would it make her a killer? There really wasn't time to think. Survival erased her doubts.

Once her mind was set, her arm was ready. Her eyes narrowed on a big fat bird lifting off not ten yards away. With all her strength, she sent a small rock sailing towards him! The bird dropped to the ground like manna from heaven.

On the path back to camp, she found that God, in His goodness, had sprinkled a handful of plump little mushrooms on the ground just for her.

Just when the sun was going to bed, proud Rifka returned to camp with her trophies. She found Meshka optimistically building the evening fire.

"A feast!" Meshka squealed in delight when she saw Rifka's bounty. She cleaned, blessed, and koshered the bird with a little of the precious salt she kept hidden in the cart.

When Meshka found this little bag of salt near one of the Gypsy campfires, she thought, Ah, dis treasure is a sign from God. He is here walking dis lonely path vid us. He vill not let us die.

Finding the salt was a good moment. Meshka's mood went from dragging her belly on the ground, to feeling a little better. She saw pearls of light even in the darkness.

Meshka put a green stick through the bird and held it up over the fire with two forked branches and a few big rocks to support them. It worked! The bird cooked and the sticks didn't burn.

Rifka put the mushrooms in their precious pot. Thank God Meshka brought the pot. She flavored the plump little morsels with sweet juices from the tender bird. When the mushrooms were ready, they tasted, deep, rich, and dangerous, like the forest itself.

Ah! Such a feast! Such a succulent meal! Every bite was a kiss from God, so delicious it was! The smell alone could almost satisfy Meshka's hunger.

The first delicious bite Rifka took, carried her back to all those wonderful meals she used to serve on Friday nights and how happy her family was. Anguish surged through her and her taste buds went numb. It was hard to take pleasure in nice things, with all the noise inside her head.

"Yum yum, dis is delicious! Vhat a vonderful night Rifka, God has blessed us."

"Are you *meshugeneh* (crazy) Mama? You call dis wonderful? Oy vay, you put too much salt on da bird. It has no taste without garlic 'n paprika. 'N you know I hate mushrooms. I only picked dem because dey va there." Rifka was so busy *kvetching*, she didn't even notice her belly was full!

Meshka felt a moment of contentment. She thanked God that they were still alive to enjoy such a good meal.

Their camp lay beside a glassy pond. Crickets charmed the night with song and frogs burped along in tune. The stars twinkled twice as bright as ever, half in heaven and half sparkling in the still waters. Standing on the sandy bank, the stars came right to Meshka's feet.

With a full belly, Meshka looked at the bejeweled sky and thought, so many pretty stars are watching over us! Heaven is helping us. Maybe now dings vill be easier. She felt a little quieter for the first time since the world ended.

Rifka looked at the same sky, but her mind went in a different direction. There are millions of holes in da cloth of heaven. *God* is lookin' through dem. He is watchin' me 'n judgin' me. She shrank beneath the spying eyes of God.

The Gypsy girl did not even see the stars.

CRCRCR

Rifka went hunting every day now, but did not always re-turn with dinner. There were still berries in late August and nuts for the gathering, but a few days passed with scarcely enough to eat. Rifka set out to find whatever gifts the squirrels left behind. With a little luck, she might even get a squirrel. The day was the perfect kiss of summer's end -- warm and breezy.

Dis is a good day to wash clothes, thought Meshka. Joya, as always, stared into her darkness.

Meshka took off all her clothes and wrapped her long thick shawl tightly around her. Knowing she was naked underneath made her feel very naughty. Her old knees creaked when she lowered herself down onto the rocky bank. She settled herself on a sunny rock beside the pond. The cool wet stones felt solid beneath her.

Her aged hands knew a lifetime of scrubbing. How com-forting it was to do something she had done all her life. If Meshka closed her eyes, she could be back in her village, wash-ing clothes and gossiping with her favorite neighbors, Hanna and Sophia. But Meshka dare not close her eyes for fear the ghosts of Hanna and Sophia would come to haunt her.

When she leaned forward to swish her clothes in the wa-ter, she felt the *mezuzah* jiggle under her shawl. She remembered the day Yonkela, only eight years old, carved the little wooden box. He was such a bright boy and so good with his hands!

The memories were sweet, but they *schlepped* (dragged) bags of sorrow. Waves of tears made her face as wet as her hands. In her mind, she saw herself standing next to Yonkle and the Holy *Torah* at his *Bar Mitzvah*. Her heart swelled with pride. Her first born son was becoming a man! *Oy*, how hand-some and brilliant he was!

"Oy Yonkle," she spoke out loud to his spirit. Her soft words drifted on the morning breeze. "At your Bar Mitzvah, you looked so grown up. Such a *mensch*! (a gentleman) Vhen da rabbi called you up to read da *Torah*, (Bible) you said every word perfectly. Oy vay, did I cry! I vas so happy! Everyone said such nice dings about you. After da big fancy dinner vee talked, remember?"

Her mind was far away, but her hands kept at the work she knew so well.

"I said, 'Yonkle, I am so proud of you. Now is a new time. Never have I been da mama of a man before. Vhat do you need from me?' You va always so wise. You said right den 'n there, 'Support, advice 'n freedom.'"

Little golden fishes wiggling through the water caught her eye. She watched the little golden slivers swim gracefully around her scrubbing hands. Several golden fish hovered close to watch her, but when Meshka swished a long skirt around in the water, they all darted away and her mind drifted back to Yonkle.

"You know Yonkle, 'support, advice 'n freedom' vas a good answer. I held those words close to my heart many times in those young man years. Vee survived your broken bones 'n your liddle acts of rebellion."

More fish came. Watching them filled her mind, so no more sad thoughts could sneak in. As the day grew warmer, she grew dreamier. The fish disappeared and with nothing to fill her mind, bittersweet memories of Yonkle returned. She wanted to remember, but it made her feel like she was falling.

"My son, my wonderful son, on your last birthday I asked you, "Now dat you are turning twenty, you vill take a wife. Please give me new words, so I can be a good mother to a married man, just like I vas to da boy. 'N you said, 'I vill think on it.' You never gave me an answer. Now you vill never take a wife. You vill never…"

"No!" She shook head to make the thoughts go away; but her heart still yearned for Yonkle.

"No!" Remembering brought too much pain! A terrible picture jumped into her mind! Yonkle lying in a puddle of blood, his body twisted and broken like a thrown away doll.

Meshka desperately searched for a comforting memory to block out the bad one. Yonkle was such a cute little boy. "Oy Yonkle, how you loved to lie in da bed all day on Shabbos, always reading a book.

"You knew all about da world. Your mind vas hungry, like a starving person goes for food. So much you wanted to know. I used to say, 'Go out 'n play' but no, you vanted to stay in bed 'n read. I am sorry I tried to take you away from da books!"

"No! No regrets! Meshka shook her head harder, but the feeling would not go away. "Regret is a bitter poison. I have enough pain, without regret."

Scrub. Scrub. Scrub. She liked the scrubbing. She could not wash away the pain, but she could make the clothes clean. Doing something, anything, made her feel less helpless.

While she was washing a wide fluffy petticoat, a big fat fish swam close by. Meshka watched him wend his way through a maze of blooming petticoats. She could kick herself for not bringing a fishing stick.

The big fat fish was charmed by the sunlight filtering through the gauzy fabric billowing everywhere. It lured him deep into the folds of Meshka's petticoats. She swished the clothes this way and that and the fish got tangled up in them. The poor rainbow fish was all confused and tried to find a way out, but he was trapped in soft clouds of cotton.

Meshka grabbed the ends of her petticoat. Suddenly her hands shot out of the water! She lifted the fabric straight up into the air with a strength that came from God knows where! The fat glittering fish struggled for a bit, but then surrendered to his fate.

Meshka was so excited! It had been days since they ate that wonderful bird and the rattling in her belly had become all too familiar.

When the washing was done, Meshka tried to stand up. Her creaking stiff body was not helping. The pain in her back brought a stifling wave of hopelessness rolling over her. Meshka sighed and *plotzed* down again, "Helplessness, you ugly demon, put down your stick. Stop banging me on my head already!"

On her feet at last, Meshka looked around the thick forest for a tree in the sunshine to hang the clothes. She found an ancient oak with barren branches near the bottom. The barrenness of the tree she understood better than all those frivolous birch and maples boasting colorful leaves.

When all her clothes were hung, Meshka stepped back to *kvell* over their cleanness. The sparkle of the apron warmed her heart. It was full of wonderful Shabbos dinners.

Now my whole life is gone, she sighed. I have nothing left only these tiny liddle pleasures, but *dayeynu* (they are enough for me). I am grateful to have dem.

Meshka waddled along the bank of the pond on her way back to camp. "Oy Yonkle," she sighed again and again. "There is a big hole in my heart just your size. I could not tell you vhen you va alive, dat you va perfect - a liddle arrogant maybe, but perfect." A bittersweet pang shot through her.

"I did not see it until after you va gone. All da mischievous dings you did dat made me so aggravated, now dey look like bright colors in a dull day.

"Oy how I wish I could see you again!"

A strong breeze blew and Meshka drew her long shawl more tightly around her body.

"Mama," came a soft whisper. She looked around, but no one was there.

"Mama," she heard again. Her eyes gazed into the water and saw Yonkle standing behind her. Humph! It is just a play of light, she told herself.

"Mama," she heard clearly, "All da words 'n all da ideas in my books never prepared me to face those angry killers. Their eyes va wild vid hate. I vas stunned! Suddenly dey va on top of me. I fought vid all my might, but you know I vas never much of a fighter 'n dere va so many of dem!

"Now vee have a choice mama – you 'n me." Yonkle explained in his grown up teaching voice. "Vee can choose hate or forgiveness. Hate vill tie us to our enemies forever. Forgiveness vill set us free."

"But how do I forgive da unforgivable?" Meshka asked through her tears.

"By stretching your mind Mama. If you look, you can see dat vee are all liddle fishes caught in a net. Look at da net! It is woven from da dings people believe. 'N it has some *meshugener* (crazy) knots in it. Guilt 'n blame – those kinds of knots - dey make people meshugener."

"Oy Yonkle, I miss you," her heart ached painfully.

"Mama do not miss me. Keep me vid you. Make a liddle nest for me in your heart. I can live inside you 'n whisper wise dings in your ears." The voice faded away, or maybe her daydream ended. A terrible longing was choking her.

Meshka was already wet from the washing, so she put a fat little foot in the chilly water and shivered. It was so cold; her goose pimples had goose pimples! Burr!!! She quickly splashed herself clean and jumped out! Despite the bitter sting of the cold water, it felt wonderful to be clean. For a moment at least she was free from the dirt soiling her down to her soul.

Clouds rolled in. The sky faded into darker shades of gray. Meshka returned to find Rifka already kindling the evening fire. On a rock in the fire sat their precious pot, dented and old. In it simmered a tasty soup of forest mushrooms and wild asparagus, prizes Rifka picked. There were also some grains of who knows what, but they added a good taste. Rifka complained that she could not find more and Meshka was grateful they had something.

Meshka showed Rifka the pretty fish and they admired his shimmering scales. Then she put him on their cooking stone in the fire. The delicious aroma of frying fish wafted in the evening air. She thanked God for these simple gifts from this strange land.

Food was scarce at times. Meshka never complained, Rifka never stopped complaining, and Joya never said a word. She just sat like a piece of wood until Meshka fed her. The soup smelled so good, Meshka's mouth twitched imagining that first luscious bite.

After dinner, Meshka collected her fresh clean clothes and put them all on. As soon as the sun set, the day stopped making believe it was summer and showed its real blustery, almost autumn, nature.

Joya sat on her bundles watching the sun set, just like she watched the sun rise in the morning. If Meshka did not tell her to walk, she would not walk. If Meshka did not feed her, she would not eat. All the time she sat and stared. Joya was like a rag doll; so agreeable, she had no will of her own. These strange *Gadji* (non-Gypsy) women and the changing landscape were not real to her.

Joya's real life was back in her caravan sitting around the evening fire. Memories came to visit. The story of her short life replayed itself over and over, day after day. She was only fourteen. No matter how far she sank into herself licking her wounds, eventually the dark or the light, the cold or the wet, something dragged her out of her dreams.

ରୁରୁରୁ

Rifka practiced throwing rocks every day and soon she got pretty good at bringing back dinner. Her aim was especially true when she pictured not the animals she wanted to kill, but the angry mob. There was a fire boiling in her belly all the time. It percolated behind every thought and spiked every word.

An angry wild turkey surprised her one day in the forest. He lunged at her from behind a tree. She tripped backwards and fell to the ground. Both her arms flailed outward to break her fall. They landed sharply on rocks. Her hands gripped two stones. The turkey went to peck her in the throat. Rifka clapped the two stones together and crushed his head between them. Then she struggled to get away from his body.

She reached into the folds in her dress for another stone and found the little rag doll instead. Suddenly the earth opened up and swallowed her. She was tumbling into an abyss. Her legs paced in circles and her eyes saw only flames. Terrible wailing shrieks were ripped from her throat and her hands began pulling out handfuls of her beautiful black hair.

Rifka uttered her first prayer since the world ended, but it was really a curse. "God, You should bless all of dose crazy murderous men vid three people in deir lives: von to grab dem, da second to stab dem 'n da third to spit on dem!" Poi! Poi! She spat on the ground.

A stray branch dared to intrude on her woeful tirade and it quickly became the target of her rage. She broke the branch into a million little pieces. "If only I could strangle those murderers! I would do it vid my bare hands." She raged loud enough for even God to hear.

To tell the truth, in Rifka's eyes, the sun was now always too feeble, the wind always bitter and biting, and the cold pierced her to the bone. Gentle warm days like this one, she never even noticed. Her eyes saw only shadows. Her sky was always gray and the light of day always too dim.

One day Meshka saw Rifka shaking her fists, but no one was there. She was screaming at the villagers who burned her house. "You miserable monsters! May God Grant you Pharaoh's plagues and Job's misfortunes."

"Poi!" Poi!" She spat on the ground.

She beat on her chest and screamed crazy accusations at stupid people who believe in demons and infidels, and at herself, who now believes in nothing.

The women bypassed the *Gentile* (non-Jewish) villages because they were afraid. In the few Jewish villages they came to along the way, they found death and destruction. Sickness, invading Turks, and *pogroms* like what Rifka and Meshka had experienced defiled these lands as well.

Nowhere was safe. Every moment was a test to see how much they wanted to live. There were many days when not a word was spoken. The three women had plenty of words for the demons in their minds, but between them lay a heavy silence.

ଓଃଓଃଓଃ

Chapter 3

Survival

A farmer and his three sons were moving across a field of hay swinging their sickles in rhythm to an old harvesting tune. They sang the same song their grandfathers and their great-grandfathers sang before them.

It was early morning. The three weary travelers had walked all through the night. Hungry and tired, they laid down behind a hay mound to rest. Meshka was dizzy and *farmisht* (exhausted). Curled beside Meshka was her living puppet staring blindly, always staring at someplace else. The poor girl looked a little green around the gills. The big purple bruises on her face and body were fading, but she still looked ashen and gray.

Like little squirrels, they made little sleeping nests and burrowed into the hay. The fluffy mounds promised a good morning's sleep after last night's long trek.

When their bodies hit the hay, their eyes closed and sleep swallowed them up; until Rifka's sneeze woke them. Before they fell asleep again, they heard the singing.

The farmers were cutting hay just a few feet away.

Rifka crouched behind the haystack, desperately trying not to sneeze! The hay was tickling her nose. She pinched two fingers over her noble nose to keep the little blasts quietly in her head. She was afraid they would hear! With a racing heart, Rifka waited minute by minute, fighting sneeze after sneeze.

If the farmers discovered them! What would they do to frightened women hiding in their fields? Fall upon them? Kill them? Or worse, give them to the army!?!

The women were trapped! Rifka was so glad she hid the cart and the goat in the shadows under the trees before they collapsed in the hay.

The three exhausted women, hidden from the farmers' view, could do nothing but wait for the men to move on. Meshka and Joya slept on and off all morning.

The sweet fragrant hay reminded Rifka of the warm dry barn and the fat cows she and her husband Chaim, used to milk back in her village. Those cows gave the world's sweetest milk; at least, in her memory they did.

The warm sun overhead woke them at noon. They were thirsty and hungry but dare not try to sneak away. It would be crazy to run. The farmers would surely see them crossing the open field to the edge of the forest.

The old farmer looked up at the bright sun, wiped the sweat from his neck with a clean rag, and sat down to enjoy his lunch. The oldest boy opened the picnic basket. The most delicious aromas wafted through the air and attacked Rifka's empty belly. It growled loudly in protest. Did they hear!?! Her senses were getting sharper. She heard the growl as a roar!

God bless the goat, they had milk every day. Some days it was the only thing standing between them and starvation. Rifka was definitely getting better at hunting. She made a sling out of a stocking and practiced throwing it. Every day she practiced hunting; some prey she hit, some she missed, some days they ate, some days they went hungry. Yesterday was not so good. Today was not looking better.

The farmer and his two older sons did not talk much, they just chewed. When the old farmer was finished, he gave his belly a satisfied pat and stood up. Rifka felt weak with wanting. The three men picked up their sickles and returned to work.

The youngest son, a huge man who weighed as much as his two older brothers put together, just sat there and kept on eating. Rifka watched him chew each bite with the eyes of a hawk. She prayed passionately to God begging Him to make the *chazzer* (gluttonous pig) leave some food in the basket and go back to work; but no, he kept on filling his face.

The older brothers grumbled, "We do all the work and you just get fatter. Put the food down. You already ate enough to feed three men. Now is the time to earn your keep. Pick up that sickle."

The father said nothing, but he cast a disapproving eye upon his son for the Bible spoke ill of gluttony. The fat young man lowered his head in shame, closed the basket and rose to his feet.

Excitement bubbled in Rifka's blood. Her busy little brain was planning how to snatch the basket. She never stole anything in her whole life but she was desperate.

Maybe I can quietly tip toe out from behind dis hay mound vhen their backs are bent to their task.

No, if a blade of hay crackles or dey happen to stretch, dey vill see me 'n heaven only knows vhat dey would do to us. Ve are so helpless.

Rifka figured, Da risk is great but my hunger is greater! All her senses were now riveted on the basket.

The men were singing again, swinging their sickles in rhythm. Rifka slid slowly around the hay mound on her belly. She was moving very slowly so no one would notice her out of the corner of their eyes. She edged closer to the picnic basket at an agonizingly slow pace. The aroma of delicious warm home cooked food made her parched mouth water. Inch by inch, her heart pounding with terror, she moved soundlessly towards her target.

Suddenly fat boy snickered, "You are just jealous that I am so much stronger than the two of you. It is wrong to waste food. What should I do, leave it for the animals?" He gave an ugly laugh and headed back to the basket.

With his ample chin pushed forward and his tiny brain pushed back, he taunted, "I am going to finish every bite of food in the basket. Try and stop me! I will crush you both with my big hands."

The older brothers grumbled and the farmer laughed. He was proud of his bountiful farm and his quarrelsome sons. It reminded him of his brothers and how they used to bicker. He believed, growling pups make tough dogs.

The *chazzer* (gluttonous pig) put his hands on his hips and puffed out his chest as though daring his brothers to stop him. Triumphantly, he reached for the basket.

Rifka was only inches away! Scrambling quickly, she slid out of sight behind the mound, just as his big hand descended upon its prey. She was forced to watch as her leg of lamb disappeared into the gaping maw of his face. Her fresh baked bread, her hunk of cheese, her potatoes; he ate it all!

Silently, Rifka shook her fists at him! The galling nerve of that *mamzer* (!*!),

"Onions should grow from your bellybutton!" Rifka muttered to herself. "Poi! Poi!" She spat on the ground.

The farmers worked until dusk. Then they lifted their sickles onto their shoulders and quietly walked back towards the cozy lights of their little cottage where a warm supper was waiting for them.

CRCRCR

With a terrible yearning Rifka watched the picnic basket being carried away. The ghosts of foods they could have eaten left a deep emptiness behind. Never had she felt such lust as she now fixed upon that basket. In silent rage, she shook her fists.

Under her breath she mumbled to the fat young farmer, "Your belly should swell up like a mountain and your testicles should shrink down to a pea! Poi! Poi!" She spat on the ground.

Twilight descended and dark was coming on. Rifka looked at Meshka, pale with hunger. Curled up beside her was the little wooden puppet with frozen eyes. The poor child looked like those eyes were ready to close forever. Rifka had to do something!

In desperation, she crept up to the cottage and peeked in the window. The farmer's family, three sons and two daughters sat around a table. His good wife was carrying in a tray laden with a fat turkey, little crispy potatoes, and a bowl of thick brown gravy. Rifka's mouth ached to taste the delicious food. Her empty stomach felt like it was full of snakes with big teeth.

Watching the cozy family at their feast made her feel hollow and lonely. The poor hungry *miskite* (pitiful orphan) felt bitterly left out in the cold, a ghost walking outside of life.

The dog sitting at the farmer's feet sensed her presence and started barking wildly. The farmer scolded him, "Quiet you little fiend. You will be fed soon." He reached for a big juicy bone, yanked it off the turkey, and held it up to make the doggie jump. Everyone laughed and the man gave the doggie the bone, the big juicy meaty bone! Rifka moaned.

She did not realize she moaned out loud, until she saw the eldest son's eyes looking straight at her!

She ducked beneath the window, her heart racing! She glanced back at the table and was horrified! The young man's seat was empty! Did he really see her? What would he do if he found her? She imagined the worst!

The sound of the front door banging closed was softened by his hand. Holding her breath, Rifka ducked down and waddled away from the window. She listened to his slow heavy footsteps getting closer. He was stalking her! Quickly and silently she slipped around the other side of the house and disappeared into the shadows.

The young man lit a lantern and the brightness illuminated half her hiding place. She squished herself into the little darkness that remained. He was walking towards her! Oh dear! Would the noisy banging of her heart give her away!?!

She took a deep breath, lunged out of her hiding place, and dashed into the refuge of the dark forest! He saw the movement and dashed after her. Rifka's eyes darted about looking for a place to hide! There was a deep cushion of mulching leaves under a big red maple tree. She balled herself up like a boulder, burrowed under the pile, and covered herself with a thick layer of loamy earth and sweetly decaying leaves.

The light of the lantern flashed over her, but the leaves hid her well. He walked within inches of her. After a few minutes, he gave up the hunt and shrugged. Maybe it was just a ghost flickering in the candlelight, he thought, and returned to his warm supper.

When the terror subsided, a boiling rage rose in Rifka! She shook her fist at him and hissed quietly like a deadly snake, "Burning horse radishes should grow on your tongue! Poi! Poi!" She spat on the ground.

Rifka's mind was racing, I have to get us some food! Joya looks so weak and Meshka looks so drawn. I must do something. Maybe I could borrow a *biseleh*, (a tiny little bit). Rifka could not stop thinking about that big leg of meat. She was jealous of a dog!

If I take less dan dey give to da doggie, den it is not really stealin'. If I do not get food now, I vill be killin' my mama 'n da wooden girl.

"But stealin' is a sin!" her conscience screamed. Rifka never willingly broke a rule, never! Coveting food when you are hungry, does not count.

"Stealin' is a sin!" her stubborn conscience persisted.

While Rifka and her conscience argued, her hungry belly led her into an orchard where three big fat red apples suddenly disappeared into her pocket. Like Eve, she was going to give the forbidden fruit to someone she loved.

On her way back to the hiding women, Rifka passed the chicken house. One of the plump little hens got too close to Rifka's outstretched hand and even her angry conscience could not stop her.

CICICI

Meshka stretched. She was cramped after all those hours hiding behind the hay. Her back creaked like an old rocking chair. Bits of hay stuck out of her hair.

Rifka returned with the stolen apples and the plump chicken. They made a small fire with the little coal Meshka carried and cooked the chicken. She and Meshka wanted to savor the wonderful feast but hunger made them gobble the apples and meat so quickly; they barely chewed. They fed Joya in small pieces, cut with Rifka's favorite knife. Joya chewed slowly, yet she could not keep any food down. Half the time, no matter how slowly they fed her, her belly rebelled.

Rifka and her mama sat back under a big bright moon. The Moon smiled down on Meshka like a mama. It made her feel just a little safer. Rifka saw the Moon frowning with disapproval. It knew she was a *gonif* (a thief).

With full bellies they were ready to move on. They walked all through the night under the full moon. It was safer to cross the rolling fields of barley at night. Like Meshka's Uncle Heimmie used to say, "At night all cows are black."

They were little mice in the shadows, scurrying from one bale to another across fields. When they reached the spooky dark forest, they quivered seeing ghostly shadows everywhere.

The women avoided all roads and strangers. Rifka was getting really strong from pushing and pulling the little cart over rough land and through muddy streams.

As the pale light of dawn put the shadows to bed, the three wandering women burrowed into some hay stacks to sleep. They were comfortable, but Rifka could not sleep. The dream world played hide and seek with her. When she fell into a dream, after a few minutes, it threw her out with a sharp slap.

Wide awake and exhausted, Rifka remembered every little tiny detail of that last day, when the world ended. Like a thread through the sharp eye of a needle, she looked at every step but still it made no sense. She found no comfort there. She listed her virtues one by one. She counted all the *mitzvahs* (good deeds) she did for people. The list was long, but it did not earn her a reprieve from the anguish. It did not bring her husband Chaim and her babies back to life.

She ached for Chaim's tender touch. She yearned for her man. He always knew what she needed. In the evenings, he would put a blanket over her shoulders before she even realized she was cold. His wonderful strong hands would rub her shoulders at the end of a long day like this one. She yearned to feel the sweet pleasure of lying tucked in under his wing.

Meshka woke up rested as the sun beamed from the top of the sky. She peeked out of the hay and smiled up at the puffy pink clouds. It was just high noon. Meshka slowly and reluctantly wiggled out of her warm soft nest to face the gnawing emptiness rattling around in her belly. The chubby little woman was sure she could eat a horse.

Rifka crawled out of her nest, looked at the sky and grumbled, "Oy vay, another day 'n I am not dead yet." She doubted God was listening anymore.

Heavy lidded and half asleep, Rifka milked the goat and shared the warm milk with the others. She and her mama took turns feeding it to the mute girl, who looked by far the worst of them. The poor girl gagged and threw it up. How were they going to keep her alive? She could not hold down what little they had.

CRCRCR

Ambling along, Meshka walked next to the cart for a minute, then asked, "Did you steal da chicken 'n apples?" Rifka nodded.

"It vas a gift from God."

"I am sorry you had to steal," Meshka said sadly. "Thank you for keeping us alive. I know you are an honest person. You never broke a rule."

Rifka shrugged like it was nothing, like she did not beat herself up a thousand times over this sin. She answered lightly, "Dey had too much 'n vee had too liddle, so I evened it out a *biseleh.*" (a tiny little bit)

The corner of Meshka's lip curled up and she said, "My rascally Uncle Heimmie used to say, "If you have to do something wrong, at least enjoy it!'"

The women walked from farm to farm, sleeping in hay mounds, begging when they could, living off the land mostly, and 'borrowing' only when they were desperate.

Joya was walking better now. She did not sway as much, or trip over twigs and rocks as often. Her lips were still sealed, but her eyes began to move from side to side taking in the world around her.

Rifka struggled to justify the stealing. All her life she was exacting and honest, but look where it got her. Nobody dinks vhen da farmer takes da egg from da hen, or da milk from da cow, dat he is stealin' from dem. So maybe it is not really stealin', if I take just a liddle from da farmers. Da eggs 'n chickens 'n apples are going to be eaten anyvay, why should it not be us?"

This was junky thinking, but hunger was has a way making its own sense. Let us just say, most days before they left the farms, they ate a decent dinner.

ಇಇಇ

Six *Shabboses* (Sabbaths) filled with little miracles, measured time as they wandered. A week of nasty days, battling cold and rain left Meshka with chills and fever. Rifka built a lopsided little shelter in the woods so they could rest while she recovered.

A big storm knocked down several big leafy branches which Rifka dragged over. She tangled them into an odd little lean-to by piling them at a steep angle against a huge boulder. It kept the wind and rain out. A fire was not safe, so they huddled together under all their blankets and clothes to keep warm through the night.

In the afternoons when Rifka went hunting, she developed a special two step attack. First she stunned her prey with a small fast rock, and then finished the job with a big one. Rifka sometimes dug a hole, filled it with dry tinder and big dead branches and cooked a bird wrapped in wet leaves, sometimes she covered a small animal in wet mud and buried it among smoldering coals to bake. Either way delivered up a tasty meal.

Rifka went hunting every day. She enjoyed coming back to their little lean-to with her daily conquests, kindling the cooking fire, and making dinner for her little family. With a routine, and people to take care of, it was almost like having a home. When Meshka was feeling better, Rifka reluctantly said goodbye to their little home as they moved on.

It was now well into September. The howling winds and crisper nights foretold winter's approach, but the days were still warm and welcoming.

"Oy Shainela, look at da moon!" Meshka said and covered her mouth in distress. Startled, Rifka looked up, but saw only a new moon.

"Shainela, da first new moon in autumn is Rosh Hashanah, da holiest day of da year! How can vee celebrate?"

"By walkin', eatin', 'n stayin' alive," Rifka replied with a not-so-nice expression on her face.

"Dis is Jewish New Year! **Adam 'n Eve** va created on dis day 'n you do not vant to celebrate it?"

"Sure Mama, vee vill get dressed up 'n go to da shul. Den vee vill come home 'n eat apples dipped in honey. Den you can blow da **shofar** a hundred times 'n vee vill wish all our friends, 'Shanah Tovah'." (have a good year)

Meshka was quiet. What could she say?

"Shainela, vee live by such a thin thread, is it wise to make God angry?

"Da Rabbi told us, 'God opens three scrolls 'n writes down His accounts. On da holy day of Rosh Hashanah, He inscribes da names of da righteous in da Scroll of Life 'n seals their fate.

"For da rest of us, He grants ten days grace until Yom Kippur, da 'Day of Judgment.' On these ten holy days, vee need to reflect, repent, 'n make amends, so He vill write a good fate for us on Yom Kippur."

"Vell Mama, last year I vent to Shul. I said all da prayers. I did lots of *mitzvahs* (good deeds), not just for ten days, but all year, 'n I vas a righteous woman. God sat on His big **throne** up in heaven, vid His fancy scrolls in front of Him, looked at all da good deeds I did all year 'n dis is da miserable fate He wrote down for me." She quickly turned away, so Meshka would not see the tears sneaking into her eyes.

For *Rosh Hashanah* Meshka prayed very quietly, so Rifka would not notice. She made up the words because she did not remember all the prayers. Usually she just repeated whatever the other women said.

Ten days later was *Yom Kippur*. Meshka wanted to throw bits of bread in the water to throw away her sins and make a fresh start. "Vee need to forgive da sins vee made 'n da sins made against us."

Rifka gave her a dirty look. But Meshka bravely continued, "Shainela, I have been throwing my sins away on Yom Kippur since I vas a liddle girl. Our family always observes da High Holy Days."

With an impatient sigh, Rifka snickered, "Mama, if you know vhere to get bread, tell me. I vill throw it into my mouth, not waste it in da water. 'N as for repentin' sins, it is God's turn to repent. He should fast 'n ask me for forgiveness!"

Meshka suggested they fast for the day, as tradition dictates.

"Sure mama, like vee va goin' to have a feast otherwise." Rifka said with a sniff.

Meshka prayed in her own made up way. Only rabbis know real prayers. Meshka asked God to forgive Rifka. After all He is older, he should know better than to be offended by her anger.

CRCRCR

The High Holy Days passed into memory so did the lush farm-land; it gave way to marshy swamps. The women sloshed through calf-deep mud with their skirts hiked up around their waists. Their shoes were tied together and hung around their necks to stay dry. Bare feet made squishy sounds, as they sloshed through thick mud.

The sky wept for them; a light misty rain. Later a fierce wind clawed through their damp clothes, raked their bodies, and left them shivering.

Rifka made up songs as she pulled, pushed, and dragged the cart along. The singing distracted her from the cold but a persistent sense of danger made her shiver!

Alert and watching, Rifka's eyes prowled over every bush and peered into every shadow. Hunting changed the way her eyes scanned the trees and bushes. Now any tiny flicker of movement caught her glance. Her ears listened for sounds in a new way. The call of several creatures and birds were now familiar to her. Even the skin on her arms felt more alive, tingling when danger was near. The short hairs on her arms were standing on end and her skin was crawling now.

Checking again that the knife was securely tied to her thigh, Rifka scanned the reeds and the water.

Then she saw it! A poisonous ribbon of bright red and black, silently slithering through the water towards them. The poisonous snake thought Meshka would make a succulent lunch.

Meshka carefully placed each foot so she would not go *plotz* in the *shmutz* (the dirt). While she was watching her feet, the deadly viper was watching her. It moved silently, slithering through the reeds. This was his world and all who entered were either foe or food!

God bless her, Rifka had eyes like a hawk. A slight movement, no more than a ripple caught her eye! She stood poised, knife in hand, waiting for the right second.

One minute she was standing still and alert. The next, quick as a whip, her knife hand shot out and sliced off his head! Rifka moved so fast, the snake was dead before Meshka even realized she was in danger!

"Dere is no end to da vays people can die," Rifka grumbled as she lifted the dead snake out of the water.

Meshka's eyebrows shot up to the top of her head! "Vhere did dat come from!?!" she shouted.

"Da snake thought you va goin' to be his lunch. He vas already wigglin' his liddle forked tongue at you, Mama," Rifka teased.

Meshka gave a hearty laugh, "Ha! Da joke is on him. Vee are going to eat da snake for dinner! He looks meaty enough."

"Mama, dat is disgustin'! I am sure da snake is *traif*," (not kosher) Rifka stuck up her nose and sniffed.

It was true that some people gave them food, which probably was not kosher. Rifka did not ask, better she should not know. But the snake was definitely not kosher.

Rifka did not care if God forgave her. She was definitely not going to forgive Him!

With a patient sigh Meshka answered, "*Mamala*, (sweet liddle mommy) maybe it is *traif*. Until vee get to a real village where people vill judge us, vee vill do vhatever vee need to do to survive. Survival first; kosher second."

With a wagging finger, Rifka said, "Mama, God is watchin' you. He sees into your heart 'n He knows dat you are trimmin' da edges of a lie to make it look like a truth." She spoke to her mother, but the words were really meant for herself.

"Oy vay, vhat can I do if God keeps judging me? I am never going to pass through da eye of His needle. My mama belly is too big!" Meshka gave a hearty laugh as she reached out and grabbed the dead snake.

Rifka was not going to betray tradition and eat forbidden food. She still believed in respecting the past. She was angry with God, not the tradition, so she walked off alone into the night. The sweet face of the maiden moon gazed down on Rifka with a mysterious smile. Sure Rifka was hungry, what else is new? But without her tradition, what would her life be worth?

Rifka went hunting, but came back empty handed. Joya and Meshka enjoyed a delicious meal. The snake tasted a little like chicken. It was all they had to eat that day but Rifka stoically endured the day without food.

CR CR CR

They were walking through murky water. Twisted vines hidden under the murky water made the going slow. The clumps of tall reeds around them were quite beautiful. These giant guardians of the swamp reached for the sky with long feathery fingers.

"Look da reeds are praying for food like us," Meshka teased.

Suddenly a wonderful idea jumped into her head! She asked Rifka to cut down several tall stalks and roused Joya from her trance to hold them. Meshka cut the long reeds into strips. Her skillful hands, having spent countless hours knitting, crocheting and weaving for her family, easily wove the tall reeds into sturdy fishing baskets.

CR CR CR

The marshlands were generous with their bounty of wild vegetables and small fish, but provided little or no dry ground to sleep on. The wide thorn bushes looked cushy enough, but there was the sinister business of their thorns. Meshka tossed her bedroll over a bush. The thickness of the rolled up clothes gave her plenty of protection and created a soft bed. Meshka carefully crawled on top and laid her weary body down, covering her weary bones with her long thick woolen shawl.

"Mama, dis is a *fercockt* (stupid) idea. No one can sleep on a thorn bush!" Rifka scoffed. But when she found nothing better, she also made her bed on thorns. Joya looked *ferblunjit* (lost and confused). Meshka was about to crawl out of her bed and help, when Joya started making a bed just like the others. It was the first time she took an action on her own. Meshka fell asleep with a smile on her face, feeling proud of her young friend.

Soon they were all asleep. They slept deeply for the first time in months. Maybe the thorns absorbed their pain. No one had nightmares and no one tossed or turned restlessly. Even in their sleep, they remembered the danger that lay beyond the boundaries of their bedrolls. Once, Rifka's leg cramped and she stretched it out. A sharp stinging nettle punished her for extending beyond her domain.

In the sacred hour just before sunset, Meshka woke up with a need; excuse me, to relieve herself. Carefully she crawled off her prickly perch and walked a little ways. Her eyes were mostly closed. Her feet walked by themselves to a small patch of solid land covered with soft tufted grass.

Meshka squatted down. A strange little animal drowsily ambled along in front of her. His little paw came right down on her naked foot! Both were startled.

The little animal looked up at the massive creature he touched. They both froze! With big eyes, Meshka and the animal stared at each other. Suddenly, like it was rehearsed, they both screamed, "Yeeeek!" at the same time and scurried off in different directions.

Joya and Rifka bolted awake!

Rifka looked at the empty 'bed,' suddenly afraid a terrible beast had eaten her mama! A wave of self-pity came over her. "Now I am ALL ALONE in dis strange foreign land." she lamented.

Rifka glanced at the mute Gypsy, who trailed after her mama, and thought scornfully, Vhat a *dumkopt* (stupid girl). She sits vhere she is put, a puppet not a person.

A soft white fog was rolling in when Meshka suddenly appeared out of the dimness. Rifka's eyeballs shot open! Mama's ghost! The line between the living and the dead was very thin to her. She had no doubts ghosts easily passed back and forth between the worlds.

"Mama?" Rifka whispered hoarsely, her throat tight with fear.

"*Momala*, (liddle mommy) I am sorry I woke you. A funny liddle creature startled me 'n I screamed. Now *geyn shlofn*." (go to sleep)

Relieved, Rifka snapped, "Mama, you should not go prowlin' around. See, now you roused a demon!"

"Shush, geyn shlofn," Meshka whispered in a soothing voice. She carefully crawled back into her cushy little nest chuckling to herself, some demon! Da poor ding vas more scared dan I vas. His terrified little face made her laugh.

ℭℜℭℜℭℜ

Back in her soft nest, Meshka thought, Suryla vould love dat liddle creature, Suryla vas so sveet vid liddle animals. Meshka's eyes grew heavy and closed *kvelling* over her sweet little grand-daughter.

When her eyes opened again Suryla was sitting beside her. She leaned over and sniffed her grandmama's neck idly twirling a finger around one of Meshka's silver curls and whispered, "Grandma, you know dis last year I did liddle dings to say good-bye vid everyone."

Meshka felt the child's touch as truly as she felt the thorn bush beneath her.

"Remember vhen Grandpa Meyer vanted me to ask da four questions at Passover? I vas so scared, I cried.

"You helped me so much Grandma. You did not scold me like everyone else. You asked, vhat made it so hard. I said, da words va so important, dey frightened me.

"Den...it vas so wonderful...you told me to close my eyes 'n you painted a picture in my head like in a dream, of me be-ing already ten years old. I did not feel four anymore. I felt how brave I vas vould be at ten, 'n dat made it easier to be brave al-ready, so I asked da four questions 'n it vas not so scary. Dank you. You helped me be a big kid 'n dat made me very happy."

She nuzzled into Meshka's neck wrinkling her nose like a baby bunny sniffing pleasantly. She always loved the smell of her grandma's neck.

Suryla gave a contented sigh and went on, "Remember how Mommy vanted me to put my toys in dat big box, but I forgot 'n left dem on da floor? Vell one day, I vas hiding in da closet vhen Mommy came in. I watched her bend down 'n pick up my toys. Vhen she stood up, she held onto da bed 'n put her hand on her back. I saw da pain on her face. I never left my toys on da floor again. I did not vant to hurt my Mommy. She vas so proud of me. I am glad I could make my Mommy proud of me before I had to go away."

"Vhat did you do to say goodbye vid me?" Curiosity led Meshka to ask.

Suryla giggled, "Nothing, I am still here!"

"I even did a goodbye vid my liddle brother. I taught him how to pump his legs up 'n down, so da swing goes by itself. I am glad he got to learn dat. He felt so grown up 'n I got to be a teacher in dat lifetime, lucky me!" She squealed and clapped her hands.

Meshka felt one of those deep warm grandmother sighs that feel so good. "My liddle flower angel, Shainela, I love you." Suryla smiled and disappeared or maybe Meshka grew so relaxed, she drifted off to sleep.

The women followed the river. Meshka was tempted to tell Rifka she saw Suryla's ghost. Would knowing her child was happy in heaven, only make Rifka sad, or angry, or both? Too bad; such visits were soothing to Meshka, but Rifka was more earthy like her father.

Life was easier now that they were eating every day. There were so many fish in the water, the handy little basket delivered dinner more often than not.

ଔଔଔଔ

Pretty autumn colors gave way to blustery November winds. The cold breath of winter left a frosty edge on the ground around them. Meshka woke up before the others and reluctantly wiggled out of her nice warm sleeping roll. She took the little mezuzah hanging from a piece of yarn on the willow branch above her bedroll, reverently kissed the little carved box, and draped it around her neck. It lay against her heart, a reminder of the God and the family she loved so much.

Meshka gathered wood, lit a fire, and put a pot of water on to heat. She made a broth from the bones of the small animal they ate yesterday. Once it was gently simmering, she found a quiet place under a nearby elm tree to talk with God.

"God," She shook her head, disapproving. "Most Holy Von, vhere is Your compassion for all da suffering people?" She spoke to God as though He were her naughty grandson misbehaving.

God, in His infinite wisdom, did not smite her. Instead He answered, "I have given your people the law." Meshka privately thought laws favor one people over another. But she could not say such a thing.

In the patient loving voice of a mama talking to her son, Meshka said, "God, dear God, if you set a good example, I am sure people vill follow. Show us how to live 'n act vid mercy 'n compassion."

God quickly replied, "Women are born with original sin, so humanity must suffer."

Meshka protested, "All-Powerful God, why did You plant da Tree of Good 'n Evil right in da middle of da garden? Why did You say, 'Eat of every tree, but not dis von?' Why would You say 'n do such dings, if not to tempt 'n taunt Adam 'n Eve? You created temptation! You created suffering! Why did it not please You in Your creation to make a gentler more graceful world? Why did You not teach people dat vee are von race - da human race? Why did You create such division?"

She said it! Still fire did not rain down from heaven.

Patiently God explained, "I have given you obstacles to push against to make you strong and worthy."

This really made her blood boil! She did not need fire to rain down from heaven, there was plenty already inside her belly. Softening her voice, she asked, "Holy One, is dat why You make us suffer sooo much? Vhat if vee become strong 'n worthy on da outside, but empty 'n guilt-ridden on da inside? Is da outside all You care about?" She wondered what God valued.

"Meshka, why must you always be so angry at Me? I warned them not to eat of the Tree of Good and Evil. I knew if they ate from the forbidden tree, chaotic forces would be unleashed, expelling them from the garden where there is no suffering. I do not want my children to suffer."

Meshka tried to push her reply back down her throat, but the words burst out.

"Holy One, maybe devout men believe such excuses, but it does not make sense to me. Even I, a liddle old woman, humble as I am, can choose vhere to plant a tree. You, all knowing 'n all powerful, could not plant da tree a country or two over, so dey did not have to look at it every day?" God let her have the last word, this time.

Meshka went back to the fire to check the broth. Her jaw was clenched. Anger was surging through her body; but she warned herself to be careful not to put anger in the food. Anger curdles food in a belly. She breathed slowly to feel the love to put into the broth. By the time the others were awake, she was calm.

After breakfast, Meshka brushed Joya's long wavy black hair marveling at its thick texture. Joya looked up at Meshka. The Gypsy girl still did not speak, but she smiled. For the first time, she reached out to someone.

CRCRCR

Part 2

Sisterhood

Chapter 4

The Seeders of Peace

It was a blustery autumn day. Colorful leaves were twirling about on a crisp breeze. The three women followed a winding animal path up the side of a mountain. Their legs were strong now.

For two months they scurried across farmlands, dared venture into the dark forests, forded rushing rivers, and lingered in sweet meadows. They skirted towns and avoided roads, choosing instead to trudge through swamps and remain invisible. Walking between the raindrops, no one knew they were there.

Sometimes they lingered for days in a pretty place beside a pond, a lake, or a river. Thinking about the past and coping with the present consumed all their energy. They did not even dream of a safe place where they could make a new life. They just put one foot in front of the other and kept on going...on the way to nowhere.

The land grew rougher and the hills grew taller. They had no choice, but to go on. They could not stay in the farmlands after the harvest was over. They could not stay in the swamps with all the creepy crawly beasts. They had no choice, but to keep on going and ahead of them were the mountains.

They followed a path cut in the hillside by centuries of sheep and goat herds.

Rifka, with a pocket full of rocks, occasionally met little animals along the path. She gave thanks for them at dinner.

Pulling the two-wheeled cart over rocks, through ruts, up the hillside, down into ravines, and across the streams with the little goat riding on top half the time, gave Rifka strong muscles and an irritable temper.

Joya was waking up more every day, eating better, and keeping it down most of the time. She felt stronger, so she put her shoulder to the cart beside Rifka and pushed with all her youthful strength. Together the two young women pulled and pushed their way to the top of a big hill. From a high perch they looked down. It was dizzying to see how far they had come!

Rifka *plotzed* down on the cold ground. She dropped her body and stretched her back. Her back muscles were complaining worse than her mouth ever did. Meshka came panting up behind her holding her chest. It was threatening to explode into a million pieces.

"Look!" croaked the Gypsy girl. It was the first word she had spoken in three months! Rifka and Meshka turned and stared at her. They were so startled to hear her speak; they did not think to look where she was pointing. The fear twisting her face, made them look.

From this high perch, they saw a large army moving up the mountain coming right towards them! They scurried around frantically looking for a place to hide. Rifka found an outcropping of huge boulders off the path. The tall boulders were broad enough to hide them, the cart, and their little goat. Securely concealed, they watched the multitude inch closer and closer up the mountain.

The strange army came near enough for the women to smell them and their animals. Daring to peek out, they saw a confusion of people.

They were not soldiers, all spiffed up in uniform, or a rag-tag militia. They were just ragged old people, women carrying bundles, and children trailing behind their mother's skirts. Even the strong men did not look like fighters. They were carrying tools, not weapons.

The frightened women watched with eyes bulging and mouths hanging open. A very odd mishmash of people was slowly winding their way up the mountain. There were more people than ants in a nest. You never saw so many!People were spread out as far as the eye could see. Meshka never imagined there were so many people in all the world!

The refugees, for that is what they were, drew closer. Never had she seen anything like this. There were giants with skin black as coal and curly hair as tight as combed felt. There were small skinny people with yellowish skin and strangely slanted eyes.

It was amazing! She saw people of every size and shape, people with the yellow eyes of a tiger, and those with eyes as green as grass in early spring. She saw giants with straight hair as pale as early wheat and little people even smaller than her. Meshka almost twittered. Nobody was ever shorter than her.

Their costumes were fascinating; a rainbow of colors, weaves and textures. The three women were stunned! Some people wore rags and others were decked out in the finest embroidered silk.

Though well hidden behind the huge boulders, their hearts were pounding with fear, lest they be discovered! Rifka fed the goat bunches of grass to keep his mouth busy for fear his usual gay chatter would give them away.

The strangers approaching the boulders were almost close enough to touch. In fascination, the women peeked around the protective boulders. Who knew there were so many different kinds of people in the world!?!

Then, shocked and startled, they held their breath. Walking before this exotic mix of people was an extraordinary, gigantic creature! A magnificent dark-haired *Goddess* wearing a short black skirt and carrying a long, silver tipped spear stood more than ten feet tall.

The majesty of *Her* bearing and the pride of *Her* step took Meshka's breath away. As *The Goddess* passed the place where the three awe-struck women were hidden, *She* stopped, turned, and smiled, *"Hello Meshka."*

Bravely Meshka stood up and faced the giant creature. Without thinking, the words flew out of her mouth, "Who are all dese people?"

In a deep resonant voice *The Goddess* answered, *"They are the seekers and seeders of peace."* *Her* words touched Meshka's heart like warm chocolate melting on a hungry tongue.

"Are you going to do something about all da suffering?" Meshka asked with more hope than challenge in her voice.

"Yes," *The Goddess* answered. Tears welled up in Meshka's eyes.

"I have come to awaken people to a new way of life. I bring new beliefs that honor and rejoice in life, rather than, force people to bring death."

The Goddess looked into Meshka's eyes, or maybe it was deep into her soul, and said, *"You and your companions are welcome to join us."*

Meshka was suddenly swimming in the most delicious exhilaration. Fresh air was blowing through her. A humming sensation lulled her whole body. When she came to stillness, she felt loved and loving, utterly content, and completely aware.

The Goddess lifted *Her* eyes to the future and continued on *Her* way.

Meshka could hardly breathe. Her feet grew roots right where she stood. "Oy vay, my God!" She was trembling.

The magnitude of what just happened, hit her square in the face. "I just talked face to face, vid someone who cannot possibly exist!"

Bolts of lightning shot through her blood! She was just catching her breath, when she remembered standing there courageously speaking to that gigantic creature. It was mind-boggling. The amazing truth was impossible. Where did she get the courage?

Meshka used to be so timid. Remember how frightened she was in the meadow with the crooked tree when she first stumbled upon the caravan and met Joya? She stood frozen with terror just because a strange girl talked to her and touched her hand. A lot of living and dying passed since then.

The little old woman, who was scared of anything outside her village, did not exist anymore. She died along the way, and this new Meshka was a very different person.

Shaking her head in amazement, Meshka thought, "Once upon a time talking to Joya vas terrifying! I vas afraid of her because she vas a stranger 'n not Jewish."

She would never forget when she was a little girl, her *Bubba* (grandma) wagged a finger at her and warned, *"It is a sin to talk vid anyone who is not Jewish!"*

"Oy vay," Meshka put her hands on her cheeks and shook her head moaning. "My list of sins is growing! I just talked face to face vid someone who not only vas not Jewish, She vas not even human!

"Can a *Goddess* really exist!?! Or are my brains falling out?" Meshka moaned again.

One last hope, "Maybe dis is only a dream. Rifka please, pinch me." The edge of Rifka's lips curled up almost to a smile as she gave her mama's arm a playful little pinch.

"Ow!" It hurt!

"Rifka do your eyes see vhat my eyes see? Is an army of strange people really walking by? Did a ten foot giant just stop 'n call me by name? Did I talk to *Her?*

Meshka's eyebrows were knitted so tight her forehead almost cracked.

"Your giant friend asked us to follow *Her* 'n walk vid all those strangers!" Rifka was trembling with fear "Vell I am not goin' to join dat mob," sniffed Rifka. "Dey are not Jewish," and put her nose up in the air.

Meshka's head was loose and kept shaking. "Rifkala," she softly said, "So vhat if dey are different? You dink maybe vee should keep walking around in circles, hiding from everyone like a fart in a pickle-barrel?

Meshka was shaking her hands palms up in helpless distress. She felt like *kvetching*, but instead she appealed to Rifka.

"Do you call dis a life? I am not a cow, you know. I cannot be content standing around eating grass. I still have a few ideas rolling around in my head.

"Heaven knows da world needs a liddle peace. I am tired of all dis *mishugass* (crazy ideas) dat make one people hate another."

Rifka was shocked! This did not even sound like her mama. "I do not care if these people are Jews or Gentiles, da same as us or different. I vant to be vid brave women who are willing to put a shoulder to a good cause. Vee are all da children of *Mother Earth*."

Outraged as much as frightened, Rifka shouted, "Mama! Dat is blasphemy!"

"Oy vay, it is a troubled world if a simple truth 'n blasphemy are one 'n da same ding. Open your eyes, Shainela! Maybe differences are a good ding, instead of something to spit on, no?"

Meshka patiently sighed, "Rifkala, please come vid me." Very sweetly she coaxed, "Shainela, I vant to do dis. Vee are family. Vee only have each other. Come let us walk vid dem for a few days. After next Shabbos, vee can talk again, nu? Vee can make a decision den."

"Mama!" scolded Rifka. Her thick eyebrows were all bunched together. "It is a sin to dwell among da *Goyim*." (foreigners)

"Rifkala," Meshka said, her shoulders drooping under invisible weight, "Are you afraid you vill be punished for your sins?"

"Of course!" Rifka roared.

"Rifkala my poor child, there is no greater punishment dan vhat vee have already suffered. Vee have nothing more to lose."

Rifka was not convinced; she was trapped! These people were a gift and a curse. Finding a way through these foreboding mountains, with winter coming on, was a daunting prospect and who knows what lies beyond the mountains? Having guides would be a great relief, but being surrounded by this terrifying mishmash of people was horrifying! In all their wanderings, no opportunity presented itself other than this one. Joining these riffraff felt somehow right and frighteningly wrong. Rifka saw no other option, so she gave in.

Joya just followed along, of course. What did she care? Everyone she knew, her whole boisterous passionate family was dead. To have survived, to be the only one left, was a dreadful curse. Each day the sun rose and accused her of still being alive.

The decision was made, but they just stood there *ferblundjit* (shocked and confused). Finally Meshka took the goat by the rope and walked on. Rifka picked up one handle of the cart, Joya lifted the other, and they fell into stride traveling along with the other people.

Shocked and amazed their eyes darted about unable to take it all in! In the next few minutes they saw more new things, than twice their lives put together! Who knew people came in so many colors, sizes, and shapes! The world was a lot bigger than Meshka thought. Her eyes saw faster than her mind could make sense of it!

When night came, Rifka could not close her eyes. She was shaking. She pushed sleep away and grabbed for it all through a long uncomfortable night.

Nights were the hardest for Rifka. She missed her family and felt lost under the big night sky. Her eyes were often ringed in red from crying through the night.

Meshka could not sleep either. Maybe it was so many people pressing in on her after the spacious silence of the journey.

It was a crisp November night. There was a special clarity and thinness about the air. Meshka crawled out of her bedroll, wrapped her heavy woolen shawl tightly around her shivering shoulders, and covered her head with the thick weave. Bundled against the cold, she wandered off. She found a quiet place to be alone by a small gurgling creek.

This night felt very special to Meshka. It was the beginning of something wondrous and new. All those months of hiding at every sound, of scurrying like rats whenever a wagon rattled down the road, always sleeping with one eye open, those days had come to an end. Something new was beginning. Sure she was scared...b-u-t...she was also very excited.

A *Goddess!* Whoever thought such a thing could exist? But then, she never imagined black skinned people with felt hair could exist either, and they were real.

Meshka looked up at the stars. For as long as she could remember, the night sky had worn these same stars. It comforted her to think that something did not change.

"Vhat comes next for me?" she wondered aloud. In the back of her mind she heard the answer, *"See the world. Know about the world. Make the world a better place."* The stars twinkled as though they were smiling at what was just said.

Did da answer come from up there? She wondered.

"God, are You talking through da stars now?" she asked. But the warm feeling melting through her was very different than the quarrelsome agitation she felt when she talked to God.

"See da world. Know da world. Make da world a better place," Meshka repeated over and over again, rolling it around in her mind. "Dat is a worthy destiny indeed."

ର୍ଉଷର

Meshka walked along with her goat, while Joya and Rifka pulled the cart behind her. Joya kept nervously looking around expecting someone to suddenly pounce on her. Rifka sang a song to quiet their pounding hearts. They were walking beside strangers, alert, and ready for a quick escape. Rifka scrutinized this mishmash of foreigners, aware that she was in the very camp of the enemy!

From time to time throughout the day, strange women fell into step beside them, smiled, and said hello. These friendly faces were a great relief to Meshka, but Rifka continued to be suspicious. Several days passed before Rifka relaxed and felt safe enough to walk freely among these ragtag refugees.

Joya, locked in a private hell of guilt and rage, still did not talk. Each day she relaxed a little more. Soon she was helping with daily chores. No one had to tell her to fetch water or clean up after dinner. She now did these simple tasks on her own.

When Friday night came around, the little family lit their *Shabbos* candles, shared a small freshly baked challah, and blessed a cup of wine.

Rifka gathered berries and mushrooms early that morning. She traded her harvest to a small yellow-skinned woman for a bag of flour. Then she milked the goat and traded a bladder of milk to a dark-haired woman with a slender nose and high cheek bones, for several eggs, a little sugar, and a cake of yeast. A few of the eggs went to a gray-haired woman with a bulbous nose in exchange for a glass of wine.

Meshka and Rifka saw how the others made an oven in the campfire using flat rocks. They tried it and succeeded in baking a fine challah! They had candles, bread, and wine. It was a real Shabbos for the first time since the world ended. After sipping the wine and savoring the fresh baked bread, they knew they were staying.

Meshka remained in state of bubbling excitement for days. Rifka's brows were permanently knitted together; trust was not her best talent. Joya was friendly, helpful, silent and withdrawn. Like a frightened deer, her eyes darted about and her body quivered sensing danger. Every new face attacked her sense of safety.

As the weeks passed, Joya slowly emerged from her dark cocoon. Then suddenly she completely changed!

Sleeping Beauty awoke from her trance on the day she heard a handsome Gypsy man play his violin. The familiar music penetrated the whirlpool of Joya's mind. Her eyes sparkled for the first time since day the world ended.

Night after night, the handsome man strolled by at sunset playing his violin. Night after night, the ice encrusting Joya's heart melted a little more.

On the seventh day, the music reached her legs! Carried away by the rhythm, she jumped up to dance. Dancing set her soul free. She desperately needed to be free. Wild passions whirled through the dance. A furious rage poured out in the snap of whirling skirts and the fierce stomping of her feet. Her young voluptuous hips undulated with hypnotic abandon.

When the golden brilliance of the sun gave way to streaks of fuchsia and dark rose, Joya's body swayed slowly, heavy with grief. Finally the sky faded into the palest eggshell blue and the dark silhouette of the trees loomed over them, Joya spread her arms wide twirling round and round. She flew into the twilight. Wild and free, she flew far away from the ugly world. When the violin fell silent, Joya collapsed into Meshka's arms and choked on a torrent of tears.

ଔଔଔ

Gilberto, the Gypsy man, lived for the evenings when he played his violin in tribute to the dying day. He played to honor the memory of his beloved family, gone now, consumed by a self-devouring world. Joya's dancing inspired Gilberto. He caressed the sweetest notes from the violin just for her. Watching her feet fly gave him an intoxicating taste of home. As days passed, he secretly daydreamed of courting his young muse; but was unsure how in this strange uncertain world.

Night after night Gilberto played and Joya danced. His bow flew over the strings, filling the air with sweet stirring melodies. The gleam in his eyes sent a wild flutter through her heart.

She danced wild flights of fancy and he played the sweetest notes on the violin. Their sparkling eyes flirted with each other. Their hearts shared a deep intimacy and a dark intense hunger, but neither one said a word. The power and the passion continued to mount, held in check by the losses of the past.

ଔଔଔ

Chapter 5

Little Old Rachel

Meshka and the goat were walking along looking at the people. They looked so interesting, if only she was brave enough to say more than hello. People fell into step beside her and smiled. When they greeted her, Meshka stared in panic, unable to answer. The exotic sound of their greetings thrilled her. She got so excited, she blushed and turned away. The poor old woman was too terrified to talk to foreigners! If only she was as brave as Rifka. Without Rifka to hunt, steal and beg, they would have starved to death.

The next Shabbos began on a clear crisp Friday night. The sun was setting and the sky was bursting into color. At the magical moment of twilight, Meshka and Rifka each lit two precious little candles to welcome Shabbos. Here they were, farmlands, forests, swamps, and hills away from home, but today was Shabbos and they had candles, wine, and challah. A touch of normal went a long way, so far from home.

The little Shabbos candles were God's eyes shining on them. Having Shabbos candles was worth the many hours of toil that went into making them; also animal fat and bits of cloth were not easy to come by. Rifka cleverly made the trades and made the candle molds by hollowing out branches with her favorite knife.

The little wicks flickered and caught flame. Meshka gathered the candle light with her hands and drew it into her eyes, three times, washing her face with God's radiance. Shabbos was a sacred time for Meshka, a time to look at things through God's eyes.

Meshka and Rifka bowed shawl covered heads and thanked God for the *mitzvah* (the blessing) of life. In their prayers, they named their family and friends up in heaven with God and asked that they be blessed too.

The candles were lit, the prayers recited, Meshka turned to Rifka and wished her a *Gut* Shabbos (Good Sabbath) like she did every Shabbos all her life...before the world ended. Meshka happened to look over Rifka's shoulder and saw a most marvelous sight.

Camped not far away was a little old Jewish woman. Her head was covered in a pretty white shawl and she was also lighting two candles to welcome the Shabbos Bride.

When the old Jewish woman opened her eyes, after saying her prayers, she saw Meshka giving her a big toothy smile. Meshka's smile could melt butter in the snow, so the woman smiled back.

Seeing a kindred spirit in this multitude of foreigners warmed Meshka's heart. This was one of those Shabbos miracles. The little old woman in the pretty white shawl ambled over and said, "*Gut Shabbos*" (Good Sabbath).

Meshka and Rifka both repeated, "Gut Shabbos" and felt the warmth of meeting a *landsmen* (all Jews are kinsmen) in a faraway land. Entering into the sacredness of Shabbos together was a wonderful way to meet.

"*Shalom*, (peace) my name is Rachel," said the old woman in a soft sweet voice. Meshka introduced herself, her daughter, and Joya who was standing off to the side quietly watching.

Rachel felt so familiar, Meshka was sure they met before, but it was impossible. They came from different worlds. The two old women chatted easily. Meshka invited Rachel to share their wine and challah.

"Real challah!? How can I say no to such a treat?"

Rifka wrinkled up her nose in distaste, but said nothing. After sharing the delicious blessing over the wine and challah, Rachel invited them to come to her fire for some real *cholent* (a dipping pot of chicken stew with grains. It simmers all Shabbos so no one has to make food.). Rifka was impressed. Real chicken was nothing to wrinkle her nose at.

Meshka and Rachel had their heads together all through dinner. Rachel was easier to talk to than God. Boy could she talk! All her words had waited for this moment. She had no one to talk to before. Meshka and Rachel were immediately old friends.

CRCRCR

On Saturday, the sacred day of rest, Meshka and her new friend were sitting by the morning fire, which Joya built. The Gypsy girl started kindling the fires on Saturdays when she noticed the Jewish women never made a fire or prepared food on Shabbos. She made a nice breakfast for them this morning of eggs and vegetables.

Rachel came over to the fire and Meshka invited her to sit down. Joya offered her some eggs, but Rachel said, "Dank you. I already ate some cholent," still she was glad to accept a nice hot cup of tea and found their pretty gourd cups charming.

Rachel shook her head and laughed. "Life is strange. Vid so many people here from so many places, vee camp in da same place. It vas *bashert* (predestined) for us to meet like dis."

With a warm smile Rachel asked, "May I ask you something personal? How do you come to be here?"

Meshka smiled a little shyly, took a big breath, and forced out the fewest words she could find. "Our village vas destroyed 'n my family vas killed. All I have now is my daughter Rifka 'n my young friend Joya. Vee walked 'n walked until vee met dese people. Now vee walk vid dem. I do not know where vee are going, but it is enough to be going." Meshka answered with a philosophical shrug.

"'N you?"

"It is nice of you to ask," Rachel replied with a demure smile. "My husband Avram, God rest his Soul, died in his sleep," Rachel put on her storytelling voice. "I found him lying peacefully; his leg vas dangling off da side of da bed like he vas just snoozing for a moment. I stood dere dinking he looked so sweet in his sleep. It took me a while to see something vas wrong. His chest vas not moving! Vee va married for thirty-six years. I vas only twelve vhen he married me, but I vas in love vid him, since I vas five. He vas so dashing."

Her eyes glassed over. Tears threatened to fall, so she stopped and took another sip of the fragrant tea. The warm gourd felt good in her hands on this crisp morning.

"Avram vas my sister's husband first. Da *shatkhn*, you know da matchmaker, arranged a marriage between Avram 'n my older sister Basha vhen I vas five. After dey va married, his family 'n ours all moved into one apartment in da ghetto. It vas very crowded, but not so bad. A lot of people had it worse. At night, dey locked us in behind da big gates. Dat horrible clank made me feel trapped 'n Basha cried every night in Avram's arms."

Rachel gave a deep sigh remembering that terrible feeling of being an animal put in a cage.

"Basha often teased me about my crush on Avram. I adored dem both. In five years, Basha had four babies. Vee laughed 'n played like brothers 'n sisters. Basha vas very weak after da last baby vas born. Da miserable life of da ghetto 'n having so liddle food, made her weak.

"Before da baby vas a year old, Basha died. Times va hard 'n many good people died. Vhen vee lost our sweet Basha, a great beauty disappeared from da world."

Meshka thought of her own sister, Raizie. She was not what you call a great beauty, not with her round pink cheeks and big belly, but her heart was beautiful. Raizie was always kind to people. She was the only person Meshka told all her secrets to. Now she was gone too. Meshka wished Raizie well in her heavenly rest and turned back to Rachel's story.

"Avram vas heart-broken. He vent early every morning to da cemetery to talk vid Basha's spirit. At da cemetery, he saw Chava, a young widow who also vent every morning to visit her husband's grave. Dey saw each other often, maybe dey even spoke once.

"Avram asked da *shatkhn* (matchmaker) to arrange a *shidech.* (a betrothal of marriage) He vas twenty-two 'n she vas eighteen. He needed a mama for his four small children 'n she needed a husband. Da wedding vas set for da following year. Dey had to wait until da mourning time vas over 'n da gravestones unveiled."

Rachel hesitated before telling Meshka the next part. Would her new friend believe her? If she did not live it, she would not believe it. Rachel finished her tea and put the cup aside, shaking her head over the strange dreams that would change her life forever.

"Vhen da wedding vas coming close, Avram had da strangest dream. In da dream, he saw Basha walking towards him smiling. She wrapped her arms around his neck 'n said, 'Marry my sister.'"

Meshka dimly remembered it was an old Jewish custom for a widow to marry her husband's brother, a practical idea, but did the custom go the other way too?

"Da next morning, Avram vas haunted by da dream. He told it to da family 'n everyone had another idea of vhat it meant. Da next night, 'n for many nights after dat, he had da same dream."

Rifka joined them by the fire and Joya handed her a cup of hot tea. While she was at it, she refilled Meshka's and Rachel's cups and poured a cup for herself. Rachel went on.

"Da wedding vas only two days away vhen suddenly Basha's liddle baby died."

"*Oy gavalt*! Dat is terrible! In my village vee put an amulet on da babies to protect dem from da Evil Eye."

"In my city too. But da *kimpet-tzettel*[2] musta fallen off her wrist 'n da Evil Eye carried da child away."

The tea was still hot, so Rachel blew on it and took small sips. Its warmth felt wonderful. She shuddered. Crisp breezes were blowing through the chilly mountain morn.

"Instead of a wedding, vee had a funeral.

"Avram put off da ceremony. A week before da second wedding day, da dreams came again. Vee all tried to interpret God's message. How could Avram marry me, Basha's only sister? I vas still a child.

"Just three days before da wedding, Basha's pretty liddle girl Leah died!"

"*Oy gavalt!* Dat is terrible! I am so sorry. Bless deir souls."

Rachel's throat tightened making her cough. She loved that little girl like her own sister; another loss, another hole in her soul.

"Avram vas so scared! Vee all va! Da whole family vent vid him to da Rebbe's house. Avram told da Rebbe about da dreams. Da old Rebbe tugged on his long thin beard several times, den said, 'Basha must feel very strongly about dis to come all da vay back from da other world, just to tell you to marry liddle Rachel. As soon as Rachel becomes a woman, you should marry her.'

"Da wise Rebbe had spoken 'n his word vas law, so a few months later vhen da curse came upon me, vee va married."

Meshka respected the power of dreams. Her heart went out to Rachel.

"Avram took my last name Birnbaum, to keep from being conscripted into da army 'n I became mama to Yacov 'n Yeshuah. I vas only six years older dan Yeshuah 'n seven years older dan Yacov."

Meshka could easily imagine Rachel a little girl one day and a mama the next. She shook her head and mused, "Women's lives are often molded by other people's needs."

---

[2] kimpet-tzettel is a childbirth amulet containing psalm 121, plus the names of angels and patriarchs

Rachel nodded in agreement, "Over da next three years I gave birth to two beautiful liddle girls: *Liba Hanna* (Love of Life) 'n Helen (Beautiful). Liba Hanna vas six 'n Helen vas only four, vhen Avram disappeared to find help."

Rachel straightened her shawl. Tears rolled down her cheeks. "Avram left…" The tears caught in her throat. It was long ago and it was only yesterday.

Rachel cried for a few minutes and then turned a bright red at the compassion she saw in the women's eyes. Meshka was not one for touching, but Rachel's quivering shoulders begged a firm gentle reassuring hand. Meshka's hand reached out with a heart of its own.

ରଔଔଔ

That evening, Meshka tried something new. She gathered thick long straight branches and tied them together to make a tent. She covered the roof with a thick layer of sticks and leaves, and the sides with blankets. She watched women around her make tents and hoped it would keep the wind out.

When she was done, she stood back and admired her handiwork. It was a sweet little tent just long enough to cover her, if she did not lay too straight.

Meshka gave a big sigh and thought, once I had a liddle box of a house 'n I thought it vas too small. Now I see it vas really a palace.

She took the piece of yarn and mezuzah from around her neck and hung it from the top of her new tent. Now I have a home. Simple as it is, it is something. *Dayeynu.* (it is enough)

Meshka was about to gather wood, but found Joya already had a fine fire blazing and Rifka was cooking dinner. She was stirring a pot of "everything" stew – everything found or bartered. Meshka was humming as she came up behind Rifka. She wrapped her arms around her daughter's waist and kissed her on the neck.

Rifka looked up and smiled, "Hello, mama. Da stew is almost ready."

After dinner, when the golden sun was sinking behind the mountains, Meshka and her daughter walked to a high place where they looked out across a great vista and sat in sublime silence.

The sky slowly faded and wild splashes of color streaked the clouds. Against the brilliant sky, they watched the silhouette of a young man in a strange sacred dance, honoring the dying sun. His long hair blew about like silken ribbons on the evening breeze. He was standing on a tall outcropping of stone. The grace and mime of his movements told a story of hope. His silhouette had the nobility of one reaching for a dream and the joy of one attaining it.

As they watched him, each was lost in their own jumbled thoughts and sad feelings. Meshka looked off into the distance and mused: Life goes on. It is amazing how our lives are sooo fragile. Vee dink, not us; bad dings only happen to bad people, but it is not true. Terrible tides crash in on everyone, but life still goes on.

So vhat really counts? She wondered. If being good does not matter, vhat does? Does God just spin a wheel 'n pick a number 'n dat tells him who vill die next?

Such private thoughts were not for sharing, so Meshka only said, "Rifkala dis a beautiful sunset, no?" She longed to say, "My liddle girl, I am so grateful dat I still have you. I know inside dat hard shell of yours, my sweet liddle child is hiding somewhere." Little did she suspect the strange destiny that was waiting for this young woman and for her as well.

ଔଔଔଔ

Meshka just stood there shaking her head, while everyone was packing up to move on. She wanted to keep the big branches. They made a perfect tent. Who knows what she would find tomorrow? She could not carry such a heavy weight and wondered if it was fair to ask Rifka to pull them in the cart.

Rachel shuffled over. Seeing Meshka's brows all knitted tight, Rachel asked, "Vhat is happening by you?"

Meshka was glad to think out loud to a friend. She used to talk to her neighbors Sophia and Hanna all the time. It usually put her head back on straight.

So Meshka told Rachel about her dilemma. Her fears sounded silly. She laughed a big belly laugh, turned away, and picked up the little goat's rope. Meshka walked on leaving the heavy tent for the next weary traveler.

"It is hard for me to leave something I like behind," Meshka apologized.

Rachel waved it away and said, "You, and me 'n everyone feels dat vay. Life teaches us to let go for better or worse."

Rachel walked beside her little one-wheeled cart. It was pulled by a little pony. Meshka walked beside her on the other side. The goat liked the cart and the way the wheels tossed up sweet tufts of grass as it rolled along.

"Rachel, can I ask you something personal." Meshka asked shyly.

When Rachel nodded, Meshka dared to pry. "How could your Avram leave you in such a terrible place, where you really needed da protection of a man? How could a husband leave a woman in a frightening place vid his liddle children?"

All the air rushed out of Rachel like she was punched. When she recovered, she said, "I vill tell you. Times va frightening. Death vas everywhere," her voice was weary. "Da children va too young 'n too fragile to risk escape. Vee already lost two liddle ones, vee could not take da chance. I vas afraid, God forbid, I might lose another child along da vay. Vee had no choice. Avram had to go alone 'n find help. I thought he would return soon 'n lead us to a safer place."

Rachel shook her head, thinking about how naïve she was back then. It was long ago. She was so young and had to be so grown up. Her lips curled up almost to a smile

"Four long years vee waited. Vhen word came, it vas not good. Someone beat Avram up very badly. Da man who told us dis, did not know if my sweet husband vas still alive. First, I worried about Avram, den I worried about my children. No one vas coming to rescue us!"

Meshka smiled warmly, her eyes soft with compassion.

ଔଔଔଔ

The little goat was dancing around in delight gobbling up the little cart's green treats. The mountain passes were rocky. Wheels and rocks are not good friends. One chaffs the other a little, sort of like Meshka's rascally goat and Rachel's stubborn little pony.

The two animals were best friends and best enemies from that first moment on. Meshka and Rachel found much to laugh about when they watched them taunt, tease and playfully romp together.

Meshka hoped Rachel would tell her more. She marveled that little old Rachel, bowed and modest, was once an amazing young woman who coped with great challenges.

With a little coaxing from Meshka, Rachel faced more of her past. "I sent my playful young Yeshuah out into da dangerous world alone at a tender age. Someone had to go. Someone had to find a vay to freedom. Vee prayed every day for God to watch over him 'n send him safely back to us.

"Yeshuah vas a funny fellow. At seventeen, he vas slender graceful 'n liked to play tricks on everyone. On *Pesach* (Passover) vhen people opened their front doors to invite Elijah in, Yeshuah slipped in da back door 'n drank all da wine in Elijah's special cup.

"One Purim, he needed a costume, so he dressed up like a girl 'n he looked so pretty in his liddle dress, a young man from da ghetto asked for a *shidech* (a betrothal marriage contract).

Meshka laughed with delight at Yeshuah's antics, but tears were hiding in the corners of her eyes.

"Five more years passed. Word came from Yeshuah from time to time, mostly through peddlers passing through. He vas in a faraway land, working hard 'n saving money. It cost a lot of money to buy da papers to open dat clanking gate 'n get us out of da ghetto."

"Five years! Oy, my poor dear!" exclaimed Meshka in sympathy. She shuddered to think of her friend starving, clawing to survive and keep her children safe.

"Yes another five years! Vee stayed fed, just barely. Many people died. Da liddle ghetto vas not so crowded anymore.

"Finally *Baruch HaShem*, (blessed be da name of da Lord) Yeshuah came back 'n vee escaped from dat miserable place, but not all of my children survived."

Rachel looked so upset, Meshka put a quiet arm around her shoulders and felt strong enough for the two of them. Losing a child is a hole in the soul, a dark place Meshka had faced as well.

ଓଃଓଃଓଃ

It was an exceptionally warm day for late November. The air was fresh and the sun was brilliant, bright, and warm. Since it was Shabbos, a day to rest and play, Meshka wandered off to explore a high meadow. She felt light-footed and kissed by life! A blush of soft cotton clouds floated through a clear blue sky, soft as a maiden's cheek.

Meshka ventured deep into a forest exploring its mysteries. Delightful mysterious feelings were stirring in her. She felt charmed by the passionate beauty of such an untamed place. She tried to name her feelings. Surprised, she realized it was 'freedom.' It felt so good she was suspicious. In the past, freedom always came arm in arm with loss.

Meshka came to a small river winding its way through dense bushes and trees. Climbing under and over thick branches, she followed the gurgling music of the water rushing down the mountain to meet its destiny. The smell of leaf mold was sweet and tangy. She took a deep breath. It seemed to clear the cobwebs from her mind.

Meshka sang softly to herself oblivious to the squawking pitch of her voice.

"Maybe dis body is wrinkled 'n old, but me, I do not age." She made up the song and sang it off key.

She followed the river as it widened. The water ran swift and shallow. A huge boulder rose majestically out of the water, just a hop and a skip from the bank. Meshka could never resist climbing rocks. Tempted, she heard the siren's call, "Come climb me and touch the sky."

Meshka scurried up the rocks. Well, maybe to someone watching, it was not exactly scurrying, but it felt like it and that was what mattered. Meshka reached the very top! She was higher than anything around her and she felt as young as she ever was! She sang in a loud scratchy voice.

"I am going to see da world
'N know a liddle about it.
Can I make da world
A better place?
I can if it is
My destiny."

Meshka sang to the sun in the sky. Whatever her song lacked in beauty, it made up in passion.

Meshka was standing on top of the world! A brisk wind blew, whipping her long dark skirts around her legs. She drew her warm woolen shawl tighter around her shoulders to keep out the sharp chill.

Intoxicated with the view, she listened to the wind whistling through the trees below and clearly heard the words, *"If you desire a world where cooperation is valued more than domination, your words and your actions help such a world to form. Cooperation is crucial to your survival."*

Meshka's head was spinning. She felt giddy. "Such big words could not come from my head!? Dey do not sound like God either! Vhere did dey come from?"

Meshka was not scared, not exactly. But there was a lot of fluttering inside her.

Carefully she crawled down the smooth stones groping for niches to grip with her fingers and toes. "Going down is always so much harder dan climbing up. How come I never remember dat?" She asked herself.

Back on the ground, everything looked a lot bigger. Only then did she realize how huge she felt up on the rocks. Light-heartedly she ambled back to camp.

On the way, she found Rachel sitting in the sun brushing her pretty little pony. Meshka gave the animal a suspicious look, but his little teeth looked innocent enough, so she sat down nearby.

"Rachel, I feel so free today. Maybe it is a liddle Shabbos magic." Meshka said with a giggle.

Rachel nodded and said, "Freedom is a rare treasure. People have paid dearly for it. I surely did."

"Rachel, vhat happened vhen you left da ghetto? How did you find Avram?"

Rachel sighed thinking where to begin. Should she start with all the bribes, all the finagling to get her and her three children day-passes to work outside the gates, or tell her of the heartache it was, to say goodbye to those who must stay behind?

"Yeshuah met Yacov by da fence near da bushes. He passed him a package 'n rushed away. Inside vas money, da important papers, 'n a message. Yacov read it to us. It said how to meet him in a secret place. Vee could not take bundles. If vee did, da guards would ask questions, so vee took only vhat vee could wear.

"Vee traveled only in da night. I vas so careful, for all da good it did me! A nasty guard saw my liddle Helen hiding behind a bush 'n took us all to a rickety old barn.

"Vee sat huddled together in da dirty hay, my liddle girls 'n my big son shaking under my wings.

"A woman sitting nearby said, 'Dey vill never let you go, not vid a boy big enough for da army.'"

Rachel shuddered just thinking of it. Remembering the empty hole that opened up and swallowed her; sinking, trapped and desperate!

"Vee all started crying. Yacov whispered… 'Shhhhh…' He took my hands 'n said softly, 'Aunt Mama,' dat is vhat he called me. He vas so sweet to me. 'Aunt Mama, dey vill not let you go if I am vid you. I should stay behind. I vill catch up vid you later.'"

Rachel could hardly breathe. The memory still strangled her. The choice. The terrible choice. Should they stay together and find a way to escape, or should she surrender her son? She could not risk the safety of the little ones; but Yacov was her childhood friend, her little brother, her nephew, and her son. Yacov was a *mensch*, a serious young man with a good head on his shoulders. She prayed for God's protective grace and cast his fate to the winds.

"I agreed 'n said, 'Be careful, very careful. You know vhere to meet us?"

"How could I leave my son!? I squeezed my three children so tight to my bosom. Dey clung to me. I vas standing in an ocean drowning in heartbreak 'n tears.

"Yacov squared his shoulders vid courage, gave me dis packet vid da precious tokens dat open da gates to freedom. He said, 'Aunt Mama, keep it safe. God villing, I vill meet you soon.' I did, but he did not."

Rachel could still hear his soft voice, gentle and strong, brave and reckless, could still feel the horror of saying goodbye. It tore a piece of her heart out.

"Vhen da guards asked me, who travels vid you? I forced da words out. Dey vanted to hide in my throat. 'Only two liddle girls, sir,' I said. My throat vas burning vid da lie.

"Dey let us go. Yacov vas conscripted into da army. He vas sent to some God-forsaken place vhere he vas shot!

"My son died so young, *chaval*! (such a pity!) He vas only eighteen. My noble Yacov sacrificed himself to save our lives."

It was years ago, but the wound was fresh. Meshka put her arms around Rachel and held her tight.

ରେଓଓଓ

Meshka served Rachel a bowl of *cholent,* took some herself and poured them each a cup of fragrant tea. In her mind she thanked Joya for keeping the pots on warm coals all day on Shabbos. Content from such a delicious meal, the two women sighed and sat together.

"Rachel, vas Avram alright?"

Rachel had never told anyone her story before. Back in her old life, it was too tender to put into words. Out here in the middle of nowhere among strangers, she finally felt safe enough to look back.

"Vid one hand God punishes 'n vid da other He blesses." She said with a shrug.

"My liddle girls 'n me, vee found Yeshuah. He took us to a faraway land vhere vee va safe. Vhen I saw Avram, I hardly recognized my poor husband. Oy, vhat dey did to him! It vas terrible! Dey broke his bones 'n his spirit. Somewhere in dis shattered man vas my dashing young Avram."

A big blue bird landed on a branch above Rachel's head. It was odd to see a bird this late in the year. He bobbed his head this way and that, like he was listening. Meshka thought, maybe birds are spirits who have returned. Maybe dis von carries Avram's spirit.

"I loved Avram all my life, but ten long-cold-hungry winters pass very slowly. I vas not da same girl I vas vhen he left. It took a long time for us to recognize each other. He vas an old man now. I vas old too. Vhere vas my sweet Avram in dis broken old man?"

Meshka thought being reunited after ten rough years was both tragic and sweet.

Rachel took another bite of *cholent* and stared at the spoon. She admired the delicate birds on the handle, another or Rifka's fine carvings and went on "I gently nursed Avram back to health 'n I began to see a liddle bit of his old dashing charm. Vee made a new home for our children, 'n eventually our grandchildren, in dat faraway land. Avram 'n I va blessed to have another fourteen years together. Den bless his soul, Avram died peacefully in his sleep 'n now I am alone again."

Meshka smiled warmly, her eyes soft with compassion. Everyone's life is such a wild adventure, she thought.

Meshka ate another spoon of *cholent* as she gathered her thoughts. Her heart went out to her friend. What could she say to comfort her?

"Rachel, you va blessed to find love at such a young age. Vhen a woman loves a man as passionately as you loved Avram, sometimes she disappears into him 'n never learns about herself - but not you.

"God made you strong. He gave you children to protect 'n feed; not such an easy task in da ghetto, nu? You are like a great mama bear. Hardship made you strong 'n your children gave you a reason to survive. A lesser woman would be bitter."

The sun was climbing the ladder of the sky and it was time to start the day, even a lazy Saturday like this one. Meshka hugged Rachel. They felt like sisters on a journey together, two women who found a piece of home in each other and they savored it.

"Rachel, you are a cat vid nine lives, a very good survivor. Next time da wind howls like hungry wolves, I am not going to lay awake waiting for da demons to eat me in da night, I am going to put my bed next to yours. Den I vill feel safe.

"You know how to walk in da eye of a storm. I vant to learn dat too."

CRCRCR

Chapter 6

New Freedoms

On *Shabbos*, Meshka usually wandered away from camp to go exploring. It was her favorite pastime for her day of rest. All other days, she walked along beside people. On Shabbos, she liked to be alone.

Meshka was strolling along with a happy young bounce. She was listening to a symphony of forest sounds. In this quiet day, she heard the squawk of a hawk circling overhead, the chattering of squirrels chasing each other, the swooshing rush of the wind tickling the trees, and the gurgling giggles of the water. She saw a rabbit run past on some important errand. A red fox, with a long bushy tail, followed her from the shadows of the trees.

Meshka bounced along feeling part of the forest. The trees thinned into a lovely clearing with a big jumble of boulders off on one side. Meshka went to investigate, lest one high perch escape her. She circled around looking for the best place to begin climbing and to her surprise came upon Joya sitting on the ground staring at a large flat stone.

"Shalom Joya!" Meshka gave a friendly call.

The Gypsy girl was staring so intently, Meshka had to call twice before Joya looked up and smiled.

Ever since the day Joya's legs began to dance, her mouth began to speak. She still was not exactly chatty with Meshka, mind you, but it was nice to ask her a question and get an answer. Meshka noticed Joya and Rifka often talked as they pulled the cart together these days. It warmed her heart to see an echo of Joya's old self, the lively young maiden in the caravan.

Joya was still shy, but she was finding ways to be helpful. She looked much healthier now that she was feeding herself and keeping the food down.

Meshka wondered what was so fascinating about the stone. Spread out on the flat rock were a bunch of strange looking pictures.

"Vhat are you doing?" asked Meshka, not sure she wanted to hear the answer.

"I am asking the cards, 'Why Del did punished us? Why does Del punish innocent people? What should I do now? Should I stay or go look for a new caravan?'" she answered matter of factly.

Meshka was shocked! "Vhat do you mean, 'asking da cards?' Are you talking to dese pieces of vellum?"

Oy vay! Da poor girl, her mind is really kaput, Meshka worried.

"These are tarot cards. This is an oracle," Joya said a little shyly. "It is like reading your palm. I interpret what I see."

"Vhat do you see?" Oops! The words jumped out and Meshka could not suck them back, even though she wanted to.

"This card is the Queen of Cups. It must be you because you arrived just as I asked, 'Should I stay with you or go look for my own people?'

'Why did you come here at this very moment?'

Meshka shrugged her shoulders.

"Because our destinies are entwined. Everything in life is connected and has a meaning. Questions come arm in arm with their answers. Since Fate brought you here at this exact moment, you are my answer. The Queen is next to The Chariot so I should keep traveling with you."

Joya closed her eyes, took a deep breath, and felt a click of certainty. When her eyes opened the issue was settled.

"I am glad you vill stay. I would miss you."

ᘓᘓᘓ

Joya and Rifka were rolling up their blankets and repacking their bundles. Each wore most of their clothes, one on top of the other, to keep warm. These mornings were getting chillier as November was drawing to a close and the dark of winter would soon be upon them. The winds grew more bitter with every passing day. There was even a tinge of frost on the ground this morning, but it disappeared as soon as the sun rose. They had no idea how long it would take to cross the mountains; and dare not imagine the harshness of winter in this rough land-scape.

Rifka tied her bedroll with her daddy's old belt and tossed it into the cart. The belt was all she had left of her daddy. Joya tied her bedroll with one of Aunt Rita's pretty scarves, a bright sky blue one, embroidered with glistening gold threads.

Rifka's skirts were all dark and she looked a little chunky with so many layers on. The young Gypsy, on the other hand, was draped in a riot of blazing colors; a delightfully wild as-sortment of bright skirts and scarves!

Joya reached into her small pack, pulled out a beautiful tor-toise shell comb and asked Rifka to comb her hair. The fancy comb felt luxurious in Rifka's hand. She had never seen any-thing so finely made.

Joya found a comfortable log to sit on and Rifka began carefully working the knots out of Joya's wild mane, just like she used to do for Molly. She and Molly often combed each other's hair. They were best friends since birth.

Rifka closed her eyes, feeling the familiar tug of the comb working its way through the long hair. With each stroke she drifted further back in time, imagining she was combing Mol-ly's hair. Each stroke combed away the years and reached behind the tears.

So many pictures whirled through her mind; Molly and her as young women being courted, Molly and her, rebellious maidens on an adventure. Molly....

Rifka leaned over Joya to comb the front of her hair. Her eyes were brimming with tears. A stray tear rolled down her cheek and delicately landed on Joya's face.

Joya looked into Rifka's soft sad eyes, saw behind her usual gruff mask, and softly asked, "Please tell me, what you are thinking?"

Rifka was about to say something dismissing, but Joya's fresh open face made her want to tell the truth.

"I vas remembering my sweet milk-sister Molly. I always loved to comb her hair, da feel of it flowing through my fingers. It vas our private time 'n vee talked of private dings.

"Vee shared da most important moments in our lives. Vhen she vas in labor vid her boys, I wiped her brow 'n held her hand. Vhen her two boys crowned, one after da other, I caught da babies. A few months later, she caught mine.

"In da quiet after da birth, I combed her hair, so she would look pretty vhen she proudly introduced her husband to his two new sons.

"My dear Molly mopped my brow 'n squeezed my hand, vhen Surya 'n Moishela va born. She hugged me and hugged me and combed my hair."

Silently, Rifka prayed to God imploring Him to watch over Molly up in heaven. "Travel safe. Travel vell. May your journey be filled vid love 'n goodness."

Joya savored Rifka's mothering touch and marveled at her patient, gentle strength. The comb massaging her head was a sheer sensual delight, an ancient ritual of pleasure, passed down from women to women through the generations. When the comb ran freely down the full length of luxurious hair, smooth as silk, the comb stopped, and the spell was broken.

Joya jumped up from the log too fast and tripped over her feet. Her arms shot out to catch herself! They landed around Rifka's neck. To cover her clumsiness, Joya hugged Rifka and gracefully whispered, "I loved having my hair combed. Thank you for your kindness."

Rifka was startled by this sudden show of affection. Her first response was rude and dismissing, but the hug felt so good, she was touched by the sweet gesture. She simply said, "It vas my pleasure," and genuinely meant it.

For a moment, Rifka felt happy, genuinely happy. Then a sharp pang of guilt stabbed her. Was happiness a crime against all those sweet ones who died; a crime of forgetting?

This was not the first time Rifka brushed Joya's hair. Back when Joya was a wooden puppet, after a day climbing through brambles and lying in soft leaf mounds; all kinds of debris would get tangled in her hair. When Rifka combed Joya's hair, the girl never blinked an eye or seemed to notice. This was the first time she had voice enough to thank Rifka.

As the world was retreating into hibernation for winter, the young Gypsy was emerging from her cocoon. Gradually she was becoming aware of herself and the new world around her. Still she had the delicate fragility of a newborn baby.

ଓଓଓଓ

The deep pile of soft needles on the ground, under the big pine tree, made a very cushy bed. Meshka was waking up from good dreams.

She rolled up her bedroll and put it in the little cart, which held everything she had. She reached for the tiny carved box hanging on the branch above her sleeping place and kissed it tenderly. She slipped the yarn, holding the pretty carved box, around her neck and tucked her little treasure securely into her dress. Protectively she wrapped her woolen shawl around it.

Joya watched this daily ritual with new found curiosity and asked, "Please Meshka, answer a question for me. What do you keep in such a tiny little box?"

"Dis is a mezuzah," Meshka answered.

"In a Jewish home, it hangs by da front door. Inside are prayers praising God, asking Him to protect da house 'n all da people going in 'n out of da house.

"My son Yonkle made dis one vhen he vas only nine years old. He learned his letters in da Yeshiva 'n he wrote da whole prayer in perfect teeny tiny letters. Den Yonkela, vid his chubby liddle hands, carefully carved these teeny tiny birds all over it." Meshka was radiant with pride.

"It vas by our front door for twelve years. Every time I walked through da doorway, I reached up 'n kissed da mezuzah 'n said hello to God. Now it is full of all dose years of kisses." She gave a big sigh aching for home.

"Yonkle vas such a good boy. He loved God. God should have loved him as much.

"Vhen he vas maybe eight, he wrote da sweetest liddle poem."

"If I va a liddle bird,
I would fly into da sky.
I would fly up up,
Oh ever so high.
Past da treetops
'N da moon 'n stars.
I'd fly right through da heavenly gate
'N say, 'Good Day' to God."

Meshka looked so sad; Joya petted her shoulder and said, "I am sorry I never met your son. He sounds wonderful." Her curiosity pushed her to ask, "Why do you hang the *mezuzah* on the tree?"

"I tore it off da smoldering doorway of my liddle home vhen it vas burnt. It is da only ding I have left of da sweet liddle house my husband built for me vid his own two hands.

"I vant God should know dis blanket wrapped around me is my home now."

Meshka looked into Joya's eyes; an understanding passed between them.

"Da *mezuzah* has all my memories in it. Vhen I hang it on da tree, I say good night to my family 'n all my friends. I ask dem to visit me in my dreams. Dis box is a spirit nest vhere my family can rest. Dey are always vid me, I see dem in my dreams."

Joya's eyes were bulging out of her head! Her heart was racing so fast! Almost too frightened to speak, she cried out, "You want *mulós* (spirits of the dead) to visit you!?!"

Joya suddenly felt chilled all over, even though the sun was warm.

"Ya, sometimes," admitted Meshka. "Vhen I am lucky, da people I love come visit me in my dreams."

Meshka felt daring, so she shared another little secret…'N sometimes dey visit me vhen I am awake."

"Who visits you!?!" Joya's shrill voice quivered.

"Vell……last night my son Yonkle did," she answered with her eyes downcast. She felt awkward and uncomfortable, like she was falling down a big hole, by saying such a private thing.

With eyeballs bulging, Joya stammered, "Are you not afraid he will harm you?"

Meshka turned bright red in the face. This was all so private. No one was supposed to talk about such things. The girl looked so scared, Meshka confided a secret.

"Yonkle 'n I could talk without words. Vhen I vas pregnant vid him, I heard his voice in my head. He told me liddle dings about himself. 'N after he vas born, I could still hear vhat he vas dinking. It vas a joke in our family dat he could never tell a lie, because I always knew his truth."

These were things Meshka never told anyone before. She felt a little giddy and a lot nervous.

"Vhen Yonkle broke his leg, I felt his pain. Feeling his pain vas much worse dan my own! I can deal vid my pain, but feeling my child suffer vas more terrible!"

She shuddered at the memory. Then her belly sank as she saw Yonkle the last time, with more than a broken leg to mend.

"Vhen Yonkle became a scholar, I could not hear vhat he vas dinking anymore. I felt sad, but I let him go. Dat is vhat mothers do, dey let go.

She gave a shrug and a weak smile.

"I watched him grow up into a good man. I used to dink, vid such a sharp mind full of knowledge he vas going to make dis world better, but he never got da chance."

Since Meshka had gone this far, she might as well go all the way. Strangely, she did not feel naked telling such private things to this young maiden. A fortune teller understands something about the otherworld: maybe she could help it all make sense.

"After Yonkle died, it vas just like it vas vhen he vas in my belly - one body 'n two souls. I still hear his voice inside me. It brings me comfort. Vhen I dink of him, I feel a warm hug inside me.

"Now vee live in different worlds, but from time to time, vee say hello. My mama heart has big arms. I can love him wherever he is."

Ever since Joya was a little girl, she was terrified of *mulós* (spirits of the dead). In the caravan, around the evening campfire, storytellers told many a scary tale of the unsettled dead returning to wreck revenge on the living!

Fear and fascination mingled in Joya as she dared to ask, "How do you know the difference between a dream and a real visit?"

"Hmmm. Dat is a good question." Meshka squeezed her chin in thought.

"Vell, dreams fade away vhen you leave dem; but a visit stays like a real memory. Last night, just vhen I vas falling asleep, I could feel Yonkle's arms wrapped around me. It felt so sweet. His touch vas as real to me as if I touched you now.

"He said to me, 'Mama, I am so big now. I can roam through da heavens 'n through time. Da veil between you 'n me is so thin. I am traveling through other worlds, but I remember vhat a wonderful mama you va. I love you. I vill always love you. Dank you for being my sweet mama.' He vas looking down at me vid those big brown eyes of his. Oy, how he could melt my heart!"

Joya was too scared to hear Meshka. Suddenly she blurted out, "But, are you not afraid he will kill you?" Joya's voice sounded shrill even to her.

Shocked by such a strange idea, Meshka stared at the girl in disbelief. "My sweet Yonkle loves me. He comes only to comfort me."

Shrieking, Joya confessed, "I am terrified that the dead will come to torture me. I think they are angry that I am still alive. I feel guilty that I was the only one to live. There were more worthy people than me in our caravan." The words rang in her ears and burned in the hollow place that was her heart.

Lightning shot through Joya's head with exploding pain, sweat was pearling in her hands, and her stomach was rocking on green waves.

Meshka's heart went out to this poor child. "God must have a special purpose for you Shainela. Your family's dreams are in your keeping. You can make peace vid your family by keeping deir special dreams alive, breathe new life into dem."

Touching was not something Meshka did often, but this moment demanded more comfort than words could give, so Meshka caressed Joya's cheek as though she were her own sad child.

"Shainela, it is a blessing dat someone in your family survived. God chose you to carry on their legacy: da bloodline, da music, da dance, da mystical knowledge 'n all deir playfulness. It all lives on in you." Oh how Meshka wanted to cradle the young girl and calm her fears.

"Maybe," Joya squeaked with half a heart. She was not going to give up her guilt that easily.

Meshka threw a lot of new ideas at her. Each one bounced off Joya's head before it sank in. Could it be possible, the dead are not a threat to the living? Can they still love you? Comfort you? Accompany you and guide you? These were new ideas for a young girl! Joya was intrigued. She took a deep breath for courage and asked. "Please tell me more about your visits with the dead."

"Vhen da storm vas growling last night, I vas shaking scared. But den I thought about how I vas warm 'n dry even in da storm. I felt blessed. Soon I vas drifting off into a very sweet place 'n da sound of da storm faded away.

"I awoke a little while later 'n turned in my bedroll to get more comfortable. There vas Yonkle sitting right next to me.

"He looked deep into my eyes. Oh, his beautiful eyes. I could get lost in dose eyes. Da rest of his face vas kind of fuzzy.

"He said to me, 'Mama, it is all about closure. Bring closure moment by moment. Be honest vid yourself 'n vid other people. Be compassionate vid yourself 'n vid everyone. Remember, life demands surrender.' I still feel a liddle of him now."

Joya shook her head trying to toss out the old beliefs. She tried on these new ideas as she would a new dress, just to see what it looked like. Even if it did not quite fit, maybe with a few alterations, it might. Could her family forgive her for being alive? She wanted to believe the way Meshka does. But in her heart of hearts she knew. If any of her dead family returned, they would come for revenge.

ଔଔଔଔ

Chapter 7

Settling In

Meshka was walking along at a goodly clip. She noticed how strong and healthy she was feeling these last few days. All this marching onward was doing wonders to strengthen her legs. Funny, back in her village, *schlepping* a few blocks to visit Rifka used to make her legs swell up like ten pound melons. Now walking miles and miles every day was making them shrink down to normal fat little elephant feet.

One day, Meshka found herself beside a young woman who was thin like a willow and a bit *fagrent* (green) around the edges. Piled on her back, she carried all her meager belongings and at her breast was a screaming baby. She was desperately trying to comfort the poor hungry thing. The woman did not look well at all. Her eyes were red and her back was bent under the heavy weight of seen and unseen bundles.

Meshka smiled at the young woman, but she was too tired to smile back. Very softly Meshka began to sing an old lullaby her grandma taught her. Its slow repetitious rhythm could lull even a wolf to sleep. The baby listened between whimpers. Soon he was blessedly asleep. "Thank you," whispered the tired mama.

Meshka did not say, "Poor liddle woman you have such tired arms, soon dey vill be dragging on da ground like a mama gorilla." Instead, she smiled at the sleeping baby and said softly, "These are da hands of a grandma, but now dey are empty. Warm an old woman's heart. Let me hold your baby for a liddle bit while he sleeps?" The young woman hesitated. She looked into Meshka's innocent eyes and then gladly poured her warm sweet little bundle into the old woman's outstretched arms. She gave a big sigh and her aching arms tingled with new found freedom.

Meshka strolled along carrying the baby. At least half a dozen old women peeked at the sweet angel sleeping in her arms. They chatted about how cute he was. By the time little David woke up and looked around for his mama's nipple, he had already been adopted by several grandmas.

A small community of women formed around the baby. Contentedly he nestled into one warm pair of cushy breasts after another. The old women took turns walking in the moonlight with little Davidka while his mama, Mary gratefully slept. The old women began to cook and sew together, now that they had a daughter to take care of and a baby to kvell over. Soon Mary was strong and healthy again.

ৎ৵ৎ৵

Meshka and her chatty little goat fell into step beside Rachel and her quiet little pony. The goat butted the poor pony and got a swift kick in return. Peace was restored for a while. After some quiet time passed, Meshka asked, "Vhat gave you strength in dose ten years vhen you va waiting to be rescued?"

Rachel thought for a moment and then replied, "I had to be strong for my children. I also had da support of my family. Vee still lived together. There just va not so many of us anymore."

Rachel looked from side to side to make sure no one was listening and gave Meshka a conspirator look. She was about to reveal a secret.

"Once, a caravan of Gypsies passed through my city 'n I met a fortune-teller. She told me some personal dings dat no one else knew. She had a real gift.

"I vill always remember her impish smile vhen she turned over a card vid a picture of a man, a woman, 'n some children in a boat on a big ocean. She said to me, 'You see! You vill take a trip across da water 'n you vill be safe on da other side.

"'But take heart, for there vill be many challenges to face first.'"

Meshka tried to hide her shock. Rachel went to a fortuneteller! Maybe Rachel could help her make sense of the jumbled feelings she had about Joya.

"Rachel, vhat do you dink about fortunetellers?" She tried to make her voice sound calm, like the question was just making conversation, but her heart was racing.

Rachel adjusted her beautiful white babushka. For a brief moment you could see one long silver braid cascading down to her waist.

When the shawl was properly back in place, she replied, "I am glad God made lots of different kinds of people. Dis vay, everyone has different skills to use in His service. Fortunetelling, making music, dancing, 'n singing, these are da gifts of da Gypsy women. Dey are generous gifts in a hard world. Dey bring joy 'n comfort to da soul. Like da Jews, dey too get kicked like dogs 'n people spit on dem."

Meshka was holding her breath. Then suddenly as the air rushed out of her, Meshka's heart got bigger; maybe even big enough to accept more kinds of people.

Rachel's face took on a soft radiance and her eyes sparkled as she said, "Everything da Gypsy woman told me came true. Each time some liddle ding happened like she said, it strengthened my trust dat one day I would be on dat boat vid my husband 'n my children. Even as years passed, my faith stayed strong, because da woman said there would be many challenges first. Each challenge drew me one step closer to da day vhen vee would sail to freedom."

Rachel closed her eyes and saw again the big ship, its sterling image engraved on her eyes forever! As though it was only yesterday, she could feel the rolling waves and smell the refreshing breeze. Ahh, the glorious memory! It was the most wondrous moment in her whole life! Tears of joy and relief came with the memory of shepherding her children onto that glorious boat and sailing away to a good new life.

"Vhat a blessing," Meshka said with a warm sigh. She was happy for her friend. They walked in silence for a while feeling safe beside each other.

Meshka squared her shoulders. In a low voice she confided to her friend, "Joya reads tarot cards. She read my cards last night."

"Vhat did she say?" Rachel was interested and curious.

Meshka wanted to tell someone, but she had to get rid of the lump in her throat first. With some coaxing, the words dared to expose themselves.

"Joya turned over three picture cards 'n dey va supposed to show my future. Da first card vas a *Priestess* sitting in front of a temple. Da second vas a rabbi vid a fancy name – Hierophant. Vhen she turned over da third card, a fourth one fell down vid it, so Joya said, 'Vhat falls on da floor, walks in da door' 'n she put it vid da rest. One card showed a man carving eight coins 'n da other vas a picture of three women dancing around vid cups in deir hands."

Meshka imitated the entranced voice Joya used when she read cards, "'Von day you vill stand before a holy initiation. *Da Goddess* vill guide your actions 'n your words. Many women vill come to help you do da work of *da Goddess*.'

"It made sense to me vhen she said it, but now it sounds a liddle *meshugeneh* (crazy). Can you imagine me talking for a *Goddess*? I am just a liddle old woman 'n even talking to plain old people scares me. Why should da *Goddess* vant me? She should ask God about me. He vill tell *Her* I am a troublemaker."

Rachel jumped back like she was hit in the face! Her eyes, always sweet and soft, now held two scorching torches! Deeply offended, angry words flew from her pious lips "There is no such ding as a *Goddess*! There is only the one God!"

Shocked at her own unnecessary show of anger, and sorry that she screamed, Rachel tried to say something nice. "Maybe da Gypsy girl vas talking about da *Shekhina* – da *Shabbos Bride*. She is not exactly a *Goddess*, but *She* is da woman part of God."

Meshka dropped her jaw and mumbled, "da *Shekhina* – da *Shabbos Bride* – there is a woman part of God!?!"

"You never heard of da *Shekhina*?" Rachel sounded shocked and immediately turned red in the face.

"No. In my village women va forbidden to study. It vas a sin. Dey said a woman who can read is a demon! Da men go off to da temple 'n study together. But women are forbidden to go dere, except maybe to bring dem lunch."

Rachel could not read either, but she knew stories, prayers, history and traditions. "In da Ghetto, our lives revolved around our Rebbe 'n his teachings," she began her story. "Every Shabbos night after dinner, our Rebbe told us stories." Rachel loved telling stories. She was delighted to have an audience.

"Da Rebbe said dat in ancient times, God told King David 'n King Solomon to build a Great Temple in Jerusalem. In da temple vas a sacred chamber – da Holy of Holies – vhere even da rabbis va forbidden to go. In dat sacred room, God laid vid da *Shekhina* every Shabbos, so love vas da law of da land."

Meshka was shocked! God had sex! Rachel could not mean dat! Dat is too messy 'n human for Almighty God!

Meshka loved to hear stories, but a *Shekhina*? It sounded like made up make-believe.

"On Shabbos, vhen vee light da candles, vee invite da *Shekhina* to watch over our lives. God created da world in six days 'n on da seventh day He rested. *Nu?* (well) Who do you dink watched over da world, while God dozed on His big cushion in da sky? Da *Shekhina*, of course."

Meshka lit candles every Friday night because her mother lit candles, and her mother's mother lit them, going back to the beginning of time. It never dawned on Meshka that there could be more to Shabbos than praising God.

Meshka's head was reeling as she tried to take in Rachel's shocking words.

"Dis is why on Shabbos vee rest, make love, pray, 'n visit vid friends. Vee are forbidden to do any work. All week long, vee labor to please God, but vhen He rests, so do vee.

"Da *Shekhina* commands us to do only dings dat make pleasure 'n peace. It is da *Shekhina* dat gives Shabbos its sweet magical spice."

Shabbos always felt quietly outside of time, a day when no one asked anything of her. Meshka relaxed and felt spacious peace. Such tranquility was always a treat after a busy week.

"Once da world vas in balance. God 'n da *Shekhina* ruled together. Now *Her* name is erased from da Torah (Bible) 'n only da mystical Kabbalists speak of *Her*."

How could God have a woman part? He was so men-only in everything He said and did! A woman part of God, this was an intriguing new idea!

"Meshka, if you vant to speak for da *Shekhina*, it vill be a blessing upon us all," Rachel said with a pious smile.

Then her face grew stern and she warned, "But beware of *shikza* (non-Jewish) *Goddesses*, 'n their graven images. Dey make God very angry!" Meshka suddenly felt very small and very scared.

ରେଔରେ

Meshka's little head stretched to think impossible thoughts. She tried to imagine the *Shekhina*! It was a strain on her brain to see God, who always played favorites with men, as actually part woman! She stopped in her tracks when it hit her that God trusts a woman to run the whole world one day every week! That was amazing! Completely amazing!

Meshka shook her head and thought, if my Meyer had a store, even a liddle store, I am sure he would not trust me to run it, even for one day a week. He would vant to keep his hand on it all da time.

God trusts the *Shekhina*!

Well one thought led to another and Meshka's mind wandered into a very open place. Thinking the impossible, she wondered what it would be like to speak for a *Goddess*, to hear a wiser voice inside her, and feel power in her words.

Immediately she got afraid and started worrying! Vhat if I do not know da difference between my own made up ideas, 'n *Da Goddess'* voice speaking inside my head? Ripples of fear iced through her body!

You know how it is. Worms eat you up when you are dead and worries eat you up alive. Oy, she got so worked up over Rachel's make-believe story, Meshka was trembling.

Then she began to laugh. She laughed at such foolish ideas. She laughed at the sheer impossibility of her ever talking for a *Goddess*! She laughed and laughed and thought, how do such meshugeneh ideas get into my head?

"*Oy, yoi yoi*," she lamented, holding her head to keep it from falling off.

But I know *Goddesses* are real! She argued with herself. A real *Goddess* looked me in da eye. *She* asked me, me liddle Meshka, to join *Her* Seeders of Peace. I hear words on da wind 'n whispers in my dreams, 'n I know dey come from da *Goddess*.

CRCRCR

After dinner was cleaned away, Joya pulled out her tarot cards and was studying them by the fire. Meshka sat down beside her and said with a teasing laugh, "So I see, you are 'talking to da vellum again.'"

"Tarot cards are an oracle. The way they work is, I open to my own wisdom and I invite Del to speak through me. After I pray for guidance, I meditate on the symbols I see on the cards and wait for an answer to arise inside me.

"I begin to see patterns. The pictures suddenly fit together perfectly. After a moment the answer seems obvious. I suddenly see the order in the chaos and the purpose in the mire."

Meshka looked skeptical.

"It is all about timing. Each moment is like a little whirlpool drawing similar things together. I look for the common thread." Joya drew in her breath and brought her gaze back to the cards.

Little Meshka, who stood only as high as a man's chest and not such a big man at that, felt as tall as the sky when she bravely asked, "Vhat is an oracle?"

"Among the Jews are there not prophets who translate God's will?" Joya asked in return.

"Tsk! Of course! Da prophets interpret dreams 'n dey tell da people vhat God vants," Meshka answered nervously.

"These cards are like those dreams. They may look like simple pictures, but they are really pockets where God puts His truths. When we look in the pockets, we see His secrets inside."

"Ah! It is like reading da palm, right?" Meshka was catching on. She looked down at her own palm, but all she saw were a lot of old wrinkles. She was surprised and delighted that Joya was talking to her at last.

"Yes, yes! The hand is also an oracle. The patterns and lines in the hands are always changing, but the overall patterns are always the same. Just like the Divine Plan, life is always changing and yet always the same.

Rifka was listening as she cleaned up after dinner. She admired how Joya spoke so easily about mystical things.

"God writes us messages all the time and He leaves them everywhere. Oracles are filters to help us read the messages. A woman has to be very wise to understand what He has written."

Meshka's jaw dropped down to her ample breasts. "Vhat are you saying? You dink all da answers to all da questions I ask God, are laying around us like liddle pebbles on da ground?" Meshka snickered.

"Yes," replied the Gypsy.

"Den vhat is there to stop me from picking up da pebbles 'n looking in da pockets?" Meshka asked, sticking her tongue between her teeth. It was an impish expression. She was sure she had Joya there.

"Nothing, only your own fear and beliefs," said Joya with level eyes like she was just saying, "pass the pudding," instead of something utterly earthshaking.

"Oy vay! Vhat are you saying? Dat anyone can read da future, even me!?!" Meshka was pacing in a circle.

"Why not?" Joya softly asked. The brilliant sun was sparkling off the little mirrors on her scarf. Maybe the sun was
laughing at Meshka too.

"Oy vay! God would never let me do dat!" Meshka recoiled.

"So your God condemns dream interpreters and prophets?" Joya challenged.

"No, wise men are very respected by Jews. But Joya I am
only a woman! Wisdom 'n knowledge belong to da men."

"That is only a belief. It is not true among my people,"
Joya shook her head and smiled kindly. "Women have a special
kind of knowledge inside them that knows more than all the
books. No book can teach you about life better than watching
the cycles of time while you dance with your Fate."

Joya tucked a stray hair under her little scarf and without
thinking, caressed the little dangling beads. This scarf was her
grandmother's. It was very special to her. Her mother died long
ago, but her grandmother more than filled her childhood with
love and magic. Joya mused about how lucky she was that
Meshka and Rifka had saved some of her most special things
and marveled at how wisely they had chosen.

ଓଃଓଃଓଃ

Most nights by the light of the evening fire, Joya looked at the
strange pictures she carefully placed on one of Aunt Rita's lovely scarves. Meshka often sat quietly and watched. Even though
Meshka's heart was thumping wildly with excitement and fear,
her curiosity was stronger than both. She asked Joya questions
and they talked about oracles. It left Meshka in a wonderful
wild mood, open to think about impossible things.

With a meaningful glance, Joya added, "It is no different
than arguing with God. I ask for guidance and you ask for action, but are we not both talking to the same Source?"

This sounded like blasphemy. On the edge of sight, Meshka saw God make another black notation in His Big Book.

Joya felt Meshka begin to fidget, so she quickly changed the subject, "Meshka you are a *Gadji* (foreigner) and yet you feel like a very special friend.

"When we first met, I looked into your palm and saw a golden light radiating from your hand. Then I looked up and saw the same golden light on your tongue."

Joya spoke softly as though she were thinking out loud.

"You were the first Jewish woman I ever met. I was curious about you. In some special way, it seemed like we were related. When I read your palm, I felt inspired. All the symbols around you seemed to call out their own answers. I did not have to think. I just opened myself to hear them.

"I should stay wherever you are.   After all, when the world ended, if you had not taken me in your arms and pulled me to my feet, I would never have stood up on my own. I wanted to die. Without you, I would have. Bless you for saving my life."

They stood up and looked at each other for a moment. Then embraced like mother and daughter.

In her mind, Meshka saw God take out His Big Book to write down another sin. She suspected there was a taboo against hugging a *shikza* (a non-Jewish girl).

ଔଔଔ

A light snow began to fall from a dreary sky. Rifka drew her homespun woolen shawl more tightly about her shoulders. Soon she felt warmer. They were pulling the cart over a rocky patch of road along a hillside, more a path than a road. Joya was pulling beside her, dressed in all her clothes; they kept her warm. Her thick black hair flowing down her back was speckled with snowflakes. At least her head was covered by a pretty little kerchief with tiny golden bells dangling along the edge.

Meshka called the little goat, Shainela so that became her name. Meshka and Shainela were walking beside the cart listening to the girls telling stories.

"Pretty scarf," *Rifka* said.

"Thank you. It belonged to my grandmother. She raised me."

"Vhat vas your grandmother like?"

Joya was a little startled by the question. Normally the Roma do not talk about the dead, but Meshka said it was safe and anyway she thought, "What do I have to lose?"

With a big breath for courage she said, "My mother's mother was a gifted *Drabardi* (fortune teller), a wise woman. She was a truly amazing! She read the future like it was an open book. She saw seeds of a truth, while they were still being sown. When someone came to her with a heavy heart, she would sit very still and breathe deeply. A light warm energy would come over her, like Del was kissing her cheek and a deeper, wiser voice spoke through her."

Meshka liked the idea of a deeper wiser voice. She could use one of those.

"My grandmother often said, 'I see in the seeds, symbols, and sensations of this day, the answer you seek is...,'. She revealed personal things she saw in their past to get their attention. Then she answered their question; right on the nose. She had no book learning, nor did she need it. She just looked in God's pockets and saw what He had written."

Joya wondered if her grandmother could hear her story being told and did it please her, or disturb her *muló*? (spirit of the dead)

Rifka was fascinated by this wild Gypsy girl, what a change from the silent puppet! Joya overcame her fear of this hot tempered Jewish woman. After pulling the cart side by side with her, Joya saw Rifka's soft side. A strong trust was building between them.

"Do you come from a lineage of Drabardi's?"

"Yes, most women in my caravan were oracles; but they were not all as wise as my Aunt Rita. Like her mama, she too was a great *Drabardi* (fortune teller). She read tarot cards, interpreted dreams, and saw the future in a crystal ball. Those were her oracles.

"All my pretty colorful scarves and skirts come from my Aunt Rita. She was a wild one." Joya shook her head and laughed.

"Do you look like her?" Rifka asked, "Did she have long black hair like you?"

"No. My Aunt Rita burst into this world with flaming red hair, a wild fiery nature, and a sharply biting tongue. No one else in the caravan had such wild desires or such a heart-softening pout. Tempestuous tides stirred the people around her. She told me amazing tales and had the scars to back them up."

"Scars?" Meshka piped in. Joya looked up suddenly aware that Meshka was there, thought for a moment and resumed, "My Aunt Rita was blessed with great wisdom and a thorough knowledge of men. She walked proudly with her head up and her eyes wide open when she wrestled with Fate's dragons. Sometimes she won, sometimes she lost, but she always lived life to the fullest. I can tell you, she tempted more than a few princes and pirates in her day."

Oy vay! Tempting princes 'n pirates? Meshka thought in amazement!

I never tempted nobody, not even my late husband Meyer, God bless his soul. I wonder how she did dat? I am pretty old on da outside, but inside I feel like a girl, free for da first time. Sweet old Meshka felt a little flustered.

"My Aunt Rita was as elegant as a *Goddess*. All she needed was a touch of makeup and that seductive look of hers. She was so glamorous, no one ever guessed her age. She was radiantly beautiful even when she was the oldest grandmother in our caravan."

Joya spoke with a twinkle in her eyes. She was very proud of her of favorite aunt. "My Aunt Rita told me many stories. We used to sit side by side on her big swing. While she rocked us back and forth, she spun the most exciting tales. She filled my head with dreams of adventure and taught me to meet life with courage. When I was older, I always went to Aunt Rita when love or luck was scarce."

As a child, Joya adored Aunt Rita and wanted to grow up be just like her. Now, no matter what Joya does, Aunt Rita will never know, never be proud of her too.

Her eyes were moist with remembering, so the fears seeped in. They clutched at her heart but no *mulós* came to kill her that night. In the morning, Joya was both relieved and disappointed.

ལཚལཚལཚ

Reading tarot cards by the evening fire, became part of Joya's nightly ritual before she went to sleep, Most of the time Meshka sat nearby watching her.

Joya often thought out loud as she interpreted the cards, and Meshka listened. She talked about the symbols in the card and how they went together to form patterns that made sense of odd happenings.

Meshka listened and watched as her own mind jumped around looking for an idea. Then something in the picture or between different pictures caught her eye. One thing led to another following a thread, until the card made sense.

Meshka had a sharp mind and learned quickly. If the critical voice in her head did not always magnify her mistakes and bang her on the head with its criticism, she might have found out that she was smart a lot sooner.

So one day Joya started talking about a picture, a tarot card and Meshka jumped right in and added some very good insights. Joya looked at her with stunned eyes. That look made Rifka put down the dishes and sit down beside them.

Joya said, "You read that card very well. If you want, I could teach you the principles of an oracle and how to interpret tarot cards. You are already learning. We are already doing it. I will give what I say a little more structure."

Shocked! Meshka's heart was racing! She protested, "You read da tarot cards! You are da Gypsy! I already worry about my words. Vhat if I accidently say something bad 'n it comes true?"

"We *Romani* (Gypsies) are only messengers for Del. That is our name for the Creator. We carry His words, we do not write them," Joya tried to reassure her friend.

"A woman can be wise. Meshka, you are wise. I see it in all the things you say and do."

"Vhat are you trying to do Joya; turn da world upside down? Everyone knows dat men study 'n women clean!"

Joya raised a questioning eyebrow.

"Vell I know some clever smart women, but dey had no book learning.

Meshka's mind was stretching to see reading oracles as natural woman's knowledge. That felt good. She liked the idea of woman's knowledge, something special.

"I am sorry. Please tell me vhat you see 'n I vill listen. I vant to know vhat God tells you, but maybe it scares me just a liddle," Meshka sincerely apologized.

ରେଓଃରେ

Meshka was so excited, and so scared, she hardly slept that night. The next morning she braced herself to ask God, if He liked fortunetellers. Why should she keep pulling her hair out over a sin, if maybe, believing a fortuneteller is not a sin? A chilly shudder went through her. She remembered the last time she believed a fortuneteller, the world ended. And yet, how could comforting people when they are suffering be a bad thing?

The next morning was ablaze with a magnificent golden amber sunrise. Meshka sat down beside a small stream, breathed in the fresh crispness of almost winter, admired the pretty frost designs along the banks, and let out a deep breath.

"God, Most Holy Von," Meshka called out. "Today you made a perfect day. Nature has so many kinds of beauty; you did good vhen You made dis world. Did You do it all by Yourself or did You have a partner who helped You sometimes? 'N also, by da vay, vhat do You dink about fortunetellers?"

Meshka brushed some pebbles off a big rock and was just settling herself down on it, when God's voice suddenly thundered, "Meshka! Oh Meshka! Thou shalt not whore after false Gods!"

That closed her mouth and opened her eyes. "Most Holy God, I do not mean to disrespect you. I am not whoring after false Gods. You know You did not make me an ostrich. I cannot hide my head in da sand. Voices are always talking in my head 'n dey do not always sound like You. I have deep feelings dat bubble up like gas 'n dey leave me vid a strong sense of knowing. I dink it is a natural ding for a woman."

In a thundering voice God commanded, "Woman! Follow the law, choose good from evil, and pray when you need guidance."

This answer did nothing to soothe her. She was determined to speak her whole truth and check out the things Joya said, so Meshka braced herself, "Most Wise Von, why do You write da truth of dings on every blade of grass 'n den tell us not to look? Is dis another von of those liddle temptations You like to throw at people?"

Meshka was suddenly sweating though the air was cold. She knew what she was saying was valid, but God dismissed her as frivolous and roared, "Follow the law, choose good from evil, and pray when you need guidance."

Meshka got so hot under her collar; she was talking before her mind could remind her to shut up!

"Holy God, Lord of my Mothers, why do You give us only two choices? Vhat about all da rest? Who gets to pick from dem? Life does not come in such neat liddle boxes. Why can vee not try more dings? Dere is lots of room between dings dat are righteous 'n dings dat are wicked. You know a lot of living falls between dose cracks. 'N vhat about all dose liddle white lies dat make a sandwich between virtue 'n sin?"

She was in the grip of a passion riding it to the end, with no thought of the consequences of speaking so directly to God!

"There is only right and wrong." God insisted. "The choice is very simple. Either you stay with your own kind and obey My laws to the letter, or you are committing a sin. My law shelters you and gives your world order. Without the law, there is only chaos."

Meshka just could not let Him have the last word. She had to go one step further.

"Most Holy Von, vhere in all dis, is listening to my own conscience? 'N vhat about da natural wisdom dat lives inside a woman's body?"

Meshka bounced back and forth between certainty and fear with a slippery foot in each.

The booming voice of God rang razor sharp and threatening.

"Beware of the body! It is full of temptation. False gods live within the flesh. People cannot govern themselves. That is dangerous. There are evil people in the world who have no conscience," God warned her.

What could she do? Every word He said was half true and yet not. She told herself, "Stop," and then kept going.

No one wins in an argument with God but that did not seem to matter at this moment. Poking out her chin a little defiantly, Meshka asked, "Vhat is dis evil business? I thought you created everything," she really wanted to know, but it did sound a little sarcastic.

"The Devil and his agents rule destructive forces," The Almighty reminded her.

If God was going to smite her dead, He would have done it several minutes ago. Maybe He enjoyed a little bantering now and then, so Meshka kept on going.

"So da Devil did it 'n you are innocent? But I am a liddle confused. I thought all da priests work for You. Are You telling me dat da Devil made da priest send Your people to kill my sweet liddle grandchildren? It does not make sense to me.

"I heard Your name on their lips vhen dey put da torch to my liddle house vhere my grandbabies va playing," She was getting very frustrated with this naughty Deity, and the state of the world made her feel very sad.

"Woman, you are talking blasphemy!" boomed God's angry voice.

"Oy God, she sighed to gather more patience. "How can You call da truth I heard vid my own ears, blasphemy?"

Meshka remembered a very stubborn man in the village who never gave in and never admitted when he was wrong. One day, he blamed a group of children for wrecking his garden, when it was obviously a stray deer. Rifka defended the children. Meshka, standing nearby heard the stubborn man say, "Woman do not bother me vid da da truth. I know vhat I vant to believe." Not that God was like that man, but something made her think of him.

"Some people are evil and they do evil things!" God insisted.

He was not listening to her, so she tried harder.

"Most Holy Von, are You saying dat dose people in da neighboring village dat vent to Church every Sunday 'n prayed to You, dat dey va evil? No, I do not dink so. Maybe if You did not make dem suffer so much, maybe den dey would not have done such a *meshugeneh* (crazy) ding. Without suffering, maybe evil would not even exist."

There she said it! Now He could throw lightning bolts at her if He wanted to. It would not change the truth.

"Some people are evil and they commit sins." God affirmed.

No lightning, no hail, not even a little fire came raining down from heaven! That was encouraging, so she pressed her point further.

"But Most Holy Von, some of Your laws, let me tell You, dey are sooo black 'n white. Sometimes dey do not match da dings dat really happen in people's lives.

"Vhen people have to tangle themselves into a pretzel to fit in vid da laws, dat makes dem meshugener. Den dey rebel 'n do sins. Maybe You could make our lives a liddle easier? Den people could maybe show You how good dey really can be." Meshka felt proud of herself for saying something so important.

"You created dis whole wide world 'n all da people in it, so why can You not make life a liddle easier? Try it 'n You vill see how people vill shine." Now maybe God will open His eyes and see the truth.

"Woman! Thou shalt obey My Commandments!" The Voice of God commanded!

CRCRCR

One cold evening in early December, the day was folding in on itself. The sky was streaked with angry clouds and strong winds pelted them with leaves and branches as they swiftly flew by. It promised to be a long night.

Rachel pulled her heaviest shawl more tightly about her shivering shoulders and said to Meshka, "I vas thinking. If you vant to put your bed next to mine tonight, vee could tie our blankets together 'n make a real tent."

"Vhat a wonderful idea!" Meshka was as excited as a young girl about to sleep over at a new friend's house.

The two old women stood side by side under a wide evergreen tree, admiring their handiwork. Rachel's blanket was thick and soft, stuffed with down. It was light, lovely and promised to be warm. Meshka's blanket was a crude weave, but the wool was thick and rich.

They draped a crude sheet liberally covered with animal fat over their precious blankets. It would keep the wetness out and their body heat in. Hand in hand, they worked together with no need for words.

A great crown of thick pine needles protected their little sanctuary and sheltering bushes cut the wind all around it.

With all the wind, they could not chance a fire. Rachel looked up at the sky. Every tree and rock took on a gaudy golden glow; the color was too rich to be real! Then it faded and the day grew eerie and dark, even though the hour was still early. A powerful storm was rolling in!

As natural as taking a breath, Rachel prayed, "*Baruch Ha-Shem*, (Blessed be da name of da Lord) dank you for giving me such a good friend.

"Most Holy Von, please watch over da two of us vhen da winds go howling around like angry wolves. Please make da lightning to strike an old dead tree somewhere far far away. Please be very gentle on our simple liddle shelter. Please *Ha Shem*, be gentle vid us. Please, no snow!"

Rachel's tone made Meshka smile and shake her head. She spoke to God with a lover's voice.

Inside the little tent, Rachel sat wrapped in her Bubba's lovely white linen shawl. It was embroidered with sparkling silver threads, sewn with a most meticulous hand. It was as regal as a king's *talus* (prayer shawl). Huddled next her, was Meshka wrapped in dark brown wool, the simple homespun weave of a peasant. There was no rank between them. They were so different and so the same. Each woman was grateful to have the other one.

As the angry storm was brewing, Meshka nervously fingered the *mezuzah* around her neck. She may have thought, God, please do not smite us in da night, but quickly erased it.

Instead Meshka said, "Rachel, God vill keep us safe. He likes you. Remember you are da cat vid nine lives."

Nervously Meshka continued to finger the little carved box. She could not trust the *mezuzah* to a tree, not with the wind grabbing everything! She could not part with it, so it spent the night lying on her heart. She hoped all the love inside would protect her from the growling temper of the storm.

The two old women created a wonderfully cozy nest. They put their bedrolls together in the center and lied down side by side. They gazed off into the darkness and could not see the other's eyes. That was comforting. Being hidden in the darkness, and only hearing a voice in the night, made it easier for them to say important and difficult things.

The winds howled and so did the two old women. They cried, they raged, and they laughed like little children.

Sometimes they fell quiet for long moments. After such a moment Meshka asked, "Rachel, you are a wise woman, vid children 'n grandchildren, vhat makes such a woman go so far away from home?"

"Dat is a good question. There is no easy answer, but I vill tell you. After Avram died," Rachel began in her story voice, "I lived in a crowded neighborhood near da boat docks for a while. Everyone there vas from da old country. Da day-to-day life vas not so different from da ghetto, except vee va free to go vhere 'n vhen vee vanted. I liked it there.

Rachel wistfully walked through the market in her mind and said, "Oy Meshka did dey have a bazaar! It vas so wonderful, so colorful it could put da rainbow to shame. Ahh! Da Food!?!" She kissed her fingers. "Everything dey made vas just like in da old country. Tsk! Such treasures – gorgeous fabrics – made for a queen – jewels - silver, gold 'n diamonds. You never saw such riches from all over da world."

After taking Meshka on a stroll through the bazaar in her mind, Rachel continued where she left off in her story.

"My children grew up. Dey got married 'n va busy vid their own liddle ones. My grandchildren, God bless dem, dey va strangers to me. Dey did not speak Yiddish or Polish, so it vas hard to talk vid dem. Dey vanted to be like everyone else in their new country."

Rachel sighed. Her face crumbled and her shoulders sank. "My grandchildren va ashamed of da vay I talked 'n da vay I dressed. Nobody needed me anymore, so I did not know vhat to do vid myself. At first, I vas all aggravated. I thought my life vas over 'n I had no purpose anymore; but den some new ideas jumped into my head 'n I got all excited.

With her chin lifted up in pride, Rachel said, "I vent to da shul to ask God, vhat I should do now? But vhen I opened my mouth to pray, I realized I already knew da answer. I knew vhat I vanted to do.

"Never in all my life did I ask myself vhat do I vant. I vanted dings as dis one's a wife 'n dat one's mother, but never did I, as Rachel, ask vhat do I vant? I never thought to ask such a question.

"But as soon as I asked the question, I knew I wanted to see more of da world. My youth vas given to duty, so now it vas my turn to have an adventure."

At first, Rachel was worried. What would God do to her, if she left her family and went away all by herself? Was her life really over? Was she supposed to fade into the background and watch her family live? She still had a good many years left; but as an old woman, nothing she did mattered anymore. She had nothing to lose.

Her heart was already full from a lifetime of happiness and love. The rest of her time was a free ride; so she got all excited about following a mystery. She held the impossible in her mind; to get on another boat and go to another faraway place.

"I yearned for all da adventures I missed living in da Ghetto, but so many doubts nagged at me.

"You know a decision is right vhen HaShem starts leaving liddle hints around to let you know He likes da idea. I saw hints.

"First, I turned a corner in da new land 'n walked right past an old man from my ghetto. He vas talking to me, 'n out of da blue, he said dat his brother vas vid some refugees who va looking for a land vhere dey could make a better life. It sounded like something I vas always meant to do."

Color rose to her cheeks, remembering how scared and excited she felt, and how sure she was that the old man was a messenger from God.

Rachel sighed and went on with her story, "Da next day, vhen I vas cleaning da stove, I grabbed an old rag from a bag of rags and put it under da oven door, you know, to catch da soap if it dripped. 'N den I looked at da rag! It vas once a dress, but just not any dress. It vas da dress I wore vhen I got on da boat.

"I looked up to Ha Shem 'n said, 'Most Holy Von, dat is number two. If you vant me to go on dis journey, make me one more sign.'

Rachel still remembered how excited she was on that day; and how sure she was that there was going to be another sign.

"'N would you believe, within two hours my Helen came to visit. She vas telling me about her sweet Hanna, such a talented liddle girl. She said Hanna has a new piano teacher. He escaped from Poland 'n vas rescued by some good people who va walking around da world trying to find a land of true peace. Dat vas it, da third sign, so I made ready to go."

She knew for sure, God was guiding her. "Ha Shem told me to go, so here I am."

Rachel and Meshka lay side by side, their heads were touching, but they were far far away in very different worlds. For a while they lay quietly, listening to the angry winds scream at each other. The tent was staked well and so far, thank God, the stakes were holding. The storm thundered and blustered outside, but inside the little shelter they were cozy and comfortable. The wet stuff stayed outside and the warmth of friendship brightened the inside.

ಞಞಞ

Chapter 8

Longing for the Past

A deep well of loneliness swallowed Joya up. She was standing all alone beneath an ominous sky looking around at the darkness closing in on her, she missed Uncle Alberto.

Oh, how she wished she could crawl into Uncle Alberto's lap, just like she used to do, when she was a little girl and Del was shaking the world with His thunder.

Wise Uncle Alberto, wild Aunt Rita and their mystical mama, raised Joya. Her own mama died bringing her into this world.

Uncle Alberto was the bravest, wisest, most powerful man in the caravan and he was her protector. How could a man with such greatness die, when stupid little me, I am still alive!?! How could the world go on without Uncle Alberto!?! Joya lamented.

Standing under the thick branches of a huge old evergreen tree, Joya pulled her uncle's heavy robe protectively around her. She closed her eyes, leaned back against the tree's strong trunk and breathed in the smoky sweetness of Uncle Alberto. The robe carried his heavy scent. Wine, cheroot, exotic incense, and manly sweat all mingled into an intoxicating perfume that quieted her heart and made her feel safe.

Joya felt grateful to Meshka for rescuing his robe. It was now her greatest treasure. When the old woman had dragged Uncle Alberto into his grave, she thought such a stunning garment should not lay buried forever. She apologized to his noble spirit.

She found him lying protectively over the body of a beautiful red haired woman with the lips of an angel pouting. Meshka thought these two strangers were the most beautiful couple she had ever seen. Even in death, dignity and nobility crowned them. She wept to see such beauty senselessly destroyed.

Joya petted the robe's soft deep purple velvet, appreciating its delicious smoothness. The luxurious collar running down the front of the robe were soft white clouds of ermine. The long full robe was embroidered with the stars and symbols of heaven.

Tall, broad shouldered, powerful Uncle Alberto had a thick long gray beard and looked like a god among the heavens in his robe of the cosmos!

The robe was much too long for her, so she kept it hiked up with a rope. Joya stood under the wide pine tree wrapped in his robe, feeling his magic keeping her safe.

Crash! A huge burst of thunder raged above Joya's head! A bolt of lightning shot down from the sky and stabbed a tree not far from her! Blue sparks and eerie light curled her toes.

Crash after crash! A sharp bolt. The swoosh of flames sizzling in the icy rain! The thunder sounded like her uncles, Petrov and Nicholas, at their endless arguments. When she was very little, she was afraid of them and their angry voices. Now she felt an icy shiver run through her.

Cold and damp, she stood alone under the tree. Rifka and the others were in their tents not far away. But she was alone with the night; alone with the *mulós* (ghosts) still traveling in the caravan through a dark, cold, barren world. The *mulós* were closing in on her! She crouched in the shadows of the tree's big roots, afraid she was not hidden enough.

She dared not close her eyes. What if ghosts followed her inside and imprison her in her mind. Inside, outside, everywhere danger lurked! The living hurt her so bad, could the dead do worse?

Joya huddled under the tree. She had no place to go to be warm and safe. She was sooo frightened.

Suddenly something snapped inside her! Her fear vanished. In dead silence, she felt the stillness of a crouching tiger before he pounces.

Joya slipped out from under the embracing branches of the tree. Guilt gripped her by the heart. The ghosts accused her of being alive, of taking the breath that should be theirs. The ghosts raged at her more fiercely than her uncles Petrov and Nicholas ever did!

The guilt drove her out from under the protection of the tree, into the freezing rain. Icy splinters stabbed her head. A cynical smile twisted her lips as she thought; if I get wet enough and cold enough, Del will have to let me die. Then I can go home and be with everyone I love.

Once this *meshugeneh* (crazy) idea got stuck in Joya's head, she was off on a mission. She felt so twisted with pain and loss, she did not know up from down. If her head were on a bird, it would start flying backwards!

Joya looked this way and that. The night was dark! Her only lantern was the quick bolts of lightning raging in abundance! Flashes seen through wavy lines of sleeting ice; it all looked unreal! Like walking in a dream, Joya put her head down and pushed her way to the cart under a thick evergreen tree nearby.

She brushed aside the protective pine branches lying on top of the cart and dragged out her bundles. Huddled over the cart, Joya rummaged around in her clothes. She chose her best and her fanciest treasures. She wanted to be pretty, to meet her family in the forever.

The skirt Joya chose was as blue as the sea at sunset. When she danced, it flared gloriously wide, twirled high, and snapped wildly. Joya put on her one special clean blouse. It was frilly, fancy, and Aunt Gertie made it for her. Aunt Gertie carefully embroidered each stitch of the bright red flowers around the edges while Joya watched her. It was Aunt Gertie's gift to Joya when she became a woman.

Meshka rescued the blouse from an overturned wagon that was hardly burned. She was stunned when she found it; it was so beautiful.

The Gypsy girl was saving it for a special day, but now nothing in life was ever going to be special again, so today she wore it. She put on her prettiest clothes to embark on her final journey.

Wild passions, swirling with the winds in the night, called to her. The sparkling gold beads, dangling off the edges of Aunt Rita's bright yellow scarf, jingled in the icy rain. She wandered off through the blustery darkness singing the songs of her ancestors.

Silhouetted in the darkness, between streaks of lightning, she saw the ghosts of her mother, father, sisters, brothers, aunts and cousins; their flying feet dancing around the campfire. Behind them, she saw her playful uncles setting everyone's feet to fancy with their violins.

Violent winds whipped her face. Her body was shivering wet and cold. Even while gasping for breath, she sang her family's songs. Roaring wind and stinging icicles of rain drowned out the words, yet still she sang on. Not until her body was numb and her legs too frozen to move, did Joya crawl under a huge bushy thicket to rest.

There, huddled close to the fragrant earth, she wept bittersweet tears, oh so bitter and oh so sweet for those she loved so passionately and missed so dismally. The night wore on and on. Joya was wretchedly miserable, her body, rigid with cold, she lay there waiting to die.

It was taking too long to die. She gave up trying and yearned only to be warm and dry. Somehow Joya stumbled back to camp on frozen feet. She heard Meshka's loud voice whispering from a makeshift tent and dragged her soaking wet body over to the sound. Her throat parched and croaking, she called, "Meshka, may I come in for a minute?"

"Come in! Come in!" came the quick reply. Joya peeled off her dirty wet clothes. Dressed in only her dry shift, she crawled into their little womb. Inside soft fluffy clothes were piled in a cushy nest. Meshka picked up a long warm woolen dress and handed it to her shivering friend. Rachel reached for Joya's ice cold feet, wrapped a cotton kerchief around those frozen icicles, and blew on each one with long slow hot breaths. Hot breath and soft cotton made Joya's little feet very happy.

Rachel and Joya had met several times before, but this was the first time since Joya began to speak. They smiled warmly at each other. Rachel and Joya both felt an instant affinity. They shared the same dark mysterious quality in their eyes. One might have mistaken them for mother and daughter, not that they looked alike, but because their eyes drew you in, in the same way.

Rachel spoke in Yiddish, which Joya did not understand, but Meshka knew Yiddish and a little *Magyar* (Hungarian), so Meshka translated.

Rachel smiled at the newcomer and asked, "So you are da fortune-teller, can you read da stars too?"

"Only those imprinted with our fate," Joya cleverly replied.

"Ah so you read dem all!" Rachel answered with a laugh. Joya laughed too feeling welcomed.

০৪০৪০৪

Rifka was lying awake in her little tent listening to the hammering sound of the icy rain, terrified by the angry winds screaming at the world. All that noise was keeping her awake! Of course, yesterday it was the silent emptiness of the night that kept her awake. Rifka was afraid to sleep. Restlessly, she tossed and turned, fitfully jumping in and out of dreams. The night was passing slowly. She was drifting in the doldrums for a long time.

Finally she roused herself to go, excuse me, to relieve herself. Reluctantly, she wiggled out of her warm bedroll made up of rolled clothes and stepped out into the blustery night.

Thank goodness the icy rain had stopped, now there was only a frosty mist in the air. She quickly did what she needed to do, and dashed back to her little make-shift tent under a big pine tree. A bolt of lightning suddenly lit up the sky! It was so bright; Rifka could see all the freckles on her hand.

Joya's voice drew Rifka's attention. She looked around, surprised and confused. The eerie blue lightning showed her mama's tent but her dark woolen blanket was tied to a fancy white one. Another bolt of lightning revealed Joya crawling into the tent.

"Humph!" She grunted for no apparent reason as she wiggled back into her tangled bedroll. It had lost her body warmth and was now miserably cold. Poor Rifka lay chilled, lonely, and awake. She imagined her mama and the other women sharing stories and felt utterly left out.

"Vell, my mama is in there, so I have a right to be in there too," she argued with herself. She tried to justify pushing herself in where she was not invited. Finally Rifka won the argument. She marched over to the tent, and said, "Mama, can I add my blanket 'n join you?"

'Yes, yes Rifkala, I am happy you vant to join us," Meshka chimed. While they were enlarging the tent, Joya grabbed some of her pretty scarves and skirts. They were gauzy, glitzy, and gorgeous.

She draped them inside the little pavilion with a creative flourish to add a touch of magic to the warm atmosphere. Joya's scarves did nothing to keep the wind out, but a lot to enliven their spirits. Rifka greeted Rachel with a chilly nod. She was jealous that her mama did not ask her to share a tent.

In the cozy little sanctuary, Meshka told a funny story about the butcher, the baker and the little dressmaker, the sweet people who lived in her little village. All her long life, Meshka thought the little village was the whole wide world.

Rachel told them stories about the big city and the narrow ghetto. Her wonderful family was shrewd at bartering. They could find a splinter and turn it into a tree. They were generous people and she admired all of them. Behind the locked gate, in the world of the Ghetto, friendship and a handshake were the keys to survival. In the crowded, half-starved ghetto, her network of exchanges and her good friends were all that stood between her and death.

Joya told them a story about traveling in the colorful caravan and her exotic life of wild exciting adventure. Oh, the sparkling sexy clothes and passionate music; the wild women and fiery men forever spun about by love and hate.

The wooden puppet could now talk and what she said was exciting! The women listened to her in amazement. They could almost hear the tender promises of the violins, the furious storms of wild tempers, and the warm companionship of campfires under starry skies. Joya's voice and her words painted pictures in their minds of beautiful dancers twirling about beneath a mischievous moon. Then she laughed boisterously, and told them how she and her family cunningly outsmarted bandits and royalty.

Once she even danced for a Prince and he said she was beautiful. And always there was the endless rocking sway of the wagons rumbling down the road from one place to the next.

Rifka was curled up next to her mama listening. She never spoke about the past. She was terrified that if one more tear escaped her guard, an ocean would pour out, and she would be swept away into madness.

Meshka wistfully shook her head and said, "Life poses some strange riddles. It is like vee are all putting together a big puzzle. There are lots of liddle pieces, which are supposed to fit together, but I dink some of da pieces are missing."

With a little chuckle she added, "But you know, no matter how *meshugeneh* (crazy) life got, I would live it all over again, because I loved my family so much."

A picture drifted through Meshka's mind of a quiet day long ago, in their little house. She was nursing Yonkle, Meyer was rubbing her feet with delicious warm oil, and Rifka was playing with her dolls on the floor next to them. It was a simple picture, yet its sweetness felt like such a tender kiss.

"My Yonkle loved to read 'n my Meyer loved to build dings vid his hands," She savored the memory. "Da house he made for me vas snug 'n vell built. Dey va good men 'n dey va good to me. I vas blessed to know such love."

"'N cursed to know such hate," Rifka mumbled under her breath.

"Da wheel of life turns so fast, too fast. Da memory of da people I loved is da treasure I take vid me from dis life to da next. Da love made it worth da journey," Meshka sighed.

Rachel agreed. Slowly weighing each word she added, "Often vhen I vas suffering, wonderful people helped me or rescued me. Sometimes no one stepped forward 'n I had to make my own vay across da abyss. Those va da times vhen I met Ha Shem, 'n felt da power of my own soul. Da Lord vas always right there beside me."

Silence, like a blanket, lay over them for a while.

Joya laughed softly to herself. Meshka looked at her with questioning eyes.

"When the world ended," Joya said, "you collected my things. Now all that remains of my old life are Uncle Alberto's wizard robe, the blouse my Aunt Gina made for me, my grandma's tarot cards, and Aunt Rita's pretty clothes with all the jewels on them. The robe still has my uncle's smell.

"It is like you somehow knew these were the things I valued most. Uncle Alberto always made me feel safe. Now sometimes at night, I cuddle up in the robe and I remember how safe I used to feel when he held me."

A small tear rolled down her cheek. She was glad it was too dark for the other women to see.

Joya asked them, "What special things did you bring for yourselves?"

Rachel liked the question, so she answered first, "Even though I collected lots of pretty dings over da years, gifts from Avram 'n da children, vhen I vas ready to leave, I took only my Bubba's shawl. It vas filled vid da strength from all da Shabboses, vhen she prayed so hard for da Most Holy One to keep us all alive. I am sure da power of her prayers convinced Ha Shem to let us live, vhen so many other people va dying."

Rachel and Joya looked at Meshka. She gave them a toothy grin and raised an eyebrow as if to say, all right I will play the game. "I took a burning coal from my kitchen stove 'n I have used it to make all my fires. Every night I take a live coal from da fire for da next time 'n I keep it in da covered cooking pot, so in dis vay, I still have some of da fire from my home. I also took dis liddle mezuzah."

She pulled the little wooden box out from its warm nest between her breasts. "It used to hang by my front door. My son carved it vhen he vas just a liddle boy." The women smiled and nodded knowingly. Tokens of home were the most precious things they had.

Since Rifka did not jump in, Joya asked, "Rifka, what special thing did you bring?"

Rifka was annoyed at being singled out and forced to answer. "My sharpest knife," she said begrudgingly. Then to justify her unromantic answer, she added, "It has a lot of practical uses."

The silence returned. Each woman drifted away on a sea of faraway memories.

After a bit, Rachel's eyes closed and her lips began to pray. Ever so softly, hardly more than a whisper, she thanked Ha Shem for the comfort she was feeling in this moment. She did not recite one of the many Hebrew prayers she knew, instead, her own words poured from her heart sounding like a song. "O Holy Lord, no greater gift could you have given me dan to be vid my sisters here. Bless these holy women, daughters of compassion. Blessed are you our Lord, Master of da Universe. Shine your goodness on our lives. Give us da courage 'n da vision to be a blessing to da world. *Aumen* (amen)."

With a wide pious smile Rachel assured the others, "Ha Shem puts da quiet in our hearts."

Meshka thought Rachel was very sweet and very naïve. Her own experiences with God brought anything but quiet.

Joya asked in a respectful tone, "Rachel, what does your song mean?" Rachel repeated the prayer and Meshka translated it from Yiddish to *Magyar* (Hungarian) for Joya. The Gypsy girl repeated each line in her own language. Words often required several translations before everyone understood.

A warm close feeling filled the tent. Meshka spontaneously turned to Joya and said, "Dank you for being here vid us on dis journey." She leaned over and kissed Joya on both cheeks as one does when welcoming a daughter.

Joya looked surprised, but she smiled and kissed Meshka on both cheeks in appreciation.

Then to Rifka's amazement, Joya turned to her and said, "Beautiful, powerful Jewess, even though you are a Gadji, I am thankful that you are my sister on this journey."

Rifka was stunned. She did not consider Joya a friend, let alone a sister, but now, come to think of it, she might be growing fond of this strange girl.

Flattered by Joya's words, Rifka smiled. Their eyes held each other for a moment. Then everyone laughed and hugged.

The winds finally stopped yelling at each other. Now they merely grumbled a little, but it was manageable. The women lay curled up together in their cushy nest. Each one fell into a comfortable sleep and dreamed of long ago and faraway places.

In the morning after breakfast, when the sun was high and the tent was dry, they took it apart. As she untied the blankets, Rachel softly sang in a lullaby voice, "Baruch Ha Shem, vee dank you for protecting our liddle shelter. Vee dank you for keeping us safe in da storm. May vee always be safe beneath da blessed canopy of your mercy."

The women made it safely to morning. The dark storm had passed, but in the darkness of their hearts, they knew more storms were brewing.

CRCRCR

Chapter 9

A Woman's Clan

When the next storm came blustering along, the four women tied their blankets together to make one big tent. They huddled inside cozy and warm. Every storm after that, they made a nest together. They crawled back into a safe womb where they rode out the storms and shared their secret selves.

They marked the passing of time by the storms. God usually stomped about, two days before or after a full or new moon. When He stomped, down came the icy rains or the quiet snow.

The cold breath of winter was upon them. The storm, *Oy Gotteniu*, (Oh God) was it frosty, bitter and cold! Sometime in the deepest dark, the quiet snow came down and made it warmer. The night was silent. All creature sounds were swallowed up by the silence. It was peaceful.

Big fat white flakes padded down quietly landing on their fragile shelter. Meshka and Rachel were worried. The snow was coming so fast! The heavy snow threatened to crush their fragile sanctuary. The timbers supporting the tent creaked and groaned; the blankets tightly anchored, sagged; and the women held their breath tensely listening to the *kvetching* logs.

The women took turns crawling out of their warm cozy nest into the bitter cold, to shake the snow off the blankets. Despite the sharp bite of the frozen air, there was something majestically exquisite about the pure white untouched winter land shining like diamonds on beautiful cotton clouds. Its pristine perfection ennobled the soul. Brushing away the snow was both a sacrifice and a sensual delight.

It was worth the chill to feel the glorious delight of crawling back into a cozy nest with warm friends cuddled close. The pavilion stayed warm. The snow piled up all around them. God's big white mittens were wrapped around the tent holding in the warmth.

Alert, too aware of danger to sleep, the tension inside the tent grew tighter. If the tent fell down under the snow, what would keep them from freezing? What if the tent was buried, would they have enough air? Everyone prayed.

Rachel opened her arms and said, "My friends, I know how vee can be safe. *Mein bubba* (my grandma) wore dis beautiful silk shawl, pure as snow, every Friday night in da old country. She gave it to me as a parting gift vhen I left da ghetto. She said it would always keep me safe 'n it has.

"I vill hang it above all of us, across da center, so mein Bubba's arms vill be draped over all of us. She vill protect us.

"No more worrying. Vee vill survive dis dangerous mountain, just like vee survived da ghetto. Relax. Vee are safe. Mein Bubba vill protect us."

"Dis shawl is sacred. It is filled vid her spirit, her high values, 'n her boundless love. It is a sanctuary. Mein Bubba's shawl is my home.

"On Friday nights, no matter how humble vas our home, it vas always clean 'n da best food vee could manage vas our dinner. Mein Bubba stood before her children 'n her grandchildren, 'n brought da light of God into her eyes, into her heart, 'n into her soul.

"She praised God 'n asked Him to protect our liddle family in such a dangerous time. All those years of mein Bubba's prayers are here in da shawl."

They very carefully hung the lovely white shawl, embroidered with silver threads of sacred love. Rachel's *Bubba* watched over and protected them through the night. The women took turns staying awake to guard and shake the tent. In the quiet of the snow, the soft flakes blanketed the night.

The next morning, when they woke up, they smiled at the blessed shawl. With a grateful heart, they were glad to be alive. It was so quiet. They could only hear their own breath.

Rifka opened their blanket door into a wall of snow. The blessed tent shakers crawled out of their warm beds into the icy cold all through the night, so now they had a tunnel through the whiteness. Rifka crawled into the tunnel, pushed through a thin layer of fluff, and stood up.

She looked to be wearing an endless white skirt from her waist to the trees! Wiggling and hobbling, she slowly made her way through the heavy fluff to the cart. It was just a few feet away under an evergreen tree, but it took tireless push to get there.

Little Shainela was tied to the wheel of the cart. She was safe in her own little snow house under the frame between the wheels. Rifka found her snuggled in among the leaves, kindling, and sticks.

Clever Rifka had the forethought, when the snow started, to make a dry bed for Shainela. She stored the firewood and several useful objects for easy reach, under the cart; her dented but trusty cooking pot among them. Now it became a shovel.

Rifka turned around and returned to the tent through the channel her body had carved through the snow. She crawled back in to report what she discovered. They should stay in the tent.

"Vhat do vee need to have, to stay vhere vee are?" Rifka asked. Meshka and Rachel shrugged, Joya was curled up asleep, and Rifka was full of ideas.

She dug the snow away from the sides of the tent with her trusty pot. It took a long time. Sweaty and cold, Rifka cleared away a few feet from around the tent, then a large circle beside it. Here she built a small fire with the dry wood and kindling from under the cart. When the others finally crawled out, they were greeted by a warm fire. Their hearts filled with gratitude.

ଓଓଓ

Every day was a kaleidoscope of change. They coped with twirling snow devils, icy winter rages, and blessed bright sunny days. Little by little, they formed rituals of living that framed their days and gave their lives a sense of order.

Whenever it snowed, they hung up *Bubba's* magic shawl to keep them safe. The many colors of their blankets disappeared behind its pristine purity and glittery silver elegance.

Most of the storms raged outside their little refuge; but sometimes the rage slipped inside. Rifka had a sharp tongue. When anger grabbed her by the throat, she aimed her temper at her mama. This was a problem because Rachel tolerated no disrespect under her *Bubba's* blessed shawl.

It was a cold snowy December in the mountains. The days were short and bitter cold. One frosty morning, Rifka woke up on the wrong side of the bed. The harsh weather made everyone a little grumpy. Her prickly tongue soon put her on the wrong side of everyone.

That night under a full moon, God was brewing up a storm. The winds were howling. Dirty smudges darkened the skies. The women were tying their blankets together. Rifka was working on one side of the tent, tying on her favorite blue blanket. It was given to her by her mother's sweet friend Sophie, on the day she and Chaim were married. Its soft warmth covered her and her sweet husband on their wedding night. Her love for Chaim was in this blanket.

She tied one end to a strong timber and pulled the blanket to reach the other corner. Ripppp!!!! The horrible sound made her heart skip a beat. She closed her eyes to make it not true!

Everyone stopped! They turned, looked at Rifka and waited for the worst, but Rifka showed no reaction. Anger was hot, but white rage was deadly calm. She did not react though they felt the storm gathering in her.

Meshka put a sympathetic hand on her daughter's shoulder and Rifka gave a loud threatening growl.

Rifka thought, If only I had my wonderful little sewing basket, dis rip could easily be mended; but out here in da middle of nowhere, I am helpless to fix it. My sewing kit burned to ashes in da flames like everything else! Fury gripped her bowels.

Rifka was locked inside herself, drowning in a churning sea of rage. She could not reach out, nor could she accept help. Anything and everything fed her temper. The rip went through her soul. It was a loss, one more loss, among far too many.

Rifka roared a wounded animal sound. Meshka said, "Shush Shainela, it vill be alright."

Rifka turned her vile mood on her sweet mama and hissed, "Sure Mama, a boil does not hurt if it is under someone else's arm!" She words poured out bitter and biting. Some of the fuming turmoil and misery inside her head, heart, and soul flew out and away.

Rachel glared at Rifka. She would never have spoken to her mother that way! Rachel probably never spoke an angry word. In the ghetto, she could not afford it.

Disapproving, Rachel shot Meshka a stern look. Meshka gave a lopsided smile and shrugged, as if to say, Vhat can I do?

"My Rifkala is striking out in pain. Vee all need to blow off steam from time to time, so other people can feel our pain. Today vas just Rifka's turn."

Meshka felt her daughters' struggle and her heart ached for her suffering child. She yearned to help, but Rifka kept her heart locked and her tears hidden.

Another mama would have withered under the whiplash of her daughter's sharp tongue, but not Meshka. She was not offended, but Rachel was!

Meshka whispered in Rachel's ear, "Do not worry. Rifka screams in pain. Vee can scream back 'n forth, like throwing a ball. I do not vant to do dat. I prefer to quietly soothe her wound.

"Rifka yells at me because I am safe. She knows I love her. Her fire hurts a liddle, sure, but I know how to deal vid her."

The simple truth was: Rifka really wanted to curl up in her mama's lap and cry. She wanted her mama. But the clenched muscles that locked rage inside her; also locked the tears behind her eyes. Rifka was afraid to soften even a little bit. She was afraid that an ocean of emptiness was waiting to swallow her up; so she fumed over little things instead.

ശശശ

Joya smirked and exclaimed, "I knew it! I knew someone was going to explode today. The Moon is visiting Mars in Scorpio. That is fighting energy. Rifka just got caught in their net. It could have been any one of us."

All the women stared at Joya like their eyeballs were frozen open. Suddenly, they all burst out laughing. That eased the tension, but Rifka was still itching for a fight.

"So you dink vee are puppets 'n da stars pull da strings?" mocked Rifka.

Joya was used to such ignorance. "All of life is spun from the same patterns. My people have the gift of knowing how to read the patterns that God has written everywhere."

Rifka scoffed. Each word dripping with scorn, she hissed, "So, if you know so much, how come you never saw dat da end of da world vas comin'?"

The blood drained from Joya's face. With half lidded glazed eyes, she said, "I saw it first in Meshka's palm that day, when we stood in the sunshine, in the green meadow.

"Del forgive me! I saw it coming. I told Meshka, but we did not believe it would really happen!"

Meshka felt ashamed. She kicked herself for not warning everyone in the village that danger was coming. But what could she say? *A wild young Gypsy girl told me dat da world vas going to end!* They would have laughed. No one would believe such *bubba maisse* (nonsense).

Joya lamented, "Ahhh, to know something, but not know all of it, is a terrible curse! My oracles said that the world was going to change and we were going on a journey. I knew someone was going die, but I did not know who. As a journeyer, of course I always move on, so I did not see it as a warning! I could not have imagined that I was destined to journey on without my caravan, beyond the only world I had ever known. We prayed for mercy and compassion, but Del was not listening!"

Pictures of the past flooded into her mind. Something in Rifka's rage gave Joya permission to feel all of it. Suddenly she was face to face with the horrors that pursued her.

"You cannot imagine what it was like; knowing the end of the world was coming. We sat around our fires at night sharing our visions and the warning signs. We talked endlessly about how to prepare and we did what we could. But we never imagined the power of blind hate or the violent madness it would release. How could we wrap our minds around the truth? These nice people, whose fortunes we were reading, were suddenly going to turn on us and kill everyone. In my own little world, the worst I ever saw was the occasional roaring of violent men."

Joya was shaking. Visions of horror bombarded her mind! For four long months, terrifying images haunted her. They tormented her inside. She was desperate to escape accusing ghosts. Once, she ran out into a storm to die, to escape, but failed.

Here, sitting in this beautiful nest, laughing and loving these gentle women, she did feel safe. They were kind women and they accepted her. She gathered her courage to look straight at the nightmare haunting her.

"If you hold my hands, maybe I can go back and put that day to rest; or at least get its claws out of me, so I can take a deep full breath again without trembling all over."

Rachel and Meshka took her hands and Rifka held her feet. Their touch kept her from floating away as she told her story.

"I woke up on a warm summer's day, one of those late lazy Sundays, I always loved; but on this day, everything felt wrong! The air was too heavy, too intense. A sharp bad feeling knifed through me.

"I went over to Uncle Alberto to tell him about the cramping pain in my belly. I was standing next to him for only a moment when a burst of thunder roared from a clear blue sky! A strange deep angry rumble was shaking the forest. Suddenly a raging horde of screaming men lunged towards us out of the shadows! Flames of malice flared in their eyes. Their clawing hands grabbed for our blood."

Joya was back in the past, watching them drag Uncle Alberto away from her. The men closed in on the great sage. An ugly monster stabbed him with a kitchen knife! Terrified, she stared aghast! Her bigger-than-life protector, folded over slowly and crumpled to the ground.

Taking advantage of their distraction, she ran towards the river! Desperately, she tried to escape the wild filthy beasts pouring out the forest!

To this day, in her dreams Joya was running towards the river, and still she never made it, because her feet got stuck in deep mud or she got sucked into a deep pool of blood!

The women in Joya's *Clan* listened, held her hands, and cried with her. When her story ended, the women slipped their hands under Joya, lifted her up and cradled her to their hearts. The three women stood swaying for a few minutes, then laid her gently back on the ground. The child was small and lithe buried in all her clothes.

In sweet silence Joya untangled herself from the past and found her way back into the present.

The silence ended when Rachel began to pray very softly, "*Baruch Ha Shem*, please soothe our scarred hearts. Please help us love each other more gently."

Rocking back and forth in the rhythm of prayer, Rachel implored the God she loved, "Baruch Ha Shem, please use your power to make good dings happen.

"Most Holy Lord, you know how much I love You. Please take all dis love I give You so freely 'n   put it back into da world."

While Rachel prayed, Joya slipped out. Her heart was pounding from all the secret things she said! Guilt crushed in on her. Despite the freezing cold, she could finally breathe. The frosty air purged the guilt. The frost biting her hands distracted her, so the anguish drifted away.

༄ༀༀༀ

Joya thought about facing the past and realized Rifka's roaring gave her courage. A wave of gratitude washed over her as she thought of the angry Jewess. She saw again the look in Rifka's eyes when the blanket tore! The pain that Rifka could not face!

Joya remembered the sewing kit! Suddenly she was excited. She was going to rescue Rifka from her sense of loss!

Joya made her way through the snow to the cart, which was safely hidden under a pine tree. The little goat was huddled underneath snug and warm. Joya dug around in her bundles and found the little basket. Luckily, it was near at hand.

Only a few days ago, a young mama with four small children, gratefully gave her the sewing basket. In a tarot reading, Joya assured the woman that all of her children were going to survive the winter and this arduous journey. The sewing basket was the woman's great treasure, but the reassurance was worth much more. Inside was an obsidian knife, a small pouch of delicate little fishbone needles, and skeins of dyed yarn.

Joya slipped into the tent and took a few satisfied breaths to enjoy her excitement. Then she turned to Rifka and said softly, "Thank you for opening something inside me. It is not choking me anymore. In gratitude, I have a great gift for you."

Rifka looked at her confused. Joya handed her the basket and said in a gentle comforting voice, "Tomorrow, when the blanket is dry, we will mend the tear. We can sew up the rip and I will embroider pretty flowers over the stitches to hide them. The blanket will be repaired and it will be even more beautiful than it was before."

Tears threatened Rifka, so she growled in rough appreciation. Like the sun cutting through a cloud, Rifka's smile replaced the frown. Peace had returned to their sanctuary.

ର୍ଷର୍ଷର୍ଷ

The harshness of the cold winter tested the four women every day. They faced their challenges together and forged a family. Joya called them the *Woman's Clan* and the name stuck.

It became their habit to tie their blankets together every new and full moon. On this night, Meshka and Rachel were working hand in hand to secure one side of the little pavilion. Joya carefully helped Rifka adjust her blanket in place. Then they stood back and admired the beautiful green vine snaking up one side. Pretty white daisies with golden yellow centers sparkled along the vine.

When all the blankets were secured, Rachel draped her *Bubba's* magic shawl over the ceiling. Joya draped her many colorful, glittery, gorgeous scarves around the inner walls to make their nest festive and gala. While Joya and Rachel were finishing the inside, Rifka went to secure the cart.

On the windswept ridge where they found themselves, there were no tall protective trees, so Rifka put the cart on the wind side of the little pavilion to cut the bite of the wind a bit.

In their magical little womb, filled with beautiful joyous colors, their hearts grew lighter. They sang songs from their homelands, confided stories of their great adventures and misadventures, and told the story of their lives. The little pavilion of shawls became invested with their sacred prayers and remarkable tales. They shuddered and they cried, they laughed and they dreamed, they sailed off on sweet remembered bliss.

Joya could always be counted on to tell a colorful story. Her tales were populated with fascinating characters, strange customs, and exotic things she had seen in faraway lands, when she traveled with her family in the caravan.

One cold moonless night, Joya filled a bowl with raw salt, poured in some alcohol and set it on fire. The dancing blue flames gave off no smoke and the fire made the women feel a little warmer.

Rachel looked around the circle and smiled. An old Hebrew prayer was on her lips, so she recited the words slowly and the others echoed her. At first Joya felt awkward saying these strange foreign words, but she liked the chanting sound of Jewish prayers. She had no idea what the words were, but the meaning was clear. All prayers begging God for salvation sound the same.

Offering her own gift, Joya sang a favorite song of hers, in her own language. The haunting tune touched the women deeply.

ରେଉଷ୍ଟେଉ

The Baking Circle

It was an icy afternoon in late December. Rachel and Meshka were tying the blankets with cold stiff fingers. Suddenly Rachel laughed gaily and called out, "Blessed are you O' Lord, King of da Universe, who gives us da holiday of Chanukah."

Rachel put her shivering arms around her friend and they both sang out, "*Gut Yontif!*" (Good Holiday).

Chanukah snuck up on Meshka. Between endlessly walking through snow covered mountains and the constant struggle not to freeze, Meshka had no sense of which day was which. Chanukah celebrates miracles. Everyone needs miracles, so it was a fine holiday to celebrate. With a light heart, Rachel said wistfully, "On Chanukah my children 'n grandchildren always gathered around da kitchen table in da evenings. Every day for eight days, vee lit a special candle 'n played *dreidel* (a wooden top).

"From da eldest to da youngest, everyone took a turn spinning da liddle wooden dreidel. Yeshuah, oy how he loved to show off! He could spin da dreidel upside down. Da liddle ones would squeal vid delight vhenever he did dis. On my turn, I used to give da dreidel a twist 'n drop it from a few inches above da table. It vas very dramatic. Everybody loved it.

"One by one, vee spun da top 'n held our breath to see if vee won or lost. Everyone moaned, groaned, or laughed vhen da top stopped. Did vee win da liddle pile of chocolates, raisins 'n coins dat vas our kitty?

"After a good supper, it vas time for da best part. My daughters 'n I brought out fresh holiday creampuffs. I served dem vid a nice hot cup of mulled wine, vhen I could get it."

Her story and the pavilion were finished. Rachel gave a big sigh as she returned to the here and now.

"My custom is not so different from yours," said Meshka. "On Chanukah my sisters 'n I got together very early at Raizie's house 'n vee baked creampuffs too. Raizie vas da youngest. She vas a big round sveet woman. Ahh, da delicious smell of baking creampuffs! Ahh *mekheye!* (such a pleasure)

"As soon as da pastries va ready, vee wrapped dem in a pretty cloth 'n I put dem in a big straw basket. Rifka 'n I wove dat basket, vhen she vas about twelve years old.

"Den vee strolled around da village carrying our delicious treats. Vee gave dem as gifts to all da wonderful people vee loved." Meshka reminisced. "Like you, vee also lit da candles, said da prayers, 'n played vid da liddle *dreidel.*"

Rachel felt inspired, "Maybe vee can make skinny liddle candles 'n light one every night for eight days. Rifka carves everything she touches, so maybe she can make us a liddle dreidel too.

"Da creampuffs va always my favorite part. I vonder it vee can make dem? I have a liddle flour. Joya has some sugar. Rifka, could you find us some cream?"

"I have cream." The voice came from a tall elegant woman with hair the color of cream. She was camped a few feet away. "I would love to taste one of your creampuffs." She said with a mischievous smile, as she went on brushing the shining golden hair of a tall young woman.

Earlier in the day, Meshka watched this exotic creature and three beautiful young maidens set up their camp nearby. She heard them call to each other and noted their names.

"Dank you Sharanii," said Meshka. She was getting better at talking with strangers and was intrigued by this elegant woman.

Sharanii was dressed in a bright red silk sari of the finest weave embroidered with golden threads. From her forehead to her nose dripped chains of gold, a shining red jewel adorned the point between her eyes and her wrists were covered with fine delicate glass bracelets; bejeweled like a *Goddess*. Meshka was in awe of the *Priestess*. Even the colorful Gypsy girl looked dull by comparison. Curiosity, more than courage, made Meshka speak to such an exotic creature from a foreign world.

Sharanii walked in beauty. Everything she touched, she made beautiful and everything beautiful she wanted to touch. Sharanii made women forget their rough lives by curling their hair or darkening it, whenever Father Time made a mess of it.

"Yes, vee shall make creampuffs!" cried Meshka. She was so happy she began to hum softly to herself.

"I have a bit of vanilla I was saving for a special day," a songbird voice sang out from the young woman whose golden waves were being brushed. "It will taste delicious in your creampuffs."

"Yes, dank you, Sarina," Meshka replied with a shy smile. She was becoming a regular chatterbox with these strange women.

Meshka noticed Sarina earlier. How could you miss her? She was a stunningly beautiful blond giant, an Amazon. Earlier today, Meshka saw her walking arm in arm with two other lovely girls; one was a thin willowy waif with long straight black hair, the other was petite with bouncy blond curls. Rumor had it the three young women knew the secret art of herbs and were respected healers.

"Would you like a little chocolate to drizzle on your creampuffs?" The words rolled off her tongue with serpentine smoothness. The sensuous voice belonged to Tasjia, Sarina's black-haired friend. She was climbing down from a big beautiful wagon. In her hand was a real teapot! The design on the pottery was so carefully crafted; it kissed the eyes of the beholder. Meshka never saw anything so flawlessly perfect!

The cute little blond with the bouncy curls, Maya, was taking care of a big white horse grazing nearby. He was grazing a little too close nearby for Meshka's comfort. When the horse nickered, Meshka's skin crawled. Not that she had anything against horses, except they do have such big yellow teeth!

That evening, the *Woman's Clan* (Meshka, Rifka, Rachel and Joya) invited Sharanii, Sarina, Maya and Tasjia to share their evening fire. Everyone contributed something and they had a delicious feast! After taste buds and tummies were happy, they started to talk. Ideas tossed about like flipping coins. Everyone took a turn and tossed in an idea. Before you knew it, they figured out how to make creampuffs in a simple fire pit. Between them, they had everything they needed.

If you were a fly buzzing around watching them, you would have been amazed! Everyone jumped in and talked like they were old friends.

The next morning the two *Clans of Women* gathered their supplies and makeshift tools to bake the sweet delicacies together. Maya, the cute little blond with the bouncy curls, had no cream or chocolate to offer, but she shared a gift that brought a creamy pleasure to the soul.

Maya played a little lap harp. Her crystal-like music gave an extra twinkle to the day. It lightened hearts, set feet to tapping, and put joy in their hearts.

The best part of baking was having a hot fire in the daytime. It was a rare treat, indeed. Usually they kept warm by walking fast. Between the hot fire and the wonderful music, they were warm and happy.

It was a joyous day. The baking was a delight. Maya's music set a playful rhythm and dancing hands kneaded the dough. Everyone had flour on their noses and funny stories on their tongues. The laughter flowed freely. It was a rare and wonderful day.

Meshka and Rachel made tiny candles, Rifka carved a beautiful little *dreidel,* and the creampuffs came out great! They lit candles, spun the top, won and lost, and enjoyed a delightful feast!

The elegant Sharanii licked a smear of cream from her upper lip and exclaimed! "Hmmm nummy, food for the Gods."

The term "gods" shocked Rifka! It rubbed her the wrong way. Her face grew red and her blood began to boil. She felt she should defend the One God…b-u-t she did not want to ruin the festivities. Pleasure was such a rare treat in their lives.

They were celebrating a miracle. Rifka took a few deep breaths. Each breath stretched her heart a little more, and soon she was able to let the anger pass. She accepted the peace she felt as her own personal miracle.

When Meshka heard Sharanii say "gods," she looked at Rifka and Rachel. Their faces were twisted with shock, so she whispered to them, "You know there is only one God. Everyone knows dat. Let these confused women call each side of God by a different name. Vhat harm can it do? All I know is dat dis is a good day for a feast."

Rachel decided Meshka was right. She thought about people worshipping "gods" and shrugged. Everyone has their *mishugass* (craziness), their own personal beliefs. She figured one was not better than another.

Only a few lucky people, like herself, were gifted enough to know that there can be only One God; One God with many faces. So if some people think one of those faces is a separate god, their ignorance was not her problem.

The *Rebbe* taught Rachel to see a bigger picture, not just to look at the surface of things. He also taught her that narrow minded people see the same picture as she does, but only understand a little piece of it.

The Baking Circle, as they came to call themselves, met from time to time to celebrate their holidays. It was not so much a mutual acceptance of each other's religion, as a chance to pool resources and share a feast. In the end, it amounted to the same thing. They each got to see how the others worship. It was scary to watch the pagan women celebrate a pantheon of gods and *Goddesses*!

If each woman had a different reason for celebrating, it was not Meshka's problem. She was celebrating the blessing of friendship, nothing more. Reassured that God was not going to punish them for their little pleasures, they continued to share food.

୧୨୧୨୧୨

Even in the foothills, winter was harsh. The mountains were behind them now. The women in Meshka's *Clan* pushed against billowing winds moving at a snail's pace.

Rifka was strong from pushing and pulling the cart over rocks and through streams. Joya, beside her, added her youthful vigor. Even so, one day the wheels got stuck in a small stream. They pushed and they pulled until they were blue in the face, but the wheels did not budge. Rachel harnessed her little pony to the cart and pulled it free.

The rocky landscape got so rough Sharanii invited Rachel and Rifka to tie their carts to her wagon. Shainela rode on the cart, the women all rode in the wagon, and the little pony trailed on a line behind. Meshka's *Clan* was grateful to be free of the struggle.

The inside of Sharanii's wagon was surprisingly beautiful, as exotic as she, a temple on wheels.

The women stayed in one place for several days to scrounge the countryside for food and barter with nearby villagers. Among the refugees, people helped each other, so no one starved. That was a miracle in itself. The blustery winds and blowing snow of early January forced the refugees to make camp outside a small town for a few weeks. The people in that town eyed them suspiciously, but nothing bad happened.

The women in the Baking Circle traded the villagers delicious pastries for yarn. Maya gathered hard wood branches and Rifka carved them into straight knitting needles with her sharp knife. The women nestled in together and knitted warm sweaters.

Meshka liked knitting, so she made extra blankets and sweaters for some of the children running around. Seeing their little bodies all snug and warm made her feel warmer. Each day, when Meshka woke up and found that she did not freeze to death in the night, she praised God for His mercy. She could hear prayers chanted in many languages all saying the same thing.

The temperature was just above freezing in the mountains. You know what they say about the mountains in winter? They are like being near God. Sometimes they take your breath away with their extraordinary beauty and you feel you are in heaven. Other times, their awesome power tries to kill you. So it was with great relief that they passed out of the mountains, climbed down the foothills, and finally reached a wide flat basin.

ଔଔଔଔ

The morning chores were done and it was time to embark on the day's march, but no one was moving. People were standing around waiting for something. The Baking Circle was near the front of the procession, so tall Sarina climbed up on the wagon bench to have a look.

The blood drained from her face as she climbed down and faced the curious women. "I saw soldiers carrying terrible weapons marching around pushing people!"

"Do they look like Turks?" Sharanii asked; her voice higher than usual. In shock, the women all turned to look at Sharanii. No one ever saw her composure shaken before.

"The Turks are gobbling up this part of the world and their methods are harsh." Sharanii shuddered, remembering a narrow escape not long ago.

Climbing back up for another view, Sarina confirmed, "No, not Turks, maybe Italians."

"Ah yes, we have reached the border." Sharanii let out her breath and her shoulders relaxed.

Once the people started moving, it took little time to pass through the check point. When Meshka reached the invisible line between one country and another, it hit her like a sharp slap in the head. Little old Meshka had lived a long time. All the seasons of her life were in one little village, always with the same people. Now suddenly she was leaving her homeland and everything she ever knew! It felt like she was walking off the end of the world.

Meshka's feet stopped! Roots started growing from the bottom of soles. They were not going to move; and her heart? You never heard such banging like that! She stared down at her big fat feet in their torn and patched shoes. For the first time, she was glad that so much of her was touching the ground.

"In dis land, my mama 'n my mama's mama va born. How can I leave it? On da other side, who vill I be? A wanderer without a home - a stranger," she muttered to God and to anyone else who could hear her.

Then she snickered, "I am already a wanderer without a home, a stranger among strangers."

Meshka's *bubba* once told her about her own grandparents, Her great-great-grandfather came from Spain, where he was a respected scholar. He performed many *mitzvahs* (good deeds) by teaching and preserving God's holy words.

He was a very learned man in a time when thinking was a mortal sin. Anyone who dared to question anything was killed in the town square for public amusement. It was a terrible time, so Meshka's great-great-grandparents fled Spain and wandered north into Hungary, where they were safe...for a while.

Bittersweet joy thoughts of Passover reminded her of the *nachas* (the happiness overflowing her heart) of sitting around *Bubba's* big table with all her *meshpokha* (family), celebrating the precious gift of freedom, just as God commanded them to do. Every springtime, her aunts, uncles and cousins all poured into *Bubba's* little house to fulfill God's commandant to give thanks that they were no longer slaves.

Passover celebrated the end of winter, the blessed birth of spring. God once commanded that all Jews on this night should tell the tale of long ago, when their people were slaves in Egypt. So Meshka's ancestors were refugees too.

Passover was her favorite holiday. She and her family never took their freedom for granted. She laughed in disbelief. "Who would have thought even freedom I could have too much of?"

Meshka realized her people did not always live in Hungary; once upon a time they lived in Spain and even before that, in Egypt.

Also, her son Yonkle once told her about a book that said, after their sojourn in Egypt, the Jews were taken into captivity in Babylon. A Persian General named Cyprus set them free. That was just before her ancestors went to Spain, where they were safe…for a while.

"Dat means my family has lived in Hungary, Spain, Egypt, Babylonia, 'n of course, da Holy Land," she touched each finger as though she could count.

For a long time Meshka stood there near the border staring at all the scary soldiers marching around in their uniforms.

She turned to Rifka and whimpered, "Oy, look at all da soldiers, it is enough to turn my hair gray!"

Rifka giggled at how silly her mama was acting. "Mama your hair is already gray 'n it has been gray for a long time,"

Meshka laughed too and that lightened her heart a bit. She remembered chubby old Uncle Heimme saying more than once, "Our people, vee survive. Vhat else can vee do?"

"If my Meyer va here," she thought, "he would say, 'Go on. Our roots do not go so deep in Hungarian soil. Be a *balabusta!* (powerful woman) Go!'"

Any time she thought about her sweet husband, it made her feel safer. He died a long time ago, but to Meshka it was just the other day.

With a shrug and a sigh, she said to herself, "A mama's mama does not a lineage make. So vhat does it matter if I am an old woman; I am alive 'n dat is all dat counts in dese terrible times."

Meshka took several deep breaths and pictured her brave ancestors. She felt their dreams alive in her. After all, they were not so different. She too wanted a better life in a safer place.

"God vent out of His vay to keep dis cranky old woman alive, so He must have a plan for me." The thought made her feel better. "*Le chaim!*" (To life!) she said with great bravado and decided to walk forward.

"I am not going to move!" said her feet.

"Why are you in such a hurry?" said her mind. "Look at vhat you are doing! You could be killed!"

Her courage dribbled away and her feet stayed right where they were. She was not going anywhere. This was her homeland.

It was a Friday morning and that night would be Shabbos. Rachel was all excited to greet the Shabbos *Bride* in a new land, but when she saw Meshka standing there like a tree sending down roots, she decided they should make camp instead. The new land could wait for a few days.

Rifka and Joya started making camp. Sharanii and her three lovely maidens noticed the others setting up. They hung back wanting to stay close to their friends and prepared to stay the night.

By now, the women were very experienced at making and breaking camp. Everyone knew their role and they pitched camp quickly.

By early afternoon, they were ready for their Friday ritual of baking challahs (sweet braided bread). After all these weeks of baking together, the women moved in perfect rhythm, like the workings of a clock.

Maya played a lively rhythmic tune on her harp to guide their hands as they kneaded the dough. Keeping the fluffy mounds warm enough to rise was a challenge.

They covered the bowls and set them in sun, which today was blessedly warm. While the dough was rising, their weekly custom was to do a *mikveh* (a Jewish ritual bath). Only three of the women were Jewish, but it was a wonderful ritual and everyone loved it. Throughout the week, all the women looked forward to it.

Every Friday, Maya, Sarina and Tasjia filled their pots with the water that Joya and Rifka drew from one of the many creeks, streams, lakes, rivers, and waterfalls, flowing abundantly in this land.

Meshka kindled the fire and the women set the water to warm, while Sharanii prepared a special little bathing spot for them. She draped thick blankets between the trees to block the wind.

Each lady luxuriously stood inside under steaming hot water. Ah *mekheye,* to be warm on such a cold day! The girls poured the water over each woman ever so slowly. They mastered the art of pouring just enough water to stay warm while making the pleasure last as long as possible. This ritual was a delicious slice of heaven here on earth.

Rachel warmed towels and blankets by the fire. The moment the girls stopped pouring, Rachel dried the woman and wrapped her in hot cloths to stay comfy warm.

Now fresh and clean after the toil of the week, the Baking Circle prepared to greet the *Shabbos Bride*. Even the women who were not Jewish loved Shabbos and were all excited. *She* enchanted one and all with *Her* magical spice - that special soothing delight that comes over you on the eve of a day totally dedicated to pleasure and relaxation.

Meshka fed the fire while Sharanii carefully gathered and arranged the stones in the flames to create her baking ovens. They braided the loaves, glazed them with egg and honey, and put them in the ovens to bake.

Rifka, Rachel and Sarina, cooked a delicious dinner. Long before dinner was ready, the challahs came out of the ovens. The aroma of the fresh baked bread enveloped them with a warm feeling of hearth and home. The Baking Circle always made a basketful of extra little challahs.

Now it was time for their favorite Shabbos ritual. They strolled around giving away hot braided loaves of bread to people who were hungry, especially to children and old people.

Exactly at sunset, Rachel, Rifka and Meshka took out their precious little skinny tallow candles. Tallow is a nice sounding name for stinky old animal fat.

The whole Baking Circle gathered around the candles. The Jewish women covered their heads with their shawls and lit the candles. All the women scooped the light of the *Shabbos Bride* into their eyes three times. Then they cupped their hands over their closed eyes to keep the light inside them. Their minds went inward to speak with *Her Presence* within them.

The Jewish women recited the customary prayer over the candles aloud and the circle of women echoed each strange word, which were now familiar to them all.

With eyes covered and heads bowed, each woman silently thanked her own *Divine Source* or *Sources* for all her blessings, especially the gift of health and life. *The Shekhina* filled their hearts with peace.

Joya was charmed by all this praying. Her own people had more of a working relationship with *Del* (God), one that did not require so many fancy words.

Rachel, as usual, was the first to start saying her prayers and the last to finish them. There were so many things she was thankful for and so many people to bless.

Meshka enthusiastically prayed, "Dank you God for bringing us safely to dis new land. May vee find peace 'n a better life here. Watch over dese wonderful women who are so kind to me. Vee are all your daughters."

Rifka felt empty and hollow. After reciting the customary prayer, what more could she add? "Dank you for killin' my kind husband, my sweet children, 'n for destroyin' my peaceful liddle village," such words she could not say. There was nothing else she wanted to say, so she just said, "*Aumen.*" (amen)

Memory echoed something Chaim used to say, "If you have nothing good to say, say nothing." So Rifka mumbled the prayer and swallowed the anger.

In this sacred moment, the busy work-week drew to a close. Opening before them was a restful day to be lived in peace.

The flames of their little candles flickered desperately, trying to survive the chilly breeze as darkness descended and the night grew quiet.

A whirlwind of hugs and kisses followed as everyone wished each other, *"Gut* (good) *Shabbos"* or, *"Shabbat Shalom* (Peaceful Sabbath)."

Sarina stood up and sang a simple Hebrew song that Rachel had taught her. Everyone joined in singing, "Shabbat Shalom Shabbat Shalom, Shabbat, Shabbat, Shabbat, Shalom."

Sarina's voice was so lovely and creamy; it made all the women sound beautiful. The singing soothed their souls and added a sparkle of delight. Their joyful song was sung as one beautiful rich voice praising this day of peace. Sweet little Maya played her harp like an angel.

Rifka lifted up a golden challah still warm from the stone oven. Each woman held a braid of the golden crusted loaf and echoed Rifka's words as she recited the customary blessing. When they reached *"Aumen"* (amen), they pulled the fresh sweet bread apart and fed one another. It was amazing how wonderful fresh baked bread tastes from the hand of a friend! Feeding each other bread fed their souls as well. Everyone's love level lifted.

In lighthearted play Maya challenged Sarina, "Open your mouth. I want to throw a piece of bread into it." A disapproving brow shot up to Rifka's forehead. Was her sacred ritual being mocked? Maya aimed well. The bread landed right on target; in the mouth, right on the tongue. All the women laughed and applauded.

Maybe nobody else noticed the grimace on Rifka's face, but Rachel did. As Rachel was walking around feeding women a piece of her bread, she came to Rifka. Very respectfully, she put a piece of sweet bread to Rifka's lips, leaned over, and whispered softly in her ear, "Dey are not Jewish, so vhat does it matter? It is enough dat dey share bread vid us."

Sharanii passed a wineskin of sweet fragrant wine around, one of those treasures hidden in her beautiful wagon. Where she got such amazing things no one knew. But then Sharanii was a magical creature who always surprised them.

Sharanii poured a small amount of the precious liquid into each cup and recited,

"May all the benevolent forces of the universe

watch over us and protect us
as we enter this new land.
May the gods and goddesses
of Heaven, Earth and the Underworld
bestow upon us a land
where peace is freely shared by one and all."

In the face of real wine it was hard for Rifka to stay angry at her friend for believing such crazy things. Rifka recited the Jewish prayer for wine and her temper cooled.

Real wine! Such a treasure deserved to be savored and savored it was. First, they filled their senses with the delicious fragrance; then their exploring tongues dipped into the cool sparkling liquid. The flavor, taken in tiny sips of sweet ambrosia, lazed around on their tongues. They made the pleasure last as long as possible.

Hearts full, the Baking Circle sat down beside a nice warm campfire and shared the delicious Shabbos meal they had prepared.

After dinner, Sarina sang a song in Magyar, her native tongue. Maya, who knew the tune well, wrapped the notes of her harp around Sarina's lovely voice. Soon toes were tapping and no foot was still.

Tasjia took each woman by the hand and danced with her. Her sensuous movements made everyone feel younger. She made it so easy. They were up and dancing before they could make up an excuse not to.

Soon the Baking Circle and every woman camped nearby, was standing in one long line. Slowly, very slowly, with hips touching hips, like one long snake, they danced around in a circle. One step forward, a bit to the right, one step back. Small steps, arm in arm, the women swayed gracefully.

Tasjia increased the tempo. It was a simple movement, easy to follow. The serpentine dance expanded wide, then shrunk down to a cluster, then expanded again; one long flowing tide of feminine beauty. The repetition of this one simple movement wove a contented trance around them all.

After the dance, Rachel sat down by the fire feeling warm and content. She thought the *Shekhina* must be very pleased with them for all the joy they were creating.

Rifka, sitting beside Rachel, was lost in her own thoughts. She was wondering if God was offended! Was it wrong to share the sacred Shabbos meal with *Goyim* (non-Jews)?

Meshka sank down on an old rotted log by the fire. She was all hot and *farshvitst* (sweaty) from the dancing. Sarina began to sing a song, one that Meshka knew. Just for fun, she sang along in her loud and scratchy voice. The women smiled at Meshka's enthusiasm.

Rifka lifted a critical brow, but Meshka ignored it. Meshka was not worried. She figured God was too busy to notice anything they did.

 felicidad

Flushed and excited, the women returned to their warm fire beneath a star studded heaven. Maya excitedly asked, "Rachel, please tell us a story?" and the others took up the call.

"Vhat kind of story do you vant?" Rachel asked flattered by the invitation.

"*Nu?* (well) Do you know any stories about brave women?" asked Rifka.

"Vell yes, I know a few,"

In her best storytelling voice Rachel began her *megillah* (long story). "A long time ago, there lived a great prophetess of God 'n her name vas Deborah. Nebuchadnezzar, da king of Babylon invaded da Holy Land. He captured all da Jews 'n took dem back to his city. It vas during dis time, during da Babylonian Captivity, dat Deborah lived."

Back in the old country, it was always the Rebbe who told the stories after dinner, now it was Rachel. That could never have happened if she stayed in the old ghetto in Poland, but out here in the world it seemed natural.

"God spoke to Deborah 'n told her dat da Jews should be free. He said she should go to Barak, da General of da Jews, 'n tell him to shake off dis yoke of captivity.

"Deborah vas dignified as she stood before da great general. A light vas radiating from her face dat gave power to her words, 'God has spoken to me. He said you must free us from da Babylonians.'"

Rifka watched the fire and added more wood to keep the flames high, while she listened to Rachel.

"Barak knew dat if God vas vid dem, dey would win, so he said to Deborah, 'I vill lead da people in a rebellion - if you, God's messenger, vill stand beside me in da battle.'

"Deborah vas a very brave woman. God talked to her, so she knew she vas safe. She stood right next to da general through all da bloody killing. Da Hebrews fought vell 'n dey killed all da soldiers except for one, da Babylonian General, Jabin. He ran away.

"Of course, our brave general Barak vent running after him.

"Jabin vas wounded 'n exhausted, so he looked for someplace to hide. He needed to rest, so he slipped into a tent. Dis tent happened to belong to Yael, da wife of da Hebrew General, Barak."

Maya was curled up in a blanket on the ground. Her head lay in Sarina's lap. They were listening intently to the story, while Sarina absently combed her fingers through her sweet friend's hair.

"Jabin said sternly to Yael, 'Woman, bring me something to drink! I am very thirsty.' So Yael gave him some milk.

"He said, 'Woman, I am cold.' He vas shivering, so she covered him vid a warm blanket. He said, 'Go woman! Stand by da door. If anyone comes 'n asks, say there is no man in here.' So, Yael stood by da door.

"She stood there for a long time watching da General sleep. Her eyes looked closely at every object in da tent, wondering vhat she could use to fight da big Babylonian general. She vas no traitor to her people."

Rachel paused to build the suspense, and then continued.

"Standing at da door, Yael noticed da iron tent peg at her feet vas loose. Quietly she knelt down 'n pulled da heavy metal peg up vid her two small hands. She pulled it very slowly to make no sound, den she tiptoed into da tent 'n quietly picked up a hammer dat vas lying in a corner. Quiet like a mouse, she vent to da bed vhere da exhausted general vas snoring. She took a big breath 'n held da tent peg above da man's head.

"Her heart vas making such a racket, but da General vas too asleep to hear it. In her mind Yael recited, 'Shamah Israel, Adonai, Elohanu, Adonai achad.' (Listen Israel, our God is one.)

Even in her stories, you could count on Rachel to work in a prayer praising God.

"God make her arm 'n her courage strong, Yael gave da sharp peg a very hard k-nock vid da hammer! Dat iron nail vent right through da general's thick head. One clop 'n he vas dead!

"Vhen Barak came home, Yael said proudly, 'Husband, da man you are looking for is in da tent.' He pulled back da cloth covering da door 'n there inside vas da general vid a big nail in his head.

"Da Jews va freed from da yoke of captivity by two very brave women, Deborah 'n a Yael."

Everyone loved Rachel's story. This was such a wonderful, joyful night; it was a pity to let it end; but the next day promised to bring Shabbos with its sweet lazy peace.

They all felt sorry to let the night end. They curled up in their bedrolls and were soon asleep. Sharanii and the three girls slept in the wagon. Meshka and her *Clan* were in their makeshift tents.

Meshka did not fall asleep right away. The night was too beautiful, so she stared through a little hole in her blanket at the stars above. In her mind she pleaded, "*Shekhina*, bring me a *mitzvah* (blessing). I need your help. Tomorrow I must be very brave."

Maybe she was dreaming when she saw one star start to shine more brightly than the rest. As she watched, it began to swirl around in a spiral. Other stars fell into place behind it. The dancing stars spiraled out from one center point to forever. Through the little hole, Meshka watched the dancing stars until it felt like chubby little hippos were sitting on her eyes and her lids fell closed.

I am not sure which side of a dream she was on when she heard a voice echoing through the heavens. *"Meshka, you will make your life better."* She felt the words as much as heard them.

"I am not a puppeteer sitting on a cloud pulling strings. But for each person I have decreed a special destiny, a bashert. Destiny lies in the people you meet and the events that come to pass. Seek your bashert and good things will happen."

Not that long ago, Meshka never imagined she had a destiny. She expected to spend the rest of her life washing clothes and sweeping her house.

"Take the reins of your destiny, or Fate will run away with you. The past and the future live inside you. Use them wisely. If you want a better life, make it better. You can do it with the help of your friends."

Meshka woke up happy. She was sure that her experience - be it a dream or not - was a sign. The words of the *Shekhina* came back to her, *"Make your life better. You can do it with the help of your friends."*

Meshka felt good. All her worrying flew away and she stood up a little straighter.

Rifka and Rachel were packing away their bedrolls when Joya came over to warn them! "Hide everything you have of value in your clothes!" She was familiar with border guards.

This morning Joya looked like a rainbow drunk on color. She was wearing all her pretty scarves and brightly colored skirts. She said it kept her warm and everyone believed her, except Meshka. She knew better.

All those clothes were there to hide Joya's spreading waist. Meshka was the only one who suspected Joya's secret. Rifka, having had two babies, should have recognized the signs, but she saw very little outside herself. Her grief made her blind.

"Hide my valuables?" Meshka laughed. "Vhat do I have dat anyone would vant?" As she walked towards the soldiers, she said to herself and anyone within earshot. "I carry da wisdom of da prophet Deborah in my soul 'n da courage of Yael in my heart. I can do dis. I can enter a new land 'n be da kind of person dat makes life better."

Chest up and shoulders back, Meshka walked with conviction. She stood straight and tall, as tall as her scant four feet would allow. Rachel took Meshka's arm and Rifka took the other one. Arm in arm, the three women walked forward. Their chins were raised as they bravely stepped up to the guard.

The guard was a skinny man with an ugly snarl who looked at them like they were vermin, and asked a lot of questions. Then he handed them some scripts and waved them on. The three women walked right through the checkpoint, crossed the border. Not one soldier bothered them! On foreign soil, Meshka took her shoes off and wiggled her toes. The pebbles felt just like the pebbles in Hungary! She took a deep breath, amazed that the air here smelled just like the air in Hungary!

"God 'n da *Shekhina* followed my ancestors vhen dey fled from country to country, so maybe these make-believe borders do not really mean so much. God vill be vid me in dis new land too.

I dink vee live in one big world, but men vid liddle minds draw lines between one group 'n another. Dey are like liddle boys who make up silly rules 'n squabble about dem."

Rifka crossed the border. She was immediately overcome by an intoxicating sense of freedom. At the last moment, she turned and spat on Hungarian soil. "Poi! Poi!" She blamed Hungary for creating the evil that befell her, as though such things did not happen elsewhere.

Rifka was proud and defiant until she looked back and saw the ghosts of her husband and children waving goodbye on the other side. Bitter tears came over her. She pulled her hair and wailed. "Freedom!?!"

"Poi! Poi!" She spat on the ground. "It is poison without my family."

The moment Rachel reached the other side, she started praying. She prayed, just like she did in Poland and in Hungary. Rachel was excited to thank God for bringing her safely to this new country. She found the world very exciting and everything that pleased her was another reflection of God's greatness.

Maybe the guards did not notice the three Jewish women, but Joya was not so lucky. The guard turned an interested eye on the beautiful young Gypsy girl. His hand reached up and caressed Joya's soft pink cheek. She found his touch so repulsive, her stomach fell out of her all over the guard's polished boots. He waved her on with an angry gesture.

When the mysterious pagan *Priestess* stepped forward, the guard looked her over slowly. He took in her costly silk sari trimmed in silver, the glittering jewel that crowned the sacred point between her eyes, and the dangling golden chains gracefully falling from her crown to the side of her nose.

She did not look Hungarian. The guard demanded to see Sharanii's papers.

Sharanii was expecting that. From a fold in her skirt, she drew out a collection of oddly shaped papers and tokens. Wearing a humble expression, which muted her noble features, Sharanii handed the pile to the guard.

As he flipped through this odd assortment of things, Meshka saw stamps from various countries, and was intrigued by this brief glimpse into Sharanii's mysterious past. She wondered about the elusive *Priestess* and her hidden secrets. After a bit of discussion between two officers, a lot of eyebrow raising and a few ugly smirks, the men waved her on, one jewel lighter.

Sharanii's three bright young maidens stepped forward. Sarina smiled innocently at a handsome young soldier. He frowned and looked them over a few times.

"Step over here," he said. Maya did not realize she was holding her breath, until it made her light-headed. Tasjia suddenly felt a hammer banging in her head. Sarina stood taller than the men and looked down on them with disdain.

The guard looked the girls over very carefully. Inflating his voice with authority and power, he announced, "You will be detained for a few days."

"What is wrong!?!" Sarina demanded to know, but the officer ignored her and waved them away. It was clear that such beautiful women would be detained for a long time.

Amidst tears and farewells, the Baking Circle was breaking apart. Their musical heart was left behind. In silent sadness, the other women walked on. They made camp not far down the road and waited for their friends to join them.

The days passed slowly. Shabbos came again. The Baking Circle gathered as always to make the challahs. A heavy silence hung in the air. Where were Sarina's happy songs? They kneaded the dough with lousy rhythm. It had to be lousy without Maya's harp to set the pace for their hands. Sharanii sang softly, but the emptiness swallowed up her song. All they could think about was Sarina, Tasjia, and Maya. The spirits of the three muses were present in every minute.

Amidst all this sadness, it was a wonder the bread rose at all. Without Maya's sweet harp, Tasjia's wild sensuous dances, and Sarina's songs, it was too quiet. With three bakers gone, fewer loafs of bread were made. Some of the little ones went hungry.

At *Shabbos* dinner, they recited the usual prayers, but no one sang beautiful songs and no one coaxed them to get up and dance, so everyone went to sleep early.

Come Sunday morning, Sharanii reached a decision. She was going back to see what happened to her friends. The rest of the *Clan* would not let her go alone; so, for a second time, Meshka crossed the border.

The women all dressed in dull dark colors. Sharanii wore an old dress of Rifka's over her flamboyant sari. She hid all her jewelry in the folds of her dress. The plain looking travelers approached the border from the other side. The soldiers let the women pass without a fuss.

The *Clan* made their way over to the pen where they found the three beautiful muses huddled together in fear. The girls were prisoners here, surrounded by watchful soldiers. The situation looked hopeless. The visitors offered the three muses hopeful words, reassuring hugs and a basket of roast chicken and challah. When it was time to leave, Rifka reached for Sarina and hugged her tightly. Her angry eyes were bright with held in tears. "My friend, vee vill not desert you. Vee vill rescue you. How? I do not know, but vee vill dink on it."

Sarina laughed, but there was no humor in it. After traveling so far, was their journey going to end in this wretched prison; and how long would the lecherous guards stay at bay?

രുരുരു

Chapter 11

The Rescue

Meshka dared not breathe until she was back in camp. Even though it was time to kindle the evening fire, she just sat there staring at the ground.

"I have crossed da border three times already! Dat vas not so hard. I could do dat again," she laughed and stuck her tongue between her teeth. It gave her a very impish look.

She turned to Rifka and shook her head. "Rescue!?! Vhat do vee know from dis rescue business? Nothing!" Meshka was worried.

Thinking out loud she said, "Right now I do not hear a peep from God so maybe Deborah I am not. There is no vay I am going to put a nail in a man's head, so I am not Yael either. Vhat are vee going to do? How can vee rescue our friends?"

Rifka's passionate loyalty lifted its head and she roared, "Mama, da words just jumped out of my mouth. I do not know. Vee are not women heroes, but vee have to do somethin'! Deborah 'n Yael va not da only heroes dat ever vas, va dey?"

The words came out more forcefully than she meant. Everyone looked at her startled.

"Rifka you are right. Other Jewish women va heroes too," Rachel announced. All eyes were on her. "Remember da story of Judith?" Rachel looked around the circle. All the women nodded no. "Ahh, she is a favorite of mine. Not only vas Judith a great hero, but she did it vid elegant style."

Rachel's eyes twinkled when she thought about Judith. She was such a daring woman!

Maya always asked Rachel to tell the stories. Her joy and delight drew the tales out of the storyteller. But Maya was gone. Joya, as the youngest, invited the storyteller to take them on a journey into another world and time.

"Oh please Rachel, tell us the story of Judith."

Meshka echoed, "Ya, please a story might make us feel better. Right now I feel so sad. Vee have to jump over a big wall out in da middle of da wilderness 'n vee have no ladders."

Sharanii had the fire built in a poof. The women cozened comfortably in for warmth. They loved Rachel's stories. She knew so many! Her mind was like a Rebbe's, full of God's words. She learned His holy books from listening at the knee of her *zaideh* (grandfather), a respected Rebbe in his day.

Rachel put on her storytelling voice, deep and slow, and the story unfolded. "In da time of da *Torah*, (Bible) there lived a very brave woman."

The tone of her voice wove a dreamlike calmness. They felt like children in the safety of a bedtime tale told by the fire. Her words transported them to a place and time when all crises have happy endings.

"Da Assyrians attacked da lovely city of Bet Ulla. Out of nowhere there came dis terrible army led by General Holoferns, may his name be forgotten.

"Poi! Poi!" Rifka spat on the ground to curse him.

"*Da bulvan* (a coarse boorish ox) had so many soldiers! Dey surrounded da pretty liddle city 'n cut da people off from all food 'n water. Da people va afraid dat dey va going to be kilt or worse. Afraid to die, dey panicked! Vhat could a small city do in da face of such a big force bent on destroying dem!"

The twilight gave way to darkness. No one noticed. No one cooked dinner. They were not thinking about food. They were all back in Bet Ulla worrying about the starving people.

"Surrounding da liddle city, swarms of terrifying soldiers made camp. Day after day da soldiers burned Bet Ulla's fields, so da belly of da city dried up. Night after night, da air filled vid da sweet aroma of roasting meat. Da invaders va eating up all da herds 'n da people in da city va starving."

Meshka's stomach growled and she smiled sheepishly at the others.

"Some food 'n water vas always kept in reserve within da city walls. Dat is common sense. But it vas not near enough to last thirty-four hungry days 'n thirty-four frightening nights. Dat is how long dey va in da grip of dat monster! Dey lived every day not knowing if it vas their last. Thirty-four days living vid those hungry wolves gnawing at dem from every side.

"Someone had to do something! There vas almost no water left to drink! Dey savored each drop. Food vas but crumbs 'n bits from da back of da shelf. Da old people, da frail wise ones va dying. People fell down dead in da streets 'n va covered in clouds of flies.

"Everyone vas so scared 'n no one knew vhat to do, so dey did nothing, at least nothing dat worked."

Rifka took a breath and looked around the fire at all the women wrapped in their shawls cozy and warm. She wondered if the girls in the detention camp were sitting by a fire comfortable and warm.

When Rifka visited the girls today, they put on a brave front, but she looked beyond the smile and saw that they were dirty, hungry and scared. At least the food she brought would keep them from starving.

The other young women in the pen looked quite gray. Rachel's voice brought her back to the story.

"Judith vent to da leaders of da city 'n begged dem to do something, but no one vas brave enough to face such a big army.

"So vhat did Judith do? She took her handmaiden Abra, 'n dey bravely walked out through da city gates all by themselves!

"Abra vas a strong young girl. Over each able shoulder she carried a large straw basket. One vas filled vid warm loaves of bread. In da clay pots va da most delicious foods da townspeople could pull together. Everyone took their last few crumbs 'n instead of putting it in their own mouths, not to starve, dey gave it to Abra to make into a feast."

Sharanii quietly put a pot of water on the fire to warm and sat down to cut meat and vegetables into small pieces while she listened.

"In Abra's second basket vas da softest silks, da sweetest perfumes, 'n several bottles of da strongest wine.

"Da city gates creaked opened 'n everyone held their breath as da two beautiful women walked right out into da soldier's camp all by themselves! Da surprised guards brought da two women to da general."

Everyone was totally listening to Rachel and did not even notice Sharanii. Her pot was boiling away with meat, vegetables and a few choice spices to tempt and tease the tongue.

"Da beautiful Judith tossed her head like a mare shaking herself free, smiled up at da big ugly general ever so sweetly 'n his brains fell into his pants.

"Judith whispered in a deep soft voice, 'Mighty General, please do not attack my beautiful city. I vill stay here vid you 'n vee vill make peace together.'

"Vhen a man dinks vid his pants, he vill say yes to anything."

The women laughed and nodded in knowing agreement, though their experiences with men were more imagined than real. Sharanii did not laugh, but one eyebrow curled up mischievously in a high arch and a mysterious twinkle played on her lips.

"Judith looked up through her lush dark lashes 'n cooed, 'O Mighty General, I ask only one small favor. Every night please let me 'n my maid take our dings 'n go alone down to da river to bathe. I vant to be fresh 'n smell sweet for you in each morning.'"

Rifka wrinkled her nose at the idea of flirting with the enemy, "How repulsive!"

Joya found it frightening, but she was only a child of fifteen.

Meshka smiled, but luckily no one noticed.

"For three days da people made weapons inside da gate, while da soldiers polished theirs outside it. Judith stayed vid da Assyrian general, may his bones rot in hell.

"Poi! Poi!" Rifka spat on him, down in hell.

"Dat night after dark, Judith carried a torch to light da vay 'n her handmaiden carried da two baskets. Dey vent down to da river to bathe. Da general told da guards to let dem go. He vas sure she would not escape."

Meshka was wondering what Judith did with the General, other than feed him and dance for him. Rachel did not say and Meshka was much too shy to ask, but she wondered.

"While Judith bathed in a lush pond, Abra slipped away to a small door in da city gate. Hidden under a thick bush of vines, da wooden door opened into a garden. Over by da fragrant red roses she passed her message on to da people. Word spread at lightning speed from mouth to mouth. Every man, woman, 'n child in da city vas holding their breath, praying dey would live one more day."

Rachel took a breath to build the suspense. She sniffed the delicious stew and was surprised! No one saw Sharanii make it so the food just appeared out of nowhere.

"After da third night, da guards va used to Judith 'n Abra coming 'n going to their ritual bath."

The dainty hands of the elegant Sharanii were at home in everything she did, even something as mundane as cooking.

"Abra prepared a special feast for da general 'n da lovely Judith arranged herself. Her long silken hair floated in amber curls over her voluptuous young body draped in spun gold. Sweetly scented vid sensuous perfume, Judith fed da fat ugly general tender bites of food 'n poured for him cup after cup of very strong wine. Hungrily he devoured it all."

Between the tempting aroma of the stew and all this talk of food, the women were getting hungry.

"Vhen da bottle vas empty, da general passed out. His eyes va closed 'n he vas snoring. Judith vas scared, but she vas also very brave. Vid trembling hands, she picked up his sword 'n raised it high above his head. Vid all her might, she brought da sharp blade down on his neck!

"His head vent flying off 'n rolled under da bed. It vas really disgusting!"

Rifka was shocked. Again when the man falls asleep, the woman hero goes for his head! Is there no other way for women to overcome men? Rifka thought Judith should have used poison. It was a lot less messy.

"Judith picked up da ugly head, wrapped it in a tablecloth, 'n put it in one of Abra's baskets. Den she 'n her handmaiden stepped out of da general's tent into da night, just da vay dey always did.

"She greeted da guard 'n said nicely, 'Da general does not vant to be bothered until morning.' Vid a sweet smile 'n a knowing wink she added, 'He drank a lot of wine 'n vhen he wakes up, he is going to feel mean.'

"Den da women walked away as though dey va going to da pond to bathe, but really dey vent back to da city through da hidden garden door.

A light flurry of snow began to fall, but the women paid it no mind. After December in the mountains, no one noticed the snow until it began to pile up on their noses.

"Inside da city, da people hung da general's head from da front gate. Vhen da soldiers woke up in da morning 'n saw da dead general's eyes staring down at dem from da gate, dey va so scared, dey ran all da vay back to their own faraway land.

"Judith 'n Abra va real heroes! Their courage saved da lives of a whole city!" Rachel sighed deeply. Telling stories always made her feel a little light-headed. Sharanii applauded Rachel and rewarded her with a bowl of delicious steaming stew.

When everyone had a warm bowl on their laps Meshka said, "Rachel, my dear friend, dat is a good story. Dank you for telling it. It made me feel braver. I wonder which one of us is going to seduce da guard 'n cut off his head? It has been a long time since any man vanted to slip under my skirts," Meshka joked and everyone laughed.

Joya shuddered at the thought of a soldier touching her.

Rifka was utterly sickened by the story. "War is disgustin'!" she muttered to herself aloud.

"Maybe vee are not all like Judith, but vee are each brave. Let us dink on it 'n see vhat vee can make up," Rachel proposed.

Meshka put in her two cents, "You know, Judith I am not, but a handmaiden, maybe I could be. I like da part vhere she vent to bathe every night. Being so familiar vid something can make a man blind. Dey dink dey know, so dey do not look."

The *Om Shante'* (blessing of heart), which Sharanii put into everything she touched, made her stew warm their souls as well as their bellies with every bite.

ରେଉେଉେ

The three Jewish women, the Gypsy girl, and the pagan *Priestess* all took turns crossing back and forth into Hungary to visit the three young maidens held captive. They each choose a different time of day, so soon they formed a clear picture of the soldiers' daily routine.

The following Shabbos, Rifka, Meshka, and Rachel walked slowly across the border to visit the girls. When they were leaving Hungary, Meshka leaned close to the young guard and said sincerely, "You look like a nice young man, like my son, Yonkle. He vas kilt. I am visiting some very sweet girls. Do you have sisters? Yes? Vell, these girls are good girls, like your sisters. Please help dem. Make da problem go away, so dey can come vid us."

The guard laughed and said, "It is not my decision. It is up to the general and he will not see you."

With make-believe surprise Meshka cooed, "Such a smart young man, I thought you va da general!" The young guard laughed at the silly old woman, but he was flattered despite himself. She smiled and handed the border guard one of her famous delicious challahs, fresh from the oven.

Rifka, Meshka, and Rachel walked together the next day. On the way back, Meshka asked the same guard his name. "Gasper Fernetti," he said smartly, with an edge of authority in his voice.

"Gasper, I am pleased to meet you," Meshka gushed. "You look like a good man. May I introduce you to my daughter Rifka 'n my dear friend Rachel? Ladies, say hello to da nice young man." Then with a girlish giggle and fluttering lashes she asked, "Do you vant to see my papers?"

He replied firmly, "Yes!" She handed him her papers.

While he was looking them over, she twittered to the other women in her most charming voice, "Every day vhen I come by, I say hello, 'n Gasper here asks me to show him my papers. He cannot remember from one day to da next who I am. He needs to see my papers every day. Does Gasper dink one day maybe I vill be different? Maybe I vill become young 'n pretty 'n all these wrinkles vill go away."

The women laughed and the young soldier blushed. He pretended not to hear them. He gave their papers a quick glance and waved them on.

The next day, the three women approached the same guard and Meshka said very very sweetly, "Hello Gasper, are you having a good day?" With a fawning look she added, "Do you vant to see my papers again?" Then turning to the others, she added coquettishly, "Every day Gasper looks at me 'n my papers. My late husband, Meyer, God rest his soul, did not look at me as much as dis nice young soldier does." She looked up into the young man's eyes and said in her sweetest teasing voice, "Gasper do I still look da same?" The soldier did not respond. He barely glanced at her papers as he waved her on.

The next day when Meshka was leaving Hungary, she smiled sweetly at the soldier and asked excitedly, "Hello Gasper, how are you? Do you vant to see my papers again?" The young man mumbled, "Yes."

As the women walked away, another guard said teasingly, "Who is your new girlfriend?"

The changing of the guard came predictably every day at twilight. The three Jewish women walked across the border into Hungary sometime in the late afternoon, but always came back a short while afterwards carrying some bundles in their arms. It was on those return trips in the evening that Meshka made eyes at the guard. He became used to seeing them go by.

Joya always walked across the border alone with downcast eyes. Plumped out with layers of clothes, she quietly showed the guards her papers and drew very little notice.

The day came, under a bright and beautiful sunset, when the soldier waved them on without a word or a glance at their papers.

The time to rescue their friends was at hand! The next day, Tuesday was cool and damp. After an icy rain there was still a wet chill in the air. The morning edged by in nervous seconds. In the late afternoon, Meshka, Rifka and Rachel gave Joya the old dress they were wearing and their shawls. Joya gathered them up and put them all on. On top of that, she wore all her colorful scarves. Wearing so many clothes made her look really chubby.

Rachel freely gave Joya her dress, but found it hard to part with her *Bubba's* shawl.

Joya waddled jauntily along enjoying the adventure. This was the first time since the world ended that she felt really alive! She approached the guard with downcast eyes. Uncle Alberto taught her well. He used to say, "When you want to fool a pompous man who thinks he rules the world, keep your eyes and chin down. Let him think you are meek, so he pays you no mind. The more he thinks you are nobody, the more he will help you rob him."

Joya sauntered past the guards. Inside the camp she found the three lost maidens huddled together, too keyed up to speak. Despite the wild pounding of their hearts, they sat together until twilight cast its illusions. One by one, the Hungarian girls quietly slipped behind the outhouse and put on the clothes Joya brought them.

Sarina was tall and graceful. Lucky for them, Rifka was tallish. If Sarina hunched down a little, it was almost a match. Well, maybe not as much a match as they hoped. It worried them a bit.

Maya and Tasjia were both small, but not as short as the two old women, so they had to hunch down even more. For the next hour they practiced waddling around like old ladies. Their exaggerated gestures were ridiculous. Joya wanted to laugh, but of course she did not. This was serious business. If they were caught escaping, the soldiers might shoot them!

After a while their waddling looked sort of real. Time was running out, so Joya decided they were ready.

"I hope he doesn't hear my heart. It is banging against my chest like a desperate bird," Maya said breathlessly.

"Do not worry, Meshka's heart often sounds like that," Joya reassured her.

The three young Magyar women slowly *schlepped* (dragged) along towards the border guard. They were waddling a short ways behind Joya. The Gypsy girl showed her papers to Gasper and said excitedly, "What strong hands you have! May I read your fortune?"

With a quick wave of his hand, he gestured no, but she persisted. "Ahh, too bad, I see a lot of money written there."

The guard looked around to see if his superiors were watching. Reassured that no one would see, he opened his palm to Joya. "I see you holding a hand of cards and you are winning a lot of money. What a nice love line you have." He listened with great interest. The three hunched women, with their shawls drawn tight across their faces waited impatiently behind Joya. Gasper waved them by with hardly a glance. He was too busy giving his full attention to the fortuneteller.

Breathless and intoxicated with their freedom so close at hand, the young maidens fought the urge to run. With great restraint they slowly, very slowly waddled down the road to the place where the other women were waiting.

CRCRCR

Sharanii and the Jewish women were packed and ready to go. Everyone was anxious to get far away from that place, but first, Rachel had to put on her *Bubba's* silk shawl. She was so nervous. She felt terribly naked and exposed without it.

Rachel held the pure white shawl lovingly. Warm relief moved through her as she prayed to her dead grandmother for forgiveness. She apologized for letting a *shiksa* (non-Jewish female) wear her shawl. Then Rachel wrapped her shawl, her *Bubba's* arms, tightly around her shivering shoulders.

The girls changed back into their own clothes. No one noticed that Meshka and Rifka both looked at their shawls for several long minutes before they covered themselves up again.

Meshka picked up the goat's lead rope and walked on.

Rifka picked up the handles of the wooden cart and pulled it along.

Rachel and her sweet tempered pony trotted behind the cart.

Next in procession came Sarina sitting on the wagon bench with the reins in hand, and the other maidens once again hiding in Sharanii's wagon, fleeing for their lives.

Joya changed into her most invisible clothes and Sharanii wore no jewelry, other than the Jewel of Wisdom between her eyes. The two humbly dressed women lagged behind the others watching for soldiers.

When darkness was beginning to swallow up the day, the Baking Circle made camp beside a creek. They put up one large shelter between four tall wide pine trees and huddled close inside for warmth and reassurance. The women were too exhausted to celebrate, everyone fell sleep early.

CRCRCR

Meshka was wide awake. She lay huddled next to Rachel who was a little furnace, she was warm and comfortable, but much too excited to sleep.

A churning power was welling up in Meshka. She wanted to explode! She disentangled herself from her sleeping partners and carefully inched her way over and around the sleeping women to go outside.

The land was still covered with snow. Meshka felt the absence of little creatures scurrying about in the unearthly stillness of this snow covered night. Its beauty cast a dreamlike spell over Meshka.

A great white owl in a pine tree above the tent stared down at her. Minutes passed as both stood motionless gazing at the other with piercing stares. The majestic bird gave a commanding "Hoot!" and flew away under a great expanse of wing.

Meshka watched him fly, fascinated by the vastness of God's sky. That was how big this day was for her. The magnitude of this day hit Meshka on the head like a stick.

Pictures of this wild crazy journey flashed through her mind. Meshka found a comfortable green tuft of grass under a big tree beside the stream and *plotzed* down (drop from exhaustion).

She looked up at the heavens and bragged to God, "You see, I am not such a useless old person after all." A sense of power was surging through her. Meshka grew several inches taller right on the spot, at least in her own mind.

Meshka and her small band of women were camped alone on a cold dark night in an unknown foreign country and Meshka was not scared.

She was utterly horrified and totally delighted by what she had done! The icy cold absurdity of their little band rescuing the three girls from the guards, tickled her. Meshka laughed. She laughed and laughed until the tears ran down her face in joy.

The rescue plan was her idea and it worked! Pride rippled through her chest.

Meshka looked at how the plan unfolded and savored each moment. She woke up the morning after hearing Judith's story knowing what they had to do. It was her idea, sort of, not really. You see, when she went to sleep, she asked Yonkle to tell her a wise thing to do to save her friends. In the morning when she woke up, the idea jumped into her head in Yonkle's voice. At breakfast, Meshka shared the plan with the women and they agreed to do it.

It really worked! She was so excited; she had to tell someone so she called out, "God, I need to talk vid You. Do You still know me? I am Meshka, remember me? I hardly know myself anymore.

The brisk chill of the pure fresh air made her feel alive!

"All my life, I vas dis liddle person dat everyone pitied. Now look at me, I am a hero person! Dis life You gave me is so amazing!

Meshka was buoyant! She may be an old woman, a penniless peasant, and a vagabond, but she was also a hero.

"God, You would not believe all da amazing dings I have been feeling. First I vent round 'n round dinking dis plan vas not going to work. I vas afraid vee would all be kilt 'n dead right now!"

She watched the water gurgle under a thin sheet of ice in the stream for a minute before she spoke again, "I never said a frightened word to anyone. You know me God, I cannot keep a secret for even a minute, but all through da rescue, I said only good dings to make everyone feel brave. I did not lie. I just stretched da truth a liddle thin."

Meshka had an urge to crack the ice and hear it tinkle, just for fun, like she used to do when she was a child.

"God, dis afternoon I had to save my friends, so I took off my shawl, she confessed. "You know, I wore dat shawl every day of my life since I became a married woman. I vas sixteen den 'n You know how old I am now! I thought dis is da dime vhen old women disappear into da woodwork 'n nobody knows from dem anymore."

Meshka's hand touched a rock. She threw it hard into the water. The ice shattered in a musical symphony of tinkling and gurgling sounds.

With a snicker, she said, "God, I do not understand You! Your plan is dat I lose everything 'n den I find myself! Do not get angry now," she put her hands together in respect, "but I dink dat is a mean joke. I used to have a good family - a husband, a mama, a papa, children, grandchildren, 'n lots of *mishpokha*. (relatives)

Meshka picked up a piece of cracked ice and began sucking on it. She was thirsty and it felt refreshing on her lips. She felt a little drained as she thought about the past.

"You know, my family 'n I va like threads woven together in a net. I held my thread 'n everybody else held deirs. Each thread stayed in its place. Together vee wove da net dat vas our lives.

"Den Your wild forces tore da net. Dere va no more threads to hold onto. God, look! You cast me out into dis wild country. You know, I am not holding those threads anymore 'n dey are not holding me!

"Now for da first time I feel different. I tell you, something really amazing happened to me! God, do I look different? Am I still me?"

Meshka felt a little bruised; a chick cracking through its own shell, all matted and disheveled on the verge of being beautiful.

"Maybe it is like Rachel said. I could ask myself, vhat do I vant to do? God, would You let me do dat?" She giggled like a young girl and tingled all over.

Lightning did not strike her, no bush started burning, not even a shower of hail stones rained down, so Meshka figured God did not mind, which was almost the same as having His permission.

A sense of freedom came over her in chilling waves. She shuddered. This was so frightening and so exciting! Meshka felt the solid support of the grass beneath her *tush* (backside). She wrapped her arms around her knees and rocked back and forth like she used to when she was a girl.

Meshka's mind sailed back to this morning. It was a long time ago. The day started on the run. She was up and doing before her eyes were open. When she removed her shawl, she expected to feel awkward and exposed like Rachel who *kvetched* (complained) about feeling naked at least three times.

Although Meshka would not admit it, not even to Rachel, she felt thrilled! She assumed it was wrong to feel so good and it bothered her a little. The world looked brighter without the blinders of the shawl. She felt young and free as though anything could happen. For this one day Meshka felt fearless.

CRCRCR

The Baking Circle woke up joyfully chattering. They were free!

Sarina was laughing, "The soldiers will not pursue us, why should they care? We are not important. They can always take more women. Why waste their important time searching for us?" She was ready to celebrate! Maya plucked the strings of her sweet harp ringing with the flutter of angel wings. Her mama always said, "The perfect way to start a day is by making music."

Sarina sang a joyous song to freedom and they all happily joined in singing the refrain. Even Meshka sang with gusto.

The lovely Tasjia sensuously swayed and whirled. Her lithe body rode the waves of music. Her spirit soared to crests of joy in leaping waves of folly.

Sweet Maya taught the *Bakers* the funny words of an old Magyar tune. The song told of a fox that disguises himself as a chicken, but could not find a way into the henhouse. The funny, fumble silliness of the fox, made everyone laugh heartily. The women were in a sparkling light mood.

Danger! Their songs stopped! Their heartbeats stopped! The sound of swift running horses turned them to stone. They quickly scrambled off the road and crouched down low beside big branchy logs.

Rifka pulled, pushed, and wedged the little cart under thick crimson bushes. Sharanii hid the big wagon in the deep shadows of the forest, behind a thick stand of trees. Rachel's heart was pounding; where could she hide her pony and little cart?

"Come hide in the shadows of my wagon," suggested Sharanii. "You will be safe."

The horsemen rode close by, but the women blended into the silhouettes of the forest. Of course Joya's vivid colors could be seen for miles, so Meshka draped her dark woolen shawl over Joya and she too disappeared into the ground. Each woman struggled to shush the loud throbbing of her heart.

The men rode right past them! Nobody breathed for a long minute. Then they all sighed with relief and climbed out from their hiding places.

They were picking twigs and leaves out of their hair and brushing them off their skirts when Sharanii said, "The soldiers will be back, we must change clothes again."

Sharanii had a basket of eggs and a plan. The eggs came from a young Russian woman as a gift to the *Priestess* for curling her hair. Sharanii mixed up the eggs with a handful of dirt and smeared the ugly mixture all over the young women's faces. In a few minutes the eggs dried, hardened, and cracked. They looked really sick and ugly.

Poor Rachel had to surrender her precious silk shawl again. *Oy, a shkandal!* (oh, what a scandal!) Being parted from her shawl was like being torn away from her *Bubba* and from her home. Inside the shawl, Rachel felt safe no matter where she was or who she was with; but being naked like this was really scary!

Meshka was thrilled! She was excited to put on Tasjia's wide swirling green skirt and pretty peasant blouse. There was a definite skip in her step. Sharanii even brushed her long wavy silver hair one hundred strokes, so her hair shimmered like silk. She was both glad and disappointed that there were no men around to admire her.

The poor young maidens were having a hard time resisting the urge to scratch their faces. The muck felt awfully itchy.

They traveled until mid-afternoon, by then everyone was tired. Rifka scouted around and found a small clearing in a grove of elm trees. It looked well hidden, a safe place, so the tired women curled up and were out cold in a flash.

No one slept very much the night before with all the nervous excited excitement, so the exhausted women fell into a deep afternoon snooze. They were still sleeping when the horsemen returned!

The sound of snorting horses clopping along woke them up. Before they could move, the men rode up to them.

Sharanii was the first to wake up. She jumped to her feet. Thinking fast, she shouted. "Welcome soldiers. Have you come to protect us from the robbers? I saw three suspicious looking people running through the bushes. I was afraid they were going to rob us."

"No," answered an officer in a fancy uniform. "We are looking for female criminals who escaped from a detention camp. Everyone stand up and let us have a look at you!" the officer ordered.

Before the groggy women could respond, Sharanii cried out, "Kind Sir, I beg you, let the old ones stay in their bedrolls, they are very sick. I am afraid they have the plague."

Meshka opened her eyes and saw a whole bunch of huge horses with big yellow teeth, looming above her huddled body! That got her heat beating! Even so, Meshka stood up gracefully for she was wearing a young maiden's clothes and felt beautiful.

Rachel, Rifka and Meshka rose to their feet. Rachel kept her bedroll wrapped around her head and shoulders to hide her naked head. Even though Rachel was fully clothed, without her shawl, she felt naked and vulnerable!

The fancy officer looked at Sharanii. The exotic *Priestess* was bedecked in a fine silk sari adorned with tiny stitches of gold. Golden chains dripped from her crown to her nose, a small brilliant emerald sparkled from her Eye of Wisdom. Her face radiated a force, a radiant light, a noble grandeur that was daunting!

The fancy fellow shrank before her. He quickly turned his attention on softer prey. His eyes ran over the three Jewish women.

When he came to Meshka, she was standing proudly with her chin defiantly raised. His eyes widened. They lost their usual carrion glare and took on a saucy sparkle. She looked like a magical creature out of a fairy tale with her great abundance of youthful silver curls flowing over her pretty shoulders.

Seated on the horse next to the fancy officer was Gasper! Hot terror shot through Meshka's veins! She struggled to keep her breath even and her composure calm.

Would he recognize her? He had seen her many times at the border. But did he ever really see her? She was a bent old woman hidden in a colorless shawl. She bore no resemblance to this wild looking creature in a bright green ruffled dancing skirt, a pretty white blouse with puffed sleeves, and a tightly laced tunic decorated with embroidered flowers.

The officer, a self-important man, turned to Gasper. "Soldier," he spat out the words, "are these the missing women? His angry tone made it clear, he was holding the young fellow accountable for the loss of the prisoners. Gasper shook his head and formally replied, "No Sir!"

The fancy officer waved his hand and towards the huddled women crouching in the grass. "Check those women! See if you recognize them."

V-e-r-y slowly Gasper moved towards the huddled lumps wrapped in their shawls. He was terrified! Everyone had heard the rumors that a horrible plague was sweeping across the land.

The three figures lying curled up in the grass tried to really look sick. A good thing they were so scared, otherwise someone would have laughed. Maya was drooling. Her lower lip was hanging loose and stupid. Tasjia, who had trouble looking anything but gorgeous, was sunk deep into the folds of her shawl. Her golden cat eyes were crossed and looking upward. Sarina was smiling like an idiot, covering all her fine white teeth with her tongue.

Finally Gasper was standing over the three huddled figures. He took a deep breath to quiet his nerves. He did not want the officer see how scared he was, but he was really terrified of touching these dark ominous lumps of cloth.

"Go ahead soldier. What are you waiting for?" The fancy officer sounded threatening. Gasper reached out and pulled back Maya's shawl! He froze with shock when he saw her face! She smiled that stupid drooling smile of hers. Gasper jumped back in horror at her hideously wart encrusted face!

If you heard his screams, you would have thought the Devil himself had burned him. Gasper's legs could not take off fast enough.

"Plague! Plague!" Gasper shrieked as he jumped onto his horse. The soldiers galloped quickly away without even a word of goodbye.

CRCRCR

Chapter 12

The Goddess Speaks

Free and safe under the brilliant light of a full moon, Meshka's body was comfortably tucked into her warm bedroll. Now that the Baking Circle was safe, she was free to travel through to the faraway land of dreams.

In the magical realm where mind and spirit dance, Meshka was no longer an old woman! She was just a little *pitsele*, a little waif, a baby cradled in her mama's arms rocking back and forth.

Her sweet baby body felt fuzzy and warm as little Meshkala listened to the creaking runners on the old wooden rocking chair and the crackle of the fire in the hearth beside them. A warm glow of love filled her whole body and made her yawn contentedly.

The dream pictures changed.

The blissful feeling was still there, but now she was older, a maiden brushing her hair beside a clear still pond. She was looking at her reflection in water, as still as glass, and smiled at her own beautiful young face.

As the lovely young Meshka, she caressed her silky hair and admired its many shades of copper and gold. Each bouncy curl framed her pretty young face. It was a quiet peaceful moment.

Suddenly an angry lion jumped out from behind a bush and roared at her, "Vain woman! Vanity is a sin!"

Startled, the young woman looked up into the ferocious eyes of the beast and laughed in such a charming way that the lion roared one more time with all his dignity and then slinked away.

Her eyes returned to her lovely young reflection. With an old woman's heart, she tenderly savored the flawless dew of her youth. The lovely young maiden closed her eyes savoring the sweet perfection of this moment.

When she opened them again, She was gazing down at the earth from the sky. Soft pink cushy clouds floated around Her. From Her high perch, She looked down upon a young maiden sitting by a pool. A strong wave of compassion washed over Her.

With a mama's heart, She yearned to ease the young maiden's journey through the losses that would come. She felt the regret all mamas feel when they realize they cannot soften their sweet children's paths. Each person must walk their own destiny according to Fate's decree!

From high in the sky, Meshka said, "Sometimes da hottest fires forge da strength to survive." The maiden looked around. She thought she heard something.

Meshka's breath came out like a breeze carrying Her words from above. "Be safe. Walk between da raindrops." Again the maiden looked around and wondered if she really heard words on the wind.

From *Her* lofty perch, *Her* cloak slipped off *Her* shoulders and floated on a light breeze down to the earth. *She* gazed at it questioningly. It was no longer a cloak. It appeared to be a mask of some kind.

From on high, *She* reached down to pick it up and found it was not a mask at all! It was an empty shell of skin from an old woman. *She* had the distinct feeling it was someone *She* knew, but *She* could not remember who.

Speaking to the maiden by the pond, from Her place among the clouds She said, *"My dear Meshkala, I have given you da gift of beauty. I want you to celebrate your life. Do not scorn My gifts. Do not hide dem. You are not vain, you are lovely."*

Meshka woke up with a start. The dream was so real! Her body tingled in the sweetest way. Wonderful warm feelings tickled her. She remembered being both the girl and *The Goddess*.

A dark cloud passed through her mind. She worried that her thoughts were blasphemous! She fell back onto her pillow. Well, not really a pillow. It was just her long heavy underpants and an underskirt rolled up together, but Meshka found it downy soft.

Slowly the enormity of her dream sank in. Meshka's eyes fell closed. She floated back into the dream. Again she felt her mamma's arms embracing her, warm cushy breasts cradling her, a baby loved and adored. A warm creamy feeling melted through her whole body. Content, she yearned to crawl back into the dream and stay there forever.

ଔଔଔ

The frosty dawn was waiting. A hearty bird with a noble blue crown of feathers was singing, rejoicing in the wonder of a newborn day. He was calling Meshka, inviting her to wake up and join in this glorious life. She was reluctant to leave the dream, but excited to meet the day. Meshka crawled out of her bedroll and put on a couple of old woolen dresses to keep warm.

On her feet, she took a deep breath, stretched, and grabbed the water bags. She was half way to the stream before she realized, she had forgotten to put on her shawl.

Meshka settled herself beside the gurgling water and watched the current rush in and out of ice caves in the stream. She was filled with a wonderful joy just being alive.

The crisp air and clear blue sky heightened her pleasure. In this happy mood, she sat down for her morning talk with God.

"God, I had da most amazing dream!" She exclaimed as she lowered a water bag into the stream.

Quietly she sat waiting for her water bag to fill, listening to the crackling of leaves dancing in a sudden swirling breeze. Angry words crackled among the leaves, "Woman, beware of the Devil's tricks. Dreams can tempt you in wicked ways."

Meshka's heart sank. As fast as she could, she filled the other water bag. She had no desire to linger. As soon as both bags were filled, she scooped them up and stomped back to camp.

All the way up the side of the ravine, she *kvetched* to herself. She grumbled about God's attitude, men's attitudes, and women's never ending enslaving yoke.

Meshka loved her dreams. They were like windows into another world. The pictures in her dreams helped her understand life better. Without their guidance, her life would never make sense. She really liked the sweet, sometimes erotic pleasure that lingered long after the dream ended. Such a dream could spill over into the next day and paint a plain morning in delicious colors. How can dreams be evil? They added so much to her life.

"Give up my dreams!?!" Meshka was all chewed up with aggravating thoughts, so she was not watching where her feet were going. She should have paid more attention. After all, she was carrying two heavy water bags and scrambling over sharp rocks. I guess it comes as no surprise that she went *plotz*, face down, right in a big mud puddle. The dirty water splashed all over her!

Sputtering muddy water, Meshka lifted her dripping face and clearly heard God say, "Thou shalt not Kvetch!"

Meshka wiped the mud from her eyes and started to laugh. What a sight she must be! The laughter made the anger disappear. She grabbed the bags and tried to save a little of the precious water, but it all spilt out.

Back to the stream she went, lowered her bags into the water for a second time, and leaned back against a tree to wait for them to fill. The sun was just peeking over the horizon in a riot of colors.

Meshka closed her eyes and tried to slip back into the delicious feeling of this morning's dream. She was just sinking into warm creamy comfort, when she felt someone watching her. At first she thought a woman had come to the water to bathe, but the presence did not move, so she opened her eyes.

Now whether those eyes opened into the day or into another dream, I cannot say for sure. But there standing before her was *The Goddess*, the same giant dark-haired beauty who invited her to join the refugees.

Gazing down at the sweet little woman sitting by the creek, *The Goddess* said in a powerful voice, **"I am The Goddess, Mother of Life. Do not shrink yourself to fit the molds of Gods or men."**

Meshka jumped to her feet awkwardly. Flustered, embarrassed, and so itzy-bitsy next to this magnificent giant, she timidly asked, "*Goddess*, are you da woman part of da Holy Von?"

"I am The Mother of Life, Mother of the Earth, and Mother of God." *She* whispered softly and still its ringing echo resounded through her senses.

In a humble voice Meshka apologized, "Oy, *Holy Mother*, please forgive me."

"There is nothing to forgive, My child. You are a delight, just the way you are. I ask only that you fill each moment with love. When you miss the mark, know an ill wind blew you astray. Try again.

"Life has its cycles. Some moments are chaotic. They just are. Anything that happens in those moments will be difficult; any words spoken will easily miss the mark. Notice and know it is not you. It is just the color of the moment. Do not mistake the messenger for the message."

Meshka was so drawn into The Goddess's amazing dark eyes, she forgot to be frightened. She just listened, like a child enchanted listens at her sweet grandma's knee.

"Life does not have separate moments. Every moment is part of a bigger pattern. Every part of your life is part of your path. Challenges polish you into the kind of person you need to be to fulfill your destiny."

Meshka looked so young at that moment, a little woman with a sweet simple expression on her face and the freshness of a child.

In a small voice Meshka asked, *"Holy Mother,* vhat do you vant vid me?"

"My daughter, feel My love. I want to radiate love into the world through you. You will inspire and guide women. Midwife My daughters. Help them give birth to themselves. Help them do it over and over again, because their lives are going to keep changing."

Meshka felt the meaning of these words deep in her heart but her mind was *farblondzhet* (lost and confused). Reality was spinning! The meaning of the words were so important, she could not hold them inside her mind! But she could feel them. Each word was etched in her heart.

"I want you to create a more loving world. Women can put an end to all the conflicts! Learn to make peace inside yourself. Learn to make peace with the people around you. After that; you will be ready to make peace in the world."

Meshka's back was bent, weary, and tired. She was already carrying the weight of the world on it, so she kvetched,

"Oy, *Goddess,* I am just a liddle old woman. Vhat can I do!? Before you choose me, you should talk vid God. He vill tell you vhat a troublemaker I am.

"Maybe you should pick someone vid a liddle more *saykhel* (common sense) or maybe someone vid more spring in her step. You know I am no spring chicken."

Smiling at the adorable little creature before Her, *The Goddess* said softly, *"You are whatever you think you are. Inside you is My Eternal Presence. I am the love that lives within you. I am the love that hungers to be shared. I am the Life Force pouring through your veins. I am the turbulent process of life."*

The image of *The Goddess* quivered gently and faded into a wisp of mist. The soft mist floated pleasantly up Meshka's nose. It kind of tickled. Meshka looked down at herself and saw a soft glow radiating from her *pupik.* (belly button) Confused by all the sweet feelings sloshing around inside her, Meshka gathered up her water bags and returned to camp.

All the people were awake now, busily going about their preparations for the new day. Meshka looked at the people so intent on what they were doing no one noticed the soft glow radiating from each person. The people wore many different costumes, represented many different cultures, different religious ideas, and different races, and yet, the same wonderful glow of spirit was shining from each one! All these people were just like her. They too were driven by needs and desires. They too were being spun about by their tails riding surging tides of *Life.*

Meshka put the water bags down and leaned back against a tree to think on this. Once the lids dropped, she dozed off! A few minutes later she opened her eyes and the people just looked like they normally did. She wondered, did they change or did she lose the ability to see the glow?

ೞೞೞ

The three escaped women woke up in a buoyant mood after a sweet night filled with intoxicating dreams of freedom.

Sarina dreamed she was sitting on a swing hanging from the heavens. All around her were the star strewn heavens. The swing rushed forward, she laughed, and kicked a twinkling star.

Tasjia found her beloved Petrov waiting for her in a sweet dream. They were floating, just the two of them in a sailing ship on a wide wide sea. The shimmering blue of the sea gave her a tingle. Blue like his eyes and the deep well of love she saw in them.

Maya dreamed of Marji. They were picking herbs in a wet marsh. Marji's feet became tangled in the weeds, but Maya set her free. They found their way onto dryer land and skipped along holding hands.

The three muses woke up thrilled to be free. Everything felt alive and rich on this special morning. Even, and especially, the fresh air they breathed.

They gathered round the campfire and found Meshka sitting there giggling to herself. She was tickled to be alive. There were so many times yesterday when she thought she was going to be killed.

What intrigued Meshka most, from all her adventures yesterday, were her feelings. She was tickled to shed her shawl. It felt great! She felt a rush just thinking of Tasjia's bright green skirt with its frivolous ruffle along the hem and its saucy sway when she moved. Oh how free she felt! No heavy woolen skirts to drag through the mud. No more hiding in a dark cavernous interior of her shawl. Meshka craved the sun outside the shawl!

She liked bouncing around in Tasjia's pretty skirt and frilly blouse, making believe she was a young maiden. It felt exciting to be exposed to the world like that! Everything was brighter! Everything looked closer! Everything was different. She did not want to peek out at a scary world from inside a dark shawl. She wanted to be a part of life, not a watcher of life. Such feelings! It scared her, but it was a nice kind of scared. Her heart stood on edge and she liked the feeling.

Meshka had a charming little skip to her step. If years have weight, a few just fell off her shoulders.

ଓଯଓଯଓଯ

They walked with a new spring in their step. Without all the crowds of people around them, they moved pretty fast. Even the stubborn little goat seemed to skip along without much coaxing. In just a few days they reached the stragglers following behind the great procession. The day was drawing to a glorious end. Any day spent in freedom after tasting bondage is glorious.

The women were relieved to be with the *Seeders* again, safe again. They made camp quickly before dusk surrendered them into the darkness of night.

Meshka set to kindling the fire and Rifka soon had a stew-pot bubbling on the flames. Meshka was stirring the pot so the bottom would not stick. She liked the feel of the big wooden spoon in her hand. Rifka carved it, of course. Rifka was always carving little designs on everything.

Meshka drank in the wonderful aroma. She idly watched her hand go round and round stirring the bubbling pot. Her mind drifted off and away, skipping from one memory to another, stepping stones through a stream of good feelings. As she idly watched her hand go round and round, a beautiful voice called her name. She looked up to see which of her friends called to her, but she was alone. That was puzzling.

Meshka waited to hear her name called again. All was quiet. She went back to idly watching her hand go round and round in the big bubbling pot. A beautiful soft voice of creamy smooth honey whispered, *"You are My daughter."*

Meshka sat bold upright! Her eyebrows jumped to the top of her head! Her eyes got so big! Her mouth was open catching flies! She looked around for the joker playing tricks on her!

"My beautiful daughter, be yourself, in all your raw beauty."

Meshka was sitting by a campfire no more than a spitting distance from someone else's campfire. She was terrified and angry, and awestruck, all at the same time.

It was one thing to secret away to a private place where she felt the sacredness, far away from people, to talk with God. It was quite different to hear *The Goddess* talking to her right in the middle of cooking dinner! Surrounded by a crowd of people, she felt on display. This was more than being naked! Everyone was staring at her, or so she imagined. It was scary!

"You are talking to me right here in camp!" She shouted in her mind, but did not say a word. She smiled at the people around her hoping her friendly smile would mask the madness. "*Goddess*, people vill see! Why are you doing dis to me?" She whispered under her breath.

Her eyes darted to a tall black couple on one side of her. They were busy making a fire. Then she glanced over at the little almond eyed people putting up a tent on her other side. Could they hear the voice too!?! They were all busy with their tasks and paid neither her nor *The Voice* any mind.

"My daughter, you will be beautiful all the days of your life, if you allow your natural beauty to shine and you make yourself a vessel of love. Accept whatever forms your beauty takes and you will always be beautiful."

Meshka felt beautiful and young.

"My daughter, know that I love God, and know that I love you. Open your heart and love Us both."

Like a sunburst in a storm, understanding hit her! "How can I be *Your* daughter? Dis is *meshugeh!* (craziness) Da daughter of a *Goddess* is a *Goddess!*"

These words jumped off her tongue before her mind could catch them by the tail. Meshka spoke the words out loud and sheepishly grinned in her elfish way at all the people around her.

No one even noticed. Craziness was an accepted thing in this mish-mash of people. Women often started crying for no visible reason or they stared blindly ahead for hours. You never knew when someone was going to start screaming. Grief had no manners; it demanded expression at the strangest times.

ଦ୍ୱଦ୍ୱ

The next morning was unseasonably warm. A few confused birds thought it was spring and flew around singing. Here in the foothills the snow was gone and even though it was only the middle of January, the good weather gave them a teasing taste of the spring to come.

Meshka felt happy for no reason at all. She crawled out of her bedroll on the right side of the bed, feeling years younger. The warm day required a light dress and no real need for a shawl.

Meshka looked at the dark cloth for a minute. Rifka walked by and saw the sneer on her mama's face. She wondered if her mama was looking at a dead rat, and was surprised to see it was only the old shawl.

At breakfast the shawl accidently slipped off Meshka's head and lay demurely on her shoulders. By the time the breakfast mess was cleared away and everything was packed up for the day, the shawl accidentally slipped off her shoulders and lay draped around her waist. Well, maybe it was not so accidental.

Meshka's conscience told her to go back to the way life was. But her hands had a will of their own. They folded up the shawl and put it in her bundle. After a tense minute, she changed her mind and pulled the shawl out again. She looked at it with her nose all wrinkled up like it was a dead rat. A shudder ran through her and she packed it away again. She stood there betwixt and between, holding her breath. Finally she felt that click of firm decision.

Meshka turned and walked into a new life. The shawl was safely tucked away. She escaped the demanding grasp of the past. Each step she took without the shawl, made her grow younger and bolder. She walked around with her naked hair showing and felt deliciously daring!

The blond Norwegian family camped beside her said, *Git Morgen* (good morning). She smiled back and said *Shalom* (peace). No one understood the other's words, but the meaning from the heart was clear. Meshka walked away and turned a rich shade of magenta with embarrassment.

Meshka wandered down to the creek to draw a bag of water. On the way she passed a rough looking young man who turned to her, gave her a wide friendly grin, and said "Вітаю" (hello in Ukrainian). Lightning bolts shot through her veins!

Meshka was kneeling down kindling the morning fire, when a big Scottish man with a huge mane of red hair and a bushy face walked by. He stopped to give her a flirting eye; that nearly made her heart stop beating altogether!

As soon as Meshka was alone again, a raging argument broke out inside her head. All through the day, minute by minute, she justified and bargained with her fears.

"Being exposed like dis is not really a sin. After all, look at all da women around here who expose their faces. Da liddle Oriental women, da big Swedish women, da petite French-women, all of dem have their heads uncovered," the young woman in her argued.

"Not da Arab women, not da Indian woman in their saris, not da turbaned African women, 'n not all dose women who wear hats," her conscience argued back.

She yearned to be free, but the voices of tradition were yelling at her. She desperately needed to justify her desire, but she could think of no one her conscience would accept. Sharanii had her sari, the three maidens and Joya were unmarried so they were allowed to bare their heads.

"Vhat about all da strangers traveling beside me? Look at dose women! Dey have husbands 'n children, but dey wear nothing on deir heads, nothing at all!?!

"Vhat am I dinking! Dese ideas are blasphemy!" Of course, the old threat roared at her. It always did. Only this time, it did not make her tremble.

The big shawl was Meshka's cocoon and her oldest friend. She wove it in preparation for her wedding day. Each stitch held a prayer for health, happiness, enough to eat, healthy babies…a lot of stitches holding a lot of prayers. The long square of rough homespun yarn protected her. It proclaimed to everyone that she was a married woman.

When Meshka was fifteen, her older sister got married, so now it was her turn. Weaving her shawl was an important part of becoming a woman. Oy, making that shawl was a *gantseh megilleh* (big deal). She started from nothing. First her sister Raizie asked her to come cut the wool from her fuzziest lambs. Meshka washed the wool, carded it, dyed it, and spun it into yarn. It made her hands so soft!

Her Meyer made the sturdy spinning wheel as a trousseau gift. He was always so gifted with his hands. Rifka takes after him like that.

Young Meshka dyed the yarn a deep dark green, like the forest at twilight. Oy! Her hands were stained green for weeks! That was the first shawl she made. She wove another, a lighter one for the summertime, just before Yonkle was born.

She never went outside without a shawl and if there was even a little chill, she wore it in the house as well. It covered her head every day, in every temperature, every year since she was married at fifteen. Leaving it behind was not easy.

Half the day was gone by the time the grumbler in her head got tired of nagging on her. She walked around with her head held high even though it was naked and everyone could see her face. It was wonderfully terrifying!

It was a glorious day! Of course, as soon as the sun went down and the winds whipped up, she was securely wrapped in her warm woolen shawl once again.

The next morning was even warmer. The sun rose in golden splendor! Meshka popped out of her bedroll filled with a new sense of daring! This time the shawl never left her bundles and never made a squeak.

What an amazing day! The first time a fresh breeze slapped her right in the face, she was startled. It was so brash and she was so exposed! It took a while for her to get used to the wind's chilling touch. It was thrilling. Meshka was bursting with excitement!

Sharanii's wagon rolled on down the road. Maya held the reins and Sharanii sat beside her on the wagon bench. Rachel was sitting on the back of the wagon dangling her feet, her little pony followed behind.

Rifka and Joya pulled the cart.

Sarina and Tasjia danced down the road arm in arm. The packed dirt surface was pleasantly smooth. The sun was high in a flawless blue sky.

Meshka marched along boldly growing taller and taller by the minute. Maybe the carpenter's ruler still showed four feet, one and a half inches, but in her heart, she was ten feet tall. She needed to be ten feet tall, if she was going to fulfill the new destiny Fate was designing for her!

Giant little Meshka walked around naked like that in front of so many people! All day a steady stream of travelers appeared beside her. Some hurried past and some lingered for a while and talked to her before drifting on. Such an interesting flow of people moved past her.

Free from the shawl, people saw her warm friendly face lit with delight and felt free to talk to her. A kindly old woman with only a couple of teeth fell into step waddling beside her.

The old woman smiled at Meshka and started chattering away in some strange tongue. Meshka gave her a friendly smile, listened, and nodded like she knew something. Every few words, the woman hit herself on the chest and called her "Dah-ling." Meshka found the rhythmic song of the language intriguing. She did not know what the woman was saying but it was pleasant to share a moment together.

Bouncing along the road Meshka looked at everyone she passed with a smile in her eyes. The people walking by smiled back. It made her feel nice and warm and happy.

Why would people not want to talk to her? She was lovely. Her long thick curly silver hair cascaded over a compact little muscular body, toned after seven months of travel.

Meshka walked differently today. She stood taller with her chin raised and her shoulders back, no more being hunched over. Her face was raised to the sunshine drinking in its glorious warmth and delighting in the pleasure on her cheeks of the sun's delicious touch.

Everyone saw her true face! She felt so exposed after so many years of being invisible! For the first time, she felt like she was a real person, not just a servant. The surging power of being a woman was amazing! Shocked and pleased, she walked around open and ready to accept and appreciate whoever walked past her. The people she met that day all shined back at her.

People were friendly. A group of elegant Japanese women dressed in stunning silk *kimonos* touched her hair. It was falling in a thick profusion of silver curls. The women chatted excitedly, obviously praising its shimmering beauty.

It felt strange, like a cool breath tickling her neck. No one ever complimented her before. Of course, everyone always raved about her famous chicken matzo ball soup, but this was different. People were going out of their way to say nice things about her and her pretty hair.

Her great mane was a silver waterfall. It was actually very long, very curly, and very silver. Secretly, she had always thought she had beautiful hair.

Such a thought in the old days always came with a slap of guilt. The Judge in her mind always wagged a finger at her and barked, "Dis is vanity. God vill punish you for vanity."

But this time the idea that maybe she was pretty was not so frightening. Actually, this new Meshka did not feel that all-tangled-up-inside feeling over God's wrath.

When night came Meshka was reunited with her shawl. It was draped over her head and wrapped around her shoulders. Reluctantly her face and hair were once again hidden away. The shawl kept her warm as the cold winds blew. Meshka felt different. She knew she would never be the same again.

෬෬෬෬

Chapter 13

Easing the Suffering

The people trailing along at the end of the procession of refugees were a sorrowful lot. The sick of mind and heart, the wounded in body and soul, ambled along in the rear. These ragged people were the lost ones abused by the powers of the world. They were walking onward for no reason, just to be going somewhere.

The Baking Circle was shocked! Before the women's detainment at the border, they naturally were walking at the front of the multitude. All the *Bakers,* except Sharanii, were shaken. Never had they seen people with so little and so much misery. Sharanii calmly looked at each person she passed with deep compassion. Who knows what horrors the *Priestess* had seen in all the lands she traveled?

Meshka froze; her lower lip gasping. She struggled to breathe. There was not enough, there was not enough air to breathe. She never saw anything like this before! Her whole life was lived in one little village, where neighbors made sure everyone had enough to eat. Traveling with the Baking Circle, it was the same. They naturally took care of one another. Was that not what peace was all about?

These abandoned lost souls were different. A ragged desperate hunger added an edge to the look in their eyes. Each one scrambled for what he could get. The *Bakers* saw it etched in their faces.

Sharanii's fine wagon and beautiful white horse drew covetous stares or glaring hostility. Meshka walked along behind the wagon leading her mischievous little goat, always ready to play or prod!

Meshka said a nice word to everyone she passed, smiled at each stranger, and looked for something to praise about them. She remembered the wise rabbi in her village telling her, "If you learn to praise dings instead of complain about dem, all these terrible dings vill never happen again."

So praise became her new art. Meshka looked at each person for the light glowing inside them and praised the beauty she saw in each one.

"Vhat pretty eyes you have. Dey make me wish I painted pictures," she said to a little blind girl. The child fluttered her long silky dark lashes and imagined herself as beautiful.

Suspicious frowns softened when they felt the warmth of Meshka's simple innocent toothy smile. She always found a special quality in each person and praised it with all sincerity. The little crippled girl had the most beautiful golden hair. The madman, whose eyes seemed to roll around in his head, sang the prettiest songs. Even though defeat dulled their eyes, each had their virtues.

Meshka's open heart left them feeling good. Soon her compassionate heart was invested in everyone. The thin veneer of "cripple" or "madman" disappeared from her sight. She saw only good people bent with struggle.

"Vhat else is new in dis life?" she would say. "*Nu* (so)? Struggles? Everyone has struggles. Vhat matters is da compassion 'n da love vee bring to dose struggles. Dat is vhat counts," she liked to say when someone *kvetched* to her.

Meshka looked at this horde of riffraff and tried to see their virtues. By the end of the day, all her prejudice was worn away. The next morning, she was already making friends.

Roly-poly little Jeannie came from Ireland. She was a *pisser* (very funny person). Meshka laughed so hard at Jeannie's funny joke that a few drops of pee ran down her leg. It was the silly price she paid for living so long.

A bright light beamed from Jeannie's smile. She was funny, witty, and horribly lame. She spoke longingly about her beautiful land. She yearned for Ireland, sparkling like an emerald in the sun, swimming in a sea of diamonds.

It was a chilly afternoon. The sun was deceptively bright but offered little warmth. The air was crisp and fresh in late January. They were drawing closer to the sea where the breath of winter was gentler.

Meshka was standing by her fire cooking her famous chicken matzo ball soup. *Oy*(oh)! This soup! It was magic food, not only did it taste wonderful, fill you up with a warm belly, but when you breathed in its steamy goodness, it wrapped its arms around your heart and warmed you. This soup chased away sore throats and sneezes and felt really soothing going down.

Meshka dropped a handful of carrots into the pot. Those carrots were a find. She traded somebody who traded somebody who got her the carrots.

A little *miskite* (a sad little orphan) waddled over to Meshka and sat down beside her at the fire as though he belonged there. The child was very sweet, very tiny, and wore a deeply furrowed brow of worry. He sat by the soup watching it simmer for hours. The sweet little fellow snuggled up next to Meshka, close by her warm fire and the promise of food.

Oy! The soup smelled like heaven, it was so delicious! The aroma of her wonderful dinner wafted through the air, a curling finger of invitation. It drew quite an audience of hungry children. As each new face joined Meshka's fire, she added water and a few more vegetables to stretch the broth a little further.

Even before the chicken soup was ready, the wonderful rich aroma fed their souls. Meshka filled those hungry little *pupiks* (bellies) with soup and bread. Sitting around the fire, the *Bakers* savored Meshka's delicious chicken matzo ball soup and fresh challah, while her new little friends wolfed down every bite and licked their plates clean.

After dinner, Timmy, the tiny fellow with the worried brow, curled up next to Meshka and fell asleep contentedly. His long lashes fluttered a little and he moaned softly when she scooped him up onto her ample lap. She hummed to him as she rocked back and forth, just the way she used to rock her own children and grandchildren. The soft purring of his breath was sweet music to her aching heart.

When Meshka was ready to crawl into sleep, she made a little nest for the child and curled up with him tucked in beside her under a warm blanket inside her tent.

Meshka was exhausted after a day that was like rubber - it seemed to stretch on forever. Today she did so much walking, talking, and cooking, she was spent, but still sleep ran away from her. Meshka tossed and turned for hours.

Eventually sleep grabbed her and threw her into a dream where she was haunted by hungry mouths! Every time she fed a child, she saw another little face looking on longingly. The children in the dream, like the ones at dinner, were so empty it was hard for them to swallow.

Meshka lay awake gazing up at an endless expanse of heaven through a glaze of wet tears. Among the stars Meshka saw a *Goddess* with twelve breasts and fourteen hungry children. She was trying to nurse them all!

CRCRCR

Icy winter winds were wailing on too long for Rifka. She hated being cold and now she was chilled most of the time. Rifka was an angry young woman who walked around in her own empty world. Day after day, she snarled at people for no good reason. Night after night, she cried in her sleep and woke up choking on tears.

Week after week, when she dared to close her eyes, she was raked raw by the cold claws of ghosts and by painful memories that jolted her awake sweating in terror. She was being devoured by grief; that's why she bellowed angrily and *kvetched* (complained) bitterly.

Rifka looked at all the sorrow and suffering of these ragged people and something snapped inside her. The rawness of aching humanity pierced her cocoon of protective hostility. First she was angry with God; then she was angry with herself. Churning with rage and helplessness, she desperately wanted to change the way the world worked, even if such a task was impossible.

When Rifka saw all the dirty, miserable, abandoned children waddling along, eating whatever handouts they could find or steal, it made her yearn for her own little ones.

In a rare moment of compassion, Rifka wanted to reach out and touch a little boy. She wanted to pet his soft cheek and tousle his hair, but her hand refused to move; and tears got stuck in her throat. She hungered – body, mind, and soul – to be home again, nesting in soft sheepskins by the fire with her sweet babies wrapped in her arms. Holding her babies was the greatest joy she had ever known.

Rifka ached so sharply for her own lost children that she felt bruised by these sad little ones and their meager existence. She could not bear the sight of them. She desperately wanted to crawl inside Sharanii's wagon and keep her eyes closed. Rifka anxiously needed to get away from all the dirty children following after Meshka.

It was a *Shabbos* miracle when that hollow person disappeared, and a new Rifka stepped into that empty shell. She was not happy like the old Rifka who had a home and family. She was not the grieving ghost churning with passion. The new Rifka felt a sense of power in the toned firmness of her muscles, was thrilled by her new sense of daring, and was secure in the firmness of her will.

The new Rifka was born on a *Shabbos* morning. It all started with a little boy squealing, "Mama, mama." A bright frosty sun was shining on his face. Recognition stabbed her through the heart. "My liddle Moishela!" she cried!

The little fellow scampered past Rifka and jumped into his mama's open arms. She was a short, chubby woman with dark hair.

Confused, Rifka looked down at her own empty arms. "O my liddle Moses, vhen you va born, I thought you va goin' to lead our people into a bedder life. How can you be dead? If you are dead, den I am dead too." These words were choking her. She stood frozen in silence. Her eyes drooped and her chin sank down to her chest as she watched the child snuggle into his mama's cushy embrace.

Rifka wrapped her arms around herself and closed her eyes. Time melted away. For just a moment, she could feel the weight of her little son's body solid in her arms.

When she opened her eyes, the mama and the child were gone. Maybe they were never there. She turned and walked away from her camp. Wherever she looked, there were so many people; she felt like they were suffocating her.

Rifka found an inviting outcropping of stone and climbed to a safe perch. In the echoing winds rising from below, sounds and voices drifted upward in bits and pieces.

Someone was calling her name, or was it the whimsical voice of the wind?

The sound was so soft; she wondered if she heard it at all. A child's voice echoing on the wind blowing through the trees whispered, "Mama do not cry. I am free 'n I am vell." Tears welled up and filled her eyes.

"Shush, Mama. I vill alvays be right here near you. Vee vill never be parted. I sent dat liddle boy to you. It vas my vay of sayin' hello, so you would know I am here. Every child you see vill have some of da sparkle from my eyes. Kiss dem 'n know you are kissin' me. I can feel you Mama. I have been vid you since da beginnin' of time. Bein' near you is heaven for me. Love me even if I have no body. Vee can hear each other's thoughts. Vee are still one person, one soul."

In the following silence, she felt quiet. A strong gust of wind rustled the leaves and carried the words, "Mama, I am comin'. Wait for me."

Rifka felt like she was waking up from a long dream. She looked around her, and really saw things for the first time since the world ended. She felt refreshed, ready to face life, and ready to do something!

Later that day, she found herself walking next to an old man and tried to be nice. "Gentle father, let me take dat heavy bag off your shoulder. Trust me gentle father, rest your bundle in my cart 'n walk vid me awhile."

His wizened old face made her feel young and strong. When he said that she reminded him of his daughter back in Russia, her mind wandered back to the garden of her childhood to the many times she walked beside her papa on the way to market to sell milk from the family cow.

ജ്ഞജ്ഞ

Dancing was in Joya's blood. She gathered a cluster of little ragamuffin girls and turned them into princesses. Not that long ago Joya was a little ragamuffin girl.

She remembered those days when her mama took her to the big rich houses. Her mama read the palms of the fancy people and she danced her fantasies, sang traditional songs, and collected shiny coins.

The rich people were dressed in such beautiful clothes! Little Joya felt bedraggled. She looked at herself through rich people's eyes and saw a dirty pauper dressed in rags, a little lost waif and felt ashamed.

Joya turned little wandering paupers into spritely dancers. With joy and delight she wove her magic over these little waifs and their hard lives drifted away. She opened a door into a realm of fantasy and thrills.

In a flurry of splashing colors, Joya turned glittering scarves into pretty little costumes. Silky ribbons and bits of string decorated wayward curls. Little girls with big wide smiles dressed up like a garden of flowers.

Joya set the lovely, gleeful, giggling girls to twirling, leaping, and spinning like colorful tops. These charming little acrobats fluttered their soft wings and glided gracefully to the music of Joya's sweet voice.

Some little dancers had mamas who loved and cared for them, others were just bits of flotsam floating on the waves of Fate. Joya danced beautifully with her little angels. Under her magic, each delightful little dancer became a fairy princess.

On a perfectly wonderful warm winter day, the sparkling music of young girls giggling brightened the mood of each passing soul. Many people stopped to watch the little dancers leaping gracefully and curtsying sweetly. They walked away feeling a bit more joy. Joya's little dancers were a blessing to one and all.

Some tired mamas took this time to put down their heavy bundles and rest, others played with their other little ones.

Maya was bent over her cauldron brewing healing potions for many long hours, but it was never enough. Being in the midst of so much need felt overwhelming.

Sarina fed the medicine pot. She took boys and girls wildcrafting in the mountain meadows nearby and taught the children to gather the roots of healing plants for Maya's magical cauldron.

While the little Alchemist mixed her potions, Sarina disinfected oozing sores and deloused a motley brood of stray children.

At the end of each day, the Baking Circle fell into their bedrolls exhausted, satisfied but exhausted. They should have fallen asleep instantly, but they were too engaged to relax. A part of their minds kept spinning new ideas. It kept them awake.

Maya's herbal teas, tinctures, poultices and salves were in constant demand, so was Sarina's medical knowledge. As children, Maya and Sarina were apprentices to the village midwife, Marji. They began studying healing with the wise woman when they were seven.

Tasjia had only a passing knowledge of herbs and healing. Tasjia's art was her passion for touch. She felt everyone was starving for a gentle touch. While the other maidens applied medicines, Tasjia's warm tingling healing hands massaged bent backs and brought relief to sore feet.

Her magic fingers read each body like a book and skillfully spoke its language. She enjoyed the pleasure she gave. After several hours, her strong arms were pleasantly tired, but her body was surging with energy.

While the three maidens eased suffering bodies, Sharanii inspired and enlivened their spirits. Sharanii walked in beauty and everyone she touched was made beautiful.

In the bare existence of these wretched people, a pretty head of curls or shiny clean hair were rare and wonderful luxuries. Sharanii worked her magic on sad waifs. She turned them into lovely *Goddesses* with her magic wand - her brush. Each woman radiated an inner elegance that felt wonderful inside and out.

Rachel knew nothing of herbs or cosmetics. She walked in the light of God. This was what she had to offer, and it was no small thing. Reverently she washed the feet of the lame and praised God with every stroke. She saw the world through Divine eyes, investing every breath with reverence. These people were the discarded of humanity yet to her, they were sacrificial lambs of noble worth. She washed and massaged sore feet with a soft cloth that not so long ago was her pretty petticoat, but felt this was a far better use for it.

Rachel had a beatific look in her eyes, for she saw herself washing the feet of God in His human form.

Each Baker in her own way contributed her skills to ease the suffering of those around her.

 প্রপ্রপ্র

Days turned into weeks very quickly. The Bakers fell to their work early in the morning and crawled into their bedrolls late at night.

Meshka was aggravated. It did not seem right that these people were desperately fending for themselves.

One evening, Meshka and Jeannie were joking about the odd mishmash of people around them and somehow their jokes turned into a serious idea.

The two women invited a bunch of strange people to a dinner party. They asked everyone to come early to help gather and prepare the food. At dinner, everyone feasted on laughter as much as soup. Jeannie was skilled at cutting a chicken into pieces with one hand. She had a strange, but effective way of holding the bird with the stump of her right arm, while cutting it with her good left hand. It was amazing to watch and funny to hear her describe it.

At dinner, everyone was invited to tell a story, a joke, sing a song, or do a dance. The evening was a riot of laughter. There were precious moments of sheer joy, a rare experience in such sparse lives.

The evening was so wonderful, Meshka and Jeannie gathered more people for dinner the next night and every night after that. Guests always came early and contributed something. These dinners did more than fill empty bellies; they warmed hearts and added pleasure to ordinary days. The cozy intimacy in these dinner circles was as healing to lonely souls as Maya's herbs were to ailing bodies.

With a little push and encouragement, Meshka convinced Jeannie that God wanted her to bring people together and teach them how to help one another. It took a lot of convincing before Jeannie came to believe that someone like her could have a destiny!

Meshka gave her friend a steady stream of encourage-ment and did half the work. Jeannie set up dinner circles every night. A varying group of people regularly prepared meals together. They did not have much, but with a little flour, a couple of eggs, a few vegetables and some odd bits of chicken, they made a decent stew.

Separately, they did not have enough to quiet the hunger rattling around in their hollow bellies, but now that they were feeding each other, the food contained enough *"Om Shanti,"* (spiritual blessing, as Sharanii called it) to fill them up. Soon, these isolated, lonely people became friends.

Meshka and Jeannie worked well together. Their dinners were wonderful. Strangers became friends and friends became a *Clan*, just like the Baking Circle became a *Clan*. Bringing strangers together and helping them become a community, a *Clan*, seemed to happen so naturally, Meshka figured the urge was just waiting for permission to happen.

Soon these little groups formed *Dinner Clans* on their own. People were realizing, when they shared food everyone had more. Friendships evolved. In the *Clans* each lost person wasn't so lost anymore. In these small family-like *Clans*, they had a place where they belonged. Meshka and Jeannie had set tops to spinning. Every night a new group of guests learned to fill their bellies and their hearts together.

CACACA

One Friday the Baking Circle gathered a bunch of women and taught them to make little challahs. A great many hands kneaded dough. Many stone ovens were built. The wonderful robust aroma of fresh baked bread wafted everywhere. Each woman baked two challahs, one for her family and one to give away.

Tasjia wiped a smudge of flour off Maya's cheek, laughed and said, "I think Jesus would be very proud of us. Not only do we give hungry people bread to eat, but we teach them how to bake it."

Sharanii nodded and smiled, "Yes Tasjia, I agree. We have done well for these people. Maybe our work here is done for now."

As quietly as these few words were spoken, a decision was made. Their time of sojourning among the wounded was coming to a close. It was understood without words, after the next Shabbos, the women of the Baking Circle were traveling on. The first day after Shabbos, when everyone was at their freshest, was a good time to start something new.

Meshka hugged Jeannie and all her new friends many times over the next few days. She baked challahs only on Friday, so Friday came several times that week. Meshka baked a lot of little tiny challahs and ran around giving them to the children. For someone so unpracticed in leaving, she was becoming an expert.

On their last Shabbos dinner together, Meshka announced the Baking Circle's decision to move on. She lit the candles and invited the *Shekhina* to watch over all these people. She recited a special prayer asking *The Mother* to protect all the little *Clans* and *Friendship Circles*. Who knows, maybe God-willing, she might return and see them again someday.

After they shared a wonderful meal, where of course, everyone contributed something, Meshka put a big thick log on the fire and all their guests gathered round to hear another of Jeannie's famous silly jokes! The first joke in Gaelic was repeated again and again in ten or fifteen different languages until everyone was holding their bellies and laughing so hard, it brought tears into their eyes.

She recited the next joke in her high Irish brogue. "A little duck waddled into a market. He asked the grocer, 'Excuse me Sir, do you have any duck food?' The grocer man said, 'No, we have no duck food.'

"The little duck took two steps, turned, and asked, 'Sir, do you have any duck food?' The grocer was getting annoyed. 'I already told you no, we have no duck food'!"

"The little duck waddled two steps, turned and asked, 'Sir, Sir, do you have any duck food?' Now the grocer was angry. He said, 'No. We have no duck food. If you ask me again, I am going to nail your webbed feet to the floor!'

The little duck left.

"The next day the duck came back. He asked the grocer, 'Sir, Sir, do you have any nails?'

'No!' replied the grocer."

'Good,' said the duck, 'Do you have any duck food?'"

The guests laughed with delight and full bellies. No one could remember when such a warm and wonderful evening was had by all. In this simple act of sharing food, seeds were sown that would one day grow beyond Meshka's wildest dreams.

ଦ୍ରଦ୍ରଦ୍ର

Part 3

Spiritual Awakening

Chapter 14

A New Life

Joya felt so alive! She often walked around quietly singing sweet tunes in her own language. Her spirits were high, even though her anger seemed to have settled in her belly, for it was often upset. She seemed to have a problem almost every time she ate.

As they moved forward through the crowd, Joya craned her neck this way and that looking for Gilberto. She missed his passionate violin, the wild emotions it released in her, and the way his beautiful music sent her feet flying! She yearned to feel that wild freedom and wings on her legs.

Joya looked like her lively old self, but nights were hard for her and mornings were even worse. She slept fitfully or not at all; and the haphazard diet of travel was making her miserable.

One sleepless night under a full moon, she moaned, "What is ailing me? Why is it so hard to keep my food down?" Restless and tired, Joya climbed out of her bedroll.

She added a few logs to the dying embers of their evening fire and soon had a comfortable blaze going. She sat down beside the warm flames and mixed the cards as she prayed. "Holy Del, I have recovered from the shock and the losses, but I still have so much pain. Please help me find a way to get well." She turned over three tarot cards on a pretty yellow scarf.

225

The first card was *The Empress,* next was *The Sun,* and the last was the *Six of Cups.* Joya stared at the cards for a long time, unable or unwilling to see what was plainly obvious. *The Empress* was relaxing on a bench holding her abundant belly. *The Sun* card showed two children playing in a circle and in the *Six of Cups,* two children were sharing cups.

Either she was retaining too much water, sick from too much sun, or pregnant. The first two answers were very unlikely and the third was totally unacceptable. Joya scooped up the cards grumbling that they were not well mixed and angrily put them away.

She was hoping the tarot reading would bring clarity and help her sleep, which did not happen. She was more awake and agitated than before. Most of the night she sat by the fire, lying to herself, coming up with absurd excuses, and mastering the art of denial.

Finally when the darkness surrendered to a blood red dawn, Joya opened her mind enough to admit that her moon blood had not visited her since the day the world ended. "After all the shock I have gone through," she told herself; "it was just to be expected." She shored up the borders of her blindness with lots of illogical excuses, but still she felt edgy most of the day.

ଔଔଔ

The Baking Circle made their way through the crowd. Sharanii's fine wagon rolled along slowly drawn by her beautiful white horse wearing a fine bejeweled headdress. Seated above the world in all her gracious dignity was the *Priestess* elegantly draped in a fine blue silk sari.

For contrast, the rag clad feet dangling out the back of the wagon belonged to Rachel. Her little pony trotted along pulling her cart behind.

The three beautiful maidens danced along with lovely songs on their lips.

The little wooden cart pulled by Joya and Rifka came along next. The two women moved together, pulling and resting in the same rhythm. They were quietly attuned to each other. Joya enjoyed singing and Rifka enjoyed listening. Joya's lovely voice added a musical sparkle to Rifka's day. No longer was her heart filled with darkness.

Bringing up the rear was Meshka, a silver haired woman with a thick long curly mane flying wild in the breeze. She was strolling along holding her mischievous goat on a rope in one hand and the chubby little hand of a small boy in the other.

After a long day of riding, pulling, and walking, the Baking Circle's little procession arrived at the front of the multitude and recognized several familiar faces. They felt a sense of homecoming merely returning to their place within the order of things.

That evening, a wild riot of rose and purples splashed across a twilight sky consorting with a flaming sunset! The women were staring wide eyed at God's lavish design, when they heard Gilberto's sad violin wafting on a breeze. Joya, bursting with excitement, ran to find him!

The Gypsy man missed his muse. After Joya disappeared at the border, his music lost its luster and took on a bitter sadness, as did the man. His violin wept with such musical sweetness, it broke hearts to hear it.

Gilberto caught sight of Joya and suddenly his violin rejoiced! He fiddled a lively tune in celebration of her return. His joyful tunes and wild rhythms set her legs free from reality's madness. The dance lifted her like a leaf on the wind. She twirled through the air and landed with a loud thump, thump, thump. As the evening wore on, her dance grew wilder and wilder. An air of exhilaration radiated from every movement.

The Bakers were delighted to see Gilberto again, especially Meshka. She wanted Joya to be her old sparkling self again, the Joya who read her palm by the crooked tree in the Gypsy camp.

A wedding would be a blessing to everyone. The refugees were so busy surviving; very few of them were envisioning a future.

The next morning over breakfast, Meshka said lightly, "Joya, Gilberto is a very handsome man. *Nu?* (well) Do you dink so? I saw him carrying wood for old Mrs. Juarez yesterday. Vhat a nice ding to do. He seems very helpful 'n easy tempered."

In a sudden flair of anger, Joya barked, "Meshka, are you playing matchmaker? Well stop it! Gilberto does not know me and if he did, he would not want me." She turned her back and walked away. The discussion was definitely over.

Meshka refused to take the hint and kept talking. "Vhat foolishness is dis?! Give me von good reason why you vill not talk vid him."

Meshka was shocked by her own boldness, but something was pushing her to keep going. "Give me von good reason."

Joya's eyes filled with tears and she blurted out, "Because I am with child."

Ah! It was out in the open; finally Meshka could talk about it. "A child is a wonderful ding 'n a liddle von needs a papa." Meshka was not being a *yenta.* (a busybody) Her heart was in the right place. She sincerely wanted to help the sweet girl.

"Men do not want dirty women or their scandalous offspring. Oh why did the mob did not kill me? There were five ugly monsters. The vile creatures spat on me, cursed me, and defiled me with their clammy hands and slimy manhood. Now I am *marimé* (impure)."

The strength of her bitterness seemed strange in one so young. Even the rage twisting her lips and the nasty way she spat out the words could not make her look ugly. Quite the opposite, pregnancy had filled out her face and made her even more beautiful.

The firelight was sparkling in her tears and the sunshine glittered off the tiny mirrors dangling along the edge of her scarf.

"One beast left his evil seed in my womb to remind me forever of that accursed day. How can I bear a child conceived in hate? O' Meshka, why did you save me? It was the cruelest thing you ever did. Now I must bear this shame!" Joya burst out crying. Suddenly the floodgates flew open and all the tears she never shed came rushing out.

Meshka weighed her words very carefully before she spoke. "Joya my free-spirited waif, vhen da world ended a door slammed shut. Vee left everything back dere behind dat locked door. Vee all carry da scars. Now vee are making a new life.

"Our families are gone. Rifka is all I have left in dis world 'n you are alone. You are young 'n you have your whole life ahead of you. Dis baby vill be blessing to you.

"She is da flower dat grows from da mud. God is giving you a child to love. No von can fill your heart 'n make it burst vid joy like a liddle child. You vill teach her to dance 'n read tarot cards. In dis harsh world she vill be a great comfort to people just like you."

Nice words, but they meant nothing to Joya. A dark cloud settled over her head and nothing anyone said or did could make the horror go away.

It was almost February. Soon the days would rapidly grow longer and the precious warmth of the sun would not run away so fast. Here in the flat land at the base of the mountains, the winds were calmer.

Joya's belly quieted down soon after that. Once she admitted the truth, she no longer felt sick to her stomach. In fact, now she began to eat and eat and eat. She was desperately trying to fill a hole in her soul. All the women in the Baking Circle cooked special foods for her. She had a constant craving for sweet cream. All day long as she pulled the cart, she imagined herself eating big bowls of fluffy white cream.

One day, she confided her obsession to Rifka. The next morning at breakfast, like magic, Rifka served her a big bowl of fresh sweet cream!

Night after night Joya tossed and turned, unable to sleep. The little person inside her belly was craving hot spicy foods. She may have hungered for cream in the day, but this baby demanded hot spicy food at night. Sharanii whipped up her favorite spicy recipes just the way she made them back in the old country. One dish was hotter than the next!

Rifka's hard crust continued to melt away. When no one was looking, she quietly did kind deeds. Most nights after pulling the wagon with Joya, she rubbed the girl's swollen feet, pressed down on her sore back, and massaged her tired shoulders. Whenever they passed a farm along the way, she stopped to do a good day's work, so she could keep feeding Joya sweet cream.

One night at dinner, Rifka watched Joya gobble down a bowl of vegetables covered in fiery spices concocted by Sharanii.

"Joya dis is foolish! You should not eat spicy food. It is not good for you!"

The Gypsy laughed and offered Rifka a bite. She expected hot, but this was a lot worse. Her mouth was on fire! Rifka guzzled down huge gulps of water, but that did not help. She ran around with her tongue hanging out fanning herself; that did not help. She was blinded by the water pouring from her eyes.

Sharanii watched with a curl of a smile playing on her lips. Quietly she handed Rifka a cup of goat milk. She guzzled it down and the fire subsided.

With a wagging finger, Rifka warned Joya, "If you continue to eat all dose spicy foods, dis baby vill be as hairy as a monkey."

CRCRCR

Rifka rarely picked fights anymore, even with Meshka. She made believe she did not see her *meshugeneh* (crazy) mama running around without a shawl like a young girl.

The wanderers emerged into a lush green valley leading down to the sea. The blustery chill of winter was more subdued in this protected land.

Meshka's step took on a light skip. Her days felt brighter. They were not easier, mind you, just happier. She patiently endured Rachel's wagging finger. As a religious woman, Rachel had strong views on Meshka walking around with a naked head! Rachel felt hell-bent with a mission from God to make her friend see how ridiculous she looked. Rifka shared the same opinion, but she kept it to herself.

"Without a shawl you are not a woman!" Rachel scolded and crossed her arms in front of her chest.

Meshka raised her palms up in helplessness, shrugged her shoulders, and chided, "Not a woman! Vhat am I, a big round challah?" Meshka playfully refused to enter into Rachel's seriousness.

"Only young girls go around vid no modesty!" Rachel blurted out. Her hand jumped to cover her mouth, but she could not pull back the words. Rachel valued tact so she was sorry she spoke so strongly. Her forcefulness was a measure of how dedicated she was to saving Meshka's soul.

With a twinkle in her eyes, Meshka shot back, "Savoring whatever last shreds of youth I have, is not such a bad ding!" She laughed lightly and pointed her chin right up Rachel's nose!

"You are committing a sin. God vill punish you!" Again with the wagging finger Rachel warned. She loved Meshka enough to save her from making this terrible sin.

Meshka laughed with a crystal ring. "Sin, shmin. God has already punished me. Now I am going to create my own self. I am no longer my papa's daughter. Dat thread is broken. It set me free from da vay life vas. My mother held me in her loving arms. Dat thread too is no more.

"Now no von holds me. I am free to mother myself. No husband. No liddle vons. No threads to hold me to any von vay in dis life. I vant to see who I can be, beyond a daughter, a mother 'n a wife. I vant to be da best Meshka I can be."

Rachel shook her head and it kept shaking like a gate dangling off its hinges. She just could not believe a woman who she loved like a sister could do such a blasphemous thing!?! How could Rachel in good conscience, be friends with such a person? But how could she give up Meshka? Meshka was one of the most important threads she had in her life. What should she do? What did God want her to do?

The two close friends were being pulled in different directions, torn between the beliefs of the past and a yearning for the future. It was very sad. Finally there was no choice. They agreed it would be better not to talk with each other anymore.

The next few days were strange. Meshka and Rachel walked side by side, they slept side by side in the storm tent, and they cooked dinner side by side in the evenings, but not a word passed between them. They laughed together when Maya imitated Francois, a self-important man they had seen strutting about earlier. They cried together when Joya spoke of yearning for her Uncle Alberto. The young girl missed him so much! Rachel and Meshka missed lots of people so much, so they cried with her. They shared one heart, the heart of the Baking Circle.

Meshka could hear what Rachel was thinking and it stung her. But she breathed into her heart, opened into a sense of understanding, and forgave her friend. Meshka held no anger. She thought only of how much she loved Rachel, how much they had shared. They were sisters of the soul and that is a rare and precious gift indeed!

Every barb from Rachel was met with a smile and a laugh from Meshka. Sometimes, just to plague Rachel, she would sneak up behind her and give her a little hug, and then walk away.

Eventually Meshka won. Rachel found it harder and harder to stay angry with Meshka when she was being so sweet, patient, and loving.

"How can I be angry at such a *ponem* (face)?" She gave up and squeezed Meshka's grinning cheeks. With these words, the feud ended. Rachel never stopped being shocked by Meshka's boldness and Meshka never let little minds keep her from growing.

ርቃርቃርቃ

Meshka did not exactly win Rachel over. They made peace but inside Meshka there was little peace. She was still feeling naked and exposed without her shawl. Her belly often felt like snakes were wiggling around in there and she argued with herself until it gave her a headache. Every morning when she got up, it took setting her will and mustering her courage to ignore the accusing shawl.

Every night she tossed and turned. In her dreams, she was pursued by doubts. Whenever she closed her eyes, she got screamed at by her mother, her father, and every dead relative. Everyone had something to say. If Jews care about one thing above all else, it is tradition. Her ancestors were not going to let her abandon their precious tradition without a fight.

As a child, if little Meshkala ever dared to challenge her mama, her mama always said the same thing. She too liked to wag the finger, "My mother did it 'n my mother's mother did it. Dat is why you vill do it!"

On one of those tossing turning nights, as hours dragged on and dawn was edging near, Meshka finally floated off into a ragged dream. Before the dream could spin webs over her mind, she snapped awake again!

Meshka desperately needed rest. She was exhausted but could not relax. Her mind kept looking for a safe comfortable haven. Her relationship with God, felt neither safe nor comfortable. The arduous journey and the needs of so many people took the juice out of her. In what part of her life could she just let go and be taken care of? As old as she was, she wished she could curl up in her mama's lap, but she was an orphan.

The night was quiet even if Meshka was not. The quiet embraced her and her mind wandered back to *The Goddess's* words. *"See the world. Know the world. Make the world a better place."*

Remembering *Her* words brought peace and quiet so Meshka drifted off into the elusive land of dreams.

Morning arrived much too soon. Meshka was roused by the busy sounds of the camp waking up. She was groggy from too little sleep and still floating in the good feelings of a nice dream. As Meshka was journeying back from dream to day, in the oasis between the worlds, a surprising visitor came through this magical rift in time.

Looking at her with a twinkle in his eye and a curl of humor on his lips was Meyer, may he rest in peace. The sweet man she married was standing on the edge of her sight nodding his head and smirking the way he always did when she amused him.

"Ah, my *balabusta*, (powerful woman) so you are seeing da world. Vhat are you learning about life? So you are going to make da world better, *nu* (well)? How is dat going?"

Meshka was so startled to see him, she jumped! This broke the thread between their souls and he disappeared before she could answer.

On and off all day, in between all her of women's circles, Meshka thought about her husband's question.

Her life was busy these days. There was making *challahs* in the Baking Circle to give away on Shabbos, knitting a soft yellow bunny suit for little Davidka in her Grandma Circle, kindling the cooking fires every day, sometimes cooking dinner for the Baking Circle, and there were all the children who needed their boo-boos kissed.

Meshka figured all little children need *bubbas* (grandmas) and all old women need *kinderlech* (children) to fuss over and keep them young. Whenever she found a sad little child, she brought the little one to meet some old ladies. Every child should have a few grandmas to pamper them.

To her credit, Meshka already created six circles of adopted *bubbas*. These old women were no longer lonely. Now they shared the pleasure of loving a child.

That night after dinner in the quiet of the evening, the Bakers were sitting around a warm fire sharing stories and songs, but not Meshka. She walked off to think about her husband's question.

Alone on a dark moonless night, she wandered over to a little stream. The gurgling of the water covered the sound of her voice. Softly she called out, "Meyer, my sweet husband in da other world, dis would be a good time for us to visit."

It was such a dark night; she could see nothing, so it was easy to imagine Meyer walking towards her. Behind her eyes, she could see him.

"Meyer, it vas so good to see you dis morning, in da window of my dreams. It made me happy all day. I hope dey feed you enough in heaven, you looked a liddle thin.

"I vas dinking today about vhat you asked me. Da *Goddess* told me I should, *'See da world, know da world, 'n make da world a better place.'*"

This was the first time Meshka said it out loud. Just repeating what *The Goddess* said; made her insides sparkle.

"Have I seen da world? Yes, I am looking at da world a liddle. But vhat is da world? If it is all dose liddle farms 'n pastures vhere da cows all face da same direction, I have seen enough to know one village is not so different dan another."

She sighed, thinking how people and cows are not so different.

"But Meyer, if da world is da vay people treat each other, oy vay! Den da world is a boat floating on a rocky sea. People have so many different beliefs.

"Dis beautiful land vid all its colorful flowers 'n big mountains, it makes me feel so alive. But I meet people who say dis world is just a test; some kind of contest to see who is going to heaven 'n who is not! Can you believe dat!?!"

A deep wave of emotion took her breath away for a second, but the words kept coming.

"Meyer, you would not believe it! Some people really dink dis promised heaven is better dan real life! Dey believe da Devil is everywhere 'n in deir panic; dey do da Devil's work."

Her mind was so open, too many thoughts rushed in. Then one rose above the others, "You know Meyer, it is strange. Vid all da people I meet dese days, I do not see so much da differences as da simple vays people are da same."

Meshka was surprised to hear such thoughts coming from her own mind. How did she know this? Maybe she always knew things, but doubted them. Maybe she had more wisdom than she thought!?!

Shaking her head in amazement, Meshka called out, "Are you still dere Meyer?" In the dim shadows, she saw his silhouette and relaxed. She made herself comfortable on a log and said to Meyer, "Let me tell you a story. Remember my Uncle Heimme? God bless his soul, he vas a rolly polly man vid a big smile who vas always making liddle toys for da children. You never could tell Uncle Heimme's age; he vas alvays old.

"Sometimes, I am sure I see Uncle Heimme here among dese people. His spirit is in different bodies, *farshtaist* (you understand)?

"Once he vas Polish, another time Spanish, den French, 'n once even Scottish. Each man looked different on da outside, but inside, I could feel Uncle Heimme; da same kind smile 'n da same sweet goodness!"

She was so excited! These ideas came to her from Meyer's questions! She was looking out on a new horizon from a very wide point of view.

"Remember my Aunt Ruthie, may she rest in peace? Remember how she talked 'n talked faster dan anyone ever? I have seen a lot of Aunt Ruthies. Vhen I meet one of dese women, vid da same nature as my aunt, I know dem. 'N dey recognize me too.

She saw a smile playing on his lips as he gazed at her lovingly from the shadows. Maybe her eyes saw what they wanted.

"Have you met anyone in heaven like my Aunt Gertrude? May da angels watch over her, she vas as big 'n as powerful as a solid wall. My aunt vas very good to me, but you never vanted to get her angry. Aunt Gertrude had a big heart, but she expected dings to be done just so.

"I met a couple of women who feel just like Aunt Gertrude. Dey va walking, no marching like generals in da front of dese people." Meshka admired and respected these women. When she marched beside them, she felt a little safer and a little more solid in herself.

A chilly breeze rippled across Meshka's neck. She shivered and instinctively reached to wrap the shawl around her head and shoulders. Her hands had done this motion a million times before. Now it was pure habit. For a second, Meshka was surprised to find no warm shawl waiting there. She shrugged and spoke to the silhouette among the shadows.

"Meyer, I have seen da world inside women's hearts. Oy so much beauty, 'n so much pain. Some of dem are made of starlight. Dey hardly touch da ground. Dey charm our hearts. 'N vee? Vee hold da string, so dey do not float avay."

She shivered and hugged her shoulders to keep warm. She was not ready to return to camp just yet.

"Meyer, believe me, some women are made from ripe fruit 'n live to share life's sweetness. Dey vant to be savored, but instead dey find a hungry beast in deir bed. Maybe dis world is really under da thumb of da Cosmic Joker. He drops liddle hints all da time to warn us of da mischief he is about to make. But most of da time, vee can only see da clues vhen vee walk backwards. Da Cosmic Joker does not let life get too quiet."

The moon was shining her shy maiden smile above a graceful fan of dark clouds. The flaming light of the dying sun was radiating up from behind her fan making her look elegantly eerie. Meshka glanced up at the charming maiden, felt a tantalizing wave of hidden mystery, and shuddered. In that second of distraction, the thread between her and Meyer was dropped.

Meshka returned to camp with a lighter step. She suddenly saw clearly. She was walking her own path. It was scary and exciting! In the village, she was told how to live, what to do, and how to do it. These became familiar fences in her mind that kept the wild forces out.

Nevermore would she be dragged from event to event by a puppet master. She was on her own destined path. Now it was Meshka and her *Divine Source*. Together they would carve out her path. She was excited to see what Fate would bring now that she held her own strings.

ଔଔଔ

Life seemed to unfold by itself the next day. Meshka did all the things she needed to do and it all got done, but she was not there. She was with Meyer walking around in a dream.

That evening when all her duties were done, Meshka wrapped herself in a thick blanket and wandered off to a special place at the foot of a waterfall. Sharanii took her to this special hideaway just yesterday.

Beside the falls was a soft tuft of grass. In delight, Meshka *plotzed* down in the grass and let out a deep breath of contentment. She looked up at the frothing falls framed in sky. It was a long way up to the top.

Here, at the foot of the falls, was a wide deep pool. In peaceful fascination, she lay in the grass looking upward, watching the wild bubbling waters cascade down over huge rocks in a daring frothy plunge. At the base of the cliff, the heady froth ebbed outward in soft blue ripples to the far edges of the pool. She was sitting close enough for the fresh cool mist to touch her face. Such a lovely place!

"Meyer where are you? I feel you somewhere nearby. Come, let us share dis beautiful place. It vill be sweet. Please let me see you."

The air grew sweeter with something like perfume, but more intoxicating. She gazed into the rushing falling waters until she saw him! A tingling excitement bubbled up through her veins!

He was there. She saw his beloved image through the sunlight playing on the water. She gazed through the light and diamond sparkles of the falls and saw his soft dark brown eyes looking out at her through the cascading waters. He looked sad.

"Hello Meyer," she sang out, grateful to feel him near. "Dank you for coming. I miss you so much."

The mist caressed Meshka's face. She fell into Meyer's familiar dark eyes. Their hearts reached for each other through a churning veil of tears.

"I hope God is treating you vell in heaven. You know, He could treat us bedder down here. Remember how Yonkle used to say, God plays tricks on us? I am not so sure God is really holding all da power. Is God really so nasty dat He purposefully made people angry, ignorant 'n cruel? If God has a choice, why does He not choose to reward people who reach for high principles 'n are gentle vid each other?

"If God had a choice, why did He choose to kill our beautiful babies 'n destroy such a sweet liddle village? I hope God does not hold all da reins. If dis is really His doing, I have no use for such a God!"

Shocked! Horrified! How could she say such a thing!?! Icy waves shivered through her.

The softness in Meyer's eyes was infinitely forgiving. She breathed in his forgiveness and released the clawing guilt starting to strangle her.

"You know Meyer, maybe there is more dan one God. Maybe dere is three: Da God of my foremothers, da Cosmic Joker who plays vid us sometimes very cruelly, 'n da Messiah who vill teach us how to create a better world."

She gazed at the hidden face of her beloved through the rushing waters, listened to the song of the waterfalls, and breathed deeply of the fresh moist air.

"Meyer. Dere is a Messiah, a Prince of Peace. I am sure I see him in some young men. You know, our Yonkle vas such a prince. Dere vas nothing fancy about our lives, but vhen Yonkle walked straight 'n proud, he vas like a king.

"Dose times vhen he talked wisely to me, 'n helped me to deal vid people gently, instead of always vid such a quick tongue, I knew den, dat dere vas a liddle of da Messiah in him."

Soft ribbons of silver moonlight danced on the waves as twilight descended into night. Every tree and rock cast a shadow making a hidden place where other-worldly beings like to hide.

In the dappled shadows, Meshka saw the silhouette of her sweet husband. His smile was so bright, it shimmered on the edge of her sight.

Meyer laughed as leaves began to flutter.

"Meshka, vhen did you become such a philosopher!?! Vhen did you start dinking so much? I am content vhere I am. Da food is not as good as yours. No one makes chicken *knaidlech* (matzo ball) soup like you, but I am satisfied."

The evening wind rippled across the water laughing with Meyer's laugh.

Meshka closed her eyes, listening to his voice whispering on the wind, "I vant you should know, I see Yonkle sometimes. Vhen he crossed over to dis side, I vas there to greet him in da tunnel of light."

Beneath the moonlight, sweet Meyer flickered in and out of rocky shadows. He looked so young! She was surprised that he was ever so young! She looked into the soft brown eyes of her sweet husband. Those eyes always melted her heart like honey butter.

The wind was not blowing and the leaves were not rustling, but still she heard his voice.

"I do not know about your three Gods, da one I met is very nice, but I cannot promise He is da only one. You might be right about da others. I vill look around heaven 'n see. May your gods 'n your *Goddess* bless you my kitten. I am happy your poor swollen feet do not trouble you so much anymore."

Meyer was so gentle, so tender, and so young. When he looked at her with those young man eyes, she felt like a maiden again, full of excitement and sweet mysteries.

A golden thread of light bound her soul to his. The more she remembered how much she loved him, the brighter the golden thread was shining.

A ragged dirty cloud swallowed up the moon. In the darkness Meyer drifted away.

Meshka's body was tingling. Despite the sharpness of the cold, the night was fresh. She savored each breath! She felt alive in all her senses!

On the way back to camp, Meshka chuckled. It was months since she thought about her feet. "Vhen I only had to walk down da street from my house to Rifka's, my feet swelled up like ten pound melons. Now I *shlep* around all day 'n dey are just big fat elephant feet dat work just fine, dank you."

Meshka felt good. A soft cloud of magic hovered around her head and a wondrous sense of *Presence* enveloped her.

అంఅంఅం

A few days later the moon was just past full, dangling among diamonds on a black velvet sky. Meshka wandered off again to court the night. Through the lantern of the moon, she made her way to the rocky outcropping above the waterfall, high over the valley. Now that was an impressive climb! She came to a big flat rock, a perfect place to sit and dangle her legs over an expanse that went on forever. Meshka was becoming pretty agile after all the scrambling over rocks she was doing these days.

The fresh cool air was intoxicating! Her spirit longed to fly! If only she had wings! But even without wings she took flight and oh how she soared!

Charmed by the night, Meshka looked out across the valley. Lacey wisps of smoke rose into the sky from hundreds of campfires. Way down there, all the refugees were clustered around their evening fires sharing warmth and companionship. Long lazy curls of smoke drifted up into various shapes before softly fading into the night.

One fire belched up a big puff of gray smoke. It was the same motley gray as Meyer's scraggly old beard. She laughed remembering how his beard used to tickle her when he kissed her; and how sweet those kisses were.

Meshka returned to camp late. Rifka was sitting beside the fire waiting for her to return. Her daughter was staring into the flames. Meshka sat down opposite her to share the quiet. She gazed into the flames marveling that the flickering tongues of fire were the same coppery amber as Meyer's young-man beard.

As soon as Meshka recognized the color of the flames, the thread between their souls touched. Standing behind Rifka was her young papa. Meshka was barely breathing. Seeing her beloved and her daughter in the same view was blissful.

Meshka fell into his joyful sparkling eyes. I tell you, that man took nothing seriously. Those eyes of his were still laughing and his smirky lips wore the same teasing smile.

In the dim light of the flames, no one could see the faraway look in her eyes. Meshka looked past her daughter and saw only her Meyer. His voice echoed in her mind.

"Meshka, you would not believe all da amazing dings I discovered in heaven! You thought maybe there va three Gods? Hold onto your hair! There are twelve!" He excitedly announced!

Meshka darted a glance at Rifka to see if she heard his voice, but Rifka was still staring blankly into the flames.

"Excuse me, Shainela I have to find a bush," she mumbled and disappeared into the shadows. Being with someone alive, and someone in spirit, was a weird mixture of feelings. It made her head spin. Once she was safely hidden behind a bush, she felt a lot better.

"Twelve! Oy vay, I vas having a hard time vid one!" The words jumped out of her mouth before her tongue could stop them. Her lips were trembling in awe! "Vhat am I going to do vid twelve!?!"

A silhouette of Meyer as a young man flickered in the shadows. Meshka was enchanted by his handsome face and slim figure. A dreamy smile played upon her lips as she listened to his story.

"In Heaven, I saw six *Goddesses* 'n six Gods. Their magic force pours into everything dat lives. You va right! Your Messiah 'n da Cosmic Joker, dey are two of dem.

"Da twelve Cosmic Beings each have a different nature. Da Jewish God, Yahweh, He is a warrior God. Some people here call Him Jehovah, others call Him Marduk. He has a lot of different names, but do not be fooled, always He has da same fiery nature."

She gazed into the shadows at his wonderful young handsome face and listened to his gentle voice. She wondered if she was sleeping and marveled at the strange stuff her mind made up!

Then the most amazing words came from Meyer, stuff she could not possibly make up!

"Six *Goddesses* live in heaven too! One is *Inanna, Goddess of Love and Passion*. Oy! *She* is such a pretty ding! *She* walks in beauty 'n sunbeams of love pour from *Her* into my soul. Like everybody here *She* has many names: *Ishtar, Astarte, Aphrodite, Venus* 'n many more. "My favorite is da *Mother Goddess* – Oy vay! Is *She* wonderful! I dink maybe *She* is da *Shekhina*. Da Greeks called *Her Demeter* 'n da Canaanites worshipped *Her* as *Asherah*; but those are just different names for da same *Goddess*."

Fireworks were exploding in Meshka. Her head was spinning.

"Oy Meyer, how are vee going to deal vid all of dem?" She whispered.

Meyer melted away her fears with his steady warm gaze. In the dark, she felt hidden and safe but still a little dizzy.

Meyer reassured her, "Liddle Kitten, vee just discovered dem, but dey have always been here.

"Vee just thought everything came from God. It vas a shock to see He is a member of a whole family of Gods. Da others Deities are not better or worse, just different."

Meshka put her hands on her cheeks and shook her head.

"Vee Jews, vee worship Yahweh 'n ignore all da others. Da important ding I learned up here is dat da cosmos is big enough for lotsa different Gods. Different vays to live is a good ding as long as people do not fight about it."

Meshka was reeling with shock!

"Twelve Gods! Oy vay! Do dey get along vid each other?" She whispered the words out loud; then wondered if it was a sin to ask such a thing.

Meyer answered with a sad shrug. "As good as people do."

Meshka could see Meyer as one sees vague images in a dream - there - but not really.

"Do dey fight vid each other?" She whispered under her breath, so it would sound like a sigh.

"Worse dan dat!" Meyer cried out! "Dey send their anger into people 'n da people fight battles for dem. It is amazing how people willingly obey their God, no matter how harsh or cruel His demands are. Mostly dey follow out of fear." Meyer hesitated and then added, "*Chaval!*" (What a pity!)

Meshka was trembling in the dark of the night, far from anyone's sight, at least of this world.

"Meyer, vhat should I do? Should I make-believe there are no other Gods, just one God, or should I try maybe to meet these other Gods?" She whispered softly under her breath, so the night would not notice.

Meshka savored Meyer's precious presence. "Sleep on it, my Kitten. Your dreams vill tell you vhat to do."

He smiled. The warmth spreading through her was real.

"Dank you Meyer. I vill say a special prayer for you next Shabbos. I vill pray to all da gods 'n *Goddesses*, to all da good forces of heaven 'n earth, 'n ask dem to watch over you 'n protect you. You va a good man 'n you va good to me. I miss you, my sweet husband. It has been too many years."

A funny thought popped up into Meshka's head.

"Husband, would you like to be born again?" she asked.

Meyer smiled mischievously, gave her his best flirting eyes and said, "Not right now. If I vas born now, I would be too young for you. I dink I vill wait until you join me in heaven 'n den vee can start da next journey together." That is just what Meyer would say!

Playfully she teased, "Good. Next time maybe you can be my son, so I can love you all your life."

As he faded into the shadows, she heard him say, "Oh. I thought maybe next time you could be da husband 'n I would be your wife." That was just like Meyer to have the last word.

Meyer as my wife!?!

The image of Meyer as a woman, running around in a frilly apron, made Meshka laugh so hard, she started hiccupping.

Meyer went back to his world and Meshka was alone again. A mysterious smile played on her face. As she walked back to camp, she replayed a favorite night of hers in the theater behind her eyes. It was long, long ago, when Meyer was a young man full of vigor and righteousness.

One night he was making love to her with such playful joy, she said in jest to tease him, "New husband I have never seen a man's body. You always wear a nightshirt. Is that to hide you from my eyes? I am curious. Can I look at you?"

Of course, modesty demanded they always wear a covering gown even in bed together. She was young, full of questions, and filled with great bravado. Meyer wanted to shock her, so he took off his nightshirt, boldly he stood before her and invited her touch him - anywhere!

She was scared, intrigued, charmed by his daring, and by her own, so she agreed to play his game. Such a deliciously exciting night; it was a pleasure worth remembering again and again! Her first child, Rifkala was conceived that night.

CRCRCR

Chapter 15

A Portal in Time

The day dawned fresh and cold. Even the sun found it hard to get out of bed. Flurries of snow softly covered the land, dancing like drunken fairies swirling sideways in the air. Meshka was sick of herself and cramped from lying on the ground for so many empty hours. She groaned and turned over in her twisted bedroll. Eventually the need to relieve herself forced her to get up. Maybe it was the dreary weather or maybe she just did not want to remember that it was Yonkle's Birthday. Back in the old village he would be twenty-one today.

Meshka wanted to run and hide, mostly she just wanted to disappear, anything to escape the pictures in her head. The first little tear rolled slowly down her cheek. The rest raced each other down her face in mad escape. Then she melted into a puddle of tears.

Feeling all the years in her bones, she crawled out of her little tent. Maya, Sarina, and Tasjia were already up. They had a hot fire blazing and were bustling about like little bees. Even though it was not Friday, they were already cooking and baking. It was probably a holiday in someone's religion.

Briefly Meshka wondered if they were going to light a *yahrtzeit* (memorial) candle for Yonkle, but brushed the thought away with a shrug. No one except Rifka knew this was a special day for her.

"Good Morning!" Meshka called to the three busy young women. Each one smiled and returned the greeting. "Is today a holy day?" Meshka asked.

"Yes, it is Mid-Winter's Eve," Sarina sang out, "half way between winter and spring" as she pounded fragrant herbs in a little wooden mortar beneath the protective branches of a thick pine tree.

"We are going to have a wonderful celebration," added Tasjia dropping an armload of branches beside the fire.

"We are preparing for tonight's ceremony and feast." Maya called over her shoulder as she added some fragrant sage and thyme to the pot. A delicious aroma rose from her cauldron. It was a refreshing change from her usual medicinal concoctions.

"Vhat kind of ceremony?" Meshka was curious.

"We are going to rededicate ourselves to *The Goddess* and to Her path of service. Would you like to join us?" Maya asked with a hopeful look.

Meshka was flustered by the invitation. She mumbled an excuse and waddled over to the stand of bushes set aside to be their potty. Once she went to relieve herself, she could think better. She was shivering, but ignored it. She did not want to wear the woolen shawl.

Meshka put on all her heavy dresses and a sweater she knitted; that made her feel much warmer. She felt a little lost. Tasjia already gathered the wood. Maya already kindled the fire. There really was nothing for Meshka to do. She could sit down by the warm fire and drink some morning tea, but she felt too restless so she wandered off to be alone.

Her feet were wrapped in booties made from strips of sheep leather. The fur inside kept her toes warm. They were a gift from Rifka. That woman was as handy with the needle as the knife. She wandered over to the river. She felt patient, wanting neither comfort or inspiration, she just wanted to unburden her heart.

"Yonkle," she called out. Her voice held a touch of loneliness and yearning. "Yonkle, I miss you so much, it feels like my heart is cracking into pieces. Come talk vid me." Silence reigned.

"Yonkle," she sang in the sing song voice she used to use when he was little to make him eat his vegetables. "It has been a while since you last visited me. Dis would be a good time to show up. It is your birthday."

She listened closely to a whispering breeze tip toe through the trees. All was silent, except the rattling sound of her own breath.

The other-world, which had sustained her for so long felt gone. A dam inside her heart broke. Rivers, no oceans of grief flooded in on her. For the first time, she realized how utterly alone she was among all these strangers.

"Yonkle," she cried out in desperation to the trees and the sky. Between sobs she begged, "Yonkle, do not abandon me! I need you! Please say something to comfort me!" She held her breath, but only emptiness surrounded her.

Meshka pulled herself together and returned to camp. She made her way past a multitude of strange faces. Along the way, she saw people with black, yellow, red, and white faces, a rainbow of strangers bustling about their morning chores. The air was alive with everyday sounds, but Meshka felt strange and distant from the world around her.

A big hole opened inside her soul and it ached. She was falling, falling down a long dark well and no loving hands reached out to save her.

In despair, she was falling with nothing to grab onto. She was lost, cast adrift far from the safe shores of her real life. No one from the other world came to calm her fears. No one made the falling stop.

"Yonkle, I need you right now! Speak to me!" Her hollow heart silently cried out in anguish.

Her legs took her back to camp. Her tears cascaded down her bright rosy cheeks. Her breath breathed itself in soft white puffs of vapor and no one was looking out through her eyes.

ርጸርጸርጸ

Meshka's face was streaked with misery when she arrived in camp. Maya smiled sweetly when she saw her distressed friend and guided her to sit by the fire. Meshka gazed sightlessly as Maya poured hot water from a heavy iron kettle over tranquilizing tea leaves. She put the steaming cup in Meshka's frozen hands.

"Drink this. It will warm you," she gently coaxed.

The lonely old woman sat staring and silent for several minutes, her hands gratefully wrapped around the warm cup. The sweet tea was creamy smooth and comfortingly warm. Waves of steam caressed her face.

Maya put her arm around Meshka's shivering shoulders and hugged the sad old woman. At first, Maya's touch was gentle and reassuring, then stronger, to pour strength into her friend.

"Meshka, this is an intense day for you because today is a portal in time, a sacred day. A holy portal is open today and powerful forces are being unleashed. It is Candlemas. We are half way between winter's harsh challenges and spring's rebirth.

"Any seeds sown on February 2nd, will take root in the year to come. We attune to the glory of life and sow our seeds carefully for the portal is open.

"Sensitive people feel the churning, but most of them interpret what they are feeling personally.

"We host a ceremony, as a vessel to contain the power and direct its flow in good directions. We would like it very much if you would join us."

"We will align our minds, bodies, hearts, and souls with the flow of the Life Force. We go to meet destiny, rather than surrender to Fate and wait to be abused by its possible harshness."

Meshka said in a small voice, "God vill punish me if I whore after false Gods."

"Does that mean He also rewards you for your love and obedience? Does He reward you for your compassionate service?" Maya asked without irony or malice.

"Okay, so God is not even looking 'n He does not care about me anymore," Meshka blurted out in despair.

Maya saw the pain Meshka was carrying.

"My old teacher used to say, 'Papas strengthen your back and Mamas point out the path.' Worship your God, but also be open to *The Goddess*. She can illuminate and ease the path before you."

Meshka shrugged her shoulders as if to say, "Maybe."

"At sunset, we will gather in the meadow." She pointed her chin towards a clearing.

"We will have a big fire. You will be warm. Come! Sing, dance, and pray with us. We will each recall this last year and speak aloud what we want for the year to come. Each woman is picking a word or phrase to hold onto as a guiding light. It helps us find our way through the problems, obstacles, and opportunities we meet on the path ahead."

Meshka was trying to pay attention, but fear was pounding like a hammer on her head. It was making too much noise for her to listen.

Maya refilled Meshka's cup with more of the warm comforting tea and smiled warmly.

"Last year I chose 'Trust.' Marji, my teacher, used to say, 'Root yourself only in your own soul and trust those roots to nourish you while you dance with Life.'"

Meshka was staring at Maya like she was crazy.

"Sarina took 'forgiveness.' She said it was an 'onion' word. She meant it took many tears to peel it down to its core.

"I hope you join us. If the other women in your Clan want to come too, they are also welcome."

Meshka stared at her unsure how to make sense of so many new ideas. She was frightened and intrigued. With an eerie shiver she suddenly felt very cold. She gulped down the tea, jumped up, nodded in thanks, and dashed away.

CRCRCRCR

Meshka's Clan was not around for her to talk to about the ritual. Rachel and Rifka were up early as usual to earn their daily bread. Most mornings they went off to find work right after a simple breakfast of eggs and vegetables. With all the women contributing to the pot, they stayed well fed.

Rachel traded the skill of her fine darning needle for hunks of cheese and meat. Rifka was on a nearby farm with her strong hands firmly wrapped around smooth udders. Joya was asleep.

It would be a while before Rachel or Rifka returned. Meshka felt all alone, weighed down by this big decision.

Joya usually woke up at the crack of noon; and even then, she was very slow to start moving. It took hours before the fog cleared in her head. Then she went off to read people's fortunes. She was in much demand and often brought home impressive amounts of food and gifts.

Meshka did not have a specific skill. She knew how to sew, but her stitches were not very even. She was not much of a cow milker either.

But Meshka had a way of taking care of people, helping the old ones lift and carry, cooking for the sick ones, or just being an extra pair of hands ready to help with whatever was needed. For her loving smile, her generous help, and her uplifting words, people enjoyed giving her food and gifts.

Putting the scary ritual out of her mind, Meshka went to her grandma circle. She sat among these sweet women smiling absently. She was not listening to the excited talk about Davidka's first new tooth and hardly heard their heated debate over teething remedies. She was listening to the clicking ring of her knitting needles and watched her fingers dance with the yarn while her mind ran around in circles – to go – to not go.

Little Timmy, a miniature child, tiny from a lifetime of hunger, crawled into her lap and nestled down to sleep. From the first day, when he tasted her chicken matzo ball soup, Timmy adopted Meshka as his mama and that was that.

Meshka rocked his soft little body and hummed an ancient lullaby. The song came from her mama's mama. Maybe it stretched all the way back to the first Eve. Who knows? Sometimes Meshka gave her lullabies words, but mostly they were just rolling sounds, full of a mama's loving heart, her tenderness, and her hopeful prayers.

She savored the warmth of the sleeping child tucked in against her soft belly. Rocking back and forth on the log amongst the grandmas, Meshka mused, how strange! Right now I feel content. Only a few minutes ago, I felt utterly alone. Meshka rocked the sleeping child and it lulled her into a sweet melted quiet place. Little Timmy squirreled in deeper and whimpered softly.

"Yonkle, dank you for pushing da child over to me," she whispered quietly under her breath, in case he was listening. "I know dis child is your 'hello.'"

Drifting in idle thoughts, lulled by the rocking, her mind wandered back to yesterday.

She was sitting in the sunshine with Joya studying tarot cards!

Meshka shook her head in disbelief thinking of the events that led her to learn to read tarot cards, even though magical oracles still scared her. She peered at the strings of Fate puppeting her. She shook her head, marveling at how events led her so far away from the customs of her little village.

Maybe it all started vhen Rachel vas wagging her finger at me for not wearing my shawl; or maybe it started dat day vhen I put on Tasjia's pretty skirt 'n it made me feel so beautiful; or maybe I became a bigger person vhen I helped save da girls. Dey dink I am a hero," her eyes fluttered with pleasure.

"It is strange, but for da first time in my whole life, I vant to try new dings!" she mused.

Meshka knew Rachel was not the only one judging her for putting aside the shawl. Some of the grandmas lifted a sharp eyebrow when she showed up at her *Knitting Circle* with a naked head.

Not all of them, mind you. The old wispy Irish woman and the robust Dutch woman do not wear shawls, so they thought nothing of it; but the sturdy Russian woman and the chunky old Polish grandma were definitely shocked.

They did not say a word. They did not have to. It was written on their faces.

Meshka smiled and greeted all the women like nothing was amiss. She sat down and began knitting her little sweater until Timmy crawled up on her lap and cuddled in.

She was thinking about the women judging her and it struck her! Anyone who does not hide inside the traditional covering has to stand up and make her own decisions.

"No matter vhat other people say," she reassured herself, "I have to trust myself 'n make up my own mind. If I dink for myself, small minds vill condemn me. Dey vill try to stop me from growing. Bigger minds are busy carving out their own dings. Maybe dey vill appreciate dat I am a carver too."

As a carver, she made her first decision.

"I vill look at dings as clearly as I can. No more hiding. I vill look at all da parts, no matter how ugly or scary. Den I vill ask myself one question, just one, does dis help people or harm dem? Dis vill be my measure."

Yesterday, around mid-day, when Meshka was having lunch with Timmy, Joya sat down by the fire beside her to eat breakfast. Meshka started talking to Joya and one word led to another. Soon she found herself confessing all the scary feelings inside her. Out of nowhere she was suddenly sharing her deepest feelings with Joya. She confided that she wanted to think for herself and try new things. She even admitted that she felt like a new, bigger person.

One word followed another and led them into talking about dreams and oracles. Meshka asked, "Do dese dings help or hurt people? Do you really dink dese pictures make dings happen!?!"

Joya shook her head and said, "No. They are just lenses to look through; just pieces of paper reflecting the patterns underlying our lives. Tarot cards open your eyes to see more of what is happening around you."

Meshka rubbed her chin, wrinkled her brow, and was chewing on her lower lip. She was thinking about all the sides to the question.

Finally Meshka answered, "I do not know," and shrugged. "But I dink maybe knowing 'n being prepared to meet your destiny is a good ding. Facing da future vid open eyes has to be a good ding, so I guess da tarot is helpful. It is like you once said to me, 'Oracles are God's pockets vhere He keeps all da secrets.' If He offers dem to us to read, why should vee turn our back on His gifts?"

This thinking thing was making Meshka feel powerful. She decided for herself that tarot cards were good.

Joya nodded approvingly. With a mischievous twinkle in her eyes, she challenged the Jewish woman, "Are you willing to learn to read the tarot cards? Are you willing to look in God's pockets? You never know what you will find."

Meshka flushed red as a beet. The new *Goddess* part of her screamed, "Yes!" Her old shawl-wearing part screamed, "No!" Both sides were yelling at her. Her head was spinning so fast she could not think. The words, "Yes!" "No!" raced to her tongue. It came to pass, the mouth decided.

"So now I am learning to read tarot cards!" Meshka shook her head. "Who would have thought such a ding vas possible!?!" She chuckled to herself, "I vas never taught to read words on a page 'n now I am learning to read picture cards, amazing!"

The grandmas heard her chuckle and looked up at her questioningly. She gave them an innocent smile and returned to her thoughts.

"In da village, dey believed dat learning made a woman a demon; but I know I am a good person, not a demon. If someone ever told me I vas going to learn new dings, I would have laughed in their faces. Who knew I had *saykhel* (smarts) enough to learn something new."

Timmy sucked his thumb with soft smacking sounds, in dreams he was nursing at his mama's breast. The little fellow gave a deep sigh and burrowed in against his new mama's belly. He was so sweet. Meshka felt alive again! She felt new and fresh. She felt open to whatever came along to make her life and Timmy's life better. Then a thought hit her sharp as lightning!

"I am going to use my mind 'n learn da secrets of life. Maybe dinking is not just for men. Vee women can do dis too, vee are just not allowed! Yes, I can do dis!" A little giggle popped out. The other grandmas looked at each other questioningly. Meshka smiled at them and shrugged.

She was feeling pretty strong until her shawl-wearing part started screaming at her. As always, it threatened her with hell and damnation. Little Timmy mumbled in his sleep, tossing and turning. He could feel her mood. Meshka petted his head slowly and gently. Soon he calmed down. His bad dream went away.

Meshka listened to the women discuss weaning. The words passed through her. While her head was nodding agreement to the Russian woman who was talking, she was listening to a terrible argument inside her head. "Look at Sharanii, she can read 'n she is an angel. Joya is not an angel, but she is not a demon either."

The new *Goddess* part of Meshka was turning cartwheels in her stomach as she imagined entering the forbidden realm of knowledge. It was alright for women to have wisdom. It was their compensation for suffering under the yoke of men, but knowledge was something very different. It was the key to power and men hoarded power to themselves.

Meshka was amazed at all the new ideas bubbling up from her mind all of a sudden.

"Wisdom I have," she accepted. "God knows da pain it cost me. All dose hard clops in da head dat life gave me, left me vid wisdom. Look at me, I am dinking! Dis is amazing!"

Her head nodded, she petted her chin, and another chuckle rippled through her. The grandmas looked up and caught Meshka's eyes. Caught with her hand in the cookie jar, she began to laugh a big belly laugh. Soon all the women were laughing with her. They assumed Meshka was laughing at them for getting so serious about teething and weaning. Anyway they needed a good laugh. Their lives were too serious.

They were all experts on teething, weaning and everything about being a mama. They raised their own children and life taught them many important things.

Each came from a different part of the world, so they carried different ideas. The laughter brought them back to the joy of grandmothering, the important thing they shared. Each one admitted to herself, maybe just maybe, there could be more than one right way to take care of a child.

Serious little Timmy woke up and blinked. He was surprised that everyone was laughing, so he laughed too. Meshka kept shaking her head and laughing at her own thoughts. Each had their own reasons for laughing, Meshka hugged her little boy. He threw his tiny arms around her neck and gave her a big kiss. He made Meshka feel brave.

The child jumped off her lap and scampered off to play. She took a deep breath and thought, "So Joya is teaching me to be an oracle! Now God 'n I can talk in another vay. Maybe da pictures vill help me understand God better."

Now that Meshka had no shawl to protect her, no place to hide, and no way to be invisible, she had no idea what was coming next!

ଔଔଔ

Meshka gathered up Timmy and her knitting, said goodbye to her *Circle of Grandmas,* and waddled back to her campsite. The sun was high in the sky and her little boy's belly was empty.

Meshka gave Timmy a big hunk of challah and a chunk of smelly cheese. She took some for herself, and sat down on a fallen log.

Joya wobbled out of her sleeping tent and sat down beside them. For Meshka it was the middle of the day and for Joya it was sun-up. Her body woke up slowly, her eyes took a little longer and her fuzzy mind took its sweet time getting clear. Joya could wander around in a daze for maybe an hour before all her pieces came together.

Joya set about kindling a fire to brew some tea. It took a while because she was trying to do it with her eyes mostly closed. With one eye open she reached for a piece of bread. It floated in her hand as her eyelids drooped close. Both eyes slowly opened as she reached for some cheese. Joya savored her simple meal in silence beside Meshka.

While Joya was busy with her fire making and Timmy was concentrating on his food, Meshka was off marveling at the craziness of life.

"Dis is really *meshugeh!* (crazy) As soon as I agreed to learn a forbidden art, da very next day, I am invited to a heathen ritual. Vhat am I supposed to do!?!"

Meshka looked at Joya, all fuzzy with sleep. Yesterday she was not a sleepy, hungry, pregnant girl, but a temptress holding open a forbidden door, a teacher beckoning Meshka to learn, to grow, to become something amazing!

Yesterday, when Meshka was listening to Joya's words, she feared lightning would strike her out of a clear blue the sky.

Nothing happened.

Joya put the tarot cards in Meshka's hands and said with a twinkle, "The lesson begins."

Meshka stopped breathing! Shocked! Meshka looked down at the cards in her hand like they were writhing snakes. Her eyes darted around the camp looking for a burning bush. She scanned every shadow. Where was the raging lion that would jump out and roar? Birds chirped, leaves fluttered, flies buzzed, all was quiet.

Excited and flustered, she held the tarot cards like they were made of the sheerest glass about to break in her hand. Meshka looked down at the thin goatskin parchments, weathered and yellowed, smooth and warm in her hand.

The Gypsy girl reached over and turned the top card up and showed it to Meshka. The picture on it was of a tall slender man, dressed in a long black cloak, standing with head bent grieving over three spilt cups. Two full cups were hidden behind him.

"This is the Five of Cups. There are four suits, four different families of cards: the cups, swords, pentacles, and wands." Joya explained.

"The cards with pictures of cups are of the water family. They are full of feelings. The cards with pentacles show the physical world of money and goods. The cards with swords show ideas, beliefs, and the problems people face. The wands show us strength of will and point us in the right direction.

"This card," she said, putting it face up on the stack of cards in Meshka's hand, "is from the family of cups. There are five cups. Every part of the picture has a meaning. The three cups spilling on the ground are the things he has lost and he is grieving them. The two cups hidden behind his back, these he does not see. He only sees what was lost. The card tells us to look around and see all that still remains."

This card was not new to Meshka. She often saw it when Joya read cards by the evening fire. Meshka liked to watch Joya. She was fascinated by the strange pictures.

"There are two different parts to the Tarot deck. One part deals with everyday events and the other part reveals sacred knowledge. In the everyday part, there are the four families: cups, swords, pentacles, and wands."

"Every family has an Ace, a leader to point out a new direction. The number cards tell us about the day-to-day experiences we meet in life. There are court cards in each family. They are the people in our stories.

There is also a sacred part of the Tarot, twenty two sacred cards that map the realm of spirit. We Roma have read tarot cards since…"

Meshka interrupted, "Vhat is dis Roma business? I thought you va a Gypsy."

"Being a Gypsy is like being a *shikza*. It is what outsiders call us." Joya patiently explained and returned to what she was saying, "We Roma have read tarot cards since the beginning of time. The meaning of each card is not fixed. It changes with circumstances.

"Each card has a basic meaning, but our feelings and insights add deeper understanding. The Five of Cups reminds us to stop weeping over what is lost and turn around, see the good things that are waiting."

Meshka's mind returned to the present. Timmy finished his lunch, drank his milk from a hollow gourd, and curled up in the grass to play with a little black bug. Meshka watched Timmy. She was charmed by the funny story he was telling the bug.

She understood what Joya was saying yesterday. The meaning of the card was clear to her. If she was reading cards for someone and this card was turned over, she would know just what to say. Meshka was shocked that she was actually smart enough to learn!

She smiled and thought; "I am reaching for da hidden cups right here, at this moment. Da past is gone. I am choosing to look for da good dings dat are left."

It struck Meshka that only fear was holding her back from growing even more. With a surge of newly budding bravery, she decided to go to the pagan ritual.

She looked down at the sweet little orphan playing at her feet and thought; "Dis child is a full cup 'n he makes me feel full too. He is one of dose hidden cups." Loving this child made her feel even braver.

As soon as the decision was made, Meshka prayed, "Oh Most Holy Von. Do not get me wrong, I am not whoring after false Gods! I am just going to take a liddle look. I vill never be von of your heavenly angels, you know dat.

"I am just a woman made of sweat, blood 'n aging flesh. My fat feet belong on da earth 'n my loyalty is to dese women. If you really vant to forbid me from going to dis ritual, den show me a sign right now! I am waiting for your sign." There, she left it up to God.

Nothing happened.

The sky was blue, the fire was warm, and all around her the world carried on, so Meshka turned to Joya and asked her if she wanted to come to the ritual too.

A strong wind suddenly picked up and blew a dirty smudge of dark cloud over her head. It passed in front of the sun. Was that a sign!?! Meshka waited with bated breath.

If one flake of snow fell on her naked head, she was not going to the pagan ritual, she was not going to study the forbidden tarot cards, and the old shawl was going right back on her head!

The sky grew darker. A large angry cluster of clouds hovered above her head. Suddenly a strong wind blew the clouds apart and a circle of blue sky opened in the middle. The sun sent a shaft of light like an angel's slide shining through the bright hole in the dark clouds. A soft ray of light, straight as a road, beamed down to the land below. If that was not God reaching out His hand to her, nothing was.

The opening in the clouds looked like a doorway to heaven with a shining lane leading right up to it. Another strong wind blew. The clouds closed in and the shining ray of rainbow light vanished. The moment passed. It came and went very fast. Maybe it was never there. Who could tell? Her eyes were always playing tricks on her.

It was a good sign. Meshka was excited and scared. She was going to learn to read tarot cards and she was going watch a real pagan ritual!

ᘓᘓᘓᘓ

Joya finished her breakfast around noontime and wandered off to earn her daily bread. She returned a couple hours later with a basket of food. "Timmy, I am going to make something special for you. Would you like to try a Roma dish? I am going to make *mămăliga*."

The little fellow nodded enthusiastically. He liked any and all kinds of food.

"Meshka, would you like some too?"

"Vhat is it? Meshka wrinkled her nose. Taste strange *unko-sher* food!? Then she caught herself being afraid to take a risk, so she quickly added, "Dank you Shainela, vhatever it is, vee vould love to taste your Gypsy food. Vee never ate anything you cooked before."

"I do not like to cook and all of you are so much better cooks than I am, but I had a craving for **mămăliga**. By a stroke of luck, I did a palm reading today and was paid in cornmeal."

Meshka smiled to herself; "Joya is cooking! Dis is a good sign. Da girl is mending."

Meshka watched Joya prepare the **mămăliga**. The young Roma put cold water and a bit of precious salt in the old dented pot, then the pot went on the fire.

While they waited for the pot to boil, Meshka asked, "Do you know vhat is dis Candlemas ritual?"

Joya replied, "Candlemas? Is that what they call it?"

"Dat is vhat Maya called it."

"We celebrate Imbolc at mid-winter. Most religions have a holiday at this time of the year to contain and give form to the natural forces that come through these powerful portals. The midway point in each season is an opening to great forces, a time of change. Be careful what you wish for on Candlemas. Today it can easily come true, but not necessarily in the form you expect.

"Last Imbolc, I wished to 'expand beyond the boundaries of my world' and look what form that took!"

The water was boiling. Joya scooped up a handful of corn-meal and let it flow through her fingers into the center of the pot where it made a little mountain.

While the **mămăliga** cooked, Meshka gathered her courage and asked, "Vhat is a portal? I thought it vas something on a boat?"

Joya laughed. "A year has four seasons, right? In the middle of each season, there is a day when a doorway opens. This doorway, this portal, is a sacred day full of blessings and magic."

Joya drained off the water, put the pot of **mămăliga** back on the fire and mashed the lumps in the thick dough with a wooden stick.

She cooked it until it was thick and hard to stir. Then she added a tiny bit of water, loosened the edges around the pot and put it back on the fire to release the steam.

Mămăliga was a simple food, but one of Joya's favorites. It had the flavor of her old life in the caravan. She savored the familiar taste of the past.

Sensing the food was ready, little Timmy jumped up on the log beside his new mama and proudly handed Meshka his squiggly bug. Meshka did not like bugs but the child did, so she took it graciously and smiled. He looked up into Meshka's kind eyes and giggled. Seeing his serious face lit up with childish giggles was a precious gift indeed!

Meshka put the little crawly thing back in the grass, so he could go back to his mommy, and handed Timmy a bowl of delicious corn mush. Meshka tasted a tiny little bit and crunched up her face expecting it to taste bad. She was pleasantly surprised by its delicious nutty flavor.

Meshka's little boy finished his food and scampered off to play with some children. He was well rested, well fed, and happy for the first time ever.

As the afternoon rolled on, the day grew comfortably warm. Meshka busied herself with people. She walked around and did whatever she could to make life a little better for the people she met. By the end of the afternoon, she diapered a baby, pushed a crippled young woman in a child's pram, cooked some fresh eggs (from a dubious source) for a clever bunch of children, and made them laugh with the duck joke she learned from Jeanne.

That was the one joke she remembered; the only one she could tell without putting the last line first and the first line last.

While her hands did all these things, her mind was busy thinking about portals. By sunset, Meshka was full of ideas about *Priestesses* and magic. Thinking about strange exotic things kept her from feeling the panic hiding inside her.

A golden sunset crowned a long day. Meshka felt calmer after hours of pouring herself into everyone else's needs. The busyness kept her safe from the raw feelings bubbling inside her.

It seemed like forever since she rolled out of bed this morning. Yet one minute she was holding Timmy at the knitting circle, and the next moment was now!

With a quivering heart, Meshka straightened her shoulders, lifted her chest and stepped out of the world she knew into one she never imagined!

CRCRCR

Chapter 16

Sacred Ritual

Meshka brushed her soft silver lamb's wool curls. She was pleased that her hair was still thick and full.

When the sun dropped down to the horizon and cold winds blew in from the sea, Meshka wrapped a thick blanket around her shoulders to keep warm, but the blanket was bulky and awkward.

She should have put on her woolen shawl. That heavy shawl, wrapped tightly around her shoulders, would have kept her nice and warm. But Meshka had only recently set herself free from her little prison of invisibility and was reluctant to crawl back in. "Dis is silly," she told herself. "Am I going to freeze to death just to prove a point?"

Still she wrapped her arms tightly around her shoulders and rubbed hard. She walked around the camp very fast to warm up her blood. She daydreamed about summer and that helped a little. But her hands were trembling. Finally, she could ignore the cold no longer. After pouting and shivering, Meshka put on the old shawl and felt like she just lost a tug of wills with God.

The thick warm shawl lay bunched around Meshka's shoulders. Her head was uncovered as a last act of defiance. Drawing in its familiar warmth around her neck, wrapped in her past, she set off to the ritual meadow.

On the way Meshka met Rifka and Rachel returning from their labors. She told them about the ritual and asked them to come. Rifka was delighted, Rachel was distraught.

Wagging the finger Rachel warned, "*Goddesses* do not exist, 'n anyway dey make God angry!" and continued walking on.

Rifka put down her bundles, shook out her thick hair, and went off with Meshka to the meadow. Joya was already there standing by the fire with Sharanii and the three maidens.

Meshka's skin was crawling like someone was staring at her. She looked around. There was Rachel standing at edge of the meadow, frowning at her. A minute later she was gone. The empty place where she had stood accused her.

Meshka stared at her big fat elephant feet. They were firmly planted on the ground. She knew she should leave, but her feet stood firm. Curiosity and fear pinned her to the ground.

Meshka reassured God that she was leaving soon. Over and over, Meshka told God that she was not really going to participate in a pagan ritual! Still her legs did not move. A nagging critical voice yelled at her inside, but his stinging criticism did not hurt her anymore. She noticed, the less she listened, the less the angry voice had to say.

Her heart was banging like a wild animal trapped in a cage. She looked at the faces around her. She knew and trusted each of these women. They survived together! These women were her circle, her *Clan*. They were a family. She belonged with them.

She was not giving up her love for God. She was not even being disloyal. Her heart felt big enough to love and respect God, while also appreciating *The Goddess*.

She was excited to learn new things and wanted to make life better. Her loyalties lie equally with these brave women and the ghosts of her Jewish family.

CRCRCR

Elegant Sharanii glided slowly around the circle of women. Each reverent step drew down sacredness and wove it into a protective cocoon around them.

Sharanii's fingers, adorned with jewels, held a large shimmering blue seashell in her palm. Smoking herbs wafted lazily upward from the shell. The delicious fragrance was soothing.

Sharanii mixed these herbs from an ancient recipe. The art of making exotic fragrances she learned in an oriental country far away. Each sweet blend of incense touched the heart in a different way. These magical herbs opened the heart, so the women to felt more loving and more loved.

Gliding elegantly around the circle, Sharanii invoked the names of *The Goddess* and a God. With each reverent step, she called down the *Protectors of the World* to oversee this gathering and safeguard the women.

In Meshka's mind, God was lighting a circle of flames around her, accusing her of being a troublesome woman.

"Why is everyone in da circle smiling?" She wondered. "Are dey not afraid God vill punish dem?" Then she remembered, the only Jewish women there were her and Rifka. Only their souls were in danger, but Rifka did not look worried.

Tasjia and Sarina glided around the circle in procession behind Sharanii carrying an air of reverent devotion.

Tasjia came to stillness in front of Maya. She held up a small phial of fragrant oil and anointed the sacred point between Maya's eyes, her *"invisible eye of inner seeing."* The dark haired waif whispered a quiet prayer into Maya's ear and a warm sweet smile spread across Maya's lips. Then Tasjia moved on to anoint Sarina.

"Vhat is Tasjia doing!?! Is she putting da mark of Cain on us!?" Worried Meshka was getting more frightened by the moment.

Tasjia stepped in front of Meshka, whose body turned to stone. Meshka was not even breathing! She was waiting for the angry hand of God to strike her dead!

Instead, she felt Tasjia's gentle touch massaging the space above the bridge of her nose with warm oil. "Open to your wisdom. Look with your inner sight," the maiden whispered.

Meshka was shocked! This was not the mark of Cain, just sweet honest words and a little oil. It was nothing, but Tasjia's touch lingered on her forehead long after the maiden walked on.

Tasjia anointed Rifka's *Eye of Wisdom* next.

Sarina stopped before Meshka. The blond Amazon motioned Meshka to close her eyes. The little Jewish woman bravely obeyed. A thumb pressed firmly on the anointed mark and left a small silver crescent in its wake. Its curious weight, though very slight, was enough to keep Meshka's attention glued there. It radiated heat - probably from embarrassment.

Meshka quickly glanced at Rifka standing with a sweet entranced look on her face. Obviously she was not aware that she was disobeying Jehovah's laws.

But then, Meshka wondered, "Vhat commandment are vee breaking?" She was not worshipping false gods. When Sharanii invited Meshka to call forth a *Deity* to watch over their circle, Meshka called upon Jehovah. She asked Him to be compassionate with the world and with everyone in it.

Meshka stole a glance around the circle; then quickly lowered her eyes so the others would not see her fear. She felt Joya's eyes on her. Meshka looked up and their eyes met. Meshka smiled weakly. It was really more of a grimace.

Joya smiled brightly. She tossed back her thick black mane, proud and elegant as a mare. All the women seemed to be radiating an ephemeral light as though the stars were shining in their eyes and the moist freshness of the sea breeze came straight from their sweet breath.

Rifka was standing straight and proud, comfortable and at ease in this circle of women. That was very puzzling to Meshka because ever since they left the village, Rifka wasn't comfortable anywhere with anyone.

They definitely were not their world-weary selves. Within this mantle of light, each woman was transformed into a *Goddess*. Their glorious radiance took Meshka's breath away. Her trembling turned to awe.

Maya strummed the most beautiful music from her harp. Each note tenderly caressed Meshka. Sarina sang and the women sang along. Her lovely voice gave the melody the smoothness of a kiss.

The songs were prayers. Poor Meshka had trouble following the words. They were in Magyar, a language she haltingly understood. But more than that, the words did not make sense! They did not praise God! They did not apologize to God for being lowly women instead of valuable men. Rather, these songs praised *Life* and the *Sisterhood of Women*.

Meshka recoiled from the strange shocking words; but willed herself to relax and just look at it all. After a bit, she found this form of worship refreshing. Prayers praising *Life* and songs rejoicing in one united family shocked her, but they also left her feeling calm and in right-action. It was so unlike the worship she had known before, when she listened to men recite endless prayers praising God's glory.

All this "celebrating life" clashed with her picture of religion. She was shocked! She sensed God's wrath and trembled.

The singing ended and Meshka bravely looked out from behind her thoughts.

The women put their arms on each other's shoulders. Rifka's strong arm embraced her on one side and Sarina's on the other. Standing hip to hip in a tight line, they slowly began to undulate. It reminded her of the wonderful dances she used to watch the men do back in her village.

Before Meshka realized what was happening, she was dancing. The women moved together like a long snake, surging forward and shrinking back. She felt wonderfully supported and strange to have loving arms holding her! The serpent of women snaked back and forth with hypnotic grace.

The dance lulled Meshka into a sense of peaceful harmony. She forgot to be scared. As the dance drew to a close, the women's steps grew faster and faster until they were flying together. In breathless exhilaration the dance ended. The *Cone of Power* they created pulsed around them.

In the center of the circle, Sharanii held up an exquisitely carved staff. Meshka had never seen anything so regal! In a soft, yet powerful voice the *Priestess* called out, "Welcome my sisters to Candlemas, Imbolic, Mid-Winter's Eve."

The glass bangles on Sharanii's wrists jingled softly as she opened her arms to greet all the women. The fine gold chain dangling from her crown to her nose shimmered in the moonlight. Her large golden filigree earrings dangling with delicate bells, tinkled whenever she moved her head. Amidst jingling and tinkling, Sharanii looked up to heaven.

"*Holy Mother*, we reverently stand before *You* to share the sacred stories of our lives. Today we honor last year's journey. We are here to acknowledge the power we gained from our experiences and surrender the pain to *You*."

The *Priestess* beamed an angelic presence gliding in her long graceful white gown. The soft fabric swirled around her ankles playing in the breeze.

Each time Sharanii called, "*Holy Mother*," a wave of magical excitement fluttered through the women.

"*Holy Mother*, as a circle of Sisters, we are dedicated, each in our own way, to our spiritual path. We are a *Priestesshood* dedicated to preserving the well-being of all creatures. We strive for inner balance and effective action in all we do."

Silver moonlight beamed down from the diamond studded darkness. Golden amber flames danced in the sacred fire, casting a magical glow upon Sharanii.

Like a great mythical bird she raised her otherworldly wings, her arms dripping long white sleeves opened wide as she spoke for all the women.

"Holy Mother, we stand before you today dedicated to sowing seeds of right action. May they blossom in the spring. We each commit ourselves to walking the path before us with open minds and open hearts. With inner sight and outer perception, we seek to uncover the deeper meaning and process at hand, at every moment. We willingly step forth to meet our destiny. We choose sacred words today to illuminate the pathway before us. We invest these words with power. May they help us see deeper secrets lying beneath the surface of our lives."

Meshka was quivering with excitement, yet she also felt an underlying tranquility. Whatever she felt was strange and wonderful.

Sharanii stood extremely tall and regal. With graceful nobility, she closed the invocation.

"Holy Mother, please help us to see through the old illusions that entrap us. Guide us to heal the scars we bear from the trials of the past. Sustain us as we learn to appreciate the complexities, the challenges we have overcome, and the despair we have transversed in the unfolding process of our souls. Open our eyes to see the nobleness and the intrinsic order hidden in life's strange winding journey."

A soft loving glow radiated from Sharanii's eyes as she turned to the circle of women. "Please," she respectfully requested, "Repeat after me, 'I pledge to support each of my sisters on this sacred journey.'"

In a chorus of beautiful voices, they all pledged to support one another. Well, maybe not everybody. Meshka sought of cleared her throat a few times, but nothing really came out.

Sharanii lowered her winged arms, signaling Maya to walk around the circle with blankets for the women to sit on. Each woman gracefully sat down on the ground except Meshka. She just plotzed down between Tasjia and Rifka.

"Sweet Sisters, I invite you to step forward one by one," Sharanii instructed. "Hold this sacred wand. Feel it's magic. When you are ready, speak from *The Goddess* part of you.

"Take us into your world. Show us your triumphs and your challenges. Help us see the meaning and the process underlying those events. Reach beyond the drama. See the deeper meaning and message being acted out in the theater of your life.

"We will help midwife your transition from the old year into the new one. We will charge your words with power and then seed them in your body."

ଔଔଔଔ

Just outside the circle was a gnarled old grandmother tree, strong, twisted and bent under the weight of many centuries. Its gnarled and twisted roots looked like a tired old lady's boney legs. Between the roots, they placed a large flat rock as their altar. On the altar, each woman each placed an object sacred to her.

A silver chalice of fresh water stood on the altar between two finely wrought golden candlesticks. Lying beside the chalice was a pretty magenta velvet pouch, embroidered with sacred symbols. Inside were Joya's tarot cards.

Tasjia stepped forward first. The glistening blue camel beads that always graced her neck were in her hand. She lovingly looked at the beautiful necklace. Her greatest treasure lingered in her hand. Tasjia kissed the beautiful exotic beads sending the long yearning kiss to Petrov, her beloved Petrov.

"My darling, I miss you so. May you journey safely throughout the worlds."

Tasjia gently placed Petrov's beads and his exquisite love on the altar. She prayed to *The Mother of Life*. "Please cradle Petrov's soul in gentleness."

She took a deep breath for luck and reached into the embroidered pouch to take a card. She pulled out a card, turned it over and behold it was 'The Fool.' She gazed at this happy-go-lucky fellow walking off a cliff. Silly fellow, it was Petrov.

Tasjia smiled at him and knew her beloved was near. She felt his light hearted spirit. He was always off on an adventure, riding his wild horses. This wonderful man saved her life! Now he was gone and his spirit was invested in the precious beads, his gift to her on their wedding night.

Tasjia held the card to her heart and then placed it on the altar beside her precious necklace. She stepped into the center of the sacred circle. The *Priestess* offered the majestic staff to Tasjia. The maiden's fingers touched the powerful staff and a shocking jolt shot through her! The majesty of its power made her stand straighter, hold her chest higher and her chin higher still. Her willowy form suddenly appeared to have substance.

Tasjia spoke and every woman wept. Even the stars in heaven wept for the loss of such sweet love. Her tale recalled a year of shocking events, tragic losses, and terrible sadness.

In telling the story, Tasjia was honoring her life. At the end of her story, when all her words were spent, she tapped an engraved metal gong with the noble staff. The sound of its ring echoed and echoed in time. Thus her year ended on a perfect note.

Tasjia drew in a breath, squared her shoulders, and announced, "Light-hearted." This was the word she had chosen to guide in the coming year. After surviving this tragic year of pain, her feet yearned to dance, and her spirit yearned to fly.

Tasjia lay down on a soft nest of blankets in front of the altar at the foot of the grandmother tree. Sharanii placed a pure red silk pillow filled with relaxing herbs on Tasjia's chest. She slipped a large rose quartz crystal under the fragrant pillow and pressed the crystal down on the maiden's heart.

The *Priestess* also put a perfect little sapphire on Tasjia's throat and pure clear crystal on the magical point between her eyes. Their weight held Tasjia's awareness on these portals of power in her body.

The women moved in close around Tasjia to seed the word, "light-hearted," in her body. They all placed their hands on Tasjia and each massaged a part of her as they kneaded the words into her flesh.

Over and over they chanted, *"light-hearted,'* until they raised a *Cone of Power.* The sweet maiden was enveloped in a *Temple of Sound. 'Light-hearted'* echoed around her and through her. Sarina and Maya whispered the words in her ears. The voices of all these women held a great variety of cadences, sometimes chaotic, sometimes sublimely harmonic. Their united voices held great power. The women wrapped tunes and phrases around the chosen words to create a wild blending somewhere between prayer, chanting and song.

Meshka was not sure about all this touching business; but she did not want to be left out. Hesitantly, she took Tasjia's left hand and held it lightly. After a bit, she began to rub it gently. It felt nice.

Though no one gave a signal, everyone felt it when the energy shifted and they all stopped at once. With satisfied sighs, they sat back feeling they had midwifed a birth.

A few moments quietly passed. Then Tasjia sat up glowing and returned to her place in the circle.

Maya stepped forward next. She placed a tincture of arnica on the altar, a token of her sacred work, and announced that her word was "Healing."

ରଉରଉ

With simple grandeur, each woman looked at the journey she had traveled in the last set of seasons. A golden light radiated from each one's face while she spoke. Meshka was amazed!

As they each told their awesome story, Meshka could see their exquisitely wise souls! She felt very proud to be among such beautiful women! Seeing the unique richness in each amazing woman, left Meshka in awe of them!

After all these months, Meshka thought she knew these women! In everyday life, she never noticed how wise and powerful they were!

Breathlessly she thought, "People do not look like dis, unless maybe vhen dey are getting married or it is Chanukah, in a good year, of course. Most of da time people moan 'n groan under da weight of life's burdens."

Time ticked closer and closer to the moment when Meshka would be expected to take hold of Sharanii's majestic staff. Could she do it? Could she speak of the unspeakable horrors of this last year? It was such a private thing.

When the moment arrived, Meshka's fear was gone. She did not exactly feel brave, just not frozen with fear. She touched the daunting staff so gingerly, you would think it was made of glass. Maybe she was. She stared at the staff in her hand as though it was the root of all temptation.

Oy was she sorry she did not run away earlier! How could she say such private things out loud? She never said private things to anyone! At least, no one alive!

All eyes were on her! This was her moment of do or decline!

Meshka had listened to the sincerity in each woman's voice when she shared her story. No one talked from a broken place and no one cried about being a victim, so Meshka felt she had to speak with the same respect.

Slowly, she removed the mezuzah from its hiding place inside her dress and put it in the lap of the old grandmother tree. She turned, faced her sisters, and spoke. Every word she said wanted to hide in her throat. She was used to swallowing her truth and saying whatever was expected of her. But that would not work here.

If this was not the bravest thing Meshka ever did, it certainly was one of the hardest. She took a deep breath for courage and drank in the cold clean air.

In this *Circle of Truth*, Meshka was not flippant, as she often was when she got nervous. She did not moan and groan and blame God as she once did. She did not even try to look for the goodness in all the misery. Just this once, she claimed her own simple way of seeing things and spoke the naked truth about the year as she saw it.

She dared to face the memories, the stench of death, and the weariness of endlessly burying the dead. Her shoulders ached to remind her of the cramped stiffness of sleeping in haystacks and on the hard ground. She shuddered to remember the waves of creeping despair that strangled her breath away. She talked about the upheaval and the confusion that followed her everywhere. She ended by thanking all the women for adding so much richness to her life.

Meshka spoke with such sincerity that the all the women were entranced by her. This business of speaking freely, without holding back, oy, did it leave her excited!

When Meshka finished her story, Sharanii asked, "What word have you chosen? What do you wish to illuminate on your soul's path?"

By then, Meshka had already decided and changed her mind at least five times. First she thought maybe 'Expand' because she was learning so many new things. But then, God might think she wanted to grow even fatter, so she dropped that word! 'Trust' seemed good, but it was too big for her. She did not trust God and she did not trust *Fate*. It was probably better that way.

So much thinking was giving her a headache. She thought about, 'Survive,' that was hard enough! It was no small task to survive wandering through a strange land! The raw power of this year raked through her, but it was followed by a profound sense of gratitude. She was simply grateful that she was still living and breathing.

Suddenly, she knew.

"'Savor' she declared. "I vant to slow down da vay I take dings in 'n really appreciate dat I am alive! You never know if those people you love vill be dere again. You never know if you vill have another chance to tell dem dat you love dem.

"So now, I vant to pay more attention 'n notice dat I am not suffering anymore. A moment without suffering is a treasure 'n I vant to make it last as long as possible. I vant to savor everything 'n everybody."

There she said it! Oy did that surprise her! She felt proud of herself, until she realized everyone was listening and they were going to say things to her. The blood rushed to her head so fast, she felt a bit faint.

Sharanii smiled at her and said kind things. Her kindness made the fainting pass. No one ever talked to her with such kindness! No one ever really looked at her so personal like that. To Meshka Sharanii's words were kisses.

One by one each woman spoke to Meshka with respect. They acknowledged the good things she did for them and praised her for being such a wonderful woman. Not her chicken soup, or her deviled eggs, which of course everyone loved; no, they praised little old Meshka herself.

She wanted to savor each word of praise, gather them in a bouquet and revisit them again and again, but her heart was beating so loud in her ears, she hardly heard a word they said. Her mind was so busy combing their words for criticism (there was none; of course), she missed many of the wonderful things they were saying. It took a while for Meshka to calm down.

Meshka laid down without fussing or apologizing. With child-like trust, she closed her eyes. Sharanii placed the red silk pillow on her chest and put the heavy weight of the rose quartz crystal underneath. It had a good solid feeling to it. Meshka took a deep breath, opened her innocent eyes, and enjoyed the warmth of Sharanii's soft smile. The *Priestess* leaned down and whispered softly, "Close your eyes and welcome the peace." Meshka closed her eyes again.

When Sharanii place the jewels on her chakras and rang the engraved metal gong, the old war-ravaged Meshka died. She floated up to heaven in a glorious temple of chanting sounds. Angels were singing. Her pulse and her heartbeat slowed way down. Nothing mattered. There was nowhere to go, nothing to do. This moment outside of time stretched on forever.

What Meshka felt was amazing! Maybe it was peace, how would she know? When did she ever feel peace before? Well, maybe there were moments on Shabbos when she felt peaceful in between serving cups of coffee and slices of delicious chocolate *babka* to her family and all her guests.

"*Savor*," together as one voice the *Priestesses* chanted breathlessly plucking Meshka's heartstrings.

"Savor. Mama you are safe. Mama you are well. Savor. Mama, savor your life. Savor my love. Savor," Rifka sang/chanted with gusto. It was rare for Meshka to hear her daughter sing.

The sound of their voices wove a magical trance around Meshka's mind. "*Savor, savor, savor,*" they sang. Sarina was cradling Meshka's head in her hands and Joya's strong hands were massaging her poor tired feet. Such happy feet now! Meshka was amazed! She loved being touched!

Lying in the *Temple of Sound*, Meshka heard a wild symphony of praise woven around her word. Five pairs of hands were massaging her body! Oy vay, she never felt anything sooo wonderful ever! No one ever touched her, except Meyer, and he was dead now seven years. It felt sooooo good.

She felt like a puddle of cream. You see, already she was getting good at savoring.

The hands stopped and silence followed. Meshka slowly returned to her body. Every part of her felt fresh and new. She lay there for a long moment savoring the tingling feelings skipping around inside her. Meshka drifted up from her comfortable nest and rang the metal gong.

Its echoing ring brought Meshka back. It would be days before Meshka was herself again. And to tell you the truth, Meshka never was herself again. Her curiosity and this ritual, planted seeds inside her that would flower into something no one could ever have imagined.

CRCRCR

Sarina stood holding the majestic staff next. She told her story, but to Meshka it was a blur, because she was still replaying her own words over and over again, marveling that she really said all those things! How she managed to say such private things out loud remained a mystery and a wonder to Meshka for a long time.

She took a deep breath, smiled a big toothy smile, and savored the moment. Never in all those years back in the village, did anyone ever look at her so closely or speak to her so honestly. She liked this feeling.

Sarina told her story. Afterwards, Tasjia and Maya told Sarina how much they loved and admired her. Meshka wanted to say something nice to Sarina too, but what could she say? "Sorry I vas not listening; please repeat your whole story again." That was not possible, so she looked for something true to say.

"Sarina, gentle giant, you walk in beauty 'n grace. You heal da wounded 'n sing like an angel. Vee are very blessed to love you. You are a delicious part of our circle.

"I dank you for your youth. Vhen I sing vid you, I get a liddle younger. 'N you never laugh at my scratchy voice. You are truly a gift from God, *kaynahorah* (da Evil Eye shouldn't hear)."

Meshka looked around for a piece of wood to knock on, to protect her from the Evil Eye, but there was no wood, so she knocked on her head instead. It was close enough to wood.

"I hope vee vill be friends for a long time." Meshka said flashing a warm sincere smile.

After everyone's kind words, Sarina laid down and Sharanii placed the totems on her head and heart. She held Sarina's head with the tenderness of a mama. Tasjia massaged her feet, Maya rubbed Sarina's ankles, and Meshka lightly rubbed Sarina's hands.

Even though everyone was clothed and touched each other respectfully, Meshka still felt touching another person was scandalous!

Rifka sat by Sarina's head and whispered in her ear while Sharanii chanted in the other one. Two voices at once swam in her head singing her word.

Rifka softly sang in her ear, "Go forth 'n meet your destiny whole-heartedly." At the same time Sharanii sang in the other ear, "love whole-heartedly, live whole-heartedly. Whole-hearted-ly." The pleasure of their massaging hands grounded the word "whole-heartedly," in her body.

Rifka went next. Her gift to the Grandmother Tree was her favorite possession, her sharp little knife. She was waiting excitedly for her turn, but when it came her story was very bitter and very short. "Crazy men murdered my children, my sweet liddle babies. Dey killed my kind handsome husband, all my relatives, 'n all my good friends, for no reason. Dey just needed someone to blame." Then she rang the gong. There was nothing more to say.

Sharanii asked her word and Rifka boldly announced, "Yes! My word is 'Yes!'"

Rifka lay down in the nest of covers and the women came in close around her. Meshka took her daughter's hand and gently massaged it. She was surprised to realize how rarely she touched Rifka since she became a woman. That was more years ago than she could remember.

Meshka gazed down at her daughter's weathered hand. This hand cleaned her home until it shone spotlessly. That was when she had a home. This hand rocked a cradle and patted away baby burps. This hand baked golden challahs and worked hard milking cows.

Meshka's touch found its own voice and sang with great appreciation. Deeply and firmly she massaged the weathered hand. In her mind, she felt the chubby paw of her sweet little Rifkala, such a brave child she was.

Meshka joyously chanted, "Yes! Yes to life!" She even forgot to mask her squeaky voice when she chanted, "Yes to love. Yes to da future. Yes. Yes. Yes." It was a good word for Rifka.

Something shifted inside Meshka. She heard, or rather felt, a little click. A door opened inside her mind and all the fear fell out. It was gone. Completely gone!

Joya took the staff as though it were a sword. Her story was horrifying! Bravely she described being raped by a violent angry mob and left to die. She spoke of how Meshka saved her and how that was both a blessing and a curse. The Baking Circle was soothing and compassionate. They touched her very gently to ground the word, "Rebirth," in her swollen body.

Sharanii went last. Her offering to the altar was an elegant and unusual jewel, a pure white tear shaped diamond. She placed it beside the chalice.

The exotic *Priestess* stepped up to tell her story. Everyone leaned in closer, excited for a peek into the life of this mysterious woman. She talked about her beautiful white horse and elegant wagon, gifts given to her by a powerful wise woman to help her escape from the designing clutches of a Turkish Captain. She spoke of hiding in a thick forest where she first saw the three young Magyars running for their lives. She told how she hid them in her wagon and how they have traveled together ever since.

"I have journeyed through many foreign lands, sometimes with a … protector, but mostly alone. I am grateful and honored to be with such lovely *Priestesses*. You each greatly enrich to my life."

Meshka mused about the word, "protector;" imagining some dashing exotic man young and gallant or mature and powerful.

The *Priestess* chose an odd word for a refugee on the move: "Seeding." What new things was she going to seed? Wondered little Meshka.

The women took their places around Sharanii to massage the word into the *Priestess*'s body. Meshka bravely moved up to her ear, to be one of the two whisperers. As she recited the word, chanting phrases around it. This felt more intimate than even touching the woman's body for Meshka was whispering right into the *Priestess*' soul.

ભ્રભ્રભ્ર

All the women joined hands to dance. Meshka felt a chilling breeze blow through her naked hair. Giggling to herself, she wondered if it was a kiss from God.

"Vhat a stupid thought," she scolded herself. "If dis is a kiss, it is definitely not from God."

She could see God scowling at her, out of the corner of her eyes. He was standing next to Adam and Eve. Eve was wearing a chain around her neck and a shawl wrapped tightly around her head. The chain was shackled to Adam's rib. In a flash of fantasy, Eve took off the chain, threw the shawl down on the ground, and walked away.

Meshka laughed out loud and skipped over to join the dancers. Well, maybe she did not exactly skip, but she felt light footed. After a vigorous dance, all the women sat down to catch their breath.

The ritual was ready to close. The elegant Sharanii stood in the center of their circle with her majestic staff held high. "This sacred staff *is* empowered with each woman's *Goddess*-eye-view of her life. I offer up our stories to the *Holy Mother, The Goddess,* and to all the protective spirits. Thank *You* for being with us today. Thank *You* for the sacredness we have shared. We release *You* to watch over the world."

ౠౠౠ

Chapter 17

Becoming a Goddess

Meshka slept like a baby that night. The next morning she jumped out of her bedroll and walked right past her shawl without even looking at it. The sun was shining brightly inside and out.

Over by the morning fire, Sharanii was brushing Maya's bouncy blond curls. Meshka watched in fascination. She was not such a fancy person. No one ever fussed with her hair, except once on her wedding day. She was married so long time ago, right after Adam met Eve in the Garden of Eden.

"Meshka, when are you going to let me play with your hair?" Sharanii asked, reading Meshka's thoughts. It was not so hard since every thought and feeling Meshka had walked right across her face. With a wide toothy grin, Meshka boldly nodded yes.

"What shall we do with your hair?" asked Sharanii. "Do you want me to cut it?"

"Oy vay! Vat do I know from hair! How could I cut it!? Every von of dese hairs has lived on my head since I vas a liddle *pitzkala*." Meshka was so excited!

She made her decision, "Cut my hair." Then, in panic she cried, "No, do not cut da hair. Curl it."

Her hair was already too curly, "No I mean straighten it. Or maybe just braid it.

"You know, better yet, just forget da whole ding!"

While Meshka was spinning around deciding and undeciding, Sharanii finished working on Maya and started brushing Meshka's hair. It felt very nice, like she was a little girl under her mommy's touch.

"Ready?" Sharanii asked with a friendly smile. Meshka nodded and gave her executioner a wincing grimace.

"Cheer up. This is not going to hurt," Sharanii chided.

The Goddess of Beauty lowered Meshka's head back into a large bowl of warm water. With her chin to heaven and her eyes closed, she felt Sharanii pour warm water through her hair. "Ahh *mekheye!*" (such pleasure) Meshka moaned.

Warm and happy, Meshka surrendered into Sharanii's strong hands and sighed deeply as her head was being massaged. Never had she known such a tender nurturing feeling. She was melting into a puddle of pleasure.

"If I die right dis minute, I vill die content," she mumbled.

More of the delicious warm water was pouring through her hair, more of that wonderful touch. "Keep kneading my head 'n I vill follow you anywhere," she moaned.

In bliss, Meshka sat up and Sharanii wrapped a soft cloth around her head.

"What color was your hair when you were a child?" Sharanii asked noticing the ghost of sweet little freckles on her complexion.

"Funny you should ask. My head vas always covered, so no one knew I had honey blond hair. My father used to tease me vhen I vas liddle. He would say, 'Your hair is not black like mine or sandy like your mother's. Why? Because vee found you under a burning bush 'n put da fire out vid cream. Dat in why your hair is da color," Meshka snickered.

"You can still be young and beautiful. You can still have honey blond. Some women become more beautiful as they get older. It takes them a while to grow into their power."

Meshka was appalled! "No! No! If God vanted me to still have da golden hair, He would not have made it so gray."

"Oh, so you are sure you know what God wants." Sharanii asked innocently, but temptation was lurking in the corners of her mouth and in the curve of her brow.

Before God could say a word in her head, Meshka blurted out, "Okay do it."

Wide eyed, Meshka watched Sharanii pour orange, yellow, and beige powders into a wooden mortar. She pounded them with her pestle. In the pestle of Meshka's heart, terror and excitement were pounding in equal measure. Nervously she kept twisting her hands in her apron.

Hoping to make Meshka relax, Sharanii asked, "My dear friend, how did you meet your husband?"

"How did I meet Meyer? You dink I can remember dat far back?" Meshka tossed off flippantly, though the memory of her sweet husband was never more than a breath away.

She was not used to talking about such private things, but after the intimacy of the ritual, her shyness seemed silly, so Meshka confided her story to Sharanii.

"Vell, Meyer lived in my village 'n one day he vas smiling at me. Vhat a nice man he vas. He vas always good to me 'n good to everyone in da village. My mama saw us making eyes at each other. She vas a lot like Rifka. She took me aside 'n asked me, 'Do you like Meyer? Do you vant him to be your husband?' My mama vas wonderful, another mama would not have asked."

It was so long ago, yet her heart still skipped a beat thinking about Meyer when he was young and handsome.

"Vhat did I know from men? Dey va scary. Dey ordered me around 'n I had to serve dem.

"Meyer liked me 'n I liked being liked, so vhat vas dere to decide? He vanted me, I vas glad someone vanted me, so I said yes to my mama."

Meshka sighed, shaking her head she wondered, was she ever that young?

"Da *shatkhn* (matchmaker) made an offer. Den Meyer talked vid my papa 'n my papa said yes. There va negotiations back 'n forth until everyone agreed on my dowry.

"All of a sudden, I vas caught in a tornado of women. Dey va sewing dresses, picking flowers, cooking 'n baking, oy it vas such a *big megillah*." (a big story)

Sharanii poured the blended powders into a small clay bowl glazed with a lovely blue design, and added magic potions. To escape the scary image of Sharanii brewing poisonous ruin, Meshka returned to her story safely in the past.

"Da day I got married vas da first 'n da last time anyone ever played vid my hair, since I vas big enough to tie my own shoes."

She remembered how special everyone made her feel when she was getting married. The only other time in her life when someone fussed over her, was when Hanna and Sophie made her feel special after Rifka, then after Yonkle were born. Those were the most amazing days of her life!

"Getting ready for da wedding vas crazy making," she remembered. "Dis one poked me vid hair pins 'n da other one poked me vid dress pins. I vas a toy doll everyone vanted to play vid. Everything moved faster 'n faster until time spilt me out under da *chupah*. (wedding canopy) Suddenly I vas standing in front of da Rabbi vid da whole village watching me. I vas so scared 'n so embarrassed."

Sharanii tilted Meshka's head back, gathered the wild silver mane in her fist and began to work the creamy mixture into it.

The smell was pungent and strange. Meshka wrinkled her nose, but kept on talking. Better to think about long ago than to feel responsible for what she was doing right now.

"Dis is sooo strange, it must be a sin." She scolded herself, but went on with her story.

"My Meyer vas very sweet 'n soon it vas like I vas always his wife." She smiled, remembering the tickling tender thrill of being a married woman for the first time and blushed red as an apple.

"All day I washed, cooked 'n cleaned, just like always. Da only difference vas I served Meyer instead of my papa 'n I did not sleep vid my sisters anymore." She giggled.

Meshka's head was covered in cinnamon colored lather. Sharanii's strong hands massaged her scalp, and Meshka moaned softly.

"Just vhen I vas getting used to dis husband-wife ding, I suddenly vas a mama. My children va born back to back, one right after da other. I had three children in four years.

"Vhen my last baby died, I vas very sick. After dat I could have no more children. But I made peace vid dis. Two children vas enough for me."

Sharanii encouraged Meshka to go on with her story, to fill the time while the color set.

"Yonkela vas such a loveable liddle pitzkala, cute, funny, 'n sweet as honey. Rifka, you can imagine, vas a handful. Such a firecracker! She kept me on my toes. Stubborn like iron dat one, vid da dignity of a queen, 'n da temper of a fighter."

Being a good mother, Meshka taught Rifka to behave like a *mensch*, (a respectful person) but secretly she admired Rifka's chutzpa, her courage, and her daring, even though it sometimes got her into trouble with the neighbors.

A wave of sadness came over Meshka. "Vhen Meyer, God bless his soul, got sick 'n died, I fell under a dark cloud. It colored everything about my life. All of a sudden I vas an old woman 'n I am old a long time - but not today. Today I feel very young."

"Good. Life has cycles. People are always changing. Fate can turn things into their opposite. You can still be young."

"You are kidding, nu? I only get older," Meshka protested, even though she found the idea intriguing.

"Women get older and younger all the time. Only after a while the young is not as young anymore, and the old looks older," Sharanii said, shaking her head, thinking how often she made women look younger.

"But I am old." Meshka insisted. "I am no longer tossed around by da moon 'n all its mishugass. Dank God! Now my pulse beats steady 'n I do not need much anymore."

"Me too, no more moon tides," Sharanii said sadly, "I miss them. I loved those wild passionate flights of fancy that sent me yearning after my next great adventure or my next exciting lover. Now I am growing accustomed to the stable rhythm of wisdom. I never believed a time would come when I would willingly accept the course of fate. I thought I always had to create everything from seed." confided Sharanii. "How many times have I found myself crossing a river mid-stream at high tide?" Meshka listened intently, intrigued by this exotic woman.

The *Priestess* checked the color again. Time was crawling by very slowly for Meshka. Finally Sharanii washed out the stinky brew. She wiped Meshka's hair dry and fluffed it out around her face. The effect was breathtaking!

"Can I go look in da creek 'n see my reflection?" Meshka asked excitedly. "I am not being vain, you understand. Just a liddle curious," she added in case God was listening.

"Wait. I have a mirror."

Meshka was shocked! No one had a mirror. The women carried everything they needed to survive on their backs, strapped around their hips, or pushed and pulled in a cart. No one could afford luxuries. The women kept only what was essential to body, heart and soul. When their values rearranged themselves under the shifting weight of old memories, the past fell behind, and so did old treasures. Only a few lucky ones like Sharanii had a wagon.

Sharanii reached into the soft tooled leather pouch that hung from her waist and withdrew a real looking glass. It was stunning! On the back, embossed in silver, was a graceful *Goddess* dancing with four arms. The design was so beautiful Meshka could not drag her eyes away. She trembled just a little.

Sharanii turned the silver mirror around.

Meshka jumped! "Who is dat???!!!" She screamed loudly.

It was decades since she looked at herself. Usually she splashed some water on her face and twisted her hair into a bun without even looking. No one ever looks at an old lady's face buried in the shadows of a shawl, so she didn't even see herself in other people's eyes.

"Is dat my face? Oy vay, so many wrinkles!

"It does not even look like me. I could walk right past me on da street 'n not even recognize myself!" She exclaimed.

It took a while for the shock to wear off. She stared into her own eyes for a few minutes until there was a little flicker of recognition.

Sharanii fluffed up Meshka's mantle of curls. It was a little redder than she intended. "Oy vay! Sharanii! Look vhat you did to my hair! You made me a lion!"

"Good. Go out and roar!"

Meshka laughed, but it sounded a little shaky. Her hair looked so dramatic! Around her face streamed a wild ocean of soft fire. Ribbons of saffron and copper curls danced around her head like the Queen of Salamanders, Guardian of the Fire.

"Oy vay, vhat vill everyone say?" Meshka worried.

"Nothing. They will not even recognize you. Go! Walk past Rifka and smile. She will not know you."

"I look a lot younger!" She shook her head amazed and shocked. "Vell, vhat harm can it do if I am young for a liddle while, before I have to go back to being old again?" she asked Sharanii. Hopefully God was not listening.

Maybe He was not, but *Destiny* was.

ଊଊଊ

For lunch, Meshka was cooking fresh eggs with onions and spinach. She was sure everyone was looking at her.

"Oy, vhat have I done? God must be angry at me! Everyone must dink I am crazy 'n vain."

To calm down, she told herself, "No one is looking at me. Stop worrying! It is only my fear that is pointing a finger at me."

By the time Rifka returned from milking cows on a nearby farm, Meshka felt calmer. Rifka had her arms full of food. She did a good job making trades on the way back to camp. She looked around for Meshka to show off her bounty, but Meshka was not there.

Hunched over the campsite stirring a pot was a strange woman with a thick fiery mane of curls. Rifka called out hello. The women looked up. Her wild wooly red curls fanned out around her. Rifka was about to introduce herself, when Meshka gave a big toothy smile. It gave the game away.

Rifka sat down beside her mama and ran her fingers through Meshka's wild wondrous mane. She wanted to laugh and cry. "Could dis fiery creature be my old mama?"

Rifka's black hair was tightly entwined in a serious bun and hidden under her heavy shawl; her heavy brows were deeply creased, so she looked older than her 22 years.

Going the other way, Meshka's wide innocent smile and crazy hair made her look younger. At this moment, they did not look so different in age. Anyway, who could see past that wild mane of flaming curls?

Joya wandered out of her tent. One eye was barely open. She ambled over to Rifka who was staring at a strange wild woman. Rifka's mouth was hanging open and her eyeballs were falling out. Joya followed Rifka's gaze and both her eyes popped open at once! She started laughing so hard, she doubled over holding her stomach.

Meshka put her nose up in the air and went back to cooking breakfast. "If you can stop laughing 'n stop staring like dat, I vill give you some breakfast."

Gasping for breath, Joya stopped laughing. She sat down and just giggled a little.

Meshka leaned over to hand Rifka a plate of eggs and spinach. Her daughter was still staring wide-eyed with amazement. A lovely lock of Meshka's wild hair slid over her shoulder. In its escaping fall, it brushed against Rifka's cheek. The touch was so intimate, Rifka felt embarrassed.

This wild creature could not be her chubby little mama. Rifka really looked at her mama for the first time on this journey. She was not very chubby anymore, actually she was thin and shapely. The old dress hung like a big balloon on her so she borrowed a piece of rope from Shainela, the goat, and wrapped it around her little waist. Meshka never stopped to realize she was losing weight. She always saw herself the same way, the way she was in the village, but that was long ago. Now she was toned and strong; stronger than she could ever have imagined.

Rifka still had her eyes on her mama, but she also looked past her at the Old Italian man. He often camped nearby.

"Mama, da old Italian man is starin' at you." Rifka said amused. She was still scratching her head over this strange person who was her sweet mama.

Casually Meshka glanced over at the man. He gave her a big wide smile. Meshka quickly looked away. He was definitely making eyes at her!

"Vhat should I do?!" She whispered to Rifka in panic.

"Nothin'. Maybe smile back," she advised.

Meshka protested, "Rifka! I am an old woman!"

"Maybe yes, maybe no!" her daughter teased.

Meshka gave the Old Italian man a weak smile just to be polite and he took it as an invitation! He came right over and sat down beside her! Oy was her heart making a racket! Meshka could think of nothing to say.

"Hello pretty lady, I am Raoul. You are new here, right?" he asked with a lecherous grin. Meshka was shocked for a lot of reasons. What should she say? She had seen Raoul every day for weeks. He never smiled, he never noticed her. She never paid much attention to him either.

With a few mumbled grunts, she politely excused herself and grabbed a water bag, as though she urgently needed to get water from the stream. Once she was safely out of sight, she thought about what happened.

"O my God! A man is flirting vid me! Oy! Look vhat I have done! I should never have taken off da shawl! Putting color on my hair vas maybe too much! Vhat is God going to do now!?!"

It took Meshka a long time to calm her panic. When she finally returned to camp, Raoul was gone! Thank God.

She wanted Sharanii to put her hair back the way it was right this minute! But once the hot flashes of panic ebbed away, and one thought could follow another, she realized she liked the idea of a man paying attention to her.

A strange mischief was afoot that day! When Meshka was carrying a bundle for the old one armed man, as she did many times before, he put his good arm around her and rubbed her shoulder! She wiggled out of his grip, offended and delighted.

Later in the afternoon, just when her feet were feeling rubbery, a handsome man on a black horse trotted beside her. He leaned down and asked her, in a deep mellow voice, "Come ride with me." She shocked herself by saying yes.

Never mind she was scared to death of horses. That did not seem so important at the moment. Sitting in front of this strange man on a saddle aroused a lot of feelings in her body she did not remember ever having. Lars, that was the man's name, held her tight against him, so she was safe from falling. But his tight grip made her pulse race like crazy! His touch was more scary than the idea of falling. He was very polite and asked her a couple of times if she was alright.

Terror and delight surged through her when she felt something hard pressing against her back. She hoped it was just his whip!!!

Suddenly everything was so scary and so much fun. She had two minds. One was trembling with fear and the other was a kid with a handful of candy.

She rode with Lars through the tall grass at a slow gentle trot while he held onto her tightly. The pressure of his touch and his breath on her neck made time stand still and her heart race.

With a gallant flourish, Lars placed her back down on solid ground beside Rifka and Joya who were pulling their cart. He took off his wide brimmed purple velvet hat, bowed his head graciously from the saddle, and rode on.

Meshka walked along with glittering eyes, peachy flushed cheeks and a skip in her step. Joya and Rifka looked at her, blinked, looked at each other, and burst out laughing. Meshka laughed along with girlish gaiety. Her spirit was fluttering with joy.

By the end of the day, Meshka was walking with a cute little wiggle in her *tush* (buttocks). A smile was permanently glued to her face. This new person she was going to be was shaping up to be a handful.

No one recognized her and no one ignored her.

That night, long after the others were asleep, Meshka pulled out a bottle of ale. It was a parting gift from Jeannie. The Irish woman brewed it herself from an old family recipe. Whatever the ale lacked in taste, it more than made up for in punch. She was saving it for a special occasion and today was definitely something special. The ale quieted the volcanoes erupting in her belly.

For an old woman who always felt invisible, she was breathlessly excited by all these new changes! What was she going to do with all the energy surging through her?

Meshka looked up at God and said, "*Kaynahorah* (the evil ear shouldn't hear), it is not bad enough dat I have no home? Now I do not even know from who I am!"

She *kvetched* out loud to confuse the Evil Eye, and to keep God from punishing her for being too happy.

Meshka took another swig of ale, shuddered, and forced herself to swallow. "'N men like dis stuff?" Yuk! She shook her head. A few swallows later, she heard someone calling her name.

Meshka looked up at God's diamonds dangling from His heavens. Her eyes floated across a vast glittering sky and landed on an odd tree. The trunk was bathed in silver moonlight lying parallel to the ground. From the girth of the tree several long dangling arms reached to grip the soil. As the shadow of night crept over the tree, it gave the appearance of a welcoming cave. Bands of silver light streamed between its strong arms

Inside this mysterious enclosure she saw Meyer. Young and noble, he peered out at her from the shadows under the tree, smirking over something funny.

"Meshkala, you look younger dan I ever remember. Vhere is your shawl?" She heard her sweet husband say.

"Oy Meyer, da world is changing so fast. Vhen I rolled out of bed dis morning, I fell into a new life! I took off da shawl 'n a whole new world opened up 'n swallowed me!"

She took another swig of the ale and a wide smile glued itself to her face. She hardly knew herself and that was becoming a good thing.

"Meyer, I vill tell you a secret, but please do not tell God. I dink I like dis new me. I do not vant to be da old Meshka. In a strange vay, who I am now suits me better!

"I am becoming a person – not a daughter, a sister, a wife, a mama, but a separate person.

"It is so strange to dink, vhat do I vant? Not vhat is best for dis one 'n dat one, but vhat do I vant!" She giggled, burped, and covered her mouth with her hand.

"Meshka, you look very pretty. You have a nice smile. Here in heaven, people are free to be whatever dey really are. You are just practicing before you get here," he said in a soothing voice.

"You dink maybe dis is okay? You are a man. Men are always their own person, but for a woman it is different. Vhen she looks into a mirror, she sees da needs of her whole family. I vas always my papa's daughter, or your wife, or da children's mama. Dat is how I saw myself. It vas all I knew.

"But now my hands refuse to wrap da veil over my head. I vant to see vhat is happening around me. No more hiding."

A shudder ran through her as she asked, "Vhat do you dink God vill do to me for being so bold?"

"My liddle lion go roar. God does not split hairs about such small dings. Da Rabbis, dey make da rules, not God. Da Holy Von likes people to open like flowers 'n shine in da sun. He is not petty 'n jealous. Shine. Shine in da sun. You are such a pretty lady."

Meshka felt wonderful! At least Meyer approved. Maybe it will not be so bad.

"Meyer, you always make me feel so much better. Once you said to me, 'My Balabusta, go show dem how powerful you are.' I thought you va teasing because you va always teasing me, but now I see maybe you really meant it."

Meshka tossed her curls and fluttered her eyes, remembering how much he loved her.

"I remember you once asked me, 'Do you know how a firecracker is made?' It vas such a strange question; I figured you va making one of your jokes, but you said, 'A firecracker is wrapped very small 'n tight, so all da power is locked inside. Vhen it lets go, all dat pressure goes pop 'n it makes da big noise. Go be a firecracker!' 'N you laughed."

His silver silhouette laughed and said, "Meshka, my Balabusta, you va always a firecracker. Everyone knew dat except you." Meyer laughed and laughed and faded into the darkness as the moon shifted its gaze.

ରୌରୌରୌ

The bottle was empty and the lovely night was clear, so Meshka curled up by the fire wrapped in a blanket instead of crawling into the tent. She slept deeply until an hour before sunrise. Enchanted by this sacred hour of the day, she watched the world being born anew. The soft light was tranquil and peaceful. A little chilled, she rekindled smoldering embers.

Once fingers of flames were reaching for the sky, and their blessed warmth enveloped Meshka, she drank water from a hanging gourd and braced herself for her morning talk with God.

With everyone asleep, even the birds and the little industrious creatures of the earth, she whispered, "O Most Holy Von, You turn da crank dat makes Fate spin, right?

"Is it too much to ask for a liddle old woman to live out her last few years without schlepping around all dat fabric?

"You know God, now I can see You better. You feel lighter! Is dere a commandant dat says I must always hide who I am?"

She took a deep breath and waited for God to scold her.

His voice boomed in her ears, but it did not scold. "Meshka, not all man's laws are My commandments. My hand alone does not turn the Wheel of Fate. There are natural tides, which men fear. Out of fear, they make laws. Men cannot control Fate, so they control each other." God's tone was softer than usual.

Astonished, Meshka questioned, "Does dat mean you are not angry vid me!?!" She was so relieved, God was not going to smite her.

God said with more patience then Meshka was used to, "My commandments set a standard for good behavior. If you can do better, go right ahead."

"Is dis a trick?" She was skeptical. She was not going to be fooled this time.

God's voice was gone.

Meshka was stunned. He did not mention da ritual! He did not scold me for whoring after false gods 'n He vas not upset dat I am exposing myself.

Maybe God does not care about me anymore! Maybe I am going straight to hell! Maybe God dinks I am no longer worth saving.

Meshka was getting all worked up for nothing. She was trembling all over and reached for her shawl, but stopped and wondered, was God really alright with this or was He just tricking her into making a sin?

ଔଔଔଔ

The pre-dawn air kissed her face with a promise of spring. Now that it was February, the light of day grew by leaps and bounds. More sun and more warmth lightened her tasks. Following her freedom made Meshka feel young and light-footed.

Her belly rattled, reminding her to go fishing. Meshka grabbed a rough sack and her fishing stick. A strong strand of yarn with a sharp fish bone tied to the end was wrapped around her stick. A few pokes in the moist dirt rewarded her with a couple of nice fat worms. Now, off she went to catch her breakfast.

Meshka did not waddle down to the stream like she usually did. No, she walked with dignity, grace, and a cute little wiggle. After being camped here for several days, the gentle sloping path was worn by many tramping feet and easy to follow.

Where the path met the stream, Meshka found a large flat rock balanced over the water. She drew water from it yesterday. While her bags were filling, she thought about all the fish sleeping under the rock shelf and made a note in her head to come back and catch those fishes.

Places where streams pour into the sea have good fishing. In the gentle light of early dawn, Meshka sat on the large shelf jutting out over the stream and waited for the fish to wake up from their little fishy dreams.

She made herself comfortable, dropped her fishbone hook into the water, and patiently waited.

Meshka's senses suddenly snapped to attention! A large animal or small man was moving through the underbrush towards her. Fear turned her to stone! She was not even breathing, not making a sound. She closed her eyes so the creature would not see her.

Desperately she prayed, God help me! If you make dis wild animal not eat me, I vill put da shawl back on. I am so sorry!

She inched her way back behind a bush so the creature would not see her. Whatever the wild beast was, it moved silently past her, entered the stream, and crossed the cold wet stones to the other side.

Meshka was so well hidden; the creature did not even try to catch her. Alone in the quiet again, her breath rushed out in a swift sigh of relief.

Soon it was time for the fishes to wake up and eat the fat little worm on her fishbone. She threw the weighted yarn into the water again, wiggled the stick around to taunt the sleepy little fish, and settled in to wait.

She was thinking, I vas more scared, more times in dis year, dan in my whole life. Vhen I vas a liddle pitzkala 'n I vas scared, papa always used to say, "Someday da Messiah vill come 'n den you vill never be scared again." Dat vas a long time ago, 'n da Messiah is still not here.

In the quiet of this gentle hour, before the sun rose and the churning challenges began, Meshka listened to the tumbling stream splashing into the sea. The frolicking water was laughing and mumbling as it rushed along. Slowly she realized she understood what the water was saying.

"The Messiah has come. The Messiah is here." the stream gurgled and laughed.

"*Holy Mother*, is there really a Messiah? Meshka whispered quietly under her breath, lest the wild animal on the other side of the creek hear and come eat her up!

The laughing, frolicking water said, *"The Messiah is not one man, but a spirit that lives in many people. I have sent you many messiahs, humble people with kind and gentle hearts."*

Meshka worried that the talking water would scare the fish away, but they were probably still asleep.

"A messiah is not a man, but a power that rises from the soul. My messiahs inspire hearts to reach out and help others. My champions have a simple nature that draws people to them."

Meshka was sure a *Goddess* was speaking through the laughing stream because water does not talk.

"*Holy Goddess*, vhat is your name?"

"Sophia. Sophia. Sophia," the water gurgled.

"*Holy Goddess Sophia*, may I call you dat? Are you a real person like Rachel, or invisible like da air vee breathe? Are you fairy tale make-believe or alive?" Meshka whispered so quietly, it was disguised as a sigh.

"I am the Life Force. I am always with you. You can feel Me surging through your veins. I am the animating force of the breath. Sometimes I take a living form. Sometimes I move about in dreams; but I am always with you"

"Do you mean da body is to You, like clothes are to us?" Meshka was trying to make sense of all this.

"I weave the cords of destiny."

"You know, I used to have a neighbor named Sophia, are you two related?"

"We are all related My child. I am the breath. I animate life. The breath brings Life Force into your body. No breath, no life. I am essential to life. I am alive in all creation. I am the World's Mother."

"My friend Sophia vas a good mama too."

"Your Soul and your body are My temples."

Meshka was stretching her mind to follow these new ideas, but now *The Goddess* went too far. Meshka was shocked!

"You dink dis old body is a temple?! You know, da body does some dirty messy dings; how can it be a temple?" Meshka challenged.

"Your body is a holy chalice. The golden liquid inside the chalice is the Life Force, a wild and messy brew. Life Force arouses your senses and spurs you into action. Destiny leads you to fulfill your soul's design."

"I am here to inspire you to reach for a better life. Meshka, I am calling you. I am calling you. Listen!"

Meshka was shocked! "Me? You sure You vant me? I'm nobody!"

The charged quality in the air relaxed. The laughing water gurgled along saying no more. *The Goddess* was gone.

The pale blue hues of the sky were pierced by swords of gold radiating from a brilliant sun as it rose above the land.

When the sun was up, so were the hungry fish. One was nibbling on her line. Happily she pulled him in, retrieved her worm, and threw the line out again.

From her hiding place behind the bushes, she heard a strange soft humming of bees.

"Aummm."

This soothing sound echoed from the far side of the stream. It was not quite bees, but neither was it a big wild animal, so Meshka inched her way out from her hiding place. Brimming with curiosity, she peered across the stream in search of the humming. On a tuft of grass across the water sitting cross-legged was a young man.

His pale blond hair glistened in the sunlight. Meshka recognized this young man as the fellow who dances gracefully at sunset. Meshka smiled, intrigued. This strange quiet young man was chanting prayers to the dawning day. She had noticed him several times before. He was always dancing or surrounded by children.

Her fishing stick, laying on the rock like a limp noodle, suddenly burst into life. The fish woke up from their shimmering fish dreams and were jumping around like crazy. If these fish were only half as hungry as she was, she was going to have quite a catch. No more time for thinking, there were lots of fish to catch and clean before everyone was up and awake.

By the time the first bleary-eyed neighbor wandered down to the cool water to wash away the crust of sleep, Meshka's gunnysack was full with the gracious bounty of the water, parting gifts from the stream as it ran away to join the mighty sea.

Meshka walked back to camp enjoying the pleasantly heavy weight of the gunnysack. It was a good catch. They were going taste wonderful.

"Vhen I vas young," she mused, "I did not even like fish, but now, after all dese months of eating *bupkis* (nothing), a skinny liddle fish is a treat. It is better than a hollow belly. Life is strange," she mumbled to herself. Shaking her head she wondered, "Da less food I have to eat, da more delicious each bit tastes."

Meshka was grateful that she had something to eat. Little did she imagine what amazing gifts life was going to bring her to be grateful for.

CRCRCR

Meshka was changing so fast, awakening so fast, her head was always spinning. Sharanii could never resist a bit of mischief, so she added another spin of the wheel.

The *Priestess* admired brave little Meshka and wanted to give her a little gift. She also wanted to stir the pot a bit.

"I have something wonderful for you, my dear. I am going to give you one of my favorite dresses. It will look lovely on you. The length will be a little long. You can cut it shorter. It may be a bit tight on the top, but you can use the extra fabric from the hem to enlarge the top for your bountiful breasts."

"It vill be tight everywhere," Meshka joked and laughed lightly like a young girl.

Sharanii invited Meshka to enter her magical wagon. It looked and felt like a sacred temple. The curved walls were an elegant creamy rich blue silk, the color of the sky on a perfect day. Billowing clouds of brilliantly colored saris, weightless gauze woven from the finest silk and delicately embroidered with gold or silver threads, were draped over it.

Within this exotic rainbow, Sharanii beckoned Meshka to be seated on the luxuriously smooth and intricately woven carpet. The colors of the fine shimmering silk carpet changed in the flickering candlelight.

In the center was a low carved ebony table, inlaid with fragments of mother of pearl. On this lovely little table there stood a braided candlestick. Upon closer inspection it turned out to be two snakes entwined; one was silver and one gold. It was originally cast in a country as ancient as time. From the mouth of each serpent rose a long perfect taper.

Meshka marveled at the perfect whiteness of the candles. Were they made of beeswax? She heard myths of such purity, but never saw one in real life before.

Sharanii leaned over, fluffed several soft cushy pillows and handed the thickest one to Meshka for her to sit on. Then she tucked many beautiful pillows around her guest for perfect comfort. Sharanii enjoyed pampering people as much as she enjoyed pampering herself. Pleasure was a *Priestess's* gift to share.

A soft whiff of incense wafted by and Meshka took a deep breath. It was both delicious and enticing, tiny tantalizing sensations slithered through her. Meshka melted into a puddle of pleasure and sighed.

Meshka noticed that no boxes or clutter broke the perfect serenity in this rainbow cloud. In the gracious flickering candlelight, only beauty and perfect symmetry were seen. All else was either hidden or disguised.

Sharanii reached behind her and produced a large leather bag. Startled, Meshka's eyes grew wide. She never saw a piece of leather, or any object for that matter, quite so outrageous a shade of rose. Sharanii untied the leather thong binding the bag. Inside were several thinly scraped natural deerskin hides. Beautiful designs were burned and painted into the soft creamy leather. Sharanii turned the deerskin like leaves in a book.

"Is dis your art?" Meshka asked amazed, admiring a portrait of a beautiful young woman with straight black hair and white-feathered wings. She was seated on an Egyptian throne nursing a little child.

"These are pictures of our *Goddesses*," Sharanii shared.

"Dey are very beautiful," praised Meshka.

Then she lowered her voice to ask a forbidden thing, "Tell me Sharanii, do you see *Goddesses*?"

"I feel *Their* presence in my body," Sharanii replied. "What about you, Meshka. How do you know the *Goddesses*?"

Such a private question made her cheeks burn the same shade of rose as the leather bag.

"I hear their voices 'n once in a purple moon, I dink I see dem sorta," she confided.

Sharanii turned the pages of brilliantly colored and delicately drawn portraits. In the center of the pack, lying on an exquisite scene was a small cloud of delicate emerald silk.

Sharanii gently scooped up the creamy soft silk and poured it into Meshka's hand. It was a cloud of no weight.

"This is for you, my dear." Never had Meshka's rough, work worn hands ever touched anything so soft. She blew on it and the light wave of her breath made the dress slither in her hand. Meshka caressed it and moaned softly over its baby cheek softness. As it unfurled, it revealed itself to indeed be a dress. The lovely wispy little thing sparkled in Meshka's eyes. Its delicateness alone was beyond anything she could have imagined back home.

In the little village, Meshka never had more than three dresses a season, two for workdays and one for Shabbos. They were made of coarse cotton or heavy wool. In fact, every dress in the village was a dark color, a course weave, and a dull shade of invisible.

This rose-petal soft silk was created for a queen! It was luscious. Meshka remembered that women were supposed to be modestly invisible. The skillful hands that wove this precious cloth made the wearer very visible, very sensuous, and a force of *The Goddess*. Meshka was speechless in the face of its beauty and too startled to imagine wearing it.

How would she feel? Who would she be? This was beyond the pleasure of wearing Tasjia's green skirt. It was dancing with the angels. What kind of woman wears something so luxurious, so exquisite, so shockingly valuable?

When Meshka finally had breath enough to speak, she said, "Oy sweet lady, dis is much too beautiful for me! I cannot accept a present so grand?"

In a voice as soft as a whisper and as firm as a binding knot, Sharanii said, "I want you to wear it. You must treasure it as I have."

Tears welled up in Meshka's eyes. This was such a big kindness. "Vhat can I give you in return?" She asked humbly.

"My dear Meshka, this is not a trade; this is a gift. Please accept it, adore it, and wear it on special days. This lovely little dress is a doorway into *The Goddess*. When its creamy softness caresses your skin, you will feel sensuous and light-footed. In this heavenly wisp of silk, *The Goddess'* beauty and *Her* grace will shine through you; and you will be a delight to all who gaze upon you."

Meshka was stunned! Delighted! Amazed! She should say, 'thank you,' but her voice was hiding far away.

Smiling tenderly, the *Priestess* gazed down upon this simple woman. Little Meshka had such a big heart and such a simple dream of peace!

Sharanii smiled lovingly at her dear friend. In a gentle voice that rang with the power of heaven she invoked, "I give you this dress in honor of *Lakshmi, Goddess of Beauty*. It will awaken Her power in you."

ᘓᘓᘓ

Sharanii was smoothing the leather portraits back into place when the words jumped out of Meshka's mouth, "Vhat are da names of dese *Goddesses*?" she sounded so young and curious. The words surprised them both!

One soft deerskin had a delicate border of ripe wheat stalks around it. Hearty loaves of bread were etched in the corners. Within this halo of wholesome food, a fruitful *Goddess* with an ample bosom and fruitful thighs reclined in a field full of flowers, bushes, rivers, and trees. The Garden of Eden was growing around *Her*.

Delighted to be asked and always ready to teach, Sharanii served *The Mother of Life* by passing on *Her* secret sacred knowledge. That is what a *Priestess* does with knowledge; she passes it on so it stays fresh and alive.

Long ago and far away, Sharanii was initiated into these mysteries by a secret sisterhood of *Priestesses*. Like those *Priestesses*, she always wore a jewel on her portal of "inner seeing." The weight of the jewel anchored her awareness on wisdom and kept one eye open to magic.

"This is the *Minoan Goddess, Demeter. She* is the *Mother of the Three Realms* - Above, Below, and Within," said Sharanii with great respect, for to name a *Goddess* was to call *Her* forth.

Meshka looked into the world weary eyes of this abundant *Mama*. This *Goddess* she knew very well. It was with *Her* heart that Meshka fed the children. Some of Meshka's 'children' were older than her...b-u-t...at any age people need to feel safe in a mama's arms.

There are so many little ones to take care of in the world. Meshka and *Demeter* shared the same mama's heart full of love; full of a desire to take care of people. Meshka's heart went out to everyone who needed her.

The next portrait was a sad one. A lovely young woman with downcast eyes sat beside the sea. Broken pieces of a horse lay in *Her* lap and scattered pieces of a castle were lying around *Her* in the sand.

"Cassandra, Prophetess of Troy," announced Sharanii. Meshka's heart ached for this sad *Goddess*. She wanted to sit with *Cassandra* and hold *Her* hand. Such a *Goddess* would know my pain, she thought.

The next soft leaf of leather fluttered gracefully open. "*Kwan Yin, the Chinese Goddess of Mercy and Compassion*," Sharanii whispered as softly as a lotus petal. It was no more than a breath. Meshka sighed deeply and her body relaxed. A wonderful peacefulness washed over her in the presence of *Kwan Yin*.

Meshka gazed down at the picture of a serene woman standing on a big fiery dragon. *Her* robes gracefully swirled about *Her* legs in a sweeping gust of wind, while *Kwan Yin* stood firm.

"*Kvan Yin*," Meshka repeated.

Sharanii turned another doeskin over and announced, "*The Creatrix Sophia*, Mother of Judaism and Gnostic Christianity, *Mother of God*."

"*Sophia*! I know *Sophia*. *She* spoke to me!" Meshka cried out all excited.

In *Her* portrait, *She* was a tall graceful woman in a long blue gown, standing on a cloud, with twelve stars above *Her* head and little cherubs at *Her* feet.

"The *Goddess* spoke to you?" It was Sharanii's turn to be surprised.

"I have felt the Presence of a *Goddess* and I have seen them in my mind, but never have I heard one speak! What did *She* say?"

"O lots of dings. Different *Goddesses* talk about different dings. Da *Goddesses* are like husbands; *Dey* tell me vhat to do."

This was so not what Sharanii expected Meshka to say, they both burst out laughing.

When the laughing released her, Meshka asked "Tell me Sharanii do you know dis *Sophia's* story?"

Sharanii nodded yes.

"O please tell me da story," Meshka coaxed her.

Her hostess raised a skeptical eyebrow, so she added, "Please, I really vant to know."

The pagan *Priestess* sat back, closed her eyes, and began to recite the story just the way she learned it many years ago, far-away in a dry and sandy desert.

"*Sophia* is the *World's Soul*. Before time began and after time ends, there is *Sophia*. There never was a time when *She* did not exist."

Sharanii gathered a breath and opened her eyes. Though her gaze rested on Meshka's innocent face, they were peering into a world faraway and long ago. Meshka quieted her excited heart and listened to the story.

"After countless eons, *Sophia* birthed *Her* first child – Ilabrat! *She* gave Him a universe to explore, stars and galaxies to entertain Him, and laid all the wonders of eternity before Him. *She* created our beautiful planet filled with churning volcanoes, turquoise oceans teeming with iridescent creatures, and bountiful jungles. Ilabrat was entertained for a while but then grew bored."

This story was very different than the simple one she heard the rabbi tell her friend Sophia, when they were girls. The rabbi said her name meant, 'the life-giving breath of God.'

"*Sophia* created creatures of every size and shape, velvet sea animals floating in the depths, brilliantly feathered birds on the wing, industrious little insects, sensuous land animals, and mysterious reptiles. Ilabrat was fascinated for a while and then grew bored.

"*She* created humanity and bestowed upon us brilliance, beauty, tumultuous emotions, and ambitious minds. *Sophia* thought we were *Her* masterpiece.

"At first, when Ilabrat matched wits with humans He was fascinated, but after a while, He grew jealous and spiteful. He threw senseless challenges at people and made them suffer just to amuse Himself.

"*Sophia* could no longer deny the truth. *Her* son was a tyrant. *Her* heart wept for humanity. We too are *Her* children. Ilabrat was twisting people into fearful, spiteful beings like Himself.

Meshka's eyeballs were jumping out of her head. This was beyond blasphemy! Was there a *god* before the one God or is this God by another name? Was God born from a Goddess!?! How could she even ask such a question!

"*Sophia* created another creature to challenge Ilabrat, someone to help Him see the effects of His actions and teach Him compassion.

"*She* wanted a champion for humanity, someone not of pure consciousness like Ilabrat, but rather a changeling, part divine to win Ilabrat's respect and part human to sympathize with human problems.

These views of God struck Meshka like lightning!

"*Sophia* took the form of a dove and flew through the sky searching for a compassionate woman. *She* came upon a young maiden whose gentle heart encompassed the whole of existence. *She* landed on the maiden's hand.

Meshka was startled! She giggled; a living creature could change form!?! The idea intrigued her. "Too bad I am not a *Goddess*, I would change into a younger body," she mused.

"Young Mari gently petted Sophia's pretty feathers and cooed. *The Goddess* liked the sound and cooed back. It was such a lovely sound that doves have cooed as sweetly ever since.

"Young Mari's gentle touch, her sweet beauty, her kind heart, they all held the spirit *Sophia* wanted for *Her* son. *The Goddess* changed from a dove into vaporous mist - the *Holy Spirit*. Thus *She* entered Mari's body and burrowed into her womb."

Meshka was stretching her mind to take in this strange idea. *The Goddess* can become a dove if *She* wants to. The dove can turn into fertile living mist and implant a child in a maiden's womb. It was a lot to take in.

"At the appointed time common to women, Mari delivered a child – *Sophia's* second son – Joshua, the *Messiah*. From baby to manhood, He made both His mothers proud.

"The *Messiah* was raised in the manner of humans - with love, hard work and religion. He reached out a gentle hand with love. He fed the hungry, healed the sick, and spoke with wisdom."

Meshka felt a flurry of excitement, a *Messiah* came once to help people? Why did He have to leave? She wondered, but dare not interrupt the sacred telling.

"Most of the religions at that time worshipped the fierce Ilabrat under one name or another, so it was not long before the two sons of *Sophia* learned of each other.

"Ilabrat attacked! He rallied an army and sent them to destroy Joshua. Some say the boy died and others assure us that He escaped. At some point in time, the human part of Him returned to dust, while the Divine part continued to live on.

"The battle between Ilabrat's lust for violence and Joshua's peaceful spirit spanned oceans of time and still persists. Soldiers and priests slanderously distorted Joshua's teachings, yet His gentle spirit endures. It is rooted in the hearts of compassionate men and women. Humanity received the gift destined for God.

"*Sophia's* seed lives on in humanity. *Her* temple is in our Souls. *She* urges us to live to the fullest and to honor the natural dimensions of life. As Joshua once said, 'The kingdom of heaven lies within.'

"The second son of *Sophia* was born of woman, so He had a human heart filled with compassion. You can always recognize *Messiahs* by their deep compassion. They feed and heal the people around them. Jesus, Buddha, and countless others are *Her* Princes of Peace, *Her* champions. *The Goddess* charges these gentle souls to ease suffering and bring peace. Unfortunately the powers of Ilabrat often attempt to silence Their message."

In the magical womb of Sharanii's Temple, a doorway was opening in Meshka's mind. She gazed into her imagination and saw powerful forces playing out in the field of human desires.

While rabbis wait for a distant *Messiah* to come and save the world, many *Messiahs* have already come to heal it! She liked this idea. It fit what *Sophia* told her.

Meshka's eyes glazed over, seeing so many new ideas. She always tried to be accepting but of course, the journey to develop this precious 'acceptance,' was a road full of potholes and bumps. She often missed the mark, fell into commonly held belief, and felt justified in blaming someone for something, though nowadays only in her mind.

She knew if she opened her mouth when she was angry and threw her pain out at someone, it would just cause trouble. Oy, and then there was always the messy clean up afterwards. Fighting was a waste of energy. She preferred to digest the problem and heal it inside herself, before she tried to deal with another person and all their *mishugass*.

Meshka was intrigued with this idea of many *Messiahs*. It seeded a desire in her to be more compassionate.

Since every thought walks across Meshka's face, Sharanii sat back after the telling and watched sparks of sudden understanding sparkle in Meshka's 'other-seeing' eyes.

"Meshka, this is enough for now," she whispered.

The Jewish woman sort of nodded.

Sharanii enjoyed remembering the story. It took her back to a vast timeless land where eerie winds swept across the desert. It was a long ago adventure when she was young.

The *Priestess* smoothed out all the layers of deerskin, rolled them up, and tied the bundle with a crimson ribbon. The two women sat side by side in silence for a while.

Meshka was becoming quite a scholar for someone who never read a book. Ignorance no longer protected her. The question was; what would she do with her new found knowledge?

Candlemas was a powerful portal. Meshka opened her spirit and stepped through a promise. Her life vastly changed, her view of life unrecognizably changed. She walked around with her face and hair exposed, open to whatever life may bring.

Death spat her out of the grief tunnel. The world of the living called her back. The first spring of this new person was filled with discovery. Meshka savored each one. She shook out her wild mane of flaming curls and laughed like a girl.

03030308

The Prince of Peace

The mountains were behind them now and the green meadows they walked through of these last few days, now gave way to the sea. It was late afternoon and Meshka was walking along the beach in stunned delight. She never imagined there was so much water in all the world! The blue waves went as far as they could and fell off the edge of world!

Meshka's little village was far inland. She always thought the mighty sea was a myth, an exaggerated tale told to children. Seeing the brilliant blue waters sparkling in the sun was one more proof that the realm of magic was alive in the world.

The soft sand demanded she remove the leather wraps from her feet. The first time the cool lips of the sand sucked her in at the water's edge, she giggled. Wet and thrilled, she was having fun wiggling her toes in the cool soft stuff.

At the end of a little cove, Meshka came upon a group of children laughing and playing on a narrow strip of land between the water and a big stone cliff. Their bubbling joy tickled her grandma heart. For a long time she stood there basking in their youthful energy. In their bright giggling faces she saw wisps of Suryla, Moishela, Yonkela, and Rifkala.

"Bodhi, do me next!" begged a little black-skin boy. The slender blond young man suddenly scooped up the little guy and spun him round and round. The flying child squealed in delight. Meshka recognized the young man. He was the one chanting by the stream and the silhouette performing strange dances at dusk.

Watching him toss the little ones around like baby chicks made her feel young again.

"Bodhi, do me next, p-l-ease p-l-ease," a little Russian boy called out gleefully. Bodhi stalked him with a wiggling finger threatening to tickle him.

"Top or toe?" Bodhi challenged. The brave young child took a gulp and squeaked, "Toe!"

Bodhi lifted the little guy by his feet and spun him around and around upside down. He giggled and laughed, delighted by the rushes fluttering through his belly.

A little girl with bright curly red hair called, "Bodhi! Bodhi! Make me fly! Make me fly!" He asked, "Top or toe?"

"Toe, but please go real fast," she chirped hopping from foot to foot in all her excitement. Bodhi wrapped his strong hands firmly around her ankles and began to spin her slowly; then faster and faster until they were just a blur. That little carrot top, bless her heart, bent her pudgy little legs to be an arrow; closed her eyes, and flew off in bliss. All you could see was her smile reaching from ear to ear. She was soaring!

Meshka sighed. She remembered how Yonkle used to spin his little nephew and niece around like that. He also liked to tickle and tease them with the finger. Yonkle felt alive again in this young man. Meshka tenderly savored a delicious wave of remembered love.

When Carrot Top landed, all the children started jumping up and down again calling, "Bodhi me next! Me next!" Bodhi smiled at all of them, but walked over to a little moppet of a child, sitting silently tucked in among the roots of an old tree. Against all odds, this tree was growing out of the rocks at the base of the cliff.

Bodhi sat down beside the little girl. She was looking down at her gnarled and crippled hands, trying to shrink even smaller.

"Would you like me to spin you?" Bodhi softly asked. She looked into his eyes, but did not reply. One of the children shouted, "Oh she cannot hear."

In the language of dancing hands, Bodhi asked her again. With the slightest shake of her head, she gestured no. He smiled and pantomimed, "May I cradle and rock you? I will be very gentle." The fragile child hesitated, but this time she nodded yes.

Bodhi carefully scooped up the crippled girl and slowly swayed, cradling her in his arms. Each reverent step an echo of his evening dance; each movement touched with grace. He was agile as a panther and rooted as a tree.

Meshka was going to walk on along the seaside, but was reluctant to leave the sweet children. Close by stood a cluster of several huge stones jutting up from the sea. They looked inviting. How could she resist standing on such a high perch? Wisps of magic, like the fragrance of a light perfume tickled her senses, calling to her from up there; so up she went scrambling over the rocks, scrambling like a little crab determined to get to the top.

She did it! She was standing on top of the world! A vast endless sea lay before her, stretched out from horizon to horizon, a perfect gentle arch of deep blue.

The sea breeze kissed Meshka's face. Looking at the children playing down below from this lofty height made her feel like a giant! She breathed in the salty tang of the air. She was excitedly alive and inspired! Her eyes closed. She felt like she was growing bigger and bigger, just like in a dream.

The huge rough stones beneath her feet looked like a mighty dragon rising from the sea onto the land. Looking out at the far edge of the sea, she imagined herself standing on a fierce beast. The power of the ocean, the mighty stones, and the dangerous beast upon which she stood, did not frighten her.

In fact, she felt a stillness, a peaceful soft sense of 'life unfolding according to its destiny.'

She took a deep breath. The warmth of the sun and the coolness of the mist played across her face; beneath her feet was the firm solidity of the stone and a sweet sea breeze danced through her hair.

"Dis is how *Kwan Yin* must have felt," she thought, remembering *The Goddess* standing on a dragon in Sharanii's picture.

"Oy *Kvan Yin*, vee have something in common You 'n me. Vee both vant to make dis world a kinder place, vhere people choose to love instead of hate. *Kvan Yin*, I know how You felt vhen you va standing on da dragon, at peace in da middle of wild forces. Living my life is like lying on da tongue of a dragon. I never know vhen he is going to bite down."

Meshka gazed down in fascination, watching the waves crash against the rocks beneath her. The water threw itself against the polished stone and then rushed away back to the sea. She breathed in the fresh sea air and felt tranquil.

"All da rivers 'n da streams became one sea. If only people could do dat too," she mused.

A dolphin leaped out of the water to wink at her and two more sleek black creatures joined in the game, leaping through the turquoise depths to charm her.

"*Meshka, My daughter,*" whispered a haunting voice, no more than a breath of wind. "*Meshka, My child,*" she heard again more clearly.

Suddenly before her stood a tall slender woman with beautifully exotic eyes, draped in a simple white robe. She was but a wisp of an image, a misty cloud drifting through her mind.

"*My child, I am Kwan Yin, the Goddess of Mercy and Compassion. You called me? I have watched over you for a long time. Your nature is baking in my oven,*" *The Goddess* whispered and vanished.

Meshka sat down and leaned back against the cool stone of the dragon's head. She closed her eyes and floated off in sweet contentment, a very new experience for her. She sat thinking about *The Goddess*, her mission to make life better, and all the wonderful fascinating people she was meeting on this journey.

Meshka sat on the dragon's back savoring the pleasure of this peaceful day for a long time, long enough for the tide to roll in.

What Meshka did not know about the sea, could fill a book. What she did know, could fill half a thimble. Boy was she surprised to discover that the sea rises and falls!

Oy vay! She was trapped! The sea wrapped itself around the bottom of the cliff covering the lower rocks. With cold white teeth, the waves jumped up to nip at her heels! The dragon grew more frightening!

Before panic could grab her by the throat, Meshka told herself, "Kvan Yin is watching over me, I vill be fine. Da Goddess climbed off Her dragon, so I can too. I just have to move very slowly. I can do dis. It is like savoring, I just have to be very careful. I can do dis."

Thinking about Kwan Yin calmed her mind, but her heart was still banging like a bell!

Very carefully, Meshka eased her legs onto the first wet slippery stone lower down. She carefully found a good footing and moved her weight very slowly onto it. Ahhh, she landed safely! Oy was she proud of herself!

"I can do dis!" she cried out to a passing sea gull who was lazily floating over her head.

Again Meshka reached out her foot, but this time no footing could she find. A stab of panic gripped her. Then her toe touched a tuft of prickly weeds. Slowly she shifted her weight to her foot. The tuft of land held fast, so she eased herself down onto it.

Within seconds the land gave way! Meshka was falling! Her hands shot out! She grabbed hold of a thin rock shelf and dangled by her arms!

Her fleshy arms were actually strong enough to hold her. Meshka was amazed at the strength she was discovering in them. Those arms carried something for someone every day, month after month. While she was busy looking for ways to help people; she never noticed real muscles were growing under all that skin. With all her might, she gripped the rock above her head till her knuckles were bleached white!

Yes, Meshka was stronger than before, but how long could she grip a wet rock with her fat mama belly weighing her down? Her fingers were gripping as tightly as they could…b-u-t…ever so slowly they were also letting go!

She heard a terrible scream! It rang from her lips. Down! Down! Down! She tumbled!

Having such a big round soft bottom, you would think Meshka would bounce.

No! Splat! She landed on a big shelf rock. Sharp stabbing pain shot through her back as her spine twisted like a pretzel. The pain screamed so loud, it reminded her of being in labor.

She only fell four feet, but the terror and the shock made the fall much further. Rudely seated on the slippery rock, Meshka desperately grabbed hold of a small twisted bush sticking up from the wet stone. She clung to it, but her seat was sliding slowly downwards! Another terrible fall was only seconds away.

Bodhi flew up the rocks to Meshka. His two strong arms shot out encircling her waist. Anchoring his feet, rooted to the stone, his strong arms caught her as she slid off the edge! Gently he brought Meshka over to the large flat rock where he stood and put her down beside him.

Meshka was panting fast like a dog. It took a long time for the pounding of her heart to stop making so much noise!

Bodhi sat down beside her and put his arm around Meshka's shoulders. He was beaming strength into her. When the trembling in her body slowed down and her breath was not so ragged, he reached for the bola he wore over his shoulder and offered her a drink of water. Meshka smiled gratefully. Her throat was so dry and scratchy; you could rub wood smooth on it.

Meshka turned to take the bola. Suddenly screaming pain shot through her and she cried out. "OWWWW!"

Oy was she in pain!

With a concerned brow, Bodhi looked at her appraisingly. "Is the pain in the middle of your back, behind your heart?"

Meshka was hunched over writhing. It was like having labor pains. They were really bad...b-u-t...she did not want to be a burden on this young man, so she brushed away his concern. "Do not worry about me, I am fine. Dis pain and me are old friends. Vee know each other many years," she tossed off flippantly.

"I am sorry you are hurting. I can make the pain stop, if will you let me. Where does it hurt?"

Meshka shyly pointed to the place behind her heart.

The young man took a deep slow breath, closed his eyes and rubbed his hands together fast like sticks making a fire until they were warm and electric.

Bodhi looked at her with soft compassion in his eyes and offered, "I can breathe the deep power of the earth into my center and draw the golden power of heaven down. I can beam these united forces out through my hands. I will not touch you, but you will feel deeply touched. Do you want me to do this?"

Meshka could make no sense of what he was saying, but he seemed sure he could take the pain away and she like that. She was confused but willing. A little frog got stuck in her throat and would not let a word pass, so she just nodded.

"Relax," he softly whispered, "Close your eyes and breathe into the pain. Your whole body can breathe, not just your nose. Breathe into the pain..."

She felt a little silly, but what did she have to lose? So she pictured the face of a lion on her back. His big nose breathed in the air and sent it to the pain.

"Breathe into the pain. Feel it fully. Breathe deeply. Do not shy away from the sensation. Face it. "

Meshka moaned.

"Look inside and feel your deep strength."

All Meshka could feel was a very sharp pain stabbing her in the back!

"Embrace the pain with a loving heart."

She remembered holding Suryla in her arms. Her sweet little granddaughter was the jewel of her eye. With that kind of love, she faced the pain.

"Breathe into the pain. Feel it. Breathe into it."

Her breath became a guideline into and out of the pain.

"Make each breath longer than the one before."

His voice was soothing. Meshka took a deep breath and filled her lungs with the fresh sea breeze, so salty and pure.

"Feel the solid stone beneath you; supporting you."

She imagined roots going from her ample *tush* (buttocks) down into the rocks. Her roots like snakes, wound their way down to draw up the power of *Mother Earth*. Meshka saw healing water flowing up from the earth, up through the long roots, through the rocks and into her tailbone. This healing water brought a stream of comfort rising up her back.

"Breathe through the crown of your head. Breathe in the light of heaven." Meshka pictured a big golden sunbeam radiating down on her humble head.

"Feel the power of the ocean crashing within you."

She was shocked! A wonderful rushing excitement surged through her; that got her attention!

"Breathe into your heart."

She drew in several deep full breathes, filled her lungs as far as they dare, and let the breath out very slowly, ever more slowly. Soon she was melting into a comfortable warm sensation. Pain and pleasure entwined within her.

Meshka had her eyes closed as she savored a pleasurable warm sensation. After a few minutes it grew hotter! A fire was radiating on her back! Was Bodhi holding a torch near her skin? She opened her eyes just a little bit, and peeked around.

Bodhi was sitting cross-legged a few inches behind her on the big flat ledge. His eyes were closed and his palms were facing out towards her. That's all! No torch, nothing! All the heat was coming from his hands!

"G-o-o-d," he drew out the word to make it even more soothing.

"Take a deep breath and release your breath powerfully. Let it all go!"

Meshka went back to having the lion on her back breathing in deeply and released it forcefully. She drifted off enjoying the heat, while the pain throbbed on.

She felt warm, safe, and open.

Meshka was no longer thinking this was silly. She was feeling real things! Real heat was warming her back and softening the pain.

With serious respect, she took a deep full breath, held it for a few heart beats and released the breath in a rush. Her head spun!

The delicious heat held her dangling on the edge of pain and pleasure. The heat brought nourishing blood rushing to her back to do the healing work. After several long slow breaths, she noticed there was more pleasure and less pain. The twisted muscle relaxed and the pain eased.

Meshka wiggled her body a little this way and that. The pain was gone! She gave the handsome young man a toothy grin and was so relaxed, she sighed. They sat quietly for a few minutes.

"Can you move now? Are you ready to go on?" He asked.

Smiling softly she nodded yes, for she felt too quiet for words.

"If you will permit me, I would like to hold your hand for just a moment."

His words brought her drifting back from a peaceful place. He reached for her hand. She was completely flustered. No man had ever asked to hold her hand; and this one, oy vay he was so young 'n handsome like an angel. Her face turned bright cherry red, but the hand floated over to him.

Bodhi put three fingers on her wrist and closed his eyes. He cocked his head to the side like he was listening. "Good strong pulses. The shock will soon pass."

He is holding my hand! He says I am good. Oy vay! Maybe I am still on top of da rock dreaming.

"Are you ready to climb the rest of the way down?" Bodhi stood up and reached out his hand to help her up.

With a constant stream of words, Bodhi guided her feet step by step, handhold by handhold; until they came to the gnashing white waves wildly trying to bite off bits of the naked cliff.

Bodhi stood firm and solid on the lowest boulder just above the cresting waves lapping at the rocks and said, "If you will permit me, I would be honored to carry you to the shore."

Meshka was too flustered to say no. All this attention from such a handsome young man made her breathless. Her face was burning brightly.

Strong young arms embraced her. He lifted her up as if she was one of the children he spun about. He was so strong; he held her like she was a little feather. Meshka was shocked. When was she ever a feather? Never! Maybe a little elephant; but never a feather! He held her against his heart. She threw her arms around his neck and felt his strong young body next to hers. She was sooo excited!

She leaned her head back against his supple chest and closed her eyes. Bodhi carried her down the last few rocks, through the shallow water, and gently helped her to stand in the soft sand. He put a strong protective arm around her shoulder and supported her while she got her legs under her. She was sure she was in heaven.

Sweet Meshka was giddy as a girl. Her heart was making such a racket but not from pain or fear. She felt all tangled up in knots. Strangers never touched her and her family never touched her this intimately. She was thrilled to be with this handsome young man and feel his magical touch.

CRCRCR

Side by side they walked along the beach. Bodhi said thoughtfully, "Whenever I hurt myself, I take it as a wakeup call. I assume the *Divine Mother* is telling me to pay attention. Something important is at hand. Each part of the body speaks of different things. Pain is always a warning! It reminds us to pay attention. If I had a pain behind my heart, I would pay attention to my heart and ask it what it wants."

She knew about the pain behind her heart. They were old friends. The cruel pain came from losing most of her favorite people. She could not say such a private a thing to a handsome stranger; better she should be flippant.

"Vhere did you learn such *bubba maisse?"* (nonsense) She scoffed and laughed nervously. Her sharp tone did not shield her from the truth of his words.

Tears welled up, but she breathed the choking wave back down. She opened her mouth to speak and then heard her mama say just like she always used to; "If you have nothing good to say, say nothing," so her mouth shut and she shrugged.

"I am sorry. I did not mean to offend you," the lad sincerely apologized with a formal little bow.

"Nu," she said with a light wave of her hand, dismissing it as nothing. "My heart is broken 'n all da goodness in me spilt out. Maybe I am empty. You know, a lot of wonderful people once lived in dis liddle heart."

"They still do," he reassured her. His eyes were warm and compassionate. He knew of such emptiness himself.

"How does your back feel now?" He asked when they reached her camp.

"Fine, dank you," she replied.

Meshka remembered all those years of pain and how she would tell anyone who would listen, saying things like, "It feels like I am carrying da wall of Jericho on my back." But little of that cranky old woman from the old village was left in Meshka.

"My back? It feels as good as a liddle baby's back!" She exclaimed in delight. With a sprightly skip she bounced along.

"Remember to be gentle with yourself," Bodhi advised in parting. She felt younger by far than she ever had. No more wall of Jericho. She was free!

Mumbling words of gratitude, she watched him walk away.

Hours passed and night fell before Meshka remembered she was really a wrinkled old woman. For a little while, she was a young girl full of fancy feelings.

Giggling like a girl and shaking her head like an old lady, she thought, "Dis would never have happened if I vas wearing my shawl." She was right in more ways than she could ever imagine.

ଔଔଔ

Chapter 19

Kwan Yin

Two days later was Shabbos. Meshka was all excited kneading the dough. She was making special challahs, big golden loaves for Bodhi and his ragamuffin flock. She lovingly kneaded the sacred braided bread of peace.

Still warm from the makeshift stone oven, Meshka wrapped the golden challahs in clean cotton cloths and went to find Bodhi. She followed a stream of urchins to a large meadow. A motley crew of children was clustered together on the ground under a cherry tree.

Plotzing down beside them, she was about to ask about Bodhi when everyone began to cheer. She looked up and saw a magnificent cream-colored horse soaring across the meadow. Its silky white tail was floating on the wind. And there, clinging firmly to its mane was Bodhi, pale yellow hair flying wild behind him.

Man and beast merged gracefully into a magnificent golden creature shining radiantly in the sunlight. He was a real centaur come to life as though he walked off one of Sharanii's ancient scrolls.

The children shouted and cheered as the centaur leaped over large boulders, soared over a tangle of fallen branches, and sailed over a tumble of obstacles. After his magnificent performance, amidst great applause, Bodhi cantered over to Meshka breathless with wild excitement, and dismounted.

All the children swarmed around him, everyone was talking at once. Meshka scrambled to her feet and backed away.

It made her nervous to be so close to such a big animal. Do horses bite? she wondered. Dey have such big yellow teeth! Leave it to Meshka, when she saw a horse, no matter how beautiful, all she saw were the teeth.

After a while, the tide of excited little faces subsided. All the kids ran off in different directions and Bodhi took a step closer to Meshka.

He greeted her warmly with a bright smile.

Meshka told herself, she was not going to scold him for doing such dangerous tricks. If he was Yonkle, she would have given him a good piece of her mind for risking his life like that. Oy, if only Yonkle was here to be scolded. *Chaval.* (such a pity)

"Did you enjoy watching me ride?" he asked still breathing hard.

She was not going to say anything, but since he asked…the words jumped out.

"Oy vay! Are you meshugener crazy? Why do you take such terrible chances? Dat horse is so big 'n you va riding sooo fast!" The words fell out of her mouth without passing her brain.

Ooops! She locked her lips, not in disapproval, even though it did look like that. No, she had to lock her lips to keep more words from tumbling out.

What she did not say was: "You never know vhen God vill turn around 'n slam you in da head. He does dat every once in a while just because He is having a bad day. Sometimes God just wakes up on da wrong side of da bed. Vhen He gets into dat warrior mood of His, He starts poking people vid problems."

Granted she did not say these words, but they were written on her face.

Bodhi was startled. Somehow that was not anything like the response he was expecting.

He could have been offended or hurt; but he was very wise for his young years. He knew people act sharply when something sharp is sticking them from within. He saw her fear, so he did not respond. Again, more softly he repeated "Did you enjoy my performance?"

Meshka wondered what she could say without insulting him more; so she said, "It vas very brave. You 'n da big animal vid da big yellow teeth va very beautiful. I am sorry I worried so much about you getting hurt."

Bodhi smiled at Meshka. He basked in her motherly warmth and her sweetness. It felt good to have someone fuss over him and be all concerned.

Meshka reminded him of his own mama. If she were here, his mama would probably scold him too. He loved taking risks. A seasoned warrior priest at nineteen, he thought he was invulnerable. His hunger for a taste of divinity sometimes made him forget how fragile the human body is.

"I like taking risks. It makes me feel more alive. I focus on my goal and become one with my horse. The rushing swish of air feels wonderful. When death tip-toes close, life feels even richer!" His youth was speaking.

"Obstacles are good for us. They make us stretch. Loss and grief are the ashes that fertilize the future – after the scars heal, of course," he added, for he knew loss, grief, ashes, and scars himself.

Meshka snorted and said, "You mean vhatever does not break you into liddle pieces makes you grow?"

He smiled and said "Something like that. Come. Please walk me back to the stables."

Meshka walked fretfully beside Bodhi on his other side, away from the horse. She did not want to get too close. You never know what a creature with big yellow teeth was going to do.

"I came to dank you for fixing my old broken back. You got real magic in those hands. Dey are such a blessing," and she gave him a warm toothy smile.

Then just to flirt a little, she said, "I feel like a young girl now. You know how long my back as been giving me *tsoris* (trouble)? Since before you va a twinkle in your papa's eye."

She felt young and playful without the heavy fabric covering her face and constantly reminding her that she was not a part of what was going on. Now that she was free of her blinders, there was so much more to see!

Bodhi's smile radiated compassion and made her feel safe. She trusted him. Maybe if she shared one of her invisible bundles, maybe her shoulders would feel lighter too, so she confided to him, "Da other day, vhen I vas such a klutz 'n tvisted my back like a pretzel, I thought God sent dat pain to punish me for talking vid *Kvan Yin*.

"Maybe I vas wrong, maybe every bad ding is not a punishment from God. Maybe it vas like you said, 'Pain is a vakeup call asking me to look at something in my life dat I could do better.'"

Meshka shocked herself! She was embarrassed that she told him about the Goddess and yearned to take the words back, erase what she said. There was no way to do that, so she changed the subject. Maybe a distraction would make him forget her big mouth.

"You know, I vas looking at dose liddle *pitzkalas* of yours making patty cake, patty cake, right here in dis vilderness as dough it vas deir home, 'n an idea hit me on da head! Maybe every-vhere can be my home 'n everyone can be my family."

"You know *Kwan Yin*!?" Bodhi asked. She ruffled his composure. This little old woman was full of surprises.

She giggled, tickled by his stunned expression. "*Da Goddess* talks to me sometimes." Meshka was relieved to share this secret with him. "I hear *Her* voice 'n I see *Her* like in a dream, but I am avake! Once I saw a picture of *Kvan Yin* riding on a dragon!

All excited Meshka asked hopefully, "Do you know dis *Kvan Yin?*"

"I seek to know *Her* better." His soothing voice made Meshka feel safe. "I have heard *Her* story told and once in China, I watched an exotic play about *Her* life. Mostly I know *Kwan Yin* through meditation and prayer."

Meshka had so many questions; she did not know which one to ask first? Vhere is dis China? Is it a land far-avay? I never heard of such a place. How did he come to be in dis far away land? Vhat is mediation, is it like prayer?

Bursting with curiosity Meshka asked, "Do you know *da Goddess's* story?"

"O yes, I remember it well?"

"Bodhi please, can you tell me?"

He smiled and nodded. Meshka's face lit up like a sunbeam. They reached the stables and Bodhi began to rub down the beautiful white horse. As he fell into a rhythm, brushing the horse with long tender strokes, he told Meshka the story. He recited it in his wonderful storytelling voice, the one he used to enchant the children.

Children loved Bodhi, even the child part of Meshka. She sat wide-eyed as he began his tale, "*Kwan Yin was the Chinese Goddess of Mercy and Compassion. She* incarnated long, long ago." Seeing the confused look in Meshka's eyes, Bodhi reminded himself to talk more simply,

"A long time ago, when *Kwan Yin* was born, *She* chose the most powerful man in the land to be *Her* father. He adored *Her* when *She* was little, the youngest of three sisters, but when *She* grew up everything changed. *Her* older sisters married well. Their father chose fine son-in-laws, a merchant and a warrior who added to his wealth and power. A match was made for little *Kwan Yin* while *She* was still a young child."

Meshka was shocked! "Vait a minute! Are you telling me a *Goddess* vas vonce a real girl who eats 'n poops!?"

Bodhi nodded yes and tried not to laugh as he continued telling his story. "When *Kwan Yin* was old enough to marry, *She* refused. *Her* heart was set on being a *Priestess*. *Her* father was outraged. He ordered *Kwan Yin* to marry the wealthy old man he chose for *Her*, but *Her* heart yearned for a life of devotion.

"One day, *Kwan Yin* ran away to the Temple of the White Bird and became a *Priestess*."

Meshka kept an eye on the wild stallion beside her. This was the closest she had ever been to such a huge creature and it made her more than a little nervous. Bodhi's voice was very soothing though, and soon his story took up her whole mind.

"*Kwan Yin's* angry father went to the Temple and ordered the High *Priestess* to release his daughter. She wisely said that the girl would just run away to another Temple. *Her* father got angry and threatened the venerable old *Priestess*. In the face of brute force, she had no choice but to compromise. She agreed to make life difficult for the sweet girl, so *Kwan Yin* would choose to go home."

The horse sensed that Meshka was scared, so he edged closer to her. He looked innocent when he swished his tail and sharply slapped Meshka on her ample *tush* (buttocks). Shocked, Meshka jumped back, glaring at the horse and certain he did it on purpose.

She edged away from the beast and Bodhi continued his story, "*Kwan Yin* had to get up before the others, gather wood and light the morning fires. *She* did it all willingly. Soon *She* was doing most of the cleaning and cooking. Spending long hours from before dawn to well after dark, *She* worked tirelessly and in good humor. *She* fulfilled all *Her* tasks. Every night *She* fell into bed pleasantly exhausted and deeply satisfied."

Another sharp slap of his tail struck Meshka. "Nice monster, be nice. Vee should be friends. Please don't hurt me." Meshka spoke to him in her mind. She really wanted to kick him but she could never hurt an animal, so instead she gave him a lopsided smile and took another step back away from the huge beast.

Bodhi went on brushing the beautiful animal and ignored his mischief. He smiled reassuringly at Meshka and continued, "Everything *Kwan Yin* did was an act of love. *She* was never alone in *Her* labors for *She* had many helpers. Tigers carried wood, serpents fetched water, and birds collected vegetables from the garden. The regal peacocks swept the floors with their elegant feathers and the fire sparked itself into flame lit by the spirit within it. *Kwan Yin* was so kind and so gentle to every creature under heaven that all the nature spirits loved *Her* and joyfully helped."

Meshka was distracted by the horse. Bodhi's story was not about a woman like Judith or Debra, but of a *Goddess* coming into the world to live a spiritual life as a regular woman. Meshka listened wide-eyed. Her jaw hung down to her chest, she was fascinated and intrigued.

Bodhi's voice grew dark and ominous. "When word reached *Her* father that his disobedient daughter was content with *Her* new life, he flew into a wild rage and put a torch to the Temple of the White Bird. *Kwan Yin* ran into the flames and put the fire out with *Her* own small hands.

"*Kwan Yin* refused to go home! *She* went right on with *Her* quiet life of selfless service in the Temple of the White Bird. It suited *Her* well."

Meshka was listening, enthralled. Her mouth was hanging so far open that a furry little fly buzzing around the big horse landed on her tongue!

"Poi! Poi!" She spat it out utterly disgusted. Bodhi watched amused. She did not resemble his mama at all. He hid the laugh that was itching to pop out and went on with his story.

"*Kwan Yin's* father would not tolerate shameful disobedience in a daughter. He was not going to be outwitted by a willful girl, so he hired an assassin to murder *Her*."

Bodhi finished grooming the horse and the animal's withers glowed. He patted the horse and put a large gunnysack of oats around his neck. Bodhi's work was done, so he returned to his tale.

"The assassin went to the Temple of the White bird. He found the girl hard at work mending clothes for the orphan children in *Her* care. *Her* head was bent over *Her* task. The cruel assassin slipped in behind *Her* and brought his sharp sword down hard upon *Her* neck!

"Many heads had rolled beneath his mighty blade. But when his sword touched the soft flesh of the girl's neck, the blade broke in two. Shocked and frightened, the assassin gasped in horror. 'What evil magic is this?' he cried and ran away.

"The assassin returned to *Kwan Yin's* father and blurted out the strange tale of his broken sword. The frightened man begged to be released from this wicked deed. The father laughed with malice and ridiculed the big man for being afraid of a simple girl. His mood was sour.

"'If you fail to complete the contract,' the father warned, 'I will have you killed.'"

Meshka was listening, her face open with amazement! Bodhi filled the trough with fresh water from a nearby well and removed the sack of oats.

Once the stallion was contentedly drinking water, Bodhi took Meshka's arm and led her out of the barn.

"*Nu?* (well) Hurry up! I cannot wait. Did he kill *Her?*" Meshka asked jumping from foot to foot like a little girl.

"To save his own life, the assassin returned to the Temple of the White Bird and strangled the young girl with his bare hands. *Kwan Yin* was dead."

Meshka was horrified, "Dat is a terrible story! Da poor child! How could a papa treat his own daughter dat vay?" She felt sorry for the poor girl.

"We live in a patriarchal world where women suffer. *Kwan Yin* suffered at the hands of *Her* father. He loved *Her* until *She* disobeyed him. Many women must obey their fathers and live lives that do not suit them. It is the curse of the Patriarchy – a woman lives or dies by the whims of her male masters," Bodhi explained.

Meshka shook her head. It was so strange to hear a young man talk about women's problems. Never did she meet a man who even noticed what women feel.

"*Kwan Yin* descended into the world below to take care of the dead. *She* was dearly loved by the departed souls. The God of the Underworld grew jealous of *Kwan Yin* and *Her* gentle ways, so cast *Her* out. *She* returned to life and settled on a sacred island in the China Sea. From there *She* watches over the world," and so his tale ended.

"I can see how *Kvan Yin* could have such a story. *Her* father vas like a dangerous dragon. Vhen I saw a picture of dis *Goddess* on a dragon, *Her* dress vas blowing in a big vind, but *Her* face vas peaceful." Meshka felt so smart and proud of herself for knowing this.

"*Kwan Yin* reminds us to meet the wild forces and deal with the danger while choosing to not get drawn into the drama and be upset."

"One ding confuses me," Meshka cut in. "If a *Goddess* can be a real person, den you never know if you are talking to a regular old woman or she is secretly a *Goddess*!" Meshka marveled out loud.

"That is very true.

"There is one more part to the story. *Kwan Yin* returned to life another time, many years later in another country. Being wiser now, *She* did not choose the most powerful man to be *Her* father, but rather, the kindest. *She* chose to be born the daughter of Avalokitesvara, the most compassionate man in all the land. He was a Bodhisattva."

Meshka rolled her eyes. She was very impressed with all his big words. She actually knew some of these big words and that made her smile. She was getting smarter all the time.

"The Bodhisattva lived in India for three thousand years. During all this time, he treated every man with respect and compassion. But the world did not become compassionate. All those years, all those gifts of love, and still men were as hard-hearted as ever.

"The Bodhisattva became so sad. One day a little pearl of a teardrop rolled down his cheek and landed in the palm of his hand. He gazed down at it and before his eyes, the teardrop changed into a lotus blossom. The blossom opened and there sitting among the lovely petals, was a beautiful young woman.

"*She* said, 'Father, I am here to help you make the world a more compassionate place. Whenever I am called, I will come quickly to remove all obstacles.'

"Now, as the *Green Tara, Kwan Yin* worked side by side with *Her* father **Avalokitesvara** all the days of *Her* life and *She* still does. Together and separately, they inspire people to be gentle and compassionate with each other."

Meshka let out her breath. She liked happy endings. Who knows, maybe her life can still have a happy ending. She liked this young man. She never met anyone like him before. His strange ideas were stretching her mind.

Bodhi was like a gardener dropping seeds into her fertile mind. What amazing adventures would they sprout? Seeds break the soil to take on life and Meshka was breaking through some crusty parts of her mind. She wondered where life was taking her, and how far would God let her go?

ଔଔଔଔ

Part 4

A Goddess is Born

Chapter 20

The Bodhisattva

A rough and tumble cluster of orphans gathered around Meshka and Bodhi. Meshka opened the big basket she was carrying and lifted the cloth to reveal several large golden challahs and big chunks of yellow cheese. A great cheer went up as the children breathed in the warm sweet smell of fresh baked bread. It was a long time since they had eaten anything so wonderful. Meshka blessed the bread and divided her treasure among the urchins. Several of the older children turned to the little ones and fed them. Meshka smiled. A silent tear eased its way down her cheek.

In her mind she scolded God, "Hungry children, now dat is a crime against Nature."

One little oriental girl shoved the whole thing into her mouth. She swallowed it in one bite with a wide grin of delight. She had dreamed of such a pleasure for a long time. Beside her sat a little dark-skinned girl who took teeny tiny little bites to make her happiness last as long as possible.

"Good girl," Meshka said, patting the little dark one on the head.

Bodhi snickered under his breath. "Vhat?" Meshka asked with a questioning lift of her shoulders.

"You believe in good and evil," he snickered amused.

333

"Of course! doesn't everyone?" Meshka chided.

"Not everyone. Taking life apart to see only good and evil is looking through a narrow lens. Life has many shades of color, not just black and white.

"Good and Evil are just beliefs. Beliefs are made up and imposed on people. They control the mind's interpretation and reaction to life. You chose to accept this narrowing belief. You could just as well choose to see more sides of a truth."

Meshka and Bodhi were walking along the beach, watching the waves roll in. A flock of sea gulls were squawking overhead. A pair of pelicans circled above and dived into the water, caught fish, and rose again with expert grace. Meshka breathed in the salty air and felt her chest expand with the freshness of life.

"A sacred path is one of balance. The wise Orientals have a wonderful symbol for balance, 'yin yang'. It is a circle divided in half. One side is white with a black spot in the center and the other is black with a white spot. There is light in the darkness and darkness in the light. Everything and everyone has a touch of the opposite within them."

Meshka understood the words but the meaning confused her. Did he mean a person has to taste a little bitterness to appreciate the sweetness? Or does he mean we all have a little mischief in the best of us and a little purity in the worst of us?

She gave up trying to unravel the mystery and simply asked, "So vhat does dis black 'n vhite mean?"

"It symbolizes balance. Life strives for balance. We explore the extremes as we find our way to the center where harmony and peace exist. Black and white symbolize the extremes. Peace is the rainbow in the middle. The acceptance of all shades of truth leads to the center."

Under her breath Meshka snickered. She raised a quizzical brow, lifted her chin and stood up for herself.

She challenged him saying, "You say black has some vhite in it 'n da vhite has dark smudges, so nothing is completely good or completely bad. Right? All rainbows? Dat means you are saying dere is no evil!?" Fire shot out of her eyes. "Da other day I held a child vid von arm. A soldier cut da other von off. Are you saying dat vas not evil?!"

Meshka was trying not to raise her voice in front of the children, but she was bristling at this scholarly young man's fancy ideas.

"I feel the suffering of all the children," he said spreading his hands wide for emphasis. Several of the little ones took this as an invitation to run over and hug him around the knees. "It makes me very sad that such cruelty exists. I agree that it is cruel and wrong; but the problem lies deeper than one soldier's actions. There is a terrible problem with people's beliefs."

A little girl with long silky black hair and golden eyes approached Bodhi. At first she looked down shyly at her feet, then her hands did a swift little dance in front of her face and she looked up expectantly. Bodhi imitated her hand dance. She smiled, handed him a couple of frayed blue ribbons and turned her back to him. Bodhi knelt down, closed his eyes and his hands skillfully wove two tidy little braids.

Bodhi's hands neatly twisted the two braids, while he continued sharing his secret teachings with Meshka. He sensed her yearning to learn. A similar yearning had once driven him to listen and seek out these teachings at the feet of a master, high in a mountain sanctuary.

Meshka watched his hands while she listened to his words. She argued with him, voicing her doubts, before she was ready to accept such *mishugas*. "You have to admit dat opposites are real. If da opposites are really connected, like you say, how come dey are so far apart?"

"Patriarchal pride and arrogance separated God and *The Goddess*. The crystal of consciousness split apart.

"Decisions based on 'separation' began to dominate the world. Darkness became truly dark and light became unattainably bright. This separation of the one Life Force into separate fractions has caused continuous war."

Meshka smiled and nodded. It was good that someone understood this war business. She was listening very closely and nodded a lot with a serious brow, so she would look like she understood. But really, she had no idea what he was talking about.

"The split between men and women has to be healed. We have to honor all the masculine and feminine parts of our lives. If we all work together, we can heal our ancestral wounds. We can put an end to disease and destruction. We can heal the world."

Bodhi finished braiding the little girl's hair. She reached up and touched them. Then a big wide grin lit up her face. She spun around and threw her arms around Bodhi's neck. Placing a loud wet kiss on his cheek, she scampered away. He smiled as he watched her go. Then he stood up, turned back to Meshka and resumed his teachings.

"The problem is," he patiently explained, "people do not know themselves. They still get caught up in shards of illusion, hatred, guilt, blame, greed, snares of the old belief system. The Patriarchy has broken the crystal of unity, shattered it into pieces. Healing is the act of making whole what is broken."

A loud cry drew their attention. Not far away sat a little girl with a very cranky baby squirming in her arms. The little mama was no more than ten years old, but she looked weary beyond her years. Her patience was stretched thin as she bounced the heavy bundle of baby on her skinny little knees.

Meshka put the clean challah cloth on her shoulder, reached down and took the heavy baby with the sour-puss out of those frail little arms.

The tired child gave up her baby sister with a sigh of relief. Meshka gave her a sweet grandmotherly smile and laid the crying baby against her own shoulder.

With a little jiggling and patting, the baby spat up some milky mess and contentedly fell asleep. With a wave of her hand, Meshka sent the little girl off to play.

Now that they were alone once more, Bodhi continued with his story. He believed that dividing everything, rather than sharing, and separating people into haves and have nots, was at the core of everything that was wounding people. He thought of this as a rift in consciousness causing all sorts of misery. Bringing together what has been separated would be a way of healing the world, but explaining this in terms easy enough for Meshka to understand, was a challenge.

Meshka gave him a big toothy grin. This time she knew what he was saying.

"Oy vay! Have people suffered!" This she understood.

Meshka and Bodhi walked along the beach among the children, watching them play with full happy tummies.

After everyone had their share, a few pieces of bread and cheese were still in Meshka's basket. A squabble broke out between two big greedy boys. There was enough bread left to divide between the two of them, but they each wanted to eat it all. It took a little negotiating to work them through their greed so they could share.

ରେ ରେ ରେ ରେ

Something caught Meshka's eye in the sand. She picked up a perfect little heart shaped seed. A few steps later, she found another one. This seed was smaller, a speckled light and dark brown, with a black strip around the middle. She put the seeds in her apron pocket. While her ears were filled with amazing new ideas, her eyes darted about on the hunt for more pretty seeds.

They came to a patch of green grass overlooking the sea and sat down. Meshka watched the endless rolling waves rush to shore and was fascinated by the waves crashing against the rocks.

Waves of new ideas were crashing against her head, challenging everything she thought she knew; everything she thought was true, but she wanted to hear more. Even if she did not understand all he was saying, just hearing it made her feel smarter.

When they got up and started walking again, she wondered about the Patriarchy. " I used to dink God vas almighty 'n terrible, but he does not seem to be breathing fire so much anymore. He did not accuse me of arrogance vhen I said I vanted to make da world bedda. 'N He didn't make fire to rain down on me vhen I talked to *Da Goddess*. Maybe He does not care about me anymore." She cringed and an ugly shiver shook her.

Only when Bodhi answered her thoughts, did she realize that she spoken out loud. "Maybe God is no longer all powerful and vengeful? Perhaps He is old. Maybe He needs our compassion and our help. In my meditations, sometimes I see God weeping. I think He bleeds like Christ on the cross."

Meshka and Bodhi came upon a little blue-eyed boy sitting on a rock in the sand looking at his toes. His feet were dirty and covered with blood. A torn old shoe lay on the ground nearby.

Bodhi sat down beside the little guy while Meshka stood quietly swaying with the sleeping baby on her shoulder, Bodhi reached for his bola and poured fresh water over the grimy foot. Then from his white tunic he pulled out a clean handkerchief and wiped away the dirt of many miles walked in exile. Bodhi was very gentle, very careful not to irritate the sensitive skin.

The little fellow looked up gratefully. Bodhi rinsed the cloth, wrung it almost dry and wound it around the damaged foot.

"Rest here for a while and I will mend your shoes." Bodhi picked up the threadbare shoes and handed the boy a chunk of challah from his pocket. He led Meshka to a shady place and sat down.

He drew out a small leather pouch. Inside was an assortment of small useful objects, including a fishbone needle and a thread of thin dried intestines.

While Bodhi sewed the little boy's shoe back together, they returned to their discussion.

"You dink vee can help God? People are only liddle worms compared to God!" She said, shaking her head at such a ridiculous idea.

"But if those 'worms' are actually caterpillars, then one day they will change into something so beautiful, even God will smile. God is in everything, so He must be in us. Maybe we help God by healing ourselves and by opening to the great power inside us. We can afford to be compassionate."

No man had ever talked to her like this before. Oh, if only Bodhi was twenty years older, or better yet, if she were twenty years younger, she thought with a big sigh.

"Vhere do you get dese *mishuganna* ideas?" She said with a hint of a smile.

It sounded like disbelief, but it was really Meshka's attempt at flirting.

Bodhi took her question seriously and answered, "I studied ancient wisdom and mystical teachings with an old master. He was like a Rebbe. He taught me to look beyond common veils."

CROSCR

After the shoes were repaired and returned to the happy little fellow, the two philosophers continued strolling along the seaside. Meshka walked contentedly beside Bodhi, her arms full of sleeping baby. They passed a cluster of giggling girls jumping rope.

The beach narrowed and a brave tuft of grass dared to grow. Sitting on the grass was little Timmy flipping a knife at a circle drawn in the soil. He aimed, threw, and the knife fell flat. They stopped to watch him for a while. Again and again he tried, but always the knife went plop on the ground.

With a warm smile, Bodhi leaned down and placed his hand lightly on the boy's wrist. The child looked up questioningly. Bodhi's hand rode on the frail little wrist and pantomimed the action of throwing a knife. He did this several times, each one slower than the last.

Then with a sharp flicking motion, they moved faster and faster, until the two moved as one. The knife flew out of Timmy's hand with perfect precision. Bull's Eye! The little boy squealed in delight and gazed up adoringly. Bodhi ruffled Timmy's hair. They watched him flip the knife a couple of times by himself. He was so proud! They all hit the target!

Meshka was as young as she ever was, here alone with this handsome young man. He reminded her of Yonkle. Oy, Yonkle would have loved to talk about smart things with this young man.

Bodhi, Meshka, and the sleeping baby strolled on. Meshka shook her head laughing, "Bodhi, you are such a *mench* (man of integrity)!"

Bodhi smiled a little shyly and thanked her. Meshka's eyebrows jumped up in surprise. "You know vhat is a *mensch*?"

"Yes, my grandmother used to call me a '*mensch*' when she was proud of me."

"She vas not Jewish vas she?" He nodded yes and Meshka's eyes jumped right out of her head. "You are Jewish! A landsmen!"

"Meshka, Meshka, do not get so excited! I do not know if I qualify. I am only a fringe member of the tribe of Israel. My mother's family was Jewish, so her people say I am Jewish. But my father worshiped Jesus, the Prince of Peace, so I am also a Christian. Two pagan midwives delivered me, so I have a touch of them in me too.

"On the day I was born, the Karmapa died. He was the venerable head of a Tibetan lineage. At first, my mama thought I was the Karmapa reincarnated. But when all the water in the house did not turn to milk, she decided I wasn't."

Jewish, Christian, Pagan, Tibetan, what a mish-mash! All the people Meshka had known were one thing: one religion and one nationality. This Boogie person was different from anyone she ever met or even imagined.

CRCRCR

The baby in Meshka's arms began to squirm and coo a little, announcing she was awake. Small grunting sounds and a pungent smell brought Meshka's motherly attention to the needs at hand.

"Wait, I am going to vash dis dirty rag in da sea."

Bodhi took the baby from Meshka and tickled the little one into giggling.

"Da fresh warm sunshine vill give her liddle *tush* (buttocks) a good airing." He sat down cross-legged on the sand with the baby lying on its belly. Meshka washed the rag with sea and sand, then stood shaking it in the warm wind to dry.

"Tell me Bodhi, you really believe people can heal God?"

He laughed, happy in this moment. Her questions inspired him.

"In the past, God led and people followed. Perhaps now it is our turn to lead. If we work together, we can heal each other and the world. Then God will no longer grieve our suffering.

"The wise sage Confucius, once taught, 'First begin by putting your own life in order. Then make your family close. When there is harmony at home, you can bring balance into your community. In this way, the world will find its way to harmony.'"

Meshka sorta understood. "In Hebrew vee say, '*ha-call beseder.*' It means 'all is in order.' Vee say it vhen dings are fine. Maybe dis Confusion person knew Hebrew. Did he ever succeed in healing God?"

Bodhi smiled and took a deep breath to stop the laugh trying to escape, "Confucius made life better on earth and maybe it is the same thing."

"How did he do dat?" She challenged poking out her little chins.

"He taught people, 'Before enlightenment there is chopping wood and carrying water. After enlightenment, there is chopping wood and carrying water.' He meant, a wise man does the same simple deeds as his neighbor, but he does them with a different attitude. He does not have narrow beliefs and dubious entanglements. He reaches for goodness and works sincerely with whatever comes."

Meshka was skipping about at the water's edge flapping the clean rag in the breeze. It was almost dry when a big wave rushed onto the land and splashed Meshka. The sprinkle of salt water was exhilarating and refreshing. She giggled. Luckily her arms were raised high and the rag was not touched by the sea.

"Do you dink da vhite part in da black half of da circle is a God part in people?" She asked.

"God has many faces. The God part of me is a Bodhisattva." He spoke with humility, but his proud shoulders were straight and he was standing tall.

"A boogie vhat?" she asked.

"Bodhisattvas are people who live to serve others because it feeds their own soul. A part of them is healed and nourished by the act of giving."

She smirked and said, "You mean like da *Green Tara* 'n *Her* fadda, Avo-vhat-is-his-name, dey made life bedda?"

"Yes Meshka," he was charmed by her sweetness.

Meshka leaned her head a little closer and confided, "Dat is my mission too! I am supposed to make life bedda. *Da Goddess* told me to."

She shook her head feeling the curls bounce around her face. They never did that under the weight of the shawl.

"Then you are also a Bodhisattva," he said and lightly bowed his head in respect.

Bodhi let the baby crawl in the wet sand at his feet. She squealed, delighted to be free.

The baby grabbed a piece of seaweed and put it in her mouth and chomped on it a bit. It fell out when a small shell caught her eye. The shell was on its way into the same place, stopped by Meshka's quick hand.

The child scowled for a second, seized one of Meshka's fingers, and wrapped her toothless pouting lips around it. Meshka felt a sharp edge to her sucking, announcing the arrival of a proud new tooth. Meshka smiled and turned her attention back to Yonkle, I mean Bodhi, and his fancy ideas.

"*Da Goddess* told me to love God. Vhat do you dink about dat?" Meshka asked and turned a bright cherry red.

"We can love everyone, if we first love ourselves, love all the parts inside us, even the unlovable parts that make us think we are bad. We all have a wounded little orphan inside who has been bruised by the world. It lacks polish because it is a raw force. This part went up against the boundaries of life and received the hard knocks. It paved the way for our future successes."

Meshka got all excited. She was beginning to understand his crazy ideas and they were making sense.

"You mean like a *miskite*, a poor liddle orphan abandoned in da cold?" Meshka said. Her eyebrows all bunched up as she struggled to make sense of what he was saying.

Yes, a *miskite*. If we do not love the wounded, stupid, help-less parts of ourselves, we cannot have compassion for those weaknesses in others. Our own struggles and suffering lead us to compassion or to bitterness. It is our choice." For a moment there, he sounded just like the wise old rabbi in her village.

Bodhi was wondering if Meshka was following him, when she cried out, "Vait a minute! Are you saying to heal God, vee have to love our own *miskite*? I do not see how dat vill work. How can vee heal God Almighty by loving da wormiest of da worms?"

The crease in her bunched eyebrows got deeper. Under the weight of these radical ideas, her head was stretching and creaking. Never did she think like this before. She was intrigued by its strangeness. The weight of the sleeping baby lying on her shoulder reminded her of what was real and important as they returned to camp.

"We are made in the image of God. When we learn to love all aspects of God, we cease to judge. When we no longer judge ourselves, we stop judging others. If we love ourselves, we have more love to give."

Meshka laughed with a toothy grin and playfully asked, "I love myself. Vhat is not to love? Everyone loves demselves, no?"

If everyone was as loveable as little Meshka, maybe they would.

The soft purring of the baby's breath asleep on her shoulder gave Meshka a deep sense of peace, so did this strange young man with his wild ideas. The young man stood straight and proud; his eyes glazed with passion.

For just a minute, Meshka wished she was a young maiden with her whole life ahead of her, instead of a wrinkled up old woman with death waiting around the corner. This beautiful young man touched her deeply in ways no one ever had. How cruel Fate can be! How twisted its humor!

They wandered back to where the baby's sister was jumping rope with a couple of Scottish girls. Meshka watched them jump and thought the little mama deserved more time to play. All too soon she would put the yoke on again and return to her burdens..

While she waited for the game to end, Meshka asked, "Vhat is a Patriarchy?"

"It is a system of beliefs that promote and maintain masculine dominance. It creates a world run by men, based on male beliefs, male needs, and male desires. In a Patriarchy, the structure of society places one person or race above another in value and rewards. Many people suffer under a Patriarchy because all the resources filter up to one man or one race. Beliefs and values in a Patriarchy are based on one person in power who rules over everyone, favors some above others, and holds onto that power by controlling people through black-and-white rules."

Meshka was thrilled that this young man thought she was smart enough to understand such big ideas. She nodded. Maybe she did not follow all his arguments, but she understood most of it in her own way.

"You must obey its arbitrary rules, even though they do not reflect life fairly. Patriarchal religions support the rules by making people feel guilty if they disobey. Guilty people blame others and thus perpetuate prejudice."

Meshka knew well the power of prejudice. She settled in comfortably on a big root under a wide tree, patted the baby on her back and watched the little girls play. Meshka remembered, once upon a time, many lifetimes ago, being a little girl jumping rope.

Meshka had a lot to think about. If this boy put one more big idea in her ear, her head was going to break into a lot of little pieces.

ଔଔଔଔ

Chapter 21

Joya

Joya woke up around noon as usual. She stretched and purred like a cat - a big pregnant mama cat. The baby, or babies, inside her belly also woke up. They yawned and stretched. With all that bouncing going on, maybe she was carrying a litter.

Wild dreams whispering vague promises left her with a strange afterglow. Her dreams told her something important, but now that she was awake, she could not remember what.

Joya blinked at the noon day sun and struggled to get all her body parts working together. It took a lot of grunting, twisting, and pushing to get this whale off the ground and onto her feet. Getting out of a bedroll should have been a simple act, but for pregnant Joya it was so ridiculous, it made her snicker.

Joya felt utterly alone. She yearned to crawl back into her luscious dreams, but by now even her dream deserted her. The lonely girl wished she had a protector, someone very tall and very strong to lift her up and point the way.

Now that she was on her feet, she waddled over to a nearby bush to pee, something she did six, seven, a hundred times a day. She had to give up on the idea of shoes; bending over to put them on was just too hard.

It was the end of May and all kinds of flowers were raising their brave little heads. The days were getting longer and warmer. Still Joya's feet were cold, but she did not care. She was six months pregnant and weighed under by this child.

Joya was cursed. She was sure that someone who hated her had put a curse on her. She should have died with everyone else. Now she was *marimé* (impure). This big baby belly branded her as *marimé* and everyone knew. She wished she was dead.

The baby heard her thoughts and gave Joya an especially strong kick. It took Joya's breath away and got her attention. It also made her angry. She put her hands on her belly and shouted, "You little imp, stop that! Play nicely, you creepy little thing!"

The baby's spirit announced defiantly, "*I* am not a creepy little thing. *I* am a girl. *I* have flaming red hair and *My* name is '*Anath*.'"

Joya snickered. "Red hair! Aunt Rita was the only Roma I ever met with red hair and Aunt Rita was a wild one!

"*Anath*! Who ever heard of a girl named *Anath*? What kind of name is that?" She grumbled out loud to the sky.

"*An ancient one*," the sky whispered back.

With a little jumping jack doing flip flops in her belly, Joya was not comfortable lying down or sitting up, so she went for a walk. She grabbed an empty water skin to fill and slowly waddled down to a nearby lake.

Her bare feet easily followed the cold path down to the lake. It was clearly marked by the many feet that followed it over the last few days.

The lake was still with only the softest ripples from the wind's barest breath. Joya stood gazing down at an odd reflection in the lake. It was hard to imagine this strangely shaped body was hers! She felt trapped!

Wonder and repulsion welled up in her. She was fascinated by all the strange feelings, her hypersensitivities, the certainties and vast uncertainties of two people living in one body. It amazed her and terrified her.

Being so young and carrying such a big belly, always made her blush when someone looked at her. Sometimes the question in their eyes was just imagined, but still she turned a very dark shade of rose. She was completely embarrassed by her huge round belly.

A rustling behind her made Joya turn around. Sharanii came walking towards the lake carrying a bucket in her hand to fetch some water.

As Sharanii approached, she said in a voice as bright as sunshine. "How radiantly beautiful you look my dear."

"O Sharanii, I fear I will never be myself again," Joya lamented.

"True my dear, but you will have a new self. You will still have all the wisdom and skills of your old life, but with fresh new direction and purpose." The *Priestess* reassured her.

"O Sharanii, I am anything but myself." Joya confided her misery and sadness, hoping this noblewoman would understand.

"Among my people - the *Priestesses of Gaea* - when a woman is close to her birthing time, friends gather to honor her with a special ritual - a Blessing Day.

We nurture and pamper *The Goddess* in her. We also stand witness as she acknowledges her journey from maidenhood to motherhood. The ritual helps her see that she is truly herself and also more than herself. When her birthing time is at hand, our prayers and blessings help sustain her strength.

If you would like a Blessing Day, I would be honored to arrange it," Sharanii offered graciously. She flashed Joya her angelic smile and waved her elegant hand as though if Joya accepted, Sharanii would make it appear out of thin air.

Joya closed her eyes. She saw all the women of her family dancing around the fire, their long wide skirts swirling around them and their brightly colored scarves flying in the wind like the wings of mischievous angels. They danced like that when her little sister Arena, was born. No one will dance for this child, she lamented.

"Thank you Sharanii. If a Blessing Day is anything like the Mid-Winter's Eve ceremony, it is just what I need. Can we do it tomorrow? It will be Sunday and I will be ready."

Sharanii agreed. "Then tomorrow it is. *Let me fill your water skin for you, my dear.* The elegant *Priestess* knelt on the grass, kissed the earth, and said a blessing of gratitude over the water. She sat quietly while the water bag and her bucket filled. It was a space in time of peaceful stillness. Joya basked in the peacefulness as well.

Sharanii lifted the water bag. As she handed it to Joya, she asked, *"Are you sure you can carry this? It is heavy. "*

"I can carry it," Joya reassured the *Priestess*, though silently she added, "maybe its heavy weight will help my body drop this burden."

The lovely *Priestess* lifted her own bucket. She carried its heavy weight on her head with elegant grace and returned to camp.

Joya looked at the water bag lying on the ground beside the quiet lake. She was reluctant to return. She needed more time alone to think. The water could wait. She noticed another path etched into the ground, probably from the animals that came here to drink at night.

She wandered along the twists and turns of the path, drinking in the warmth of the afternoon sun. Gradually the path led upwards. It was a gentle climb up a small hill. From the top, she could see the freshwater lake below and the rolling sea in the distance.

Joya stepped to the edge of the cliff and looked down at the river dropping into the lake. She wanted to lean forward and sort of fall into the water, let it carry her away from her guilt, but the turbulent churning of the river did not look inviting; rather it looked violent and foreboding like birth.

"A woman stands on the edge of a great abyss when she enters the birthing chamber. The powers of Birth and Death walk very closely together. Will I die or be reborn?"

She had only a vague idea what was going to happen to her once the birth pains started and she dared not ask.

How can my body open like that and host the most powerful force in the universe? I wonder how it feels to have those ferocious forces surging through me!

She saw herself riding a massive wave and crashing against a huge stone wall. Waves of choking came over her.

"O *Holy Mother*, I humbly stand before you. I did not choose to stand at this gate of *Your* temple, but You called me and I am here. Please be gentle on me."

Joya shivered with a sharp inner chill, certain there would be no gentleness. Her back grew straighter and she braced herself.

"O *Holy Mother, when* I was a little girl everyone cradled me. I thought I was born to play and love. I was such a fool. When I studied the stars and saw Destiny's plan, I thought I knew something about the powers behind Fate. I was so naïve. The Divine Powers who rule our little world must be amused when we watch them. It is such a far cry from watching to knowing."

Joya felt she could not unburden her heart to any of the women, but at least she could speak to the *Divine Mother of Life*. Surely *She* would understand.

"O *Holy Mother*, I looked at Pluto and Saturn standing face to face in the heavens and assumed they were going to engage in an intense dance. I was so wrong! They were not dancers, but rather, soldiers preparing for deadly battle. As heaven's warriors, they stirred up hidden forces and released collective rage. I was a dancer caught in a war and I lost," her voice quivered and big wet tears flowed down her cheeks.

Joya breathed in the fresh moist air, felt the sun on her face, and the cold granite beneath her bare feet.

"O *Holy Mother*, please tell me one thing. Will I live through this or will I die? Is youth to be the whole of my life?"

Her bare feet were freezing, so she turned to go. A pair of squirrels ran by her chasing each other, chattering excitedly as they dashed up a small tree nearby. She laughed at their antics and that made her feel a little lighter. Maybe this was a sign saying she was going to live.

Joya closed her eyes and imagined the *Divine Mother's* arms wrapped around her. For a moment, she sank into a cocoon of safety.

"O *Holy Mother*," she whispered. "Please lead me through this abyss. Forget all those times I prayed to die. If you give me the strength and the courage to survive, I will dedicate my life to serving You."

A wave of relief washed over her and some of the terror drained away. In its wake, an image appeared. She saw Meshka leaning over a deep pit reaching a hand out to her. The old *Gadji* woman was pulling her up, big baby belly and all, up from hell.

"Yes, *Holy Mother*. I feel your strength flowing through Meshka." She was certain Meshka would keep her alive and safe.

"Meshka, my funny little guardian angel, you are a deceptive disguise for the *Goddess of Compassion*," she sang out with a smile.

Joya sat on the cliff overlooking the world. She felt safe, then frightened, then safe again, changing with each passing moment. She cried pitifully and raged angrily. She screamed at the clouds and the sky.

The flaming colors of twilight delighted her. She took in the beauty of this wide sweeping valley and felt deeply touched by the brilliant hues of the rainbow sky.

It was time to waddle back to the camp. As she made her way down the hill, she saw Meshka's friend, the strange young man with lemon yellow hair, dancing to the dying sun. With raised arms, each deliberate motion seemed to praise the glory of the day. His long straight hair floated on a light breeze as he moved very slowly, very beautifully.

Joya loved to dance. She lived to dance. She raised her arms up high like him and echoed each of his simple movements. He moved very slowly and was easy to follow. The hard part was getting the litter in her belly to stop jumping around while she was dancing. She followed the young man as best she could in her huge clumsy condition.

When the dancer stood on one foot or bent low, these she could not do, but his slow careful turns and the beautiful hand movements she seemed to know by instinct.

She felt the Dance was drawing the power of the sun down into her womb. Her heart opened as wide as her arms were spread. She embraced each movement and a quiet reassurance flowed through her. The twilight was suddenly filled with magical promise and a ray of hope entered her darkness. She was going to live or maybe not. At least she had today.

ଓଓଓଓ

Chapter 22

The Blessing Day

Sunday afternoon was pleasantly warm. A large flock of white geese flew in a tight V across a bright blue sky, casting shadows when they passed before the sun.

Sharanii gathered the *Bakers*, even Rachel joined the circle. The elegantly draped *Priestess* stood in the center wearing a long simple white robe embroidered with a touch of gold all along the edges. Its long dripping sleeves hid her graceful hands, giving them an air of mystery.

Around Sharanii stood seven torches on stalks as tall as her. Next to her was a nest of pillows and blankets where Joya lay tucked in as though it were a cushy cozy throne. Gentle hands made Joya's big ungainly body comfortable.

With slow dignity, Sharanii raised her left arm, draped in a long lovely sleeve, so all could see the long carved ebony staff in her hand. The majestic staff was capped with a beautiful polished silver globe and wrapped around the sphere was an exquisite little embossed mermaid. The *Priestess* silently lifted this awesome *Wand of Words* high. Its majesty alone commanded the women to silence.

They listened to the stillness in the meadow. Birds sang, flies buzzed, jumping fish softly splashed, and fresh new leaves fluttered in a soft breeze. The playful rhythms of the natural world and the magic of the *Blessing Day* all escaped Joya. She noticed nothing because her heart was pounding loudly with chilling intensity.

With arms raised to heaven, the *Priestess* proclaimed, "Welcome my sisters! We stand in sacredness upon this land. Together we shall reverently and lovingly prepare Joya to host the power of the Birth Mother."

Her voice was steady and soft, yet it echoed through them.

"O *Great Mother*, preside over our holy ritual.

O Compassionate One,

We beseech *You* to protect Joya

And her baby during the birth.

She is your vessel.

We are all *Your* vessels,

A challenging task in this wounded world.

We stand before *You* in our full radiance."

A huge flock of bluebirds landed on a nearby tree and set up such gay singing, Sharanii had to speak louder. Perhaps all the spirits of the caravan had come to watch.

"*Holy Mother*, I am *Your* daughter, *Your Priestess*,

The one who lights *Your* sacred fire.

Look in the flames and see the purity of our intentions.

You are the light in our darkness,

The warmth in a chilling world.

You are our refuge of tranquility during life's storms."

To their amazement, when Sharanii said, "...the one who lights *Your* sacred fire!"... a flash of blue light suddenly appeared in the palm of her left hand! The blue light flew from her palm into the sacred fire pit where the dry straw caught flame!

Everyone gasped! Joya was delighted.

Comfortable in her throne of soft blankets, Joya pulled Uncle Alberto's wizard robe tighter around her, for security as much as for warmth. She was feeling little and weak. Without Uncle Alberto's lap to crawl into, she curled up in his robe. Safely wrapped in Uncle Alberto's embrace, Joya felt a wave of gratitude toward the Jewish women for rescuing the magic robe. What a sad loss it would be if Joya had nothing left of Uncle Alberto to shield her from the harshness of life! Nothing else was big enough to reach around her big baby belly. Soon her pounding heart and panting breath slowed down to the gentle swell of a quiet tide.

"O *Holy Mother*," Joya silently prayed. "I am afraid. I do not want this child. Please release me from all this torment so it may be forgotten. Let it fade like a bad dream. If this thing lives, we will be cursed and our lives will be *marimé*. (condemned to perpetual disgrace) O *Holy Mother* please have mercy on me."

The staff disappeared into the many folds of Sharanii's robe. Her left hand now held a blue flame.

Sharanii waved her palm with a flourishing sweep. The blue flame shot out of her hand. Soaring across the open air, the fire landed in an iridescent aqua seashell sitting on her right palm. The sweet smelling herbs in the seashell burst into flame!

Everyone gasped!

"The seashell must have come from inside those endless sleeves, but where did the fire come from?!" Everyone wondered

A sweet fragrance perfumed the air. The *Priestess* raised both palms up to heaven. In her left palm hovered the flickering blue flame, in her right, the seashell wafting with the fragrance of aromatic herbs. In supplication, the *Priestess* recited an ancient blessing.

"Holy Mother of Birth!
Mother of Everything that Lives and Breathes!
We thank *You* for *Your* sustaining compassion!
Holy Mother, we welcome *You* to our sacred circle."

Sharanii lowered her arms and the flame disappeared but the shell remained! As her palms slowly sank towards the earth, the women sat down.

Rachel was sooo uncomfortable. Oy, did she want to leave. This was much too unJewish for her. All her life, Rachel walked the religious road. She never questioned and never willfully disobeyed. She feared God. She was afraid this ritual would anger Him.

If there was any way for Rachel to not be here, she would be far, far away, but Joya was part of her *Clan*. Joya was a dear friend. By the rules of friendship, she had to stand by the young maiden and help face the fiery initiation of birth. If this gathering of women and its strange rituals could help the girl live through the birth, after all she has gone through, then of course, Rachel was going to be here. As part of Joya's *Clan*, she felt being here was the right thing to do.

It was hard for Rachel to listen to Sharanii talking to God as though He were her mama. Then Rachel thought, If every time da *Priestess* says, 'Holy Mother,' I dink, 'da *Shekhina*,' it vill make me feel bedda. So little old Jewish Rachel made her peace with this pagan ritual in order to honor and support the sweet Gypsy girl. She looked up to heaven and promised God she would only watch. Even that felt v-e-r-y daring.

The women were seated in a circle. All eyes were on the elegant *Priestess* standing in the center. Sharanii seemed to grow even taller. A gorgeous white owl wing suddenly appeared in her hand. Where did that wing come from? How deep were the folds in that slender robe, anyway?

Sweeping the feather over the soft wafting smoke, Sharanii brushed the smoke over Joya from head to foot, front and back. When she drew the feather across Joya's trembling chest, the shaking stopped.

"Breathe in the sweet smoke," whispered the *Priestess*. The serpentine silkiness of the smoke relaxed Joya's tightly tangled muscles a little.

"Joya, birth is an initiation. It will challenge you to the core and empower you. Two sacred births lie before you: the child's and your own. Your Soul is being reborn. Birth is a portal into your Soul. Now you will truly come to know yourself. Giving birth is the most amazing initiation in a woman's life."

Gliding like a swan around the circle, Sharanii's gown flowed around her delicate ankles as she carried the fragrant herbs to each woman. The curling smoke and a gentle touch with the owl wing, cleansed away their worldly worries.

In a whisper as hushed as a mama cooing in her baby's ear, the *Priestess* recited a prayer over each woman. The words came from the woman's own soul. With *Priestess* vision, Sharanii gazed at their hidden divinity. Her sacred words, like her majestic staff, commanded reverence. The women grew visibly grander as they cast off unseen yokes.

Rachel was nervous about the smoke. She did not want to get drunk on strange herbs; but when Sharanii was standing before her gazing into her eyes, smiling that radiant soothing smile of hers, Rachel was soon breathing easily. She willingly filled her lungs with the pure sweet smoke.

Sharanii brushed the owl feather across Rachel's heart and womb. Rachel remembered her first birth - little '*Liba Hanna*' – 'Love of Life.' The name reflected her wondrous joy at the sweet birth.

Rachel was a good Jewish woman solid in her faith. She found all this paganism offensive, but these women were her dearest friends, so she reached inside herself and found a little more tolerance for their strange abominable ways.

Sharanii's soft voice was seductive as she waved the sacred smoke over Rachel whispering, "Rachel - Wise Woman – Protectress of Children. You are steadfast in crisis. You have served your family well. It is your time now. You have completed all the demands of motherhood and you have done them well. You who dare to claim your freedom; you are a holy woman with a rabbi's soul. May God always answer your prayers."

Gliding around the circle, Sharanii purified each woman with the sacred smoke. When she came to Meshka, the feather tickled and Meshka laughed nervously. She was worried. God would certainly have some fiery words for her, the next time she spoke with Him.

"Most Holy Von," she silently prayed, "A liddle incense 'n a feather, vhat harm can dey do? I vas just about to leave anyvay, but I need to vait until dis part of da ritual is ova. I do not vant to spoil it for everyone else," she reassured God.

B-u-t...once Sharanii was standing in front of her radiating such gentle love, all of Meshka's thoughts about leaving disappeared.

Rifka took a deep breath filling her lungs with the sweet pungent smoke. A strange feeling came over her. These foreign rituals actually felt more natural to her than a lifetime of watching men *davening* prayers.

Rifka felt as though she had spent lifetimes standing in a circle of holy women. It was a foolish thought, but it felt so real.

The women in the circle were blessed and purified. Sharanii reached up to the sky as sweetly as a child waiting to be lifted into her mama's loving arms. Her hands were free of shell and feather.

The *Priestess* invoked!
"Mother of the Waters!"
In response, a fresh breeze rippled across the still lake.
"Mother of the Sky!"
A huge flock of geese fanned in flight the sky overhead.
"Mother of the Sun!"
The bright light of day grew warmer.
"Mother Earth, Gaea!"
The fresh wild beauty of the land was vibrantly alive.

Sharanii was standing on holy ground in the middle of all these natural elements. *Celestial Powers* were watching. The air was pregnant with *Presence*. An electrical charge crackling with tension gripped the air. Each woman felt the *Divine Presence*.

Sharanii returned to the center of their circle, knelt down and petted the young maiden's face. Then the noble *Priestess* slid a supportive arm under the little waif with the big belly and gently held her. She smiled into the maiden's trusting face and softly sang,

"Welcome my child.
Let the *Divine Mother* cradle you in *Her* love.
She will accompany you through this challenging time.
Lean on *Her* for your strength.
She is coiled at the base of your spine
Her power is unleashed when the birthing begins.
Her raw force is sacred.
She has woven the pure essence of life into a conscious,
Breathing, loving child.
She spun the threads from your body and your Soul.
Celebrate with wonder and fortitude.
When you emerge from birth's initiation,
You will know the length of your courage,
And the breadth of your endurance.
The maiden will continue to live inside you,
along with the mother, born on that sacred day!"

Rachel stood transfixed. Nothing in her experience of study room-and-storytelling rabbis ever prepared her for this!

Rifka, on the other hand, was home! This was so much more exciting than sitting behind a curtain in the back of the temple listening to the rabbi and the men *davenen* (praying). Each breath she took was fuller than the last. Her chest expanded all the way perhaps for the first time in her life. In this moment, she knew who she was!

Sharanii held up one of the seven torches and turned to Sarina. She asked, "Would you like to be Keeper of the East and speak for *The Goddess of New Beginnings?*" Sarina gave a silent nod and accepted the torch. The hand of the *Priestess* touched the torch and it burst into flames!

Sharanii reached for another torch, lit it from Sarina's and stepped up to Rifka. The *Priestess* asked the eager young woman if she was willing to be *Keeper of the South* and speak for the *Goddess of Passion*. Rifka's heart fluttered wildly. Waves of excitement soared through her. After catching her breath, Rifka gladly accepted the flaming torch. She felt ten feet tall!

Rachel accepted the duty of *Keeper of the West*, but had her doubts about speaking for the *Goddess of Compassion*. She knew she was standing on thin ice! She could not let a strange *Goddess*, speak through her!?! She leaned on the torch for support and pondered the magnitude of her duty.

Meshka agreed to speak as *Keeper of the North* with a giggle. "Who vould have thought liddle old me vould be standing here in dis circle of women in a foreign land 'n I vould be speaking for *Da Goddess*."

She shook her head in disbelief. "But den life is very inventive, you never know....."

The roles of *Keeper of Heaven* and *Keeper of the Earth* were given to Maya and Tasjia. Each woman reverently took the torch and accepted the charge that went with it. Sharanii kept one for herself, *Keeper of the Soul*.

Each woman willingly took on the mantle of a powerful feminine force, even Rachel who justified it by reminding God that she was representing the *Shekhina*. When Meshka took her torch, she heard a definite grunt of disapproval from God.

Aside from Sharanii, this was everyone's first *Blessing Day*. The weight of the torch made each woman feel strong. Their spines lengthened and they looked taller.

Joya was breathing rapidly in her nested throne. A great surge of power was rushing through her followed by several mighty strong kicks.

Joya winced and doubled up. The *Priestess'* words came to her from far away,

"We are each conduits for the Life Force.

All elements come together within us.

Breathe in the fresh breeze.

Feel your naked feet standing on consecrated soil.

The sea beside us holds the life blood of the *Divine Mother*.
The fire is the flame of *Her* passion.
She is alive within you.
Feel the power of your womanhood.
Open your mind and your heart to the pulse of life.
Breathe the life force in deeply. Feel it in your body."

Sharanii charged them. "We will move through the sacred directions one by one starting with the East. Please share your wisdom with Joya."

Sharanii helped Joya to her feet and accompanied her as they stood before Sarina. The young waif leaned heavily on the *Priestess* as she looked up into the eyes of the towering blond Amazon.

Joya bowed her head and whispered, "Powers of the East, bless me on my journey."

Sarina lifted her torch high in the air, took a deep breath, looked deep into Joya's eyes and spoke right into her Soul. "May the Powers of the East speak through me. Joya, my lovely friend, you are blessed to be the seed and its fruit. Awaken - holy vessel of life - from the dream of who you have been and carve out a new life in your own image. At the moment of birth, you too shall be reborn."

Meshka stifled a laugh. She felt God breathing down her neck. "If all dis hocus-pocus makes Joya feel less alone," she reassured herself, "den dis ritual is a good ding. God does not care vhat women do to entertain demselves as long as dey let men run da world."

The women intoned, "Blessed Be." Of course, Rachel could not say that. Instead she said the Jewish, "Aumen." Meshka said, "Blessed Be," because '*aumen*' might draw God's attention. Why start trouble with God in case He does not like all this *Goddess* stuff?

Sharanii and Joya stepped before Rifka. She lifted her flaming torch high and said in a booming voice, "As Keeper of da South, I vill speak for da *Goddess of Passion*."

Before she could scoff at the idea of speaking for a *Goddess*, words filled her mind and excitement sparkled on her tongue.

In a voice far grander than her own she said, "Brin' me your rage. I can stand in da heat of your passion. I know dis place vell. Do not be afraid of your vildest emotions for I can contain dem. Turn to me 'n you vill alvays feel met."

Rifka found speaking an invocation oddly familiar, even though she never imagined such a ritual before. She felt intrigued and rebellious. Being here with these women and doing these rituals, felt very daring as she said, "Blessed be."

Rachel slowly lifted her torch and said, "As *Keeper of the West*, I speak for the *Shekhina*." She looked inside herself for worthy words with which to bless Joya and remembered a simple Jewish prayer. Reciting it made her feel she was being true to her God and her friend.

Oy vay, now it was Meshka's turn! She raised her torch high and looked at everyone in the eyes. Her panic was just beginning to surge when inspired words poured from her lips. "I am trusted to speak for da *Goddess of da North*. Vee are Joya's family now. Vee love her. Help us make da world a bedder place for her 'n her baby - for all da women 'n deir liddle babies. May da land under our feet alvays be a safe home for women 'n deir children."

Meshka's heart was pounding wildly. She shocked herself! She held her breath waiting for a bolt of lightning to hit her. When nothing happened, her knotted shoulders slowly untangled and her body relaxed. Maybe speaking for a *Goddess* is not blasphemy after all. Then she scolded herself for such a thought. She blamed the brightness of the sun and the heat of the torch for making her feel so pliable.

Maya spoke for *Heaven* and Tasjia gave a blessing for *Mother Earth*, but Meshka never heard a word they said. She was busy combing through her own words again and again. She was impressed that such an important message came from her mouth.

Meshka was startled back to the ritual when Sharanii opened her white robe and fanned it out to reveal a magnificent rainbow of colors. Beautiful as a peacock, the *Priestess* spoke for the Soul. Her words were directed at Joya, but each woman felt they were meant for her.

"*I* am *Sophia*, the World Soul.

I come to you with a mother's open heart to bring you Blessings.

You are *My* beautiful daughter,

My greatest creation.

Through you *I* continue to create life.

Love *Me* as *I* love you."

Sharanii let her robe flutter closed, planted her torch in the center and led Joya back to her nested throne. Meshka was amazed at the power pulsating through the circle. It intensified the brightness of the sun, the freshness of the water, the solid support of the land, and the preciousness of each breath.

Meshka knew how it felt to stand before God and how it felt to hear the voice of a *Goddess*, but the breathless joy she felt now was different, somehow more personal.

The dignity, compassion, and wisdom of these women enchanted her! She felt mysteriously connected soul to soul with each one and especially to the *Divine Mother*.

Joya also felt great forces rushing through her. They usually ended with a series of slamming kicks.

Sharanii, standing as noble as a beacon shining light from the center, proclaimed:

"*The Goddess* lives in each of us.

Hear *Her* words as *She* hears ours!

She guides us to constantly recreate ourselves."

"*Da Goddess* lives in each of us." Meshka chuckled at this strange idea. How can dat tall awesome *Goddess* fit inside my liddle round body? It made her feel like she was with child. She laughed at the idea of giving birth to herself, and thought about what kind of 'new self' she would create.

"Joya, we have come to the core of your initiation. Now it is time for you to face each direction and pick a stone from this basket." The one that suddenly appeared in her hand.

"Speak about a part of your life that is passing away. Invest the stone with whatever you wish to release. Bury it. Put the past to rest. Let go of these outworn beliefs. Bury one in each direction.

"Pick another stone to invite blessings into your future. This one you may keep. Invest it with the things you want to bring into your life."

Sharanii handed the basket of little stones to Tasjia. The lovely maiden carried it over to Joya and sat down beside her.

Some of the stones were dug up from the land, rough and jagged; others came from a river, polished and smooth. Joya reached into the basket and picked a smooth river stone.

Sarina stepped forward, lifted her torch high and said as *Keeper of the East*, "Look to the East my little sister. Here is where life begins. Here you get to choose a new direction. First you must close the old. Acknowledge the old beliefs you held about who you are and how you should be. Then put them in the stone and let them go."

Joya looked up at this confident young woman and some of the Amazon's self-possession entered the young maiden. The soft smile that passed between them helped Joya pull her thoughts together. At first, she felt a little awkward speaking from a throne of pillows lying on the ground, but that disappeared soon.

"I spent my youth in a caravan. When I became a woman, the women in my caravan welcomed me and taught me their secret arts. We traveled down from the mountains because Uncle Alberto saw danger looming in the future. He hoped we could hide from the danger in a peaceful meadow.

"Now I walk many roads without my family. Never would I have chosen this strange path. I forgive Del for stealing away my dreams. I will never be an innocent maiden again. I bury my innocence."

Sharanii handed Sarina a large wooden cooking spoon and took her torch. Sarina turned to the east and dug a small hole in the soft ground. Joya watched.

She felt like a big fat whale and moving to do anything was out of the question. The big wiggling mass she was carrying in her belly made it impossible.

Sarina placed the smooth stone in the rich soil and covered it. She stood up and brushed the dirt off her hands, took back the torch and lifted it high saying,

"Joya, this is a new doorway. When you go through it, you will never be quite the same again. Since you are going to be different, decide for yourself what your new direction will be, so Fate does not choose for you."

The rock Joya chose for keeping was rough and jagged.

"I am empty. I am dead. The breath breathes itself or surely I would die. I stand on land, yet I feel like I am drifting at sea. I died with my family and this shell that continues to eat and sleep is hollow and numb.

"I will keep this stone to remind me in the future to root myself in people, never in capricious Del." She dropped the rock into one of the deep pockets of Uncle Alberto's robe and mused out loud. "I was a traveler and I am a traveler still. I knew how life worked in the caravan, but now, I have no idea what tomorrow will bring. I have no idea how to be a mother. I cannot imagine passing through that doorway." Joya gripped the rock before she dare release it.

Rifka, the *Keeper of the South,* stepped forward, bowed to Joya and announced, "Sveet Joya, my dear friend, face da south ova here, 'n tell us vhat kindles your passion?"

Joya chose another smooth stone and clutched it to her heart. She said with gusto, "I loved my family and I lived comfortably within their rules. I now surrender all need to follow anyone's rules. I will live in accord with my own beliefs. I release myself from those who do not value me, yet wield power over me. No one will control my life ever again."

Joya picked a smooth stone and handed it to Rifka. She gladly knelt down and planted the charged stone in the soft ground.

Joya looked so young. She was only sixteen, ripe with child, very beautiful, and very much afraid as she reached into the basket and chose a sharp stone to keep.

"Sveet Joya, in dis realm of passions vhat do you vant?"

Holding the ragged stone tightly in her closed fist, Joya felt it jabbing into her palm and welcomed the pain. She said in a deep hollow voice, "May this stone bless the passionate relationship I will have with the child." Joya did not drop the stone into the robe's deep pocket. She gripped it until her knuckles went white and thought, if the babies in my belly all live, my life will be fierce."

Rachel, as *Keeper of the West*, stepped forward and warmly said, "Joya, please pick a stone 'n look to da vest vhere da sun sets. Tell us my dear, how you feel. You are changing in so many vays. Vee vant to know how it feels to you."

Joya chose a sharp rock with her left hand because she was still clutching the baby's stone in her right and looked to the west.

"What do I feel? I feel Rage! Hatred! Despair! Shame! Anguish! Hopelessness! Betrayed! Abused! Each word spat out bitterly. "Those are a few of the fires in my blood. I am sure there are more. "

"My dear liddle Joya, let da bad feelings pass through. Let dem go 'n be gone."

"I put all the pain in this rock and give to Mother Earth to be cleansed." With a shudder she cried loudly, "I cast off these creepy feelings." Joya looked at the jagged sliver in her hand and spoke to it, 'Go little rock, go into hell and take the men who hurt me with you!'"

Joya held the stone tightly then dropped both stones into Rachel's hands. "Please bury them. Let Mother Earth make me pure and clean again."

The baby's stone was now in the *Divine Mother's* keeping.

Tasjia held up the basket to Joya. Their eyes met and filled with tears.

Rachel's eyes were not dry either. She leaned down and put her hand on the girl's quivering shoulder. Her soothing touch was calming to the fiery girl.

"Please liddle mama, pick a new stone to hold your new dreams. How do you vant to do family from now on?"

Reaching into the basket, Joya picked a nice smooth stone and declared, "I breathe in Freedom. May Freedom always be as close to me as my next breath."

She kissed the stone before dropping it into her pocket. It made a nice clink.

Meshka, as *Keeper of the North*, shyly stepped forward and stuttered nervously as she spoke, "Joya, my dear, come look to da north. Here you can dtalk to your body. You can dank da body 'n ask vhat it needs from you? Tell us vhat you vant da practical parts of your life to be like."

Joya was slow to answer. She tried to see herself holding a baby in her arms and saw nothing. She was still waiting to wake up and discover this was a bad dream. She could not possibly be having a baby!

Reaching into the basket, she picked a smooth stone. "My body is strong. I surrender this strange ungainly form and wait impatiently for my old body to return."

Once the stone was committed to the ground, Joya sighed, chose a smooth red stone, and held it to her lips. "I will now be my own security. I will rely on myself and on you, my dear sisters, for my love and security. Your friendship is all I need."

The women standing around her echoed her words, "I will now be my own security. I will rely on myself and on you, my dear sisters, for my love and security. Your friendship is all I need."

The women planted their torches in the ground beside them and sat down on the ground around Joya relaxing in her cushy nest. Only Sharanii remained standing as a beacon of light radiating from the center. In a soft soothing voice she sang out,

"Close your eyes. See yourself crossing a threshold into your new life as a mother. May you live within the embrace of the *Divine Mother*."

"Is there something you wish to say?"

Joya prayed aloud, "*Holy Mother*, grant me a secret wish." Silently she added, "Free me from this burden I do not want."

Not knowing Joya's secret wish, the others echoed, "May it be so. Blessed Be."

Rageful bitterness pierced her words when Joya cried out, "I am *marimé* (impure). I who am cursed, curse the men who raped me. May they suffer frightening nightmares every night for the rest of their lives. May itchy oozing sores break out on their ugly genitals and may their everyday be filled with *bibaxt*." (bad luck)

With blazing eyes she added, "From this day forth, I surrender my hatred. I will not allow my soul to be bound to theirs. On the day this child is banished from my body, may my hatred for those vicious men be banished from my soul. May the purpose for my suffering be revealed to me."

In closing Sharanii intoned, "May *The Divine Mother* watch over you and bless you all the days of your life."

The women moved in around Joya to fluff up her pillows. The maiden was as comfortable as the restless fidgeting baby would allow. She relaxed and closed her eyes. With warm hands, the women opened the wizard robe and dripped a light stream of deliciously warm oil across Joya's belly. Seven pairs of strong hands touched her. Gentle hands kneaded her sore shoulders; quiet hands eased the tension from her head, rough hands massaged her tired feet, and loving motherly hands tenderly rubbed rich creams into the tight skin on her belly.

Joya floated off in a dream under the loving touch of so many blessed hands.

Joya rolled over on her side. It was hard to stay in one position for long with this litter bouncing around in the confines of their little cave.

Someone with a good strong grip was doing wonderful things to Joya's aching back. She figured it was Rifka. Inch by inch, Rifka worked the heels of her hands up Joya's sore back. Against the pressure of the baby, her hands felt fantastic.

Loving hands massaged her, unraveled knotted muscles in Joya's body, while her ritual sisters chanted sweet blessings. Everyone's eyes were closed and their hearts were open, beaming the purest love as they blessed the precious child and the wonderful mama Joya would become.

When every muscle in Joya's body was deliciously loose and she was utterly content, the women positioned their mouths inches from her round full belly and following Sharanii's lead, softly chanted,

"Welcome little one.
We are here to love you
when you come to our world.
We are your mama's sisters
on this journey together."

Over and over, making up tunes as they went along, their ringing voices wove a temple of sound around Joya. Like a rag doll she lay carelessly draped in a tumble of blankets. The last invocation they sang in harmony. Joya was floating blissfully in this sweet temple.

The *Priestesses* sat back for a moment and relaxed. The quiet was pristine. The loud silence was charged with power. The child's spirit was hovering near.

The women propped Joya up in her nest of blankets until she felt like a queen holding court.

The next ritual was a simple one. Each woman kissed Joya, handed her a small flaming candle and said a heartfelt prayer of blessing. Joya put the smoky smelly tallow candles in the bowl of sand Tasjia was holding. To these women, who worked for days to render the fat and make the tallow, a candle was a precious thing; but they valued friendship above all, so each woman gave Joya her longest candle, her very best one.

Sharanii gave the little maiden a fragrant long blue beeswax candle. The others stared in disbelief. Who ever saw such a treasure? Where does Sharanii get these things?

When Joya's little garden of flames was complete, Sharanii said, "Make a wish and blow out the candles."

No one knew her secret wish, except *The Mother*. "*Most Holy One* please save me!"

"When your labor begins, we will relight these candles and place them beside your birthing mat. Our blessings will be there radiating love upon you," Sharanii announced.

The sacred ritual came to an end. Sharanii stood in the center of the circle. She slowly turned round, with her arms upraised she intoned to heaven,

"Guardian Powers of the East, South, West and North, Powers of Heaven, Earth and Soul, *You* who protect and govern our lives, We thank *You* for being with us today. We release *You* to watch over the world. In the days and weeks to follow, please be gentle on us. Bring our dear sister Joya an easy birth. Let peace prevail here and everywhere."

Just at that moment the baby gave Joya a really sharp kick. Easy birth, thought Joya, I doubt it.

A few minutes later a miraculous feast appeared. Joya's little community of women settled in to enjoy a good meal and a good many stories.

As they ate, they praised the sweet joys of motherhood and talked honestly about how challenging being a mother can be at times. In this sacred space, it seemed appropriate to share their most private mysteries.

Joya felt a wonderful sense of sisterhood. She was connected to these women by their mutual suffering and their collective triumphs.

The nobility of their quests and the pain of their struggles gave Joya the feeling that she really was in a circle of *Priestesses*. She enjoyed playing at being a *Priestess*. The heavens laughed at her for thinking it was play.

CRCRCR

Chapter 23

Rifka and the Cave

"Rifka woke up on da wrong side of da bed," Meshka warned Rachel. Her daughter was in a foul mood. In another world and time, it would have been little Suryla's birthday. All morning, Rifka prowled around like a hungry cat. Anyone who came too close was likely to be whipped by her sharp tongue. The women sensed her pent-up rage and tip-toed around her.

Now that spring was here, nightfall came at the end of a long day. It was too long before it began. By nightfall, Rifka was completely fed up with the crush of people swarming around her.

"Why do dese people go on livin' vhen my sveet babies are dead? Why did da ignorant peasants murder dem!?!"

Looking around her at the everyday people, she wondered, "Why do dese people deserve to live? Some are old, or lame, or stupid. Why va dey spared vhen my smart, pretty liddle girl vas kilt? She vanted only to love 'n be loved. Why did she have to die? 'N Moishela was so young, he vas just a baby, cushy 'n perfect!?"

Rifka forced herself to breathe! She was suffocating.

A furious rage was chasing her. Tender sharp pains were piercing her heart. It was unbearable. She was drowning in bittersweet waves of love.

Suryla, sweet, lovely, tiny little wise woman.

Desperate longing whipped her legs. She ran, propelled by surging forces gnawing and exploding inside her.

Deep into the woods she ran, yearning for solitude and quiet. Moonbeams illuminated the path as it wound its way under twisted branches. Dappled light shimmered down through fluttering leaves on tall slender trees. Above her head, branches swayed, casting out dancing shadows of ominous silver light.

Rifka's feet hugged the path, her senses quivering. The thick forest was alive with chattering hidden creatures, but Rifka was beyond fear.

With each step, another mysterious silhouette came into view. She suddenly stopped and stared in disbelief! Confusion grabbed her, shaking all her senses loose! Was she dreaming? After traveling all these many months, she was far, far away from the old village, b-u-t...standing in front of her was the same crooked tree in the same green meadow!

A wave of shock shook her like a rag doll. Slowly she began to notice small differences. This meadow had a wall of boulders off to one side, in the same spot by the old village stood a thick stand of trees.

The old crooked tree called to her with sweet memories. It looked so familiar. The trunk was bent at the knee and curved upward making a slanted bench, exactly like the one back home. When she was a child, she loved climbing on the old crooked tree while her mama was off picking blueberries.

Rifka sat down on the crooked tree and leaned back against her trusty old friend, just like so many times before. She drifted back into the past where once upon a time, she was so happy. Her eyes closed and she made believe she was in the meadow near the village, back home again. She crossed her arms and hugged herself tightly. A bittersweet memory rushed in, so piercing that it took her breath away.

She was lying on this tree nursing little Moishela. Suryla was playing with her little angels on the ground beside her. Suryla was three then. She was holding a handful of pretty daisies which she called, "angels."

The child loved playing with flower angels. She chatted endlessly, telling stories about the angels. Her angels rescued people and made the sun shine so little children could go out and play. The angels helped the rain to fall for hungry crops. They washed the world brand-new and clean.

On one particular sunny morning long ago, the air was sweet, because the angels made it so. Suryla looked up at her mama and said ever so sweetly, "Mommy, vhen I grow up, I am goin' to be an angel 'n vatch ova da world."

Rifka wrapped her arms together under her ample breasts and imagined she felt the weight of her baby, sweet little Moishela cradled in her arms. She could hear the chiming voice of her little angel talking to the angels as the child played on the ground beside her. In that moment, lost in her daydream, the world was as it had always been. For that moment, she was content.

Out of nowhere, a large white owl appeared! With its great snow white wings extended, it glided over Rifka only inches from her face! Startled, she snapped out of her daydream! Her eyes followed the owl as he landed on a nearby branch. He sat there looking intently at her like a messenger waiting.

After a minute, the owl took flight. He swooped up, flew over a large tumble of boulders and disappeared. Rifka followed to see where he had gone. She peeked around the boulders and discovered a large cave hidden from view.

Soft foggy clouds were billowing out through the mouth of a cave. Rifka was taken back! This strange place made her body quiver with a memory she dare not remember!

Gripping curiosity drew Rifka into the cave. Inside, she found herself in a huge cavern. Its rough walls cast off a strange green glow. In the dim green light, she saw textured walls beneath a spectacular rounded ceiling.

The hard pack dirt beneath her feet was hidden in low drifting fog. The creamy white fog curled around her feet and soon she felt deliciously relaxed.

Rifka cautiously stepped forward. The green light was soothing. Strangely enough, she felt no fear. She was intrigued and enchanted.

This strange magnificent world felt somehow familiar. It held an echo of long ago, like a special place remembered from childhood. Her feet followed a familiar path.

Rifka crossed the vaulted chamber. Each step drew her closer to her destiny. On the far side of the chamber, a tunnel beckoned. Inside, she found the same green glowing stones lighting her way.

Where the fog was patchy, she could see the earth beneath her feet was polished smooth. A great weight must have swept across the floor countess times to bring it to such a high level of polished smoothness.

She arrived at a small cavern branching off from the tunnel. Its rounded ceiling was creamy white with dripping salt frozen in beautiful forms with sculptured grace.

The cloudy mist encircling her feet swelled up higher. Her head grew lighter and her heart more peaceful. A unique sense of quiet embraced her. Her breath slowed to barely a trickle. A vision came upon her. Three women were sitting on three leg-ged stools beside a fountain. She saw them here, in this cavern, right over there.

The vision left her with a strange feeling. Cautiously she walked deeper into the eerie green cavern. From the knees down, her legs disappeared in the thick foggy mist. Her body seemed to float over the chamber floor. In the very center of the cavern, the foggy mist bubbled up in a frothy fountain of clouds.

Curiosity drew Rifka towards the fountain. Slowly she glided through the clouds.

Startled! Her foot kicked something hidden in the mist. She leaned down and picked up a three legged stool. A sharp shud-der shook her.

Suddenly a wave of weariness overcame her. Without forethought, she put the stool right and sat down on it. Her eyes fell closed and her breath slowly deepened. Strange images floated through the sweet mist surrounding her. They were vague, but felt important. She yearned to know their meaning.

Rifka was wrapped in deep quiet, her heart was purring, and the cave was throbbing!

She began to feel dizzy and drained. The mist was sucking her into a spin! Wild forces were swirling around her! She was spinning! The world was spinning and spinning! And then it stopped!

Still at last, the inner clashing stopped!

She opened her eyes and gazed into another world. She was sitting on this stool, just as she had done all her life. Her dearest sisters sat beside her, deep in trance on stools just like hers.

Through the mouth of the chamber, a huge creature silently glided towards her out of the lacy fog. It was a dragon, but she felt no fear. A tender emotion washed over her.

"Noble *Priestess*, it is time for you to drink," he announced as he slithered closer, a leather bag of water in tow. At first, he was but a silhouette in the dim green glow, but as he drew near, she saw him in his full glory!

A huge ancient serpent God was coiled up in front of her! His slanted amber eyes were set in the face of a handsome man with a wild mane of black hair, broad shoulders, and powerful arms. This magnificent man had a mighty chest covered with scales and the rest of him was that of a serpent!

"Ah Python, my dear," she welcomed him.

"Drink deeply my lady for it will bring you strength and good health." She took a few sips and then he coaxed her to drink more. "What would you like me to bring you for your evening meal?" He asked.

"O' somethin' small 'n light. I am not hungry," she replied offhandedly.

"My dear *Priestess*, it is my responsibility to take care of your body. I shall bring you a meal of fruits, vegetables, nuts, and grains. We must care for your body when your spirit flies to other worlds in search of wisdom's truth." Python was being practical as usual.

The Oracle Rifka was imagining herself to be smiled at Python, thinking how much she appreciated his loving service and kind attention.

Another *naga* (half snake and half man) entered the cave carrying a message, a question for *The Oracle*. She took a deep slow breathe, closed her eyes, and as she breathed out, the question became an answer. The *naga* left to deliver her prophecy to a man waiting outside.

With the next deep breath, Rifka felt something terrifying! Danger was near!

Within moments she heard a frightening commotion outside the cavern. The sanctuary filled with choking smoke. Rifka and the other *Priestesses* ran to the entrance, their stools toppled over as they rushed to escape.

Horror stricken, eyes wide with terror! She saw Python slithering towards her. His body was on fire! A burning arrow was embedded in his side! A shrill cry rang from her trembling lips! The terrible sweet smell of living flesh burning was overwhelming! Terror and disgust raked through her. Her sweet protector was shrieking in agony!

Through the flames stood a giant God. His looming shadow filled the entrance. With the dignity and grace of a *Priestess*, she stood before Him. His golden face was exquisite. He was huge! Compared to Him, she was as tiny as a baby.

"I am Apollo. I claim this sanctuary as my own!" His booming voice declared.

Shocked, she saw this beautiful terrible God grab her sweet sister and fall upon her! In a terrible act of sexual rage, He violated her virgin purity! Then He cast her aside and turned a lustful eye on Daphne, the youngest of the three *Priestesses*.

Tearfully Daphne prayed to *Diana, Goddess of Women,* to rescue her from this terrible beast! She ran through the tunnels and out of the cave. He watched amused, then followed her out.

The *Goddess Diana* heard Daphne's prayers. Apollo reached out to grab the young maiden. She tripped. Just as she was falling over into his arms, *The Goddess* changed her into a laurel tree. The crooked tree took root, safe from the evil God's rage and cruelty.

Frustrated, Apollo returned to the cave, blocking the entrance. He focused His wild passions on the third *Oracle*, on Rifka. Looking wildly about for a way to escape, she realized in horror she was trapped!

Apollo advanced on her, his mighty hands clutched her soft flesh. Then, stabbing through her body was His sex penetrating her virgin flesh! Apollo crushed something holy in her. Darkness and desolation closed in upon her.

In the stillness afterwards, there was only pain. She tried to stand up, but an awful dizziness came over her. Black lights flashed behind her eyes. Her mind was swirling around and around. In the darkness, decades passed, lifetimes came and went, then at last the stillness returned and the pain was gone.

Her stomach was tangled in knots, but when her eyes opened, she was herself again. Dazed, she stumbled out of the cave. Out in the fresh sweet air, the lovely maiden face of the moon gazed down at Rifka with great sympathy.

Rifka's whole body was trembling. What a strange dream! It seemed so real! She stumbled over to the crooked tree. Her shawl lay on the ground where it fell when the owl woke her up. She wrapped the shawl tightly around her, but still she shivered because the cold was inside her.

Rifka stumbled through the forest back to camp. Her feet followed a path while her thoughts were far away. Soon she was lost, wandering aimlessly through the trees vaguely in the direction of camp. Her legs took the lead because her mind was *farblondzhet* (bewildered and confused), lost between the worlds wrestling with strange eerie feelings.

She struggled to make sense of her terrible dream, but a voice in her head insisted it was not a dream. She was certain she once lived in this land and was a *Priestess*.

Rifka argued with herself, "No! Dis is foolish! I am a Jewish widow who has lost her babies 'n most of her *mispokhim.* (relations) Dis is who I am. I have never lived before. God gives us only von life. Dat is enough! Dis is just da magic of da fog. It just made me drunk, nothin' more."

As Rifka stumbled along, she argued with the sky, the trees, and the little pebbles on the ground. She tried to convince them that she was a good Jewish woman and not some kind of pagan oracle. No matter how many times she repeated the words and clung to her denial, she knew she had glimpsed her Soul's truth. Such knowing cannot be erased.

Something felt shattered in her. With certainty, she knew she once suffered at the hands of Apollo. It was as real to her as Moishela's death.

Her legs eventually found their way back to camp. The hour was late. Rifka felt hollow and lonely. She did not want to be alone so she crawled into Meshka's tent. She snuggled in next to her mama. Meshka sensed Rifka's need for silence, so she made believe she was asleep. The two women lay side by side, as they did on many cold nights, but something felt different about Rifka.

Meshka could not put her finger exactly on it, except to say she felt a sense of sacredness. That puzzled her. Everyone knew her daughter was a notorious stickler for laws and rules. She pooh-poohed anything sacred.

Just as Meshka was dozing off, Rifka leaned over and kissed her mama. "Dank you for walkin' dis life vid me," she quietly whispered, thinking her mama was asleep. Meshka opened her eyes just a sliver, gazed up at her daughter and saw a stranger.

ଔଔଔ

Chapter 24

Joya and the Crooked Tree

Rifka and Joya usually walked together at night under starry skies. They were especially fond of strolling beside a pond or a lake when the moon was full, like it was today.

But Rifka was gone. She went storming off earlier today. Now the sun was going down and she still had not returned. Joya was not a worrier, but in Rifka's enraged state something awful could have happened.

"Who knows what kind of trouble she could get herself into? If Rifka met up with a bear in the dark forest at night, I would put my money on Rifka. I feel sorry for any bear that tries to fight that woman when she is in a fury." Joya mumbled as she set out to search for her friend.

The young maiden waddled along behind her big belly, enchanted by the silhouetted images of the trees and bushes in the nighttime forest. She was following Rifka's path through the shadows.

Deep into the woods she wandered. Mysterious moonbeams of dappled silver light shimmered down through fluttering leaves on tall slender trees as she made her way under twisted branches. The thick forest was alive with the chatter of hidden creatures.

Joya recoiled in horror! Frozen with fear, she did not believe her eyes!

There before her was the crooked tree! The gnarled old beast looked sinister and threatening. She backed away from the evil thing and the terrible memories hidden in it.

Time suddenly stripped away. Screaming people were running in every direction. An angry mob of men was running towards her! They were shaking pitchforks and holding burning torches! Her eyes began to water and her nose twitched, as though acrid smoke was again filling the air with foul smells.

Joya stood in horror staring at the tree. Her heart was pounding like it did when she was running breathlessly, using every bit of strength she had to escape the rageful mob of leering beasts chasing her! She was running as fast as she could but they came closer and closer!!

Suddenly one hideous beast leaped forward and grabbed her by the ankle. He brought her down like a dog upon a stag. Joya fought like a she-demon, until their pounding fists cut her spirit loose from her body and sent it far away.

She felt nothing after that. Her wounded spirit gazed down at her poor broken body from the top of the tree. Perched on a branch, she watched with cool indifference as one crazed man after another viciously fell upon her.

Her mind went blank. Somewhere far far away was a lot of pain, but she did not feel it. The world was far away; even her beautiful virgin body being ravaged savagely was far far away. She was not in that tortured body; she was the tree, stiff and cold, untouched by the madness of men.

She was barely fourteen and she always liked men. She knew how to get her way with them. But these were not men. These crazed animals were not aroused by erotic desire, but by a ferocious blood lust.

Seeing it all again brought back the terrible pain hiding in her body. The locked chamber of denial flew open and she screamed with rage! She wailed! Wailed! Wailed, and tore out handfuls of hair. Her cries echoed all around her!

Joya backed away from the all too familiar tree, until a wall of boulders brought her to a stop. A sense of dread seized her. Chills ran up and down her arms, crawling over her skin. She slowly turned, knowing she would see an entrance to a cave. It did not feel like intuition, but rather, remembering.

Soft pale foggy clouds seeped out of the cave and wound around the boulders. Joya stared at the creamy oozing whiteness with disgust. A wave of nausea overwhelmed her. The cloud looked like spent semen.

Repulsive fascination drew her into the cave. She found herself in a huge cavern. It felt strangely familiar. She remembered the vaulted ceiling, the creamy white whimsical sculptures dangling from the dripping ceiling and the strange green glowing jewels embedded in the walls. She was grateful for the dim light they cast. Looking around her at the familiar walls, everything was exactly as she remembered, even the white clouds swallowing up her legs.

She wandered through the tunnels and chamber until she came to the fountain, the source of the billowing clouds of mist crawling along the hard beaten earth. Instinctively, she knew just where to find an overturned stool. An unknown force was compelling her to set the stool upright, and sit down.

Joya froze staring in disbelief! This was the place of her childhood nightmares! The eerie green light, the upturned stools, the terror, the running, and then the silence, always in her dreams. Night after night she remembered waking up screaming. Uncle Albert always scooped her up in his arms and held her until she stopped shaking.

She could still hear her sweet uncle cooing, "You are safe my little peacock. I will never let anyone harm you," but when the nightmares became real, even he could not save her.

The fog was making her woozy. Suddenly she was trapped in a nightmare again! A giant man, bigger than anyone she ever saw, was striding in through a wall of flames. His beautiful face was masking a dangerously arrogant spirit. Terror was strangling her! Horrified, she saw Him fall upon her sister!

Running, terrified! She was esperately praying to *Diana*! Surely her beloved *Goddess* would protect her. She was running with all her youthful vigor; the terrible God still following her through the tunnels! His long muscular legs easily covering the distance between them! Running through veils of smoke and flame!

The *Goddess Diana* heard her pleas.

She ran out into the blinding light of the meadow. The evil giant closing in behind her! He grabbed for her! He was about to leap upon her as He did to her sister! She was falling and reached upward...

Her body grew heavy and her limbs refused to move. She was stuck in this twisted position. Her arms stiffened cast forever reaching upward. Her legs took root where she stood. *The Goddess* turned her into a laurel tree.

The huge vile creature looked at the tree in disappointment. He returned to the cave to vent His rage on the third *Priestess*, her oldest sister.

ଔଔଔ

Joya awoke from a dream that was not a dream. She was sitting in the eerie green chamber on a three legged stool as she had for as long as she could remember. This was her life once. It all came back to her now. She was an *Oracle* and this was her *Temple of Prophecy*.

The maiden felt a wild mixture of emotions. Mostly she was suffocating and desperate for some fresh air. She waddled out of the cave back into the moonlight. For a long moment she stared at the crooked tree, seeing it in all its incarnations.

ଔଔଔ

Chapter 25

Anath

Exhausted, Joya staggered back to camp, crawled into her little makeshift tent, and fell into a restless sleep. When she woke up some time later, she was stiff, cold, and in the first stage of labor. She draped all her clothes over her. She was chilled to the bone and totally worn out. She writhed and moaned each time the pain stabbed through her, then collapsed utterly when the pain released her. Rifka and Meshka were awakened by the sound of Joya moaning.

Meshka boiled some water, collected a bunch of clean cloths to use for swaddling and gathered whatever useful tools she could find. Rifka gave Meshka her sharp knife to cut the baby's cord. Sharanii brought over a bottle of good wine to relax Joya. Sarina lit the first of the *Blessing Day* candles. She lit only one to conserve the love and blessings of the Baking Clan so they would glow for a long time. Maya played soft beautiful music on her harp. Tasjia's strong hands pressed hard on Joya's lower back and massaged her during contractions. Of course, Rachel cooked a delicious chicken soup to give the poor little mama more strength.

Rifka sat beside Joya and held her hand. Eye to eye, she kept a steady prattle going to keep Joya focused outward, since whenever Joya slipped back inside herself, giant waves of pain and fear consumed her, before spitting her out again.

Through the day, the Baking Clan built a large birthing tent under Sharanii's guiding hand. The women, including some neighbors camped nearby, contributed shawls and blankets, so the tent was large enough to stand up in.

Inside, they made Joya as comfortable as possible. She lay on a cushy bed under a canopy of friendship. Sharanii smiled to herself. She took pride in what they had created. These scarves, shawls, and blankets came from different towns, different villages, even different countries, but together they shielded sweet Joya as she labored to birth a new baby.

The contractions grew more and more intense! Joya howled! All the emotion held in for nine long months burst out like a broken dam. The strange horrors of the night before added a sharp intensity to her screams.

The wonderful birthing tent gave Joya room to prowl. She could not lay still. The intensity of the forces surging through her propelled her to keep moving. She stomped, crouched, and even crawled around on all fours like a wounded animal. With her arms draped around Rifka and Sarina, she ambled outside.

They walked her to a strong oak tree. Joya latched onto a hefty low branch and gripped it until her knuckles turned white, she pushed as hard as she could but no baby popped out.

Restless and uncomfortable, Joya kept changing position. Her lower back felt like it was being sucked out of her, as though she was being sucked down into the earth. Ahhh, Tasjia's magical hands pressed, massaged and softened the sharp edges of the pain.

All the *Bakers* lent their spiritual strength to Joya. After only a few hours, the contractions were coming quickly. The birth was at hand!

Her body was racked with volcanic force again and again, but the birth was no closer than before.

Then the contractions stopped completely with disappointing relief!

Half an hour later, the birth pains returned even more fiercely. Now they were coming more and more quickly.

Joya's hopes rose, then were dashed. Again the contractions stopped. Joya was tired.

Rachel fed her more chicken soup. Her wonderful soup could cure anything. Sharanii gave Joya a little more wine to help her relax. Tasjia sat back to rest for a minute. Her arms were stretched down to her knees. Her fingers had gone numb a long ago massaging Joya's back for so many hours. Maya sucked on the tips of her fingers. They were raw from plucking harp strings all this time. Meshka was exhausted from helping wherever a spare pair of hands were needed.

The only one who still looked fresh and alert was Rifka. Her eyes were riveted to Joya's. She was not leaving her friend's side. If Joya could continue, then surely she could too.

Eye to eye, Rifka was holding Joya above the waves. She was Joya's one outer focus. The laboring mama held onto her for dear life. They were riding these waves together.

Time and again, they crashed up against the threshold of birth only to find the door securely locked. Each time the disappointment was harder to bear. A wave of fear began to roll in with each new surge of pain.

The baby was reluctant to be born. Rifka chatted on for hours, coaxing and encouraging. She said more words during this birth than she did all year.

Hours without end inched by. Rifka, driven by unflagging devotion, was determined to ride this to the end. It was like she too was giving birth.

Joya was sweating, panting, prowling, so was Rifka. Joya was pushing, gripping, grunting, growling, so was Rifka; and two of them were fighting a growing sense of despair.

Hour after hour, Rifka's parched and cracking voice droned on. "Liddle Mama, these pains are a mountain you must climb. Let us count how many steps to da top of da mountain. Climb Joya. Climb to da top 'n slide down da other side." What started as a smooth chant, after so many hours, became a rasping echo, "How many strokes... von... two... three... does it take ... four...five...six... to reach da top?"

During the long hours of pulling and pushing the cart up and down the mountains together, they needed something to pass the time. Joya once taught Rifka to count, now she returned the favor.

"Ten steps to the top," Joya hoarsely whispered.

"Now vee need to push da cart more dan ten steps to get to da top of da next mountain. You can do dat, right? Maybe only eleven or tvelve steps, dat is not so much. You can do dat."

When the next contraction began, the two women huffed and puffed and made it to the top. Then they slid into the peaceful oasis on the other side.

Rifka did all but push Joya up the mountain. She cooed to reassure her, "My dear liddle sister...von...two...three...you are a vonderful climber...four...five...six...to reach da top ....seven....eight.... nine.... in only.... ten.... eleven... tvelve strokes."

"Relax now," Rifka whispered. "You have reached da great oasis. You made it! Enjoy da silence after so much noise. Let go into dis endless pool of peace. Float in dis quiet place between da storms."

Rachel was sitting on the other side of Joya. Her weathered old hand gently wiped the sweat from the laboring mama's tender young forehead with a cool cloth. After the last contraction, she covered Joya's face with the fresh cold cloth. Joya moaned.

Sweet pious Rachel prayed to God. She prayed with every breath, prayed with every stroke of the cool cloth, prayed with all the devotion she felt for her young friend, for a *Baker* in her Clan. Rachel begged God to help the struggling young woman live through this and deliver a healthy baby.

Rifka's eyes were riveted on Joya. For the hundredth time, Joya's little body arched up and Rifka intoned with uncommon gentleness, "Ahhh, it is da time to climb da next mountain. You can do it…von…two…three…soon you vill reach… four…five…six… da next great oasis…seven…eight… nine… of sveet quiet…ten…eleven…tvelve…each stroke takes you closer…thirteen…fourteen…fifteen…Ahhh…

"Up 'n ova you go. You are on da other side of da mountain. Surrender my dear into dis sveet place of quiet. Let go completely 'n float in an endless pool of peace."

Rifka's palms hurt. The circulation stopped several minutes ago; Joya was gripping her hand so hard. Rifka was willing to share her friend's pain.

"You are a vonderful climber to reach da top in only twenty strokes," Rifka cooed. "Vee are von mountain closer to da end of da journey. Den you vill rest 'n vee vill all take care of you. You are safe."

Joya followed Rifka's familiar voice, as she struggled up and over ragged mountains. However, somewhere during each climb, she wanted to give up.

"Enough! Enough! Enough! Stop already!" She wanted to scream, "I want to go home. I do not want to do this anymore!"

Rifka's steady reassuring voice pulled her through the labyrinth. Joya held onto the words and they kept her above clutching waves of despair. Hand in hand, they climbed the mountains and dived into the endless oasis of delicious rest and bliss on the other side.

These two women were way past exhaustion. Holding fast to each other, one dragged the other up the next mountain.

Echoing behind Rifka's voice was the light pitter patter of rain landing on the blankets and shawls of the birthing tent. A few droplets were pooling on the cloth and dripping through, making an annoying splat on the ground.

At the end of a long night, nothing much had changed. The tortuous dance continued. Time and again, the two women came right up to the gates of birth, but the baby was forbidden to pass.

During the lulls, Joya ate more soup, walked around, and slept.

The long night drew to a close. The sun was hiding so the day never really dawned. It just oozed from night into day. At least the rain stopped. Maybe God figured He had pounded these poor people enough and gave up His little fit.

Every hour limped by so slowly, it felt like time was stopping along the way. Still the birth was no closer than before! Exhausted beyond exhaustion, Joya was waning.

As the day went on, dull and cloudy, a stream of women came by to bring salves, soups, advice, and blankets to keep the young Gypsy girl comfortable and warm.

The struggle over the mountains grew longer and harder. When they collapsed in the oases, they both felt utterly depleted.

Rifka was worried and frightened. This birth was taking much too long! Two mornings and most of a day had come and gone, what should they do? Rifka and the Baking Circle had to do something to save their beloved little Gypsy girl.

The candles from the *Blessing Day* had long ago burned away. Rifka had to do something more! She stood up and stretched her cramped and aching body. She looked down at Joya in her sweat soaked bedroll and begged God not rob her of her dear friend. Rifka was terrified. She looked at Joya's glassy eyes staring blindly in despair and vowed to find someone to help.

Every neighbor woman who knew a secret herbal formula or powerful birthing position was asked to help. Every special tonic Maya could concoct was tried. Nothing worked. Joya was getting weaker.

The mystical fortuneteller, the magical Gypsy girl dressed in wild flamboyant colors, the fanciful dancer, sweet young Joya, was she going to disappear too, like all their other loves?

Rifka desperately shook Joya to make her focus, but Joya refused. The Gypsy girl gave up. She was lost someplace between pain and despair.

Rifka firmly took hold of Joya's hands, and drew her close. She looked deep into the girl's eyes and whispered in her now croaky voice, "Vee can do dis together. Look into my eyes. Vhen I breathe out, you breathe in 'n take my strength into you. Vhen you breathe out, breathe away da pain 'n let it go."

With the strength of her iron will, Rifka held Joya by the thread of her breath. Their eyes were locked on each other, breathing in perfect rhythm. Rifka held Joya safe above the biting waves of pain with the power of her breath. They stayed linked like that for a long time…until questions started to attack them. Was this agony ever going to end!?! Was the baby stuck? Why was this going on and on for so long? Something must be wrong! Clawing doubts gnawed at them.

Rifka's face was so pale; you would think she was having the baby! Women came in with gifts and hands to help. When they left, a shadow of dread followed them out. Dread rode on tense shoulders and sat on worried brows.

None of these kind women were trained in delivering babies. Whatever they knew came from their own births. Births are intense. This one was also dangerous. It was rare for a birth to take so long. They needed an experienced midwife!

ଡ଼ଉଡ଼ଉଡ଼

The Bakers felt stuck between breaths; waiting. Each prayed in her own language. They felt so alone, empty and helpless. Through prayer, they felt the Presence of God(s) and *Goddesses* and that brought a little comfort.

Twilight approached. The stone gray sky faded into a darker gray. Meshka saw her friends praying and realized she missed her morning talk with God. She briefly thought of finding a damp tree for their talk and shivered in the chilled air. Finally she told herself, He was probably busy listening to a lot of other prayers right now, and went off to find Sharanii instead. The *Priestess* was just leaving the birthing tent with an empty soup bowl.

Meshka pulled the *Priestess* aside and quietly whispered in her ear, "Sharanii vee need an experienced midvife. Please use your magic 'n call von to us now."

Meshka watched Sharanii ride off on her beautiful white horse. Even though Meshka was not crazy about big animals with big teeth, in this moment, she was grateful they had a horse.

Meshka turned to go. On her way back to the birthing tent, she passed Tasjia and Maya, sobbing and weeping against Sarina's strong shoulders. The young women were frightened. Though Maya attended several births as an apprentice, none were as long as this one. She was familiar with the terrible forces that rack the body at the gateway to life, but this was Tasjia's first birth. Tasjia's terror was contagious. They feared for their sweet little sister's life! The Amazon sat with her long powerful arms wrapped around the weeping maidens, drawing them under her wings like a mama hen.

Meshka made herself comfortable under a beautiful cherry tree, sitting among the lovely little pink and white blossoms blanketing the ground. Tiny Timmy came waddling along behind her and crawled into her lap. He put his thin little thumb in between his puckered lips and contentedly drifted off to sleep.

"God," she called quietly, not to waken the little fellow. "Most Holy Von, I need to ask you for a favor. Please make dis birth go faster. It is taking a scary long time."

No answer.

"So God, tell me, are you dinking of taking dis sveet liddle *maideleh* (liddle girl) avay from me too? You know you have already taken so many. Dayeynu! Enough already! I only have a few loved vons left. Please Holy Von, please let me keep dis von."

No answer.

"Hello!...God!...Are you listening? I am asking you for a favor. Please do not take Joya or da baby. I need a new grandchild."

A crack of thunder roared. Lightning flashed! And the words rang out in her mind, "Meshka, if you do not like the way things are, change them." God was listening.

"God, vhat can vee do? Vhat do vee know from birth? So many smart women vid so many good ideas 'n nothing works! My babies never took two days to be born. I never did dis kind of stop, start business. I vent into labor 'n da baby pushed out. Please God help us. Please send us a really good midwife."

∞∞∞∞

Dark smudges of cloud streaked the sky. A thick blanket of silence hushed the world around them. The eerie quiet was bristling. Crickets, frogs, and birds held their breath in anticipation. The tension kept mounting. Finally as the darkness enveloped them, a soft warm rain began to fall.

Rachel silently recited Hebrew prayers, then added her own heartfelt prayer, "Most Holy God, *Baruch HaShem*, (blessed is the name) please make dis birth end soon 'n vell." In one form or another, the same prayer was on many lips, in many languages.

Rachel was mopping Joya's brow with a cool cloth. In a soft kind voice she said, "Sometimes special babies have to bake in da oven a liddle longer." Tears quietly rolled down the old woman's cheeks. She was careful not to drip one on Joya's face.

Joya barely opened her eyes but smiled weakly. A little part of her believed as Rachel did, but mostly she thought she was dying.

∞∞∞∞

Sharanii rode among the people spreading the word. Woman to woman, the news spread like wildfire. The camp was buzzing as word spread from campfire to campfire with amazing speed. If there was a midwife anywhere in this multitude, she would soon hear the call.

When Sharanii and her horse returned, she and the *Bakers* moved Joya into Sharanii's snug, warm and dry wagon.

Meshka entered the exquisite sanctuary of Sharanii's wagon. Side by side Meshka and Sharanii prepared a wonderful birthing nest for Joya. They made the girl comfortable in a queen's nest of pillows.

The midwives arrived and so did the storm. Lightning ripped through the darkness. Flashes of blue light tore through the sky. Loud claps of thunder and down pouring sheets of rain announced the arrival of a fierce storm.

Once all the midwives climbed into the wagon, there was no room left for Rifka so she stood outside in the dripping rain.

Her dearest friend was dying, tearing out what little was left of her heart.

"Joya, I vanted to hold your hand 'n go vid you as far as da road goes. Now I vill not be dere to say goodbye. I am sorry I couldn't save you from death. I couldn't save anyone from death," bitter tears flooded her eyes.

Dripping in the rain, Rifka stood transfixed staring at the lightning skewering the sky. She was praying with all her heart that these midwives would save Joya's life.

ଓଔଓଔ

"**Bon giorno**. I am Chitara, a midwife from the blessed hills of Sicily, and these are my sisters. May I examine you?" said a sweet little round woman wrapped in a dark blue shawl.

Joya gazed into the old woman's kind eyes. Weakly she smiled and nodded ever so slightly, that was all the strength she could muster. With a furrowed brow, the old woman massaged Joya's belly. Her hands were like eyes seeing through the taut skin.

"The baby is breech," she announced. With gnarled and knowing fingers, she kneaded Joya's huge belly until the sweet baby agreed to turn around. Ah, that was better.

Now that the child was more comfortable, she got down to the business of being born.

Chitara clicked her tongue loudly and the other three women: Maria, Marietta and Francesca quickly moved into action. They moved as eight hands with one mind.

Francesca, an elderly woman with eyes as clear blue as a child's, beamed a warm innocent smile and patted Joya on the cheek. She said softly, "Do not worry little birthing mother, if someone has put the Evil Eye on you, I will remove it." Then she ran a large clear crystal over Joya's swollen body and chanted strange soothing prayers.

The charming Marietta held Joya's hands. Her touch was very different than Rifka's. Her healing hands were hot and penetrating. Joya felt a warm, almost liquid feeling flowing from the old woman's arms into her.

The force roused the young Roma from her tranced-out wanderings in a fog of pain. Suddenly Joya became alert for the first time in hours.

Outside the wagon, lightning flashed and thunder roared, winds howled and a sheet of rain pounded fiercely on the thick slick cover protecting them.

Rifka was still standing out in the rain. She was too distraught to notice or care that she was getting soaked to the bone. Meshka tried to usher her into the big birthing tent, but Rifka refused to move. She insisted on guarding the wagon. This was her own personal vigil. Rifka set all the power of her will to keep *Death* at bay.

Disregarding the cold and the wet, Rifka was not going to be distracted or defeated by the rain, or by anything. She held Joya in her mind and continued to breathe life into her.

Someone was calling her name. Rifka looked around and saw Marietta leaving the birthing tent, motioning her to come inside. Poor Rifka was trembling with the cold, the wet and the fear of facing 'Goodbye.'

Rifka turned to enter the cozy sanctuary and a vision flashed before her eyes. It lasted only a few seconds. First she saw Joya as the wooden puppet she had been when they met, then as a whirling force dancing wild and free and lastly as her patient partner pulling the heavy cart side by side each day.

Rifka pulled back the wagon flap and climbed inside. Joya lie still and white. Rifka braced herself to say her final goodbye to her sweet little sister.

A terrible anger gripped her. She had no way to spit out her words. She loved the young Gypsy girl. She adored the girl's charm and wit, her beauty and grace, all the many ways Joya brightened her life. Secretly Rifka wished she could be as young and as free as Joya.

Maria helped Rifka remove her wet clothes and dry off. The midwives each gave her a piece of their clothing so she was warm and dry.

Rifka was about to say, "My sveet Joya, my sister, my best my friend, look how far vee have come since dose wooden days! Look at all vee have shared. Vill all da richness of our struggle 'n all da vays vee helped each other survive, vill it all be svept avay by death?"

Before she could speak, Marie said, "Please take the position in front of the mama, my dear, so you can catch the baby."

A tidal wave of relief washed over Rifka. Joya half opened her eyes and smiled weakly.

The woman propped Joya up. Short dark intense Maria sat down behind Joya and pressed hard on the girl's lower back. Joya arched up again as another wave grabbed her and twisted. Chitara sat beside Joya guiding when to push and when to pant.

On this dark stormy night, a shrill cry burst from Joya's lips! It was more terrible than any that had come before.

"The baby's head is crowning!" announced Chitara!

Despite utter exhaustion, Rifka's eyes were wide awake. A bright pink head covered with bulging veins peeked out almost all the way, then slid back in.

Rifka cried out and grabbed Chitara's arm to draw her attention. The midwife looked from Rifka's horrified expression to the emerging head. The cord was wrapped around the baby's neck!

Strangling! The baby was strangling!

Shocked, Rifka set her iron will to keep *Death* at bay.

Chitara's hands moved with amazing swiftness. She set the baby's neck free. Two more strong pushes and the little creature popped right out. In a rush of fluid and blood, a perfectly beautiful baby slid out of Joya's womb into Rifka's waiting hands. A squiggly little baby girl burst into the world and landed right in the palms of Rifka's hands. This was one of the most glorious moments in Rifka's life.

The lightning, thunder and pouring rain were far away. Here in this beautiful sanctuary, Rifka was holding a precious new life and her heart was overflowing with love.

Her little pink body was covered with a light layer of soft white cream and tufts of copper down. She was a hairy little monkey, just as Rifka predicted.

Maria reached out her arms and Rifka reluctantly gave her the tiny little perfect angel. The midwife checked the baby's breathing, washed her, and wrapped the precious angel in swaddling cloths and a soft cotton blanket. Once the sweet little baby was fresh, clean, and warm, Maria placed the baby in Rifka's safe embrace to be petted and cooed.

Chitara massaged Joya's womb to help her deliver the placenta and then checked to make sure it was all released.

Francesca had a needle and thread ready, but Joya was young and supple. She had only a few minor tears, nothing that would not mend by itself, so the needle was put away.

Joya's face was chalky white! A sharp stab of fear turned Rifka's face a similar color. Joya's chest was hardly moving…

…but it was moving…

…if slowly.

Blessed sleep claimed her friend. Joya was alive and well. She deserved a deep sleep.

Rifka cradled the perfect little baby for a long time. When she began to root around for food, Rifka tenderly placed the baby on her mama's breast and covered them with the softest blanket. Those little puckering pink lips found their way home and sucked happily.

In a trance of exhaustion and happiness, Rifka contentedly stared at the perfect little angel. She was just a little bulge on her mama's breast. Only her pretty little face could be seen peeking out over the edge of the soft blanket.

Rifka felt the pure perfection of the universe and the long struggle of birth faded away as a wave of exhaustion overtook her. Rifka curled up next to this sweet mountain of mama and baby and drifted peacefully off into a very deep sleep.

The midwives left the wagon just as Meshka entered. She covered her daughters with more warm blankets and left them to rest. Rifka, Joya and the squiggling baby slipped into a well-earned sleep.

CRCRCR

The hour was late and everyone was tired. Meshka invited Maria and the other midwives into the big birthing tent for some nice hot soup and fresh challah. Inside the spacious tent, the Baking Circle and the midwives enjoyed big steaming bowls of Rachel's delicious chicken soup with fluffy *k'naidlech*, (dumplings) along with a challah, and creampuffs for dessert, of course, what else?

Outside, lightning flashed and thunder roared, heralding an auspicious birth. Inside the birthing tent, the Baking Circle and the midwives filled the night with joyous songs. Little Maria with the intense eyes led the women in a welcoming song to greet the new baby. Her dark eyes sparkled as she sang.

Meshka kindly invited the Stregas to stay for the night. The birthing tent was filled with thick blankets. It was warm, comfortable, and mostly dry. The visitors were reluctant to drive their wagon at night in bad weather and so they gratefully accepted her hospitality.

CRCRCR

Joya woke up a short time later, exhausted, lost in a fog, barely aware of anything around her. She lay back against the pillows. Every part of her body ached, so she tried to ignore all sensations. She did not even feel the small weight on her chest until Maya removed the baby.

Bouncy blond Maya put the baby in the cradle Tasjia made. It was a lovely basket woven by Tasjia's gifted hands, tightly woven with thick bundles of fresh clean straw. Pretty ribbons and bits of colorful fabric were laced through the weave. The beautiful basket had a soft linen blanket. She made a cushy, warm nest for *Anath*. She also brought two delicious creampuffs for the mamas.

Tasjia massaged the baby while Maya spoon-fed the tired mama her latest and best concoction. The brew was not much on taste, but it would help her womb shrink and give her more strength.

Maria entered the wagon. She sniffed the concoction wafting in the air, "Hmmm. Good herbs. They will help. You know what works even better than herbs? Eating the placenta will make her belly shrink like that," she said and snapped her fingers.

Joya stared in dismay at the dinner plate in Maria's hand.

"Do not worry, my dear. I cooked it with onions and it tastes delicious like liver."

It sounded repulsive, but Joya was beyond caring, so she ate the placenta. It was tasty, a little chewy but not bad.

Marietta entered the tent carrying a large bowl of warm water. She bathed Joya's sore body in sweet salts and herbs. It was a joy to feel clean. Joya was so relaxed; she drifted off to sleep again.

ଓଶଓଶ

Rifka woke up happy as a lark and hungry as a bear. Joya was still sleeping, so Rifka went to the birthing tent following the enticing smell of fresh chicken broth. Rachel served her a big bowl of hot soup with a big *knedla* (matzah dumpling) floating invitingly in the middle.

Rifka was sooo tired, it took a valiant effort to sip some of the delicious soup.

Meshka was watching her exhausted daughter and her heart was filled with pride. Who would have thought this angry grumbling woman was capable of such fierce loyalty?

Rifka was holding the bowl of soup to her lips when her eyes closed and she fell fast asleep. Rifka's head drooped forward. Meshka grabbed the bowl of soup just before Rifka's head went plop into it! Then she tucked her sweet daughter into a nest of blankets and left her alone to sleep.

ଜଃଜଃଜଃ

After another sweet nap, Rifka returned to the wagon to check on Joya and the baby. She found her friend awake and fuming.

"How are you feelin'?" Rifka asked happily.

The brooding new mama merely grunted. Rifka picked up the sleeping baby and cooed in Joya's ear, "She is beautiful. She looks just like you."

Joya burrowed under her covers and started to cry.

"Vould you like to hold her?" Rifka softly asked.

"No! Never! I do not want her. Drown her. She is a curse to me." Joya screamed, drowning in rage, guilt, and shame.

Meshka heard Joya screaming and yelling as she entered the wagon with a nice bowl of warm soup for the new mama. She ignored Joya's hysterical babbling, figuring it was just the exhaustion talking and fluffed up Joya's pillows to make her more comfortable.

Meshka checked the baby's swaddling clothes and found them fouled, so she cleaned the teeny tiny little bottom and put the sweet little angel in the pretty basket Tasjia made for her.

As she left, Meshka cooed, "Joya, you did great. Da baby is beautiful. She vill be a blessing to us all."

Joya's pale face turned red, "Expose her to the rain," she screamed. "She is a curse to me."

Rifka was appalled! "Joya vhat are you sayin'!?! Just to have a baby, a healthy child, a livin' breathin' child to hold, love, 'n protect, dis is da greatest gift God can give you. How can you dink of throwin' avay such happiness?"

The baby was rooting around looking for a nipple. Joya ignored her. Rifka watched her adorable little pucker turn to a frown and tears welled up in the woman's eyes.

Rifka opened her blouse and held the sweet-smelling bundle to her breast. The baby began to suck. Rifka closed her eyes and savored the pleasure. For a minute she was home again with her baby in her arms and her little girl playing at her feet. Life was as it had always been.

Rifka looked into the child's eyes, still too young to see. But the little one looked right through her with a piercing grown-up look. It was probably a trick of the light, but Rifka felt the baby was looking into her soul. She wondered, "Vhat kind of new ideas are you bringin' vid you into dis life?" Then she shook her head like a wet dog, startled by such a strange thought.

Once the little one realized no sweet milk was coming, she began to fuss. Rifka tried to rouse Joya, but the girl refused to nurse the baby.

Meshka heard the baby fussing and came to see if she could help. Rifka told Meshka, Meshka told Sharanii, and in less than an hour a wet nurse arrived. Sharanii knew where to find her.

ରେରେରେ

The rain stopped and the clouds drifted apart to let the moon peek out. *Mother Moon* was wearing *Her* prettiest young maiden face. *Her* soft smile and round rosy cheeks beamed down through an opening in the mysteriously dark veil of clouds.

Joya woke up tired and restless. She burrowed deep in the blankets and only her foot stuck out. Meshka took the foot and started massaging it. Joya moaned in pleasure. Meshka was getting more comfortable with this touching business.

Sitting beside them was Rachel cradling the beautiful soft bundle of baby. She was petting soft pretty pink cheeks and cooing, "Hello *mamala*, I am your Bubba Rachel. Vee are going to love you so much 'n take such good care of you."

Rachel affectionately asked Joya, "So my dear, vhat are vee going to name our liddle princess?"

"*Anath*," mumbled a voice from under a mountain of warm blankets.

"*Anath*," repeated Meshka. "Dis is a pretty name."

ଔଔଔଔ

On a tall outcropping of rocks high above the wagon stood *The Goddess*. A soft smile played upon *Her* face. *Her* breath blew away the clouds, all except for a large gray one that looked like a dragon's head. Where the dragon's eye should be, was a circle of black sky studded with stars. *Mother Moon* slowly emerged from behind the clouds right into the middle of the dragon's eye.

Anyone listening to the voice of the wind would have heard, *"Anath, Anath. Welcome my daughter. Welcome back to life."*

ଔଔଔଔ

Acknowledgements

I want to thank Ruth Miller for opening the door for Meshka to enter the world. Under her loving guidance, I was able to let go of my dearest friend - lil' ol' Meshka. I pray that Meshka journeys as well in life, as she has on paper. I also want to express my heartfelt gratitude to my dear sister, Carol, my most devoted fan, who kept a recording of this book playing in her car for years. Many thanks to Marie Ruster, one of my oldest and dearest friends, who carefully combed the manuscript and coaxed me to make many dearly needed changes. Thank you to Mona McSweeney for crossing all my "T"s and dotting all my "I"s.

Once upon a time, I was afraid to share this tender story with anyone, until Julie Carpenter dragged me off to the Mountain Misfits where I read the first few chapters. Edie, John Latham and the others were graciously kind to me and gave me the encouragement I needed to keep writing and reading it aloud. I want to acknowledge my dear Madhavii Shirman who was always saying, "Well, it is like Meshka says…." as though Meshka was a member of our Qadisha. I want to thank Stephanie Spradling for her great enthusiasm for the story and Ruth Baumrucker for her friendship and encouragement. Many thanks to Charles, Elon, Vanessa, Bodhi, and Pancho for loving the Meshka in me. I am grateful to my mother, Liba Hanna, for it was her voice in my head that relayed the story. I would also like to acknowledge my grandmother, Rachel, whose true story I included in this book.

About the Author

N*I*N Sharyn Bebeau has been a disciple of the Goddess for years, spending months at a time in the woods listening for Her Voice. She has also taught and administered a graduate institute of Transpersonal Psychology, training therapists and counselors. She's been an international ambassador for peace. And she's been a wife and mother, raising her own, and many other, children in the mountains of Colorado.

N*I*N currently lives on the Oregon Coast, where she participates actively in her community and narrates her stories for s local radio station.

A Glimpse into Volume 2...

...Who would have believed it? If Meshka could go back in time and visit her old village, If she could go to the stream where Hanna and Sophie were washing their clothes and tell them, "Someday I am going to be da leader of a great multitude in a new land," they would laugh and laugh until tears ran down their faces. If the old Meshka was standing there with them, she would have laughed the hardest of them all. Life is so strange! It is so amazing! You never know what destiny is bringing you; even when it looks like it is taking everything away.

On the last day of the great celebration, with pomp and pageantry, the community's first wedding ceremony was held in the new *Temple*...

The *Sanctuary of Peace* was shining brightly under the mid-day sun. Everyone was standing in the sunbeams aglow with joyful eyes.

[The bride] looked out at the multitude around her. Time stopped. She knew this was a vortex moment in her life and she would remember it always. She was so happy to be in love... and loved by a whole community. The perfection of this moment brought tears to her eyes.

The two young lovers came from different countries and shared different religious beliefs, but in their souls, they carried the same high ideals. Both yearned for a peaceful community where they could love and be loved. They were excited and inspired by the future they wanted to create together....

Watch for <u>Meshka of Seederland</u>, coming Fall, 2018

Other SPIRITBOOKS & Titles
from Portal Center Press

Awakening, a journey of enlightenment
by Andree Cuenod

Butterfly Soup, changing your life from the inside out
by Aurora J. Miller

Deva and the Soul-Snatcher, an ecological fantasy
by Barbara Rogers Wilson

Language of Life: answers to modern crises in an ancient
way of speaking, by Milt Markewitz & Ruth L Miller, with contributions by Batya Podos

Making the World Go Away: a babyboomer's guide to end
times,   by Ruth L Miller

Mary's Power, embracing the Divine Feminine as the age of
empire ends, by Ruth L Miller

Rebecca and the Talisman of Time: a Bat Mitzvah miracle
by Batya Podos

Wake UP! Our Old Beliefs Don't Work Anymore!
by Andree Cuenod

www.portalcenterpress.com